My Highlander
A Cree & Dawn Novel

By

Donna Fletcher

Donna Fletcher

Copyright

My Highlander A Cree & Dawn Novel
All rights reserved.
Copyright November 2018 by Donna Fletcher

Cover Art
The Killion Group

Chapter One

The Highlands, Scotland late 1200s

Cree turned and draped his arm over his sleeping wife's waist and wrapped his body around her naked one. She felt good, so very good, warm and soft. He could melt into her and forever feel at peace. He pressed his face in her tousled, dark red hair, the familiar scent of lavender tickling his nose.

God, how he loved this woman. She had stolen his heart, a heart that had turned cold and felt nothing. Dawn had changed all that. She had made him *feel*, something he had never expected to do again.

He smiled, running his hand down over her stomach, the familiar slight roundness not noticeable to the eye only his touch, leftover as a reminder of the beautiful son and daughter—twins— she had given him almost two years ago.

Life was good, so very good.

He smiled again and with a gentle swipe of his face moved her hair away from her neck so his lips could nibble along her silky soft skin and begin to stir her awake. His hand drifted down along her slender body, his fingers settling in the triangle of red hair nestled between her legs, finding that small bud of pleasure he loved to tease and stir to life.

Another smile surfaced when she stirred against him. He could almost hear her soft moan, though one would never slip from her lips. It made no difference to him that Dawn had no voice, though there were times it angered him that she had been born that way. It had been so unfair to her, never able to speak a word and yet there were times he felt she made herself heard more than someone with a voice.

3

She made herself known through gestures, ones he easily understood now, though when vexed, her hands moved rapidly and he found himself lost as to what she was saying. She could have a temper, when warranted, otherwise she had an even nature, which pleased him since he was aware that his own scowling nature could prove difficult.

He smiled again when she dug her bottom against his manhood, which had sprouted to life as soon as he had wrapped himself around her and now fully blossomed against her tight backside.

That was another thing about Dawn, she made him smile, but then he had had little to smile about before she came along. Endless battles, death, and destruction had been his constant companions. No more. He had paid with his soul to finally get a title and land, and a home for his faithful warriors. Now he battled only when necessary, his days spent with his wife and children, keeping them and his clan well provided for and safe.

Always safe.

She turned in his arms, her eyes still closed as her arms went around his neck and her lips settled on his. It was no tender kiss, but then he had teased her passion awake well before she woke, leaving her aroused and in need, just the way he liked her.

He returned the kiss with equal desire while his hand gripped her backside and pushed her tight against him, his hard manhood eager to settle between her legs.

Lord, but he could not get enough of his wife. whether they coupled, simply kissed, or their hands joined, he found his need to have her near him had grown with time. Where some men found their wives irritating, he found pleasure in every moment he spent with Dawn.

Need grew in Cree like a man starved far too long from coupling with his wife. He had to have her now. He could not wait. He needed to be inside her, deep inside her, and feel her wrap snug around him.

"I need you now," he said with a hunger so strong he feared he would hurt her if he did not temper it.

Her dark brown eyes opened wide as she nodded vigorously, her need matching his.

Cree turned with her in his arms, covering her with his body, spreading her legs with his knee, and settling between them. His need to enter her grew so rapidly that he thought he would burst with pleasure before ever getting inside her.

He thrust his hips forward, having felt the wetness at her entrance, eager to slip in and become one with her. He groaned, impatient for that moment when he would feel her wrap around him, hug him tight, and finally be where he belonged.

A crack of thunder had Cree bolt up in bed—alone—his hard manhood throbbing for a wife that was not there and would never be again.

He tossed his head back and roared with a fury that had not left him since the day he had lost Dawn, three months ago. That day was forever burned in his memory. He had kissed her that morning in early April, feeling a bit jealous that she was excited to be off to help Lara and Elsa, the clan healer, collect some healing plants. He hadn't wanted her to go, had almost stopped her, but the twins had been demanding of late, not to mention his own demands, and he saw that she needed time to enjoy others besides her family.

He pressed the heel of his hands to his eyes, trying to erase the image of Lara screaming as she ran into the village.

"Dawn is gone! She is gone! Drowned!"

Sloan, his best friend, and his wife Lucerne, wed six months and now three months pregnant with their first bairn, went running with him along with most of the villagers. They reached the rushing stream to find Elsa collapsed on the ground, hugging Dawn's wet shawl to her chest, tears streaming down her face.

Cree roared to the heavens and was ready to jump in the rapidly rushing waters to find his wife, but Sloan stopped him.

"You will not find her if you die."

Sloan's words had struck him like a sword to his heart. Dawn could not be dead. He would not allow it. He ordered his warriors to comb the banks of the stream. Knowing his wife, she would have struggled to survive. She could be clinging to a branch or rock somewhere.

The search went on and when night fell it was obvious to most Dawn was not going to be found. She had been swept away. Cree had refused to give up. He had continued to have the banks of the stream searched throughout the night and day after day. And day after day there was no sign of Dawn.

Cree dropped back on the bed. He hated life without Dawn and if he did not have the twins, he would throw himself back into battle and hope for a quick death. But Dawn would not expect that of him. She would want him to be a good da to their children and that was the only thing that kept him from joining his wife.

It did not, however, stop him from getting lost in ale and wine and whatever else would help ease the dreadful pain that had shattered his heart and soul. The day he had realized that Dawn would never return to him, that she was dead, had been a nightmare. He had torn the Great Hall apart, smashing benches and tables, throwing whatever he could get his hands on until he stood in the center of the carnage, hands bleeding, sweat powering from him, and tears streaming down his face.

He had not shed a tear since his mum had died and he had not even realized he had been crying. He had wiped at his wet cheeks and wished for the return of his cold heart, but knew that was not possible. His love for Dawn was too strong, too deeply rooted inside him. The horrible, endless pain would never go away. It would always be there with him like a punishment for not having listened to himself that day and not let her go. Why had he let her go?

His only escape was spending endless hours on the practice field, whether with fists or a sword he battled day after day until one day he arrived at the practice field to find Sloan standing next to a post pounded into the ground.

"You have injured enough of your warriors. Take your anger out on the post."

Cree had done just that, the post having to be replaced each day.

He forced himself to get out of bed, standing, then dropping to sit on the edge, wishing he did not have to face another day without Dawn. He braced his hands on the bed to either side of himself, ready to force himself to his feet when he stopped, his eyes focused on his arms. With his daily sword and post bouts, his arms had grown huge as had his chest. His legs were also thick with muscles. And his strength went far beyond what it had ever been.

He spread his hand, palm up, in front of him, staring at it. He had no doubt he could easily choke a man to death with one squeeze and it would not matter to him at all.

He shook his head. Dawn would not want him thinking that way.

Dawn was not here.

The thought wrenched his gut and tore at his heart that was already torn to pieces. How much more could it take?

A crack of thunder shook the room and Cree went to the lone window and saw it was raining, not a downpour though the heavy gray skies warned it could turn into one.

He hurried into his plaid, not bothering with a shirt and slipped on his boots. He needed the mind-numbing task of battering the practice post, rain or not. Once done, he would spend time with his son and daughter. It was difficult seeing his daughter, her dark brown eyes so much like her mum's and her gentle smile as well.

Wanting the pain to stop, he hurried through the keep, those around making sure to keep their distance from him. He could not blame them. He had not been a pleasant man since Dawn's death.

Death.

He still could not believe it. How dare she die and leave him alone. He should have been the one to die, not Dawn. He shook his head. He had to get to the practice field. He had to numb his mind, think of nothing, feel nothing.

Rain sprinkled down on him as he walked through the village. He saw Old Mary, her gait slow, walking to her cottage. She had as much difficulty accepting Dawn's death as he had and still did, insisting she would have known, would have felt it.

Cree had wanted to believe her, to hold on to hope, especially since Dawn's body had not been found. Sometimes he would look in the distance, expecting to see her on the top of the hill, waving at him as she ran down it toward the village. He turned and looked now, the darkening skies hugged the hill, not a soul was in sight.

He clenched his hands at his sides, digging his fingers deeply into his palm, and walked to the practice field. The anger, the pain, he would beat the post senseless today. And he did, waving Sloan away when he attempted to approach, attempted to stop him.

The rain had turned heavier, but Cree did not care. He needed to rid himself of the agony that was tearing at him like a mighty beast that he was sure would devour him at any moment. He even heard its powerful bark and chilling howl.

Cree stopped suddenly, realizing the sound was not in his mind. He looked and in the distance by the edge of the woods stood a dog or was it a wolf? The animal was a good

8

size and all black and when his eyes met with Cree's the dog lifted its head and howled to the heavens. When he stopped, his eyes settled on Cree once again and he barked, turned to run into the woods, then stopped, looked at Cree, and barked again, and again turned to the woods.

Cree realized the animal wanted him to follow. He could not be bothered. He turned back to the post and the dog's barks grew frantic, not stopping.

Cree had no patience with the animal and with his anger near to boiling over, he rushed toward the dog. The black beast did not make a move until Cree was nearly on top of him, then he ran into the woods and Cree's anger had him following. He had only gone a short way in when he spotted the dog. He stood in a protective stance over a crumpled piece of cloth or so Cree thought until he saw slight movement.

Had the dog gone in search of help for his master?

Cree approached the animal slowly. "Your master needs help?"

The dog looked as if he nodded as he barked once in answer.

Cree took careful steps, the dog larger than he had thought and his teeth a good size. "I will see to him for you."

Surprisingly, the dog took a couple of steps back, as if giving Cree permission to approach.

Cree crouched down beside what now was clearly a body beneath a cloak. He feared he might be too late to help whoever lay beneath, no movement coming from it, until… fingers slipped out, as if the hand was about to try and crawl.

"Easy there. I will see you safe," Cree said and gently turned the figure over.

Shock had his mouth dropping open and he thought his eyes would burst from his head, and his heart explode in his chest, then he let out a roar.

"DAWN!"

Chapter Two

Dawn's eyes drifted open and her lips turned in a faint smile as she fought to mouth *Cree*. She was not sure if it was a dream like so many she had lately, only to wake and be disappointed. She prayed it was not, for it would mean she had finally made it home.

Pain robbed her body of strength, but she did not care. She fought against it to raise her hand to touch her husband to see if he was real. She gasped, though it could not be heard, when she felt him take her hand and almost cried when he spoke.

"I am here, Dawn. You are home. You are safe," he said, seeing the worry and exhaustion in her eyes. He swore then and there he would never let anything happen to his wife again. Not ever. "I am going to get you home and Elsa will heal you." He felt the faint tap of her finger telling him yes and was never so grateful to feel it again.

He eased his arms slowly underneath her, not sure of her injuries or how much discomfit he would cause her. He almost roared with anger when he watched her face contort in pain as he gently lifted her in his arms to rest against him.

"I hate causing you pain, but I have no choice," he said and kissed her brow.

Her eyes drifted closed and his heart slammed in his chest when he felt her go limp in his arms. He could not lose her again. He would not lose her again. He took off running for the keep.

"Elsa! Elsa!" he roared as he ran through the village,

His demanding shout for the healer had people pouring out of their cottages into the rain and they were shocked to see Cree running, his wife in his arms, and a beast of a black dog following behind him.

Sloan had heard Cree's desperate shouts and, worried something terrible had happened, had gone running to find him. He stopped dead, for a moment, when he saw who Cree carried. He shouted out, "I will find Elsa."

Cree nodded and hurried up the stairs to the keep, servants holding the two doors open for him. He rushed through the Great Hall, everyone there keeping out of his way and staring in shock, though prayers were heard spilling from their lips. Except Flanna, the overseer of the keep and good friend to Dawn, she rushed up the stairs before Cree, opening the door to his bedchamber.

Cree entered their bedchamber and stood a moment in the middle of the room. He had to see to his wife's care, but he did not want to let her go. He never wanted to let her go.

"She needs to get dry," Flanna said and went to the hearth to get a stronger fire going.

The beast of a dog gave a bark and went to sit by the fireplace as if agreeing with the woman.

Cree waited until Flanna had a fire roaring going in the hearth and without asking the woman moved a chair close to the warmth of the flames for him to sit. As soon as he sat, he began to peel off Dawn's soaked cloak.

"Thank the Lord, she is alive," Elsa said, entering the room, Lucerne following her in along with Sloan.

"And you will keep her that way," Cree ordered sternly.

"If I am to do that, we need to get her out of those wet garments and dry, then I can see what injuries, if any, need tending," Elsa said a slight command in her own voice.

"Whatever you need, Elsa, just do not let her die. I cannot lose her again. I will not lose her again."

"I will do all I can, my lord," Elsa said and turned to Sloan. "I need my healing basket. It is by the door in my cottage."

Sloan nodded and rushed out of the room.

Elsa turned to Lucerne. "I will need help making brews and possibly poultices. Go and have the kitchen ready and waiting for my instructions." Lucerne nodded and left the room and Elsa turned to Flanna. "Fresh towels and more blankets."

Flanna rushed out the door, closing it behind her.

"That animal needs to go," Elsa said, pointing to the dog.

The dog growled and moved closer to Dawn

"He saved her. He stays," Cree ordered and turned a scowl on the animal. "Not a sound from you or you will be gone. Dawn is safe with me."

The dog's growl turned to a low rumble in his chest as he backed away and settled down by the hearth to keep watch.

Elsa kept her eyes on the dog as she approached, the size of him and his bared teeth intimidating. Once by Dawn, the animal was a thought no more, healing Dawn her only concern.

"We have to get her out of these wet garments and into the warm, dry bed," Elsa said, her hands already busy at removing Dawn's boots.

Elsa cringed and Cree swore when they saw the raw blisters on her feet.

"She has walked far to get back to you," Elsa said a tear in her eye.

Dawn's cloak was easy to shed, but the other wet garments were difficult, sticking to her skin.

"Take a knife to the garments," Cree said, nodding to one on the chest near the bed, "I will see these garments burned."

Elsa nodded and grabbed the knife and got busy slicing at the cloth and as she did Dawn's ordeal was revealed. There were raw scratches over her arms and legs and bruises as well, but it was the dark bruise on Dawn's right side, beneath her breast down to her waist that worried Elsa the most.

It troubled Cree as well, since he had seen men die from such a bruise.

"She doesn't wake," Cree said and as if his wife heard him, her eyes fluttered open and she gave him a weak smile.

"A good sign," Elsa said with a nod and a smile of her own. "Dawn is a fighter. She will not give up. She did not give up. She made it home. Now, care, rest, and food will help heal her. She has gotten thin."

Cree not only saw it, he felt it, holding her there in his arms. She was a head taller than most women, her head reaching just past his shoulder, and she had always had curves to her and a slight roundness to her stomach since the twins were born. All the curves and the roundness were gone. She was far too thin and it troubled him what she must have suffered to have gotten that way.

"I need to examine her back and," —Elsa paused, tears gathering once again in her eyes— "I am sorry to say this, my lord, but she smells terrible. She needs to be bathed before you place her in bed to rest and heal."

Cree had noticed the foul scent when he had taken her in his arms and it was even worse now in the confined room. "Order a bath. I will bathe with her and see her washed clean."

"First, her back," Elsa reminded.

Cree lifted her gently to rest her chest to his while his other arm turned the lower portion of her body so Elsa could have a look.

Elsa gasped.

"What is it?" Cree asked, trying to see for himself, but not able to.

Elsa looked reluctant to say.

"Tell me now, Elsa," Cree snapped.

13

"A bite mark on her backside, my lord."

Cree turned a vicious scowl on the dog that had the animal baring his teeth in a feral growl.

"It is a human bite, my lord."

Cree turned such a harsh glare on her that Elsa took a step back.

"A human bite?"

"Aye, my lord," Elsa reluctantly confirmed. "The teeth marks can be seen clearly and the bruising is fresh. It has not been long since she got it." She hurried and grabbed a blanket from the rumpled bedding, seeing for herself the truth to the gossip that the servants had been avoiding Lord Cree's bedchamber for a while, and draped it over Dawn. "I will see to the bath and have your bedding made fresh."

Cree nodded, keeping Dawn tucked close against him, feeling her soft breath on him, and her ever so slight movements. He had no idea of what she may have suffered and part of him feared to learn her fate, but learn he would. He would hear all of it, then he would seek his revenge.

It did not take long before Flanna had the servants bustling in and out of the bedchamber. The wood tub was soon carried in, draped with a cloth, and filled with hot water. The servants tasked with the chore, all expressing their blessings on Dawn's return home.

After Flanna asked if anything else was needed, she shooed the last servant out the door, and slipped out closing it behind her. Only then did she let her tears fall and sent prayers to the heavens for Dawn to heal quickly.

Elsa pulled off Cree's boots and he stood, with Dawn in his arms, so she could get his plaid off him. The blanket over Dawn fell to the floor along with Cree's plaid and he stepped on the small stool to step over the rim and into the tub.

Dawn's eyes shot open as he sunk with her into the partially hot water.

"A bath, my love," he said softly and kissed her cheek.

Cree felt her sigh as she placed her head on his shoulder, and his shattered heart felt like all the broken pieces were coming together again when her lips gently brushed his chest.

"Never will you be out of my sight again," he said, sounding more a promise than a declaration and she tapped his arm once, agreeing with him, and his broken heart healed even more.

Elsa did not wait for instructions, she took charge. She got busy scrubbing Dawn's hair. "A comfrey poultice is being made for the bruise at her side. Honey will help heal the numerous scratches and a comfrey salve will see to the other bruises and swelling. I see no reason to worry about fever, but I am going to give her a brew for it anyway and—" Elsa suddenly turned quiet.

"What is it, Elsa?" Cree asked, seeing her hesitant to continue.

"I mean nothing by this, my lord, but I can give her something in case she got with child while away."

Cree looked down at his wife, sleeping comfortably in his arms. "No, I will not do that to her. She will decide that for herself if necessary."

Elsa nodded and continued to fight the tears that had threatened to spill several times since entering the room. Most men would not leave that decision to their wives, but then Cree was not most men.

Cree gently scrubbed his wife's face with the cloth Elsa handed him.

Dawn woke periodically and attempted to sit up, but she was far too weak.

"Rest in my arms, where you belong. I will see to your care," Cree said and kissed her brow.

When Elsa finished scrubbing Dawn's arms, she took her hand to clean the thick dirt embedded beneath her nails.

Cree said what Elsa thought. "She crawled. That was what she must have been doing when the dog came for help, crawling to get home."

That was it, Elsa could not hold back her tears any longer, they spilled down her full cheeks. "She is courageous."

"That she is," Cree agreed, thinking his wife was far more courageous than him since he had given up on her, believing her dead. When she had never given up. She had let no one stop her from returning home to him.

Cree lifted Dawn so Elsa could scrub her legs and gently wash her blistered feet.

"She barely moves," Cree said, after moving her around different ways so Elsa could scrub her.

"Exhaustion," Elsa explained. "Her body can take no more. She needs to sleep, to heal, to regain her strength." She handed him a cloth soaked with soap. "Gently wash her private parts since I do not know if she has suffered there."

Cree nodded and it was the first time since meeting his wife that he did not grow aroused when he touched her intimately. He was too concerned about her well-being to think of coupling with her. That would come in time after she healed, after she grew strong.

Dawn startled awake in his arms when he slipped the cloth between her legs and her hand latched onto his wrist to stop him. When she saw it was him, her chest heaved in a heavy sigh and her hand fell away and her eyes closed once again.

"She wakes still fearing it a dream," Cree said.

Elsa nodded. "Time and your arms are the only things that will heal that."

When Dawn was scrubbed clean, Cree stepped out of the tub with her in his arms and Elsa hurried to dry them both and wrap Dawn in a clean blanket. Then Cree sat once again in the chair by the fire with Dawn cradled in his lap, while servants removed the tub and other servants dressed the bed with fresh bedding.

The whole time the beast of a dog slept by the fire, looking up only when Dawn made a move and not settling down until she did. Cree wondered where and how she came by the dog. The animal was certainly protective of her and that Cree liked.

"Bring food for the dog," Cree ordered to no one in particular and one of the servants hurried out of the room.

The servants were nearly done with the room when the food arrived for the dog. He growled when the servant approached and Cree shot the animal a look that turned the growl into a low rumble.

The servant took no chance. He placed the crock of food on the floor and gave it a shove with his foot. The dog sniffed it, while keeping an eye on Cree, then devoured it.

If the dog was that hungry, he could only imagine how hungry Dawn must be.

"She needs to eat," Cree said, looking to Elsa as the last servant left the room.

"She will, but sleep is more important now. A brew will be finished soon that will help sustain her. I will spoon it into her mouth."

"I will feed her," Cree said.

Elsa nodded, having had no doubt he would have it no other way. "I was going to examine her more closely, but I think it would be best that she rests."

Cree understood what she did not say. Her examine would be more intimate, to see if she had suffered in other ways. Cree did not want to learn that from Elsa. He would rather his wife tell him what she had endured in her absence.

"You will wait until Dawn wakes," Cree ordered.

Elsa was relieved to hear his command and nodded once again. "As you say, my lord."

A knock sounded at the door before it opened and Sloan entered. "I cannot keep Old Mary and Lila at bay much longer. They are eager to see Dawn for themselves."

Cree did not want to share Dawn with anyone, but that would not be fair to her or her friends. "Give me time to settle her in bed and dress."

Sloan nodded. "They wait outside the door. Let me know when you are ready to receive them."

Elsa had spotted Dawn's nightdress on the peg by the door.

"No," Cree ordered when Elsa reached for the nightdress. "She never wears it and if she wakes with it on, she will fear she is not home."

Elsa nodded and returned to Cree's side to help him settle Dawn in bed, tucking the blankets up under her chin.

Cree donned a fresh plaid, nothing else and moved the chair beside the bed to sit close to his sleeping wife. Fear smashed into his gut, her dark red hair and the light-colored blankets making her appear far too pale and fragile.

He intended to join her in bed after feeding her some of the sustaining brew. Then he could soothe and reassure her when she woke.

"She needs to sleep, to rest," Elsa said. It was heart-wrenching and strange to see the worry in Cree's eyes since he rarely displayed anything but a scowl.

"I will make sure she does." Cree gently tucked a strand of his wife's damp hair behind her ear. "Tell Sloan that Old Mary and Lila may enter."

Elsa bobbed her head and went to the door.

The two women entered with quick steps, stopping at the end of the bed.

Lila, more like a sister than a friend to Dawn, and completely opposite in features, petite and slim with curly red hair and gentle green eyes, and a tongue that could chatter on forever, though at the moment failed to do so. She

18

stood staring at Dawn, tears streaming down her cheeks and reached for support from Old Mary, taking hold of the old woman's hand.

Though Old Mary's hand was gnarled from age, she gripped Lila's firmly, sharing her strength.

"She is well, my lord?" Lila asked.

Cree's dark eyes went to Old Mary, wanting—more needing—her to answer, since she often had knowledge of things to come. And Dawn's death had not been one of them. She had been shocked when the news came and refused to believe it, just as he had, but time had begun to leave doubt. Time, however, had been wrong. Old Mary had been right.

"Dawn's time is far off," Old Mary said.

Cree wanted to roar with relief, but remained silent.

"Please, my lord, if there is anything I can do to help," Lila said, her tears continuing to flow.

Cree knew Dawn would want to see her friend, know she, her husband Paul, and their young son Thomas were well, and have time to talk with her, since Lila understood all of Dawn's gestures easily.

"You have my word, I will send for you," Cree said.

Lila laid a hand to her chest as she said, "I am most grateful, my lord."

"I will know when to come to her," Old Mary said, looking to Cree.

"And you will be welcomed," he assured her and wondered what it was in her aged eyes that she was not saying.

With respectful nods to Lord Cree, the two woman left the bedchamber, Lila still clinging to Old Mary's hand.

The brew arrived shortly afterwards and Cree placed another pillow beneath his wife's head and a towel beneath her chin before sitting on the edge of the bed, bowl and spoon in hand, to feed her the brew.

19

"A few sips should sustain her, though more would be preferable," Elsa advised.

Cree worried Dawn would take none at all, but when he eased the spoon between her lips, she opened and eagerly took the liquid.

He and Elsa were ecstatic when she finished half the bowl.

"It is promising that she is eager to eat. She will heal and grow strong soon," Elsa confirmed. "I will leave you with your wife, though I will return in a few hours with a fresh brew for Dawn to enjoy."

"Send Sloan in, and, Elsa," —Cree paused and looked at Dawn— "I am grateful for the help you give my wife."

Elsa rested her hand to her chest, tears pooling in her eyes. "And I am so very happy that Dawn has returned to us, my lord." She turned and hurried from the room before tears fell once again.

Sloan entered and Cree stood as he approached the bed and walked to the end, casting a glance back at his wife as if the short distance between them was too much.

"That beast of a dog left good prints for our trackers to follow. Henry leads the group," Sloan said.

Cree and Sloan had been friends for some time and in that time, they had come to know each other well. So well, that Sloan knew what to do before Cree gave any instructions or commands.

"They will follow the tracks as far as they take them. Unfortunately, the rain does not help the situation," Sloan said.

"It is a start and when Dawn is well enough she can tell me all of it. Then I can decide if it is revenge I seek."

"As always, your warriors and clan stand with you."

"Of that, I had no doubt." Cree gave a quick glance at his wife, knowing she was there sleeping, but needing to reassure himself. "You and Elsa are the only ones permitted to enter this room when necessary. All others must seek permission."

"Aye, my lord."

"We will talk later," Cree said, dismissing him, eager to join his wife in bed and take her in his arms where she belonged.

Sloan bobbed his head and took quick steps to the door, and turned after opening it. "She is a courageous woman. It is good to have her home." He shut the door quietly behind him, expecting no response.

It was more than good to Cree and he had to keep telling himself that this was real and not a dream.

He removed his plaid, tossing it on the chair, then crouched down beside the bed. He eased the blanket off her some and gently rolled his wife on her side, holding her steady there with his hand. He wanted to see the bite mark for himself that had so upset Elsa.

His nostrils flared, a scowl deepened across his face, and his anger soared like a mighty bird of prey. A purple and black bruise covered the lower part of her right cheek and in the center could be seen distinct teeth marks.

He reached out to touch it when Dawn shivered, gooseflesh running over her skin. He hurried into bed beside her, easing her back to rest against his front, his arm going around her and tucking her close against him. He slipped his leg between her two just as he had done endless nights before and he rested his face against her damp hair, drinking in her fresh scent.

Cree shut his eyes tight for a few moments, then opened them again. He did that a few times, wanting to make sure yet again this was not a dream. That he would wake wrapped around his wife.

Finally, he accepted that it was real and Dawn was there with him. Still, he remained awake and watched her sleep, ready to do whatever was necessary to help her heal from the ordeal she had suffered.

There was, however, one thing he intended to see done. He would have his revenge on any and all who had dared to do harm to his wife.

Chapter Three

"Two days, Elsa, and in all that time she has barely woken," Cree said, pacing next to the bed where his wife slept peacefully.

"Her body is doing what it needs to do to heal," Elsa said, repeating what she had told him endlessly since Dawn's return. "You have seen for yourself how the scratches are fading and also the large bruise to her side. It is responding much better to the poultice than I expected."

"And the bite mark?" he asked with a scowl, aware she avoided speaking of it to him. That could be because any time she did, he got angry and snapped at her. He could not contain his fury when he thought of it. He so badly wanted to get his hands on the person who did it to her and make him linger in his suffering before he killed him.

"It also responds well to the poultice and I am confident it will leave no trace of a scar," she said, pleased herself with the results. "She eats when she does wake or when you feed her. The care, rest, and food all help her grow stronger. You must have seen how she does not struggle to move her arms as she did when you first found her. It proves she is doing well, growing stronger."

Cree nodded, trying to temper his frustration. He wanted his wife back, wanted to see her smile, her hands gesture to him, feel her touch upon him, her lips pressed to his.

Patience, he silently warned himself. Unfortunately, patience was one virtue he lacked.

"I sent for Lila to sit with Dawn for a while," Elsa said and held her hand up when he looked ready to bite her head off. "Please, my lord, you need to get out of this room for a while and visit with your children and see to your duties. Your daughter Lizbeth repeatedly calls for her da and your son Valan is unsettled, having difficulty sleeping. They miss you."

Cree had been meaning to go to his son and daughter, but he had not wanted to leave Dawn. She was safe here, two warriors standing guard outside their bedchamber and all his warriors on alert in case Dawn had escaped someone who thought to go after her.

"Lila's endless chatter just might bring Dawn awake and keep her awake longer than a few moments," Elsa said.

Cree's nostrils flared with annoyance. That was not for Lila to do, it was for him to do. He rubbed at the back of his neck taut with pain, his own fault. He needed to let things be, let his wife rest and heal and see to his duties and most of all to his children. They needed to be smiling and happy when reunited with their mum.

"You will wait for Lila to arrive while I go see to my duties and my children and tell her to take her time with Dawn, since I have much to see to today and it is already past mid-day."

Elsa was relieved that Cree paid heed to her words, and smiled.

"Send for me if my wife wakes and remains awake," he ordered and bent down and gave Dawn's cheek a kiss and walked to the door. "Come, Beast." He had taken to calling the dog Beast for lack of a name. The dog went to the bedchamber door in the morning and before evening set in to let Cree know he needed to go out. He always found his way back in, though Cree wondered how since no one would go near the beast of a dog, or dare open a door for him, and he would settle himself by the fireplace once again.

The large dog looked to the bed, looked back at Cree, then walked over to the bed and sat beside it, his thick chest expanding as he tilted his head up, letting Cree know he would stand guard.

Cree admired the dog's loyalty to Dawn and he wondered what had forged such a strong bond the animal felt toward her.

"Guard her well," he said and walked out the door.

Cree stopped halfway down the stairs and took a deep breath. It had been more difficult than he had expected leaving Dawn. His heart had hammered harder and harder in his chest with each step he had taken away from her, and it had not stopped. It had worsened the further away he got from her.

She was home and safe. He did not need to worry and yet he did. The pain of having believed he had lost her was still too raw and he never—never ever—wanted to feel it again. He had learned a lesson with his wife's death.

Life was not worth living without her.

He squared his shoulders and tossed his head from side to side, working out the stiffness in his neck. Life was finally worth living again and he planned to make sure it stayed that way. He continued down the stairs and through the Great Hall to step outside to look for Sloan.

It was a beautiful summer day and warmer than usual but that could change at any minute. As he looked over the village, he wondered if it had been the recent rain that made everything look brighter, the villagers happier, laughing and smiling, the children running and squealing in delight. Or had the constant gloom been lifted, the heart of the village beating once again with Dawn's return?

Cree turned when he heard soft laughter and was not surprised to see Sloan nuzzling his wife, Lucerne's neck at the open door to their cottage. Annoyance flared in him not at the couple, but the memories of the time he had spent in that cottage with Dawn and how he so badly wanted to share intimate moments again with her, even if it was the simplest of gestures… her hand slipping around his and holding tight, letting him know she was there and that they were one.

"My lord, how is Dawn today?" Lucerne asked, a blush rising to stain her cheeks with embarrassment that Cree had come upon their moment of intimacy.

"She does well," Cree said and his annoyance grew when he selfishly thought that he wished she would do better faster.

Sloan gave his wife a hasty kiss on the cheek and whispered, "Later." Her blush deepened and he winked at her before walking over to Cree.

"Do not be impatient. Be glad your wife has returned and heals with each passing day," Sloan said when he stopped in front of Cree.

"You hear my thoughts now?" Cree snapped.

"Your face shows more than you know since Dawn entered your life. Besides, I have known you long enough to know you have no patience except when we go into battle. Then you wait, watch, and attack at the right moment. Think of your wife's healing as a battle and attack when it is time."

"Is it time for me to attack?" Cree asked.

Again Sloan understood what he asked. "The trackers have found nothing so far, but Henry has picked up on a trail that others failed to see and he follows it."

"See he is rewarded."

"I will, but he will not take the reward. He, like all the others here, does this for Dawn and nothing else."

"I never truly realized how much the clan admires and cares for my wife."

"Even more so since they have seen what a monster of a man you are without her," Sloan chuckled.

"I feel the need for the practice field today and you shall be my partner." Cree's scowl spoke more loudly than his words.

Sloan chuckled again. "You have no time for the practice field. You have duties to see to that you have sorely neglected. Besides, you don't need to practice. Have you happened to see how huge you have grown with muscle. Dawn has not returned to the husband she has left."

"I am no different," Cree bellowed, his anger sparking.

"Sloan!"

Both men turned to see Lucerne headed their way, her lovely face pinched in annoyance.

"Have you upset Lord Cree? Has he not been through enough? He does not need you tormenting him," Lucerne scolded her husband.

Cree kept a glare on his face, but inside he was grinning from ear to ear.

"I say what he needs to hear," Sloan defended himself and wondered how his wife could look so beautiful even when angry.

"Lord Cree needs to hear that we are all here to help him and Dawn, and do whatever they need us to do," Lucerne admonished.

"Which is why I tell him what he needs to hear," Sloan said, refusing to back down from his wife.

Lucerne crossed her arms over her chest when she came to a stop in front of him. "And tell me, if it were you who were going through what Lord Cree is going through, would you wish to hear the words you said to him?"

Sloan's arm went around his wife's waist and he rested his brow to hers. "I could not bear to lose you."

"Nor I you." She kissed his cheek, then whispered, "Tread lightly with him and later I will show you just how much I love you." With a respectful bob of her head to Cree, she returned to the cottage, closing the door behind her.

"Damn," Sloan said, shaking his head.

"You have a good wife, Sloan," Cree said, "though if she were my wife I would never tolerate her speaking to me

27

that way in front of another or ever for that matter. A good reason why I never wed her, though she had been my intended. Her tongue can be far too sharp and wicked."

"I agree with you that her tongue can be wicked and I do not mind that at all," Sloan said with a grin.

Cree laughed and shook his head. "You two were made for each other. You both have quick and sharp tongues."

Sloan rested a hand to Cree's shoulder. "It is good to hear you laugh again. And if anyone was made for each other, it is you and Dawn. I am more pleased and happy than you will ever know that Dawn has returned home, and I will do whatever it takes to seek revenge if necessary."

"You are a good friend, Sloan. You tolerated me when I was not at my best and I am grateful for that. And I know I can always count on you to raise a sword along with me without question."

"Now to see to some duties that need your immediate attention," Sloan said and the two men walked off.

***

Lila had not stopped talking since arriving in Dawn's bedchamber an hour ago. She did her best not to be fearful of Beast, but he was an intimidating creature, keeping a watchful eye on her.

She sat in the chair beside the bed, reaching out to touch Dawn's hand every now and then, especially when she would chuckle or break out in a fit of laughter over something she told Dawn that little Thomas or her husband Paul had done.

She chatted on about things that had happened since Dawn had been gone, letting her know that not only Sloan and Lucerne were expecting their first bairn, but that Dorrie's time was near and Elwin was a mess with worry. She went on about how Flanna somewhat tamed the snappish and grumbling Turbett, and that the large man could even be seen smiling now and again. Some thought it a miracle, while others believed Turbett had met his match in Flanna.

Lila never lacked for something to say. She went on and on, chuckling and laughing, though what Dawn did not see were the tears that rolled down her cheeks, her heart hurting for her friend.

***

Dawn wondered over the droning buzz in her head. What was it? Where was it coming from? Had she made it home? Or had she fallen prey to someone? She feared opening her eyes, feared what she might see. And where was Beast? What had happened to him? He would not leave her side without being forced to do so.

She lay still fearful of moving, of calling attention to herself, of alerting anyone that might be around her.

Home. Home. She so wanted to be home.

Her journey had been grueling and her dreams horrible, always making her believe she had made it home, only to wake and be disappointed. The dream where she had woken in Cree's arms, his body wrapped around hers, had hurt the most. He had felt so real, his breath so warm on her neck, the bed so soft beneath… like now.

She was in a bed, but where?

She forced herself to listen to the buzzing in her head, trying to recognize it, trying to find out where she was.

She felt a tongue lick her face.

"Do not do that," a voice scolded.

Dawn felt another lick and knew it was Beast.

"You will stop that right now," the voice warned.

Again a lick to her face.

29

"You are going to get in trouble when I tell Lord Cree," the voice threatened.

Dawn suddenly recognized the voice and her heart soared with relief. She opened her eyes to another lick to her cheek and smiled at her best friend Lila.

"Oh my God! Oh my God! You are awake," Lila said, her eyes turning wide and a wider smile breaking out across her face.

Dawn's smile grew along with her friend's and she gestured to her.

"You want to sit up?"

Dawn nodded.

"We should get you in your nightdress as well before others start pouring in here."

Dawn only then realized she was naked beneath the blankets, and she nodded again.

Before Lila could do as Dawn asked, the dog ran to the closed door and barked.

Dawn pointed to the door, letting Lila know to let him out. She knew what Beast was doing. He was going to the person who had helped her the most since they had arrived here to let him know something had changed with Dawn.

And that person would be Cree.

Lila hurried to open the door and the two guards were quick to see if all was well.

"Get Lord Cree. Lady Dawn is awake," Lila ordered to her own surprise.

Dawn clasped onto Lila's arm for support as she helped her to sit up, piling pillows behind her to see that she was comfortable. She did not want to let go of her friend when she finished and Lila, realizing it, hugged her tight.

"You are safe. You are home now," she reassured her and waited until Dawn finally released her to help her on with her nightdress. "I am so glad you are home and that you are not dead."

Dawn scrunched her brow.

"We all thought you dead, drowned."

Dawn scrunched her brow again.

Lila, fearful her remarks might upset Dawn, said, "There will be time to talk about that. What matters is that you rest and get well. Valan and Lizbeth will be so happy to see you."

Dawn's smile grew wide and her eyes bright, and she did not have to gesture to ask how the twins were, Lila started chatting away about the pair.

***

Everyone in the village hurried out of the large dog's way, his bark more like a roar as his sharp black eyes searched every face.

Cree heard the bark in the distance and didn't hesitate, he ran straight toward the sound.

The animal and Cree caught sight of each other at the same moment and the dog did not wait, he turned and headed back to the keep, Cree running to follow him.

***

Dawn's eyes kept going to the open door, waiting, wanting badly to see her husband, feel his arms around her, know that she was finally home.

"He will be here soon," Lila said, seeing the anxiousness on her friend's face.

Both their heads turned at the same time, hearing the barks that echoed up the stairs.

Lila squeezed Dawn's hand. "I will see you soon." She stepped out of the way, knowing any moment Lord Cree would come bursting through the open door and not wanting to be in his way.

Dawn waited, her hands clenched in her lap, her heart hammering in her chest, her body feeling more alive than it had in months.

Beast burst in the room and moved to the side, Cree entering just behind him and stopping for a moment to stare at his wife, awake, and sitting up.

Dawn did not hesitate, she threw her arms out to him, and Cree rushed over to her.

Chapter Four

Cree lifted his wife into his arms as she clung to his neck and settled her in his lap when he sat on the bed. She curled into him, getting as close as she could and his arms tightened possessively around her. It was clear that they never intended to be separated again.

"You are home now. Safe. Never again will you go anywhere without me."

Dawn nodded and her agreeing so easily worried him. His wife was not one to obey him and his concern grew over what she may have suffered these last three months.

She patted his chest, then hers.

He kissed the top of her head before resting his cheek there and whispered, "I love you too, wife."

They stayed like that for a moment, then Dawn looked up at him and cradled her arm and rocked it, asking about her son and daughter.

"Valan and Lizbeth do well. They will be so happy to see you. I will bring them to you when you feel up to seeing them."

Dawn smiled and nodded, then rested her head on his shoulder again.

"Lila," Cree called out when he caught her inching toward the door.

She jumped and turned, "Aye, my lord."

"I am grateful for your chatter."

Lila blushed.

"Tell Elsa that Dawn is awake and she is to come immediately," Cree said, though she was probably already

33

on the way there, the whole village having seen him and the dog rush toward the keep.

"Aye, my lord," Lila said and bobbed her head and hurried out of the room, closing the door behind her.

Dawn raised her head suddenly, snapping her fingers as she did.

The large black dog was instantly at the side of the bed, his head going to rest on her leg.

Dawn reached out and rubbed behind his ear, then gave the top of his head two quick taps, then gave her chest two. The dog raised his head and barked as if he understood what she told him. She kissed her hand and placed it on the side of the dog's face and he licked it, then laid down beside the bed.

"The beast of a dog and you are attached," Cree said, a stab of jealousy poking at him. "He helped you?"

Dawn nodded and tapped the tip of her fingers repeatedly.

"Many times?"

She nodded and once again her head dropped to rest on his shoulder.

Cree was full of questions and not patient to ask them. There was much he wanted to say and wanted to ask, but he could feel her fatigue. She may have finally woken, but she had yet to fully heal.

"Then he has a new home here," Cree said, thinking that since the dog was so attached to her and protective that he might work well in helping to keep Dawn safe. "I call him Beast."

She looked up at him and smiled her approval, then suddenly winced when she shifted in his arms.

"You are in pain?" he asked anxiously.

She held her thumb and forefinger a short distance apart to let him know it was only a little pain she felt.

"You have much healing to do, wife, then we will talk."

She barely nodded in response, her head going to rest on his shoulder once again, it simply too heavy to hold it up.

He not only saw the reluctance on her face at the thought of them talking, he felt it in the slight tensing of her body. Had her ordeal been so terrible that she did not want to speak of it? He did not want to put her through the pain of what she had gone through all over again, but he wanted to know… everything. And he would know everything, then he could go after whoever caused her such suffering.

At this moment, however, his concern was his wife.

Dawn patted her chest, then patted his chest, then his arm.

"I am glad that you are here with me and in my arms as well," he said. "I have missed you more than you will ever know."

She nodded and patted her chest, letting him know she felt the same.

A sharp rap sounded at the door before it opened and Elsa entered. "It is good to see you awake."

Dawn went to smile and yawned instead, though a smile quickly followed it.

"You still need to rest and eat," Elsa said.

Dawn patted her stomach and nodded.

"I should have realized you were hungry and sent for food," Cree said annoyed at himself for not thinking of it. "I will have Flanna bring a feast for you."

"No," Elsa ordered and Cree turned a scowl on her. She ignored it and looked to Dawn. "You have been here two days. How long before that had you eaten?"

Dawn held up two fingers.

Cree cringed inside, thinking of his wife not far from home, so hungry, so alone.

"How much did you eat when last you ate?" Elsa continued.

Dawn looked as if she pinched two fingers together that she held up with a narrow space between them, letting the healer know she had eaten little.

"I have seen time and again how a person cannot eat much when they have been without food for a while. So broth, bread, and a little meat to start and we will see how you feel afterwards. We do not want your stomach protesting and ridding itself of the food when you need it to grow strong," Elsa advised. "I will see to getting you food and when you finish, I will apply another poultice to that bruise at your side. How did you come by it?"

Cree looked to Dawn's hand, impatient to hear her response.

Dawn patted her chest, then rapidly moved hand over hand,

"You took a long tumble?" Cree asked.

Dawn nodded and cringed, placing her hand lightly to her injured side, then held up her two hands as if she was holding something fairly large.

"You hit a rock?" Elsa asked.

Dawn nodded and smashed her fist into the palm of her other hand.

"Hard. You hit it hard," Cree said, the cringe he had previously kept hidden, surfacing enough to be noticeable.

"Did you walk immediately afterwards?" Elsa asked.

Dawn shook her head slowly and yawned again. She patted Cree's shoulder and laid her head on it.

"You rested," Elsa said. "That was wise of you, Dawn, and now it would be wise for you to rest again while you wait for the food."

Dawn nodded, while keeping her head on Cree's shoulder.

"I will see you after you eat and apply the poultice to your wound," Elsa said.

"I will remain here with Dawn, let Sloan know," Cree ordered and Elsa nodded and took her leave.

Dawn raised her hand to delicately trace the few lines at the corner of her husband's eyes that had not been there when she had last seen him. And the ones she did recall were set deeper now. His skin was warm and unmarred, and his lips were as she remembered them... ready to always kiss her. She had had endless dreams of him kissing her and making love to her, and she would wake so disappointed, that many times it had brought her to tears.

Not this time. This time it was not a dream.

She wished she had the strength to lift her head and kiss him, but as much as she did not want to admit it, she was too weak. She brushed his lips with her finger, then tapped her own lips.

Cree had ached to kiss her since her return. He had missed her lips, always so welcoming and so eager, like now.

He lowered his head and before his lips touched hers, he whispered, "I have missed the taste of you, wife."

Dawn slipped her hand around to the back of his neck, gripping it with what little strength she had, wanting to hold on to him and never let him go. And when his lips touched hers, tears gathered in her eyes.

She was home. She was finally home.

Cree warned himself to keep the kiss light, not linger in it, make no demands, but one taste and he was lost. He had thought he had lost her, that she was gone forever, that he would never kiss her again. And now that he could, he never wanted to stop.

The tender kiss turned powerful as if they both needed to make certain that the kiss was real, that they did not linger in a dream, that they had been reunited, joined once more.

A pain suddenly shot through Dawn's side and she gasped in Cree's mouth.

He tore his mouth away from hers. "Dawn?"

She took short breaths against the throbbing pain, her hand resting at her injured side.

Cree wanted to thrash himself for being so selfish, seeing tears begin to roll down her cheeks. She suffered in pain because of him. "Slow breaths," he said gently, though felt anything but gentle, he was so angry with himself.

The pain began to subside, though her breathing remained a bit labored. She could see by the scowl her husband wore that he was blaming himself for her suffering. She would not let him do that.

She tapped his chest and shook her head.

"It is my fault," he insisted, wiping away her tears, with his thumb, that continued to trickle down her flushed cheeks.

She continued to shake her head. She patted her chest, touched his lips, and patted her chest again.

"I know you wanted me to kiss you, and I wanted to kiss you, but I should have been more gentle in your weak condition."

She gave a silent laugh and that caused her to wince.

Cree winced along with her. "Do not laugh, it causes you pain, and what are you laughing at?"

She might be weak now, but it was her indomitable strength that got her home and she let him know that by shaking a fisted hand at him and narrowing her brow.

He smiled. "You are not weak, on that we both agree."

A knock at the door had Cree saying, "Food to make you grow even stronger."

Dawn's stomach answered for her, rumbling.

While the food tray was set on a small table a servant carried in, Cree saw to settling his wife in bed, so that she could eat comfortably. He propped a couple of pillows behind her and folded the blanket to rest below her waist.

The stone walls held a chill thanks to the cool, summer nights so a fire was kept burning in the hearth to ward it off, it being needed more so now to keep Dawn warm. He was glad for the strong fire when he saw her shiver and pull the blanket up higher at her waist.

He leaned over and whispered in her ear. "I will keep you warm tonight."

She smiled and with her finger traced a cross over his chest.

"Aye, I promise," he said and kissed her cheek.

As the last servant went to leave the room, Old Mary entered.

Dawn stretched her arms out to her and the old woman hurried over to hug her tight. "I knew you would wake today, though you need more rest."

Dawn smiled and nodded.

Old Mary turned to Cree. "Sloan will be here soon with news. I will see to feeding Dawn."

Cree was about to argue with the woman, having intended to see to the care of his wife himself.

"The news is important," Old Mary said.

Dawn gestured for him to go and let Old Mary tend her.

Cree did not like that his wife dismissed him so easily, but then he was not the only one happy and relieved with her return. There were many who were going to want to visit with her, though Old Mary was special to Dawn and he could not refuse them time together.

Sloan entered the open door and looked to Cree. "Important news." He turned his attention on Dawn. "It is good you are home. Your husband has been a beast of a man in your absence."

Cree shot him a threatening scowl.

Dawn smiled, though it was more of a soundless chuckle as she nodded.

Cree leaned over and kissed Dawn's brow. "I will return soon."

"No need to rush," Old Mary said. "I will take good care of her."

He had no doubt the old woman would. He simply did not want to be separated from his wife too long, the fear that somehow he would lose her continuing to linger in him.

He stopped suddenly as he approached the door and turned, pointing to Dawn but looking to Beast. "Guard Dawn!"

The large dog got to his feet from where he laid near the bed and took up a protective stance beside it.

Cree left his bedchamber feeling more secure that Dawn would be safe with Beast beside her.

Cree and Sloan settled in Cree's solar to talk. Tankards were filled with ale and the two men took a seat in the chairs facing the fire in the hearth.

"Dawn looks much improved than when you found her," Sloan said.

Cree nodded. "She does, but she still has much healing to do."

"Beast rarely leaves her side."

"He leaves her only when he sees to his own needs and that has been twice a day, and only if someone is there with her. He never leaves her on her own."

"He will see her kept safe."

"You have important news and yet you talk of Dawn and Beast. What do you avoid telling me?"

Sloan did not hesitate to respond. "When Henry returned with the news, I had a thought as to what he discovered. Seeing how Beast is protective of Dawn, I believe it explains what Henry found."

"And that is?" Cree asked impatiently.

"Henry came across a body of a man whose throat appeared to be ripped apart by an animal. A leg and an arm also suffered severe bite marks. I think Beast attacked the man who was about to attack Dawn or was in the middle of attacking her."

Cree thought of the bite mark on his wife's backside. "Dawn will be able to confirm if that was what happened. And if it is, Beast will definitely be rewarded." It would mean the dog saved Dawn's life twice. Would he learn of more heroic rescues once Dawn spoke of her ordeal? He owed much to the large dog and damn if it did not rankle him that an animal did what he should have done.

"Did Henry find anything else?" Cree asked.

Sloan shook his head. "No, the trail went cold soon after that."

"So we have no idea where Dawn has been?"

"Unfortunately, no, but with her awake, you will be able to learn all that has happened to her," Sloan said as if that solved the problem.

Cree thought differently. While he and his wife always spoke the truth, he wondered if this was one time she would keep something from him. He intended to make sure she told him everything.

***

"You improve and will grow strong again," Old Mary said, spooning the tasty broth into Dawn's mouth.

Dawn would have preferred to feed herself, but she could feel the weakness in her limbs and feared the spoon would not last long in her hand. Even the chunk of bread Old Mary had handed her had become heavy in only a short time.

"It was a difficult ordeal for you," Old Mary said, feeding her the hot broth slowly.

Dawn nodded.

"There is much for you to tell Cree."

Dawn nodded again and took a bite of the bread.

"I knew you were not dead and yet I could not grasp where you were," Old Mary said with a tear threatening to fall from her one eye.

Dawn placed her hand on Old Mary's, preventing the spoon from reaching her mouth, and she shook her head, then shook her finger at her, letting her know she was not to blame herself.

"I should have known, but it was so difficult deciphering the dreams, the visions. It took until your return for me to understand some of them and still I question them. Tell me about your journey so I may help you."

Dawn shook her head firmly.

"I worried that you would refuse to tell me."

Dawn pointed at Old Mary, then tapped her temple and pointed at the old woman again, and shook her head.

"Are you telling me I do not need to know?"

Dawn nodded and held her hand up, letting Old Mary know she did not want any more broth. She also handed what was left of the chunk of bread to Old Mary.

"You have not eaten enough," Old Mary scolded gently.

Dawn patted her stomach and shook her head.

Old Mary set the spoon and bowl aside and took Dawn's hand. "You need to tell me what happened so I may help you."

Again, Dawn shook her head firmly.

"Your husband will ask the same and what will you say then?" Old Mary asked.

Dawn shook her head again.

"Cree will want to know. He will demand to know."

Dawn was adamant, turning her head away and folding her arms across her chest.

"Fine, I cannot make you tell me, but your husband will."

Chapter Five

Dawn had fallen in and out of sleep after Old Mary had left, disturbing dreams waking her, only to fall back asleep and into the dreams once more. Old Mary was right… Cree would want, no doubt, demand answers. And that was the reason for her troubling dreams. There was much to tell her husband as to what had happened to her, yet there were also things she did not know if she wanted to tell him, and that disturbed her.

They both had learned how keeping things from each other could create more problems than they were worth and do damage to trust. But she wondered if some of what she had been through was not better left alone, for no one but her to know.

She was eager to heal and resume her life with her husband and the twins, and all her friends. She would prefer to forget her ordeal, not that she ever could, but she hoped the burdensome memories would fade with time and trouble her no more. One thing that would never fade from her memory was the horrible thought of never seeing Cree again. It had pained her heart worse than anything she had ever been through or could ever imagine. It made her realize the depths of her love for him and how difficult—impossible—it would be to live without him.

Dawn winced as she tried to turn on her side.

A wet tongue was quickly at her face along with a small whine.

Dawn scratched behind the big dog's ear and received more licks. She would have never made it home if it had not been for Beast, not that that was his name, but it was better than his true name.

She kissed the top of his snout and he licked her cheek again. They had fast become best friends and she did not want to lose him. She wanted him to become part of her family, but she feared his owner might think differently. And if he decided to search for the dog, she worried what might happen.

It was not that she had stolen Beast. The dog had decided on his own to follow her and she was grateful he had, the journey home having been fraught with danger.

She patted the top of his head, then patted her chest, then rested her hand to the side of his face, letting him know she loved him. He had seemed to understand what she was trying to convey from when she had first gestured that way too him, since he always responded by pressing his face to hers as if he was showing the same affection.

It was no different now. He pressed his face to hers, then rested his chin on the bed as if telling her to sleep and he would be there when she woke. Her eyes drifted shut, feeling safe with Beast there beside the bed and Cree somewhere in the keep.

***

Cree had returned to his bedchamber a few times throughout the day to find Dawn sleeping. He had not been happy to learn that she had eaten sparingly. Though, Elsa seemed pleased enough.

"She ate today and will eat more tomorrow, and more the next day as she grows stronger and stronger," Elsa had said.

Cree accepted her word, since there was little else he could do, though tomorrow he would be the one to feed her.

It was late now, much of the keep asleep when he returned to the bedchamber to find Dawn asleep once again. Beast slept beside the bed, having gone out for the night when Cree had last been here.

Cree went and sat in the chair by the hearth, a fire burning strong. A storm was brewing and the whipping wind slammed against the stones, sending a chill drifting off the stone wall. He took off his boots and stretched his feet out to the fire's warmth to toast his toes after slipping off his shirt.

The dog's sudden whine had him turning his head, then hurrying out of the chair when he saw his wife trying to get out of bed.

"What are you doing? Stay where you are," he commanded firmly, lifting her legs she had managed to slip off the edge of the bed as if making ready to stand.

She tapped her chest and pointed at him.

"You want to join me by the fire?" he asked and he grew annoyed that because she had no voice, the simple request had been denied her. She could not call out to him. Beast, however, had understood and alerted him. He liked the big dog more and more each day.

She nodded, smiling.

"I can join you in bed," he said.

Her smile vanished as she shook her head and pointed at the hearth.

She wanted to sit in front of the fire as they had done many times before and he could not deny her. He reached down and lifted her carefully, so as not to cause her pain, into his arms and walked over to the hearth to once again sit in the chair. He arranged her comfortably on his lap, pulling the hem of her nightdress down to cover her legs and feet, He felt more than simply content to have her there snug against him. He felt whole.

"I have missed this with you," he said and kissed her brow.

45

She nodded and patted her chest, then his, telling him she felt the same.

"When I thought you gone, lost to me forever, I would sit here at night and wonder how I would face another day without you. I am relieved and grateful I no longer have to do that."

She nodded and patted her chest, agreeing.

Dawn rarely, if ever, felt sorry for herself that she had no voice. It was something she had accepted since she was young. She owed that to her mum, Lizbeth, not the woman who gave her birth, but a true mum who loved her and cared for her and taught her to be brave and proud despite being different, despite not having a voice.

Tonight, however, she wished she could speak, explain to Cree what had happened, where she had been, how she had escaped, and be done with it. But her weak limbs would never allow the gestures necessary to explain it all. It would take time to tell the tale and, at the moment, she did not wish to relive some of the memories.

"I know you require more rest and I should wait to ask you what happened, where you have been, how you made it home, and in time I know you will explain it all. But at the moment, can you tell me how you manage to survive the fall in the cold, rushing stream?"

Dawn raised her head off his shoulder, her brow scrunched in question.

Cree wondered why she seemed confused. He reminded her. "You went with Elsa and Lara to collect some plants and accidentally fell in the stream. Lara rushed to the village for help and when we reached the stream Elsa was clutching your soaked shawl. Lara explained how she had reached out to grab you to try to stop you from falling in, but her hand slipped off you, the shawl caught in it."

Dawn pushed at his chest to sit up and Cree helped her. She shook her head and gestured falling and being rushed away in the water.

"Are you telling me that you did not fall in the stream?" he asked, not believing his own question.

Dawn nodded.

Cree found her response disturbing. "Then what happened to you?"

She rushed her arms across her chest, her hands grabbing opposite arms and shook her body back and forth.

Cree stared at her again shocked at what she was trying to tell him. "Are you saying someone took you against your will?"

She nodded vigorously and held up two fingers.

"Two men?"

She nodded again and raised her hands, keeping one hand high and the other low.

"A tall and a short man?"

She nodded again.

Cree gave her words thought for a moment. "Was Lara there when these two men took you?"

Dawn mouthed *Lara* then ran her fingers along her palm and held up two fingers.

"Lara brought you to these two men?"

Dawn confirmed with a nod, then tapped her chest and walked her fingers along her palm again and gestured plucking plants.

"Lara took you to where she told you there were plants to pick?"

Dawn nodded and gestured plucking a plant and wincing.

Cree narrowed his brow. "I'm not sure what you're saying."

Dawn gestured again plucking a plant and this time when she touched the imaginary plant, she withdrew her finger fast and cringed.

"The plant pricked your finger," Cree said understanding.

Dawn nodded and looked to wait for him to realize more.

It took a minute before he said, "Nettles, a prickly plant. That is where the men waited, by the nettles."

Dawn nodded, pleased he understood her, then with a shrug mouthed, *Lara*?

"Lara is still among us, though she no longer helps Elsa. She keeps to herself, speaks to know one, and wears a constant frown. Everyone assumes she feels guilty over not being able to save you and blames herself for your supposed death, but now I know differently. No doubt, she had something to do with the men who took you."

A sadness fell over Dawn's face.

"Her betrayal will be dealt with," Cree assured her eager to see to it.

Dawn yawned, the brief talk with her husband taking its toll.

"You need to sleep. We can talk more in the morning."

Dawn gave a brief nod and wrapped her arms around her husband's neck and lowered her head to his shoulder as he stood with her in his arms.

Cree tucked her beneath the blanket and when she scrunched her brow as if asking why he was not joining her, he said, "I have a matter to see to. Beast will guard you until I return, then you will spend the night in my arms."

A yawn stole Dawn's smile and she closed her eyes after Cree gave her lips a gentle kiss. She knew where he was going. He would not wait until morning to see to Lara.

Cree slipped on his boots and his shirt and before he left the room, he said, "Guard Dawn, Beast."

Cree's temper mounted with each step he took down the curving staircase. All this time he had thought his wife had been swept away in the cold stream, when that was not at all true. She had been abducted. If he had known the truth, his trackers would have found the culprits in no time. Lara had purposely misdirected them and he intended to see her suffer for her lies. But first he would learn who had taken his wife and why.

He stepped out of the keep, the wind whipping around him and storm clouds rushing past the half moon. He went to Sloan's cottage and pounded on the door.

Sloan's plaid hung half off him when he flung open the door.

"Lara lied. Dawn did not fall in the stream… two men abducted her."

Sloan called out to his wife. "Do not wait up for me, Lucerne." He grabbed his shirt that had been tossed carelessly over a chair and hurried into it after closing the door behind him.

"We need to find out what she knows," Sloan said as he kept up with Cree's rapid strides.

"You warn me not to take her life before we get information from her."

"I think of what I would want if it had happened to Lucerne. You would need to keep me away from Lara, my first thought would be to snap her neck."

"That is why you are my trusted friend and top warrior, you think as I do, and, like you, I am aware that information comes before the consequences of her betrayal," —Cree's hands tightened into fist at his sides— "as maddening as that is for me."

No more was said as they wound their way through the village, the wind growing stronger, the storm clouds thickening almost blotting out the half-moon, and lightning flashed in the distance.

They came upon the small cottage and Cree did not bother to knock at the door, he flung it open. There was no one there. He glanced around, Sloan doing the same.

"It looks abandoned," Sloan said. "Lara could have left the day Dawn was found unless someone can tell us otherwise."

"See if any of the sentinels spotted her," Cree ordered. "I am going to see if Elsa might know something."

Cree felt a splatter of rain hit him when he reached Elsa's cottage. He pounded the door with his fist twice to wake Elsa, though it was Neil who opened the door.

Neil was one of Cree's seasoned warriors. He had once been wounded while guarding Dawn and Elsa's tender care had won his heart. They had been together for almost two years now.

One look at Cree and Neil called out, "Hurry, Elsa, Lord Cree is here."

Elsa's long gray hair was in a loose braid and she wore her nightdress with a shawl wrapped around her.

Her eyes were wide with fright as she asked, "Is it Dawn?"

Cree shook his head. "Dawn is good. She sleeps and Beast guards her."

Elsa let out a relieved breath.

"Come in, my lord, come in," Neil said, stepping aside for Cree to enter.

Cree entered the cottage and while it always welcomed with pleasant or delicious scents, he gave no notice to that now. He was quick to ask, "Have you seen Lara since Dawn's return?"

Elsa's brow scrunched in thought and before she could respond, Neil spoke.

"I saw her earlier today. She came her looking for you," he said, turning to his wife. "I told her you were at the keep and she should go there to speak with you. I thought she did."

Elsa shook her head. "No, I never saw her. Come to think of it, I have not seen her in a good while. She kept to herself after Dawn was gone, feeling guilty that she was not more of a help in finding her."

"She should feel guilt," Cree snapped. "Dawn never fell in the stream. Lara walked her right into a trap. She took her to where the nettles grow and two men were waiting there to abduct her. Lara misdirected us while the men made off with Dawn."

Elsa paled. "Good Lord, why would she do that?"

"That is what I am going to find out, then Lara will pay for her betrayal."

Chapter Six

Dawn was annoyed and it made her smile since it made her realize that she was feeling much stronger today. She had woken in Cree's arms and was looking forward to lingering there with him as they had often done, though it usually, actually more often than not, lead to them making love. And while she was not sure if she was strong enough for coupling yet, she would not mind a kiss or two, but Cree had hurried out of bed soon after he had seen that she was awake.

He had dressed with even more haste and told her that he would be feeding her this morning. She had tried to tell him she could feed herself, but he refused to listen.

"You are not eating enough," he had argued.

She had been grateful when Sloan had suddenly shown up and Cree hurried off with him after ordering her to eat more and for Beast to guard her. If she heard him tell Beast to guard her one more time, she was going to scream. A lot of good it would do since no one would hear it.

Frustrated, she got out of bed slowly, testing her strength and while she still felt weakness in her legs, they felt much stronger than she had expected. She took her time, so as not to tire herself, and got dressed slowly. She found the task easier than she thought, slipping on a plain white shift and yellow tunic over it. However, when it came to her shoes, she found herself in a quandary. The blisters on her feet were healing nicely, but she worried the shoes might delay the healing. In the end, the decision was simple. She would go barefoot.

She took her time to comb and braid her long hair and did not feel the least tired when she was done, though her arms felt the effort.

She looked to Beast with a smile and waved her hand for him to follow as she walked without haste to the door.

Dawn was glad Cree no longer had two warriors standing guard at their bedchamber door. She knew it was because of Beast. He trusted the animal to protect her and so did she.

She took the stairs with careful and slow steps, Beast following behind her. Cree had promised her that he would bring the twins to her later, but she could not wait another moment to see them and she could not spend another full day in that room. She might not be fully healed yet, but it would do her no good to continue to lie abed all day.

Laughter and talk drifted down the stairs and she smiled, hearing her son and daughter talking and laughing. She stopped abruptly, her smile vanishing, and worry setting in. She had been gone three months, would her children recognize her. She had gotten thin. And would they remember her gestures that they had learned to understand and responded to?

Beast leaned against her leg, reminding her that he was there to help.

Dawn smiled, patted his head, and continued up the stairs.

"Mummy," the two little ones squealed as soon as they saw her and Dawn's worry vanished in an instant. She lowered herself down on the floor to sit as the two ran at her and threw her arms wide to greet them with a tight hug. She kissed and cuddled them close and they laughed and kissed her and hung on to her as if they would never let her go.

When the hugs were done, a bit of worry returned as she tapped her chest, crossed her arms tight against it, then reached out to poke each one of them in the chest. Would they understand her?

"Love Mummy," they both said and hugged her again.

They had not forgotten and Dawn's heart soared with joy. The two had grown in the few months she had been gone. Valan was looking more and more like his da, dark eyes, and his light brown hair beginning to streak blond. Lizabeth's hair was red, dark like Dawn's but beginning to streak blonde like her brother's. Her hair would be far more lovely than Dawn's dark red hair and her features far more beautiful, a thought that could not make Dawn happier. What gave her even more joy was that her daughter had a voice. She had not inherited Dawn's affliction.

Dawn gestured to Nell and Ina, the two women who looked after the twins, as if spooning something into her mouth and pointed to the twins.

"Aye, my lady, they ate this morn," Nell said with a smile. "They have missed you."

Nell was Henry, the tracker's wife. They had wed just before Dawn had gone missing. She was petite with a pretty face and had more patience than Dawn thought possible. Ina was a plain lass and a bit plump, with such a pleasant nature that she had men constantly after her, but none had yet to catch her eye or interest.

Lizbeth poked her mum's cheek. "You stay."

Dawn smiled. She issued orders like her da, with a strong command. Dawn wasted no time in assuring her daughter and son with repeated nods and hugs that she was home to stay. After a bunch more hugs and kisses, Dawn gestured to Nell and Ina once again, pointing outside the room.

"You want to take the bairns somewhere?" Ina asked.

Dawn nodded.

The two stepped forward and that was when Beast made himself known, entering the room from where he had kept guard just outside the door, no one having noticed him.

The two women jumped back with a squeal and Valan jumped into his mum's arms. Lizbeth approached the large dog without fear.

"Pretty pup," Lizbeth said and walked over to hug Beast who was so taken back by the little lass that he sat there while she buried her face in his fur and hugged him.

Dawn quickly patted his head and pressed her face to Beast's, then to each of her children, letting him know she loved him as well as the little ones.

Beast licked Lizbeth's face and the little lass giggled.

Not to be outdone, Valan went to the dog and hugged the animal, though not as tightly as Lizbeth.

Dawn pointed to the two women and patted her chest, then patted Beast's head so he would know the two women were to be trusted.

"He will not hurt us, will he?" Nell asked.

Ina smiled and went to the dog and gave him a rub behind his ear. "Of course not. He is a gentleman. The villagers speak of how protective and faithful he is to you, my lady."

Dawn nodded.

"He will have many friends here," Ina said.

Dawn smiled, grateful for her easy acceptance of Beast, since the large animal could easily intimidate.

Ina and Nell each scooped up one of the twins to carry down the stairs, Dawn not objecting. She had healed some, but not enough to carry either of the twins. Soon the small group entered the Great Hall and the few servants, in attendance, greeted Dawn with smiles and blessings that she had returned home.

Dawn noticed that one of the three warriors seated at a table got up as soon as he saw her and rushed out of the hall.

She had limited time before her husband appeared. The twins grabbed for her hands when the two women set them on their feet and Dawn smiled and walked them to the kitchen.

"Turbett, treat," Valan said with a grin.

Nell laughed softly. "Turbett spoils them, my lady."

"And us too," Ina giggled.

Dawn was pleased to hear that since Turbett intimidated most people. Sloan feared talking to him, but then Sloan feared losing the man as a cook, his meals exceptionally tasty.

"Who is this who has come to visit?"

"Turbett!" the two little ones cried out and broke free from Dawn to run and be caught up in the man's beefy arms.

Dawn smiled at the way the large, bald man grinned and cuddled the two close. Turbett rarely smiled, though he did at times when he looked at Flanna, the unlikely pair having fallen in love. Their dominant natures often clashed, but love always shined in their eyes.

"Have you come for a treat?" Turbett asked.

Lizbeth turned a sweet smile on him and kissed his full cheek. "See you, Turbett."

The large man looked ready to melt.

"Berries!" Valan cried out, being more direct.

"Those two have his heart."

Dawn turned and smiled seeing Flanna and threw her arms around the woman.

Flanna returned the hug. Dawn had worked in the kitchen when Flanna was the cook, before Cree attacked the castle, claiming it for himself with the blessing of the King.

"You are well enough to be out of bed, my lady?" Flanna asked with concern.

Dawn preferred that Flanna address her as she had always done, Dawn, not my lady. But Flanna had insisted it was not proper and Cree would never stand for it.

Sometimes, though, when there was just the two of them, Flanna would call her as she once did, Dawn, and it always pleased her to hear it.

Dawn smiled, patted her chest, and nodded.

"It is good to know you do better," Flanna said and nodded at the twins. "He loves those two. They can get anything they want from him, that dog too."

Dawn noticed then that Beast had followed the children and sat near Turbett as if he too was expecting a treat.

"Cree ordered the dog be fed each day. Turbett was annoyed, as usual, at first, then he was impressed by how the dog would come to the open kitchen door every morning and evening, after he was finished outside and before he returned to you and wait for his meal. He did not try to steal any food, he simply ate what Turbett gave him."

He was trained that way, Dawn thought. Food was something Beast had never been deprived of until their journey home. Then his instincts and hunger had taken over, and he had hunted,

"My lady," Turbett said with a respectful bob of his head. "It is good to have you home."

Dawn acknowledged his remark with a smile and a nod.

"Let me fix you a nice brew along with some honey bread just freshly made," he said.

Dawn nodded again, and Flanna returned her and the twins to the Great Hall to settle them comfortably at a table. A bowl of blueberries was placed between the twins and soon their little fingers were stained from snatching up berry after berry.

Dawn found herself enjoying a second piece of sweet bread, surprised how the tasty treat had woken her hunger.

"What are you doing out of bed?" Cree's strong voice thundered through the Great Hall.

Valan hurried closer to his mum, while Lizbeth scrambled off the bench and ran to her da.

"Da! Da!" she cried out with a huge smile.

Cree's scowl vanished in an instant and he scooped his daughter up into his powerful arms. Her little arms went around his neck to squeeze tight, then she kissed him on the cheek three times.

"Mum home," she said with glee.

"That she is, Lizbeth, home to stay," Cree said.

Lizbeth nodded, agreeing with him.

Cree walked over to his wife and son and saw that Beast had taken a protective stance beside Dawn.

He was about to snap at the dog when his daughter squirmed in his arms to be released and when he placed her on the floor, she ran to Beast and threw her arms around the large dog, burying her face in his fur and hugging him tight.

"Love Beast," she said, raising her head and kissing the top of the dog's snout.

Cree knew then and there his daughter would be the fearless one or perhaps foolish one, acting without thinking. Not so Valan, he was more cautious, though no less courageous, watching, seeing the best approach as he slipped off the bench and took slow steps to his sister.

Cree left the twins to play with Beast while he planted his hands on the table to lean over and bring his face close to his wife's.

"Why are you not in bed?" he demanded, keeping his voice low but stern.

She smiled, grabbed his handsome face in her hands, and kissed him.

"That is not an answer," he said, though he did enjoy the kiss and he noticed a blush to her cheeks that had not been there this morning.

She grabbed his face again and kissed him again, a bit slower this time.

Cree silently cursed, her sweet kisses arousing him.

"I assume you are feeling better since you have returned to your old ways of not obeying me," he said.

Her body shook with a silent laugh.

"Mummy laughs at you," Lizbeth said, pointing at her da, and laughed herself.

Cree was about to tell his wife she would not be laughing much longer when he saw the delight on her face and how Valan was chuckling as well. At that moment, he was never so grateful for his wife's disobedience, realizing that with her return, he had gotten his family back.

"Are you laughing at me too, Lizbeth," he said with a smile and turned from his wife to scoop his daughter up in one arm, more laughter bursting from her, then reaching to scoop his son up with his other arm, and nuzzling with a playful growl at their necks.

Dawn laughed, watching the joy on her children and husband's faces and placed a comforting hand on Beast's head to let him know all was well.

"Help, mummy help," Lizbeth shouted through her giggles.

Dawn hurried up off the bench to join them and a pain ripped through her side so fast and hard, she had to grab the edge of the table to keep from falling.

Cree saw her face pale and her hands grip the table. He quickly lowered the twins to the ground and playfully growled, "I am going to get mummy."

He had his wife up in her arms in an instant while his son and daughter playfully attacked his legs.

Flanna suddenly appeared and Cree still could never understand how the woman always appeared when needed, but was glad she did. He nodded toward the children.

"Turbett has cooked something special for you two," Flanna said and held out her hands.

Valan and Lizbeth ran to her, though Lizbeth stopped and looked to her mum and da.

"Go," Cree said. "I will stay with Mum. Beast, go with them."

The dog looked to Dawn and when she nodded, he walked over to Lizbeth.

Lizbeth smiled and patted Beast's head. "Treat, Beast."

The dog hurried off with her.

Dawn placed her hand to her side.

"Your side pains you?"

She nodded.

"I will get you to bed."

She shook her head and placed her hand to his cheek and her brow to his temple.

"You need to rest," he said gently, worried over her and hating to see her in pain.

Dawn nodded, then shook her head.

Familiar with that response, he said, "You know you need to rest, but not right now."

She kissed his cheek.

"You are stubborn, wife."

She tapped his chest.

"I am not stubborn," he said with feigned sternness and kissed her cheek before settling with her in his arms on the bench. "I am relieved and pleased that you are up and about, but you must not do too much. You still need rest and to eat more to fully heal."

Dawn turned her head and pointed to the honey bread on the table and smiled as she held up two fingers.

"You ate two slices. That more than pleases me," he said thrilled that her appetite was improving.

Dawn tapped her husband's lips, then her chest, eager to hear about Lara.

"Tell you what?"

Cree knew what she asked, but he had missed seeing her expressions that many times spoke louder than words and he smiled when she narrowed her eyes, scrunched her brow, and pursed her lips, which he knew all too well meant tell-me-or-else. It was another thing that confirmed her strength was returning.

He kissed her lips. "I have missed that look."

She gave it again to him.

He laughed. "Try as you might, wife, you cannot intimidate me."

Dawn sighed, a frown following, and her shoulders drooping.

Cree tapped her on the nose. "That will not work either, since you never give up that fast."

Dawn poked him in the chest and tapped her own repeatedly.

"Now there is my demanding wife," Cree said with a laugh.

Dawn shook her head.

"You are demanding," Cree insisted with another laugh.

She tapped his chest repeatedly, letting him know he was the demanding one.

"Stubborn, demanding, is that what you think of me, wife?" He chuckled.

She went to nod and stopped, her eyes narrowing and she mouthed. *Devious.*

"What was that you said, wife" he asked teasingly.

She tapped his chest, tugged at her ear, then tapped her own chest, letting him know he heard her clear enough. She tapped his lips again, then her chest more firmly so that he understood he better tell her and now.

Cree gave her a quick kiss. "I have so missed talking with you."

Good lord, but she loved this man, always speaking to her as if he could truly hear her words. She rested her hand to his chest and kissed him gently, showing him she felt the same.

"Lara is nowhere to be found," Cree said finally giving her the news she had been anxious to hear. "Neil saw her just yesterday morning when she arrived at Elsa's cottage wanting to speak with her. There has been no sign of her since." He shook his head. "I had been so distraught over you being swept away in the rushing stream that I did not think clearly enough. I should have seen that it was all a lie. I should have looked closer at things."

Dawn shook her head and mouthed, *Lara fault.*

"And mine for believing her."

"Lara gave you no reason to believe she lied."

Cree and Dawn both turned their heads to see Old Mary standing on the opposite side of the table. They had been so engrossed in each other, they had not heard her approach. But then she could be silent when she wanted to be.

"Lara gave none of us any reason not to believe her," Old Mary continued. "I truly believe she was sorry and regretted her actions when it was done, which was why no one ever suspected anything other than what she told us was the truth." Old Mary sighed. "If anyone is to blame, it should be me for failing to make sense of what I saw."

"Does it make sense to you now?" Cree asked.

"Unfortunately, no, but I do know one thing for sure… death comes our way."

Chapter Seven

Old Mary's words continued to haunt Cree throughout the day. Death had come close only to be chased away. Was it returning to claim what it had lost? Death was a formidable adversary, but not completely unconquerable. Cree intended to remain cautious, keep a keen eye, and a sharp ear. This time he would miss nothing.

He climbed the stairs, supper was waiting for him in his bedchamber. He would share it with Dawn. It had been a good day, having gotten to spend some time with his wife and the twins. He had insisted that Dawn return to her room to rest after speaking with Old Mary. He had felt her body grow weak in his arms. She had pushed too hard, had done too much for just getting out of bed. When she did not argue with him, she had confirmed his suspicions. She was tired and needed to rest.

He entered his bedchamber to find Dawn, in her nightdress, seated in one of the two chairs at the table that held a generous supper. He had made sure there would be more than enough food, hoping his wife would find one item more than another to her liking and eating more of it as she had done with the honey bread this morning.

He smiled when he saw that she was munching on a piece of cheese.

She gave him a you-caught-me grin and patted her stomach.

"I am glad to find you hungry," he said and went to her to give her cheek a kiss before taking the seat opposite her and breaking off a sizeable chunk of bread from the loaf.

63

"And I am pleased you did not wait. You need to eat so you can heal."

Cree was glad she was chatty as well. She gestured slowly so that he could more easily understand her, though he was more than familiar with her gestures by now. She could, however, still confuse him when her hands moved too fast.

"I see that Lizbeth can be fearless, though I worry more foolish at times," Cree said when she expressed how the twins had grown in the short time she had been gone. "Much like her mum."

Dawn smiled wide and pointed to him.

"You think she is like me?"

Dawn nodded and mouthed *fearless*.

"That would be you," he said, "fearless. Otherwise you would have never survived your abduction."

Lara, she mouthed.

"She still has not been found, not even a trace of her. I do not understand where she could have gone to. The sentinels that patrol the land has seen no sign of her." He shook his head. "It is puzzling."

Dawn turned her head, her eyes going to the flames that burned in the hearth.

Cree wondered what she was thinking. What might be troubling her.

"Dawn," he said softly and she turned to look at him. "Tell me what happened?" He had been patient, at least he had thought he had been, but he needed some answers, needed to know what she had been through."

She reached for her tankard, the brew still warm and sipped at it as if needing to fortify herself. She placed it back on the table and proceeded to tell him. She hugged herself, but it soon resembled a struggle when suddenly her arms broke free and she pumped her arms as if she were running.

"You escaped the men who took you?" Cree asked.

She nodded.

"How long after they took you did you escape them?"

She held up four fingers.

"Four days."

Dawn confirmed with a nod.

Cree worried what may have happened to her in those four days and he was quick to ask, "Did they hurt you?"

Dawn stared at him for a moment, then squeezed her breast and dropped her hand between her legs.

Cree held his breath.

Dawn shook her head.

"They did not force themselves on you," he said with a relief he could not hide.

She shook her head and shook her finger back and forth.

"Are you saying they were forbidden to touch you?"

She nodded again.

"Who forbid them?"

She shrugged.

"They never said?"

She shook her head.

"How did you get away from them?" Cree asked.

Dawn gestured jumping, then moving as if she was swimming fast.

"You jumped in rushing water?" he asked, thinking she had done what was necessary to escape them even if it had meant risking her life.

Dawn nodded, gestured swimming again, then her arms dropped as if she collapsed and her eyes closed for a moment, then opened suddenly and she rubbed her arms and sighed as if she was warm and safe.

"Someone found and tended you," Cree said, grateful to whoever it was.

Dawn nodded.

He was about to ask if it was a man or woman who had helped her when she yawned wide and dropped her head back against the chair, closing her eyes.

"You are tired," Cree said and Dawn nodded, not lifting her head or opening her eyes.

Cree stood, pleased and relieved with what she had told him so far. There was time to learn more. Now she needed to rest.

"Time for bed," he said and stood and walked around the table to scoop her up and carry her to bed. He pulled the blanket over her and she scrunched her brow and shook her head, questioning why he was not joining her.

"The candles need extinguishing and I need to shed my garments," he explained.

She smiled and nodded and turned on her side to keep her eyes—fighting to remain open—on him.

Cree snuffed out the candles with his fingers and slipped out of his clothes. His wife was nearly asleep when he slipped beneath the blanket and took her in his arms.

Dawn cuddled against him, wishing she was naked, wishing she could feel his warm flesh against her own naked flesh, but she had been too tired to shed her nightdress. Her body was beginning to stir to life again and it would not be long before she would want to make love with her husband. Something, however, told her that he might not feel the same. There was a reluctance in him, she could feel it. He held her tight, stroked her arms, her back, yet his hands kept his distance from any intimate touch. And he would have never let her in bed with her nightdress on.

That was not like him.

Her husband could never keep his hands off her. Did he fear her too fragile to touch yet? If so, as soon as she felt well enough, she would show him she was far from fragile. She had missed the intimacy they shared and she longed to share it again. And they would, she would make sure of it.

***

Three days of rest, poultices, and endless brews and Dawn had had enough. The bruise to her side was fading by the day as were the painful movements. Her feet were healing nicely, most of the blisters mended enough for them not to cause discomfort, and Elsa had assured her that the bite mark on her backside had faded considerably.

She was feeling much improved, much like her old self and she hoped Cree would start treating her as such. He was treating her as if she was fragile and fragile was something she had never been. Vulnerable at times due to her lack of a voice, but she had maintained a strength and determination that had seen her through a number of difficulties, many of which her husband was aware of, some he had even caused.

Dawn smiled at some of the memories her thoughts had stirred.

"You are not only healing well, you are also happy," Lila said, approaching the large oak tree Dawn sat under, her son Thomas running to join Lizbeth and Valan busy eating blueberries from the bowl on the blanket spread out in front of them.

Dawn nodded and patted the blanket beside her, inviting Lila to join her.

Lila did not hesitate, she lowered herself down beside Dawn. "That daughter of yours has that large monster of a dog eating out of her hand."

Dawn looked and watched as Lizbeth shared the berries with Beast. The dog had taken easily to the twins, watching them with equal concern as he did her.

With a nod, Dawn agreed with her friend.

Lila leaned her shoulder against Dawn's and kept her voice low. "I am glad you did not die. I missed you so much and I have news to share with you."

Dawn looped her arm around Lila's and pressed tight against her, eager to hear what her friend had to say.

"I am with child again," Lila said, a smile spreading across her lovely face.

Dawn broke into a wide grin and threw her arms around Lila to hug her tight, then patted her chest and Lila's and asked about Paul.

Lila laughed. "He is overjoyed and, naturally, hoping for a son. I am glad this bairn will not deliver during an attack on the village." She shuddered recalling the troubling memory of Thomas's birth when Cree and his warriors attacked, laying claim to the village.

Dawn pointed out at the active village, smiling faces, sounds of laughter, children running about in play, and smiled.

Lila smiled as well, nodding as if she heard Dawn's silent voice. "The village is a good and happy place with Cree ruling over us, and glad I am for it." She patted her stomach. "This one and Thomas will be spared the suffering of a cruel overlord."

Dawn pointed to Lila's stomach and shrugged.

"The bairn should arrive about a month or so before spring," Lila said.

"You are with child?"

Dawn and Lila looked up to see Lucerne not far from them.

Lucerne's eyes turned wide and she lowered her voice as she asked, "Was it a secret?"

"Not anymore," Lila said with a laugh and shook her head when Lucerne went to apologize. "It was only a secret until I told Dawn. I wanted to make sure she knew before anyone else." She patted a spot beside her on the blanket. "Come join us."

Lucerne eagerly joined the two women.

"Your bairn arrives with the winter, if wagging tongues are truthful," Lila said.

Dawn turned a huge grin on Lucerne, patted her chest, and pointed to her.

"Dawn says she is very happy for you," Lila interpreted.

"And I am very happy you have returned to us," Lucerne said.

Dawn nodded and patted her chest, letting Lucerne know she felt the same. She did not think anyone could truly understand how much she was relieved to be home. The three months had been sheer hell for Dawn and something she wished she could forget, yet knew she never would.

"Why did you wait until only a few weeks ago to let everyone know about the bairn?" Lila asked.

Lucerne's eyes filled with sadness. "I realized not long after Dawn went missing that there was a good chance I was with child. While it brought great joy to Sloan and me, I did not think it was a good time to share it with Lord Cree, he was suffering so much, so we chose to wait."

Lila nodded and looked to Dawn. "It was a terrible time. Laughter died along with smiles and fear once again returned to the village."

Lucerne nodded, agreeing with Lila. "I was relieved when Sloan had those posts installed on the practice field, though we have Elsa to thank for that. She told Sloan that Lord Cree's warriors were suffering far too many injures, and more than minor ones, when they practiced against Lord Cree. Sloan could not believe that a new post had to be installed daily."

"His endless bouts of practice show on him," Lila said with a shudder. "His arms are enormous with muscles and I thought his grip was powerful before, but now" —she shook her head— "I saw him grab one of his warriors and toss him as if he weighed nothing."

Dawn listened, thinking on the changes in her husband since her return. She had thought him a large, strong, and intimidating man when they first met. His recent physical changes made him even more so, though to others, not to her.

Or so she told herself.

She wanted to believe her husband had not changed, but there was something that warned otherwise. She could not say exactly what it was, she just knew something was different. It had nothing to do with his love for her. She had not a kernel of doubt that their love was eternal. So what was it that disturbed him?

The women continued to talk, Lila interpreting for Dawn allowing the conversation to flow more smoothly. Dawn felt at peace with these women, her friends, talking about everything and anything, feeling at home once again.

Valan drifted over to his mum to settle in her arms and fall asleep. Thomas did the same with his mum while Lizbeth fell asleep cuddled against Beast. Nell and Ina came to collect the twins who did not budge when lifted and carted off to continue their nap, Beast trotting after them once Dawn approved with a nod.

Lucerne gave a yawn and excused herself, announcing the bairn she carried needed a nap and Lila soon followed, cradling a sleeping Thomas in her arms as she rose to take her leave.

"I will see you soon," Lila said.

Dawn nodded and watched her friend walk off. She sat alone under the tree, thinking, not always a good thing. Her thoughts drifted, time and again, to her time away. Try as she might, she could not stop the memories from invading her thoughts.

"You think too much on it."

Dawn looked up, not at all startled by the unexpected, yet familiar voice. She smiled at Old Mary.

"You keep too much inside yourself... talk to him," Old Mary urged and groaned as she tried to lower herself to sit beside Dawn.

Dawn reached out and helped her to sit.

"These old bones are protesting far too much of late," Old Mary said with a laugh.

Dawn hugged the old woman and shook her head. She did not want to lose her. She was the closest thing she had to a mum.

"Do not worry, Fate intends to keep me around far longer than I would like."

Dawn smiled and nodded, showing she agreed with Fate.

Old Mary took Dawn's hand and gave it a comforting squeeze. "Talk to me."

Dawn's heaving chest was the only sign of her heavy sigh.

"You carry a burden, you need to release," Old Mary said.

Dawn shook her head.

"If not now, when?"

Dawn shrugged.

"What is it you fear?"

Dawn spread her hands wide, as if encompassing everything.

"Cree loves you far too much for you to lose everything," Old Mary said.

Dawn sighed again and turned her head.

Old Mary took her hand once again. "You need not fear telling him anything. Cree would forgive you anything."

Dawn patted her chest.

"You question if you can forgive yourself?"

Dawn nodded.

Shouts rang out and Old Mary called out to Timmins, the smithy, as he ran past them. "What goes on?"

"Lara has been found... badly injured."

Old Mary shook her head and mumbled a blessing for the poor unfortunate lass.

Dawn was not feeling as forgiving, though she did offer a blessing for the lass. If Lara died, the truth would not be known and Dawn was eager to learn who had wanted her abducted. And even more so... was she still in danger of being abducted again?

Old Mary struggled to get to her feet. "I will go see what I can learn."

Dawn rushed to her feet to help Old Mary, forgetting that a sudden movement could cause her pain, and it did. She pressed her hand to her side as if it would do some good and at that moment she caught sight of her husband walking toward her. While the pain tore through her whole body, turning every limb weak, she was reminded again how thick her husband's body had grown with muscle. As a veil of darkness began to descend over her, she struggled to reach out to Cree, knowing he would be there for her. He would always be there for her.

Cree saw his wife's face turn a deathly pale, saw her fight to stretch her hand out to him for help, and he ran, fearing he would not reach her in time.

Chapter Eight

Cree barely caught Dawn before she hit the ground, her head snapping from the jolt of being scooped up so abruptly in his arms.

"What happened?" Cree demanded of Old Mary.

"She grabbed her side when she stood," Old Mary explained.

"Go find Elsa and send her to my bedchamber," he ordered.

"She will be tending Lara," Old Mary said.

"My wife comes first," Cree ordered and hurried off with Dawn tucked tight in his arms.

Cree was worried for his wife and annoyed that he had not been more forceful in his demand that she listened to him and continued to rest more. It might appear that she had grown stronger, but she had yet to heal completely.

She was stirring when he placed her on the bed, her eyes fluttering, fighting to open.

"You will rest," he demanded when her eyes finally opened to look upon him.

That he sounded as if he claimed it law brought a smile to her face, though she also heard his worry and she did not want him to worry. She was feeling good. She had moved much too fast, startled by the news of Lara being found, for an injury that was still healing.

Dawn decided the best way to handle her husband was to appease him and so she nodded.

Cree brought his nose to rest against hers. "I mean it."

His warm, minty breath fanned her lips and set an ember stirring in her. She did not think, she did what was

73

familiar to her, what she had so desperately missed. She brushed her lips over his in a faint kiss that she had done endless times before and once she did, it was not enough for her. She wanted more from his lips and more from him.

That he eased away from her kiss, ending it far too soon—sooner than he had ever done—annoyed her, though she told herself it was his concern for her well-being that had him doing so. Still, it bothered her.

Dawn gestured, wanting to reassure him that she felt good, the pain her own fault for not taking care when she moved.

"Elsa will make that determination," Cree said.

Dawn wanted to argue that she knew better than Elsa how she felt, but knew her husband would be too stubborn to listen. She remained quiet, not an easy chore since her hands were itching to gesture, but she kept firm hold on them.

"You will remain abed for the remainder of the day," Cree ordered.

Dawn did not respond.

"I mean it, Dawn," he said, though it sounded more like a rumbling growl.

Dawn was glad to see Elsa enter the room, Cree having left the door open.

"What happened?" Elsa asked anxiously.

Dawn had come to know Elsa well and considered her a friend. She could see that the concern in the woman's eyes was not for her. That meant that she was worried for Lara.

Dawn was quick to gesture, resting her hand to her side, then suddenly raising it and rolling her head and eyes as if she was about to faint.

"You stood too quickly," Elsa said and Dawn nodded. "The pain is gone?"

Dawn nodded again and smiled.

"You feel good?" Elsa asked and Dawn confirmed with a sharp nod. "Good, then there is nothing to be concerned with." She turned to leave.

"Dawn needs to rest more," Cree said. halting Elsa's quick steps.

Elsa sighed and shook her head. "Dawn knows what she needs. Let her be."

Her words did not go over well with Cree. He walked over to Elsa and stood towering over her as he said, "I do not care what happens to Lara, though I would prefer she lives so I can find out who was responsible for abducting Dawn. My first and only priority is my wife as she is yours. You will tell her what she needs to do to heal since you know as well as I do that at times she does not do as she should. If you do not, you will suffer the consequences."

Elsa bowed her head. "I am sorry, my lord, Dawn does come first and it would be wise of her to rest a bit after suffering a pain that caused her to faint, though it is not necessary she remain abed for the rest of the day."

Dawn almost jumped out of bed and hugged the woman. She would have gone completely mad if she had to spend the rest of the day in bed. Besides, she was curious about Lara.

Cree turned to his wife. "You heard her and you will follow what she says and remain abed for at least three hours."

That was far too long, but Dawn nodded, already planning to leave the bed before then.

"Rest, wife," Cree ordered and turned to Elsa. "Tell me of Lara." He walked to the door, Elsa following him.

Dawn eased herself out of bed, not wanting to suffer another pain, her side having been left with a dull ache. She went to the open door, hoping to hear Cree and Elsa talking but they were already descending the staircase. She hurried over to it and caught only a few words.

"Lara does not do well."

She returned to her bedchamber, though not to the bed. She paced the room, impatient to go and see Lara for herself. She wanted answers as much as her husband did. But if Lara was not doing well there would be no answers to Dawn's endless questions. And what if she died before she could answer them? There was no one else to give them answers. Or was there?

Had he known more than he had told her? She knew little of him so she certainly had not trusted him the whole time she had spent with him. And she thought it better if Cree never knew about him, since she had no answers to the questions her husband was sure to ask.

"I knew you would not remain abed."

Dawn turned to see her husband standing in the doorway. She ran to him and threw her arms around him and buried her face in his neck, never wanting to let go.

Cree's arms closed around her tight. He wished he knew what caused her sudden fright, though he wondered if it had something to do with Lara being found.

"I am here. You are safe," he said and kissed her brow.

A shiver so strong ran through Dawn that it raised gooseflesh along Cree's arms and he scooped her up once again and carried her to bed. He tucked her beneath the blankets and sat on the bed beside her.

"You need to rest, not worry. I will find out everything and will see those suffer for what has been done to you." He leaned over and kissed her brow again. "Now promise me you will stay abed and rest for a few hours."

Dawn crossed her heart with her finger, giving her word and realizing, not that she wanted to admit it, that she did need some rest.

"Your word pleases me, wife," he said and gently kissed her lips. "Where is Beast?"

Dawn rocked her arm as if she held a bairn.

"With the twins."

Dawn yawned as she nodded and she was surprised her eyes grew heavy.

"I will go get him and have him watch over you."

She yawned and this time shook her head, letting her husband know it was not necessary.

It did not matter to Cree. He wanted Beast by her side, protecting her while he went to talk with Lara. He waited until her eyes fully closed. He had seen how the faint she had suffered left her weak, her body crying out for rest, but she had refused to recognize it. And he had seen how Elsa was anxious to tend Lara, thus not looking more closely at Dawn. He had made sure once again to remind her that Dawn came first, now and always.

He waited a few moments after Dawn's eyes closed, listening to her soft breathing. He had missed hearing it at night when he woke and was ever grateful that he would miss it no more. She was there in their bed again and there she would stay.

Beast would help him achieve that. As much as he thought to spend every waking minute with her to make certain she was kept safe, he knew it was not a sensible course of action. And Dawn would not approve of it. She would feel a prisoner in her own home and he would not have that.

He went to fetch Beast and watched as the large dog rose from where he lay at the open door to the twin's bedchamber and stand, his chest out, his head up, teeth bared, and letting loose a slight rumbling growl.

Beast ceased his growl when Cree stepped in front of him and said, "You guard my children well, Beast. Now you need to guard Dawn."

The dog went to the steps and stopped to glance back at Cree.

"I am right behind you," Cree said, walking over to him and the dog turned and hurried down the stairs.

Beast did not need any further orders, though Cree was quick to say as soon as the animal entered the room, "Guard, Dawn."

Cree left, thinking Dawn had yet to tell him where she had come across Beast. The animal followed orders which meant he had to have belonged to someone at some time. But who and where and how had Dawn wound up with him? A detail he was eager to discover.

Sloan was coming up the steps of the keep and stopped and waited for Cree, when he saw him walking down them. They walked together to Elsa's cottage.

"Lara was stabbed several times and left to die," Sloan said.

"Who found her and where was she found?" Cree asked.

"Henry found her not that far from where Dawn had disappeared."

"What was Henry doing in that area?"

"Looking for anything that might prove helpful in finding out what happened to Dawn."

Cree thought about when Henry had first approached him, asking to join Cree's warriors. He had been honest with Cree, making it clear he was no warrior, passable with a weapon, but he was a good tracker. Cree had already had two trackers, but there had been something about the quiet, almost reluctant way, he had spoken about being a good tracker that had given Cree reason to pause and give him a chance to see what the young man could do.

Henry had been more than a good tracker. He was the best Cree had ever seen. He kept much to himself, explaining he preferred the quiet of the woods and the land rather than people. Henry was kept away from battle, the warriors making sure he stayed safe ever since he had tracked down two of their wounded warriors who had been dragged off after a fierce battle with barbarians. The warriors had been well aware of what the men would suffer and when Henry told them of where the group had camped, Cree and his men had gone and got their men back and finished off the small group of barbarians.

Henry was so quiet, the warriors teased him mercilessly about never finding a wife. They were all surprised when Henry and Nell got together, but unlike others, Cree had seen the way Nell looked at Henry. The young man did not stand a chance, not that he objected since Cree had seen that Henry had looked the same at Nell.

Cree had also seen that Nell had not been the only one interested in Henry. Lara had been as well and he recalled how Lara had sulked around the village after it became known that Henry and Nell would wed.

Why that came to mind, he could not say. It did not seem probable that it had anything to do with Dawn's abduction, but then he would not make the mistake of dismissing the thought lightly.

Ann, Elsa's other helper, steps faltered as she stepped out of the healing cottage, tears running down her cheeks as she stumbled to the bench against the wall to sit. She brought her hands up and buried her face in them and wept.

Cree hoped he was not too late. He entered the cottage to find Elsa standing over the bed, her face pale and tears rolling down her cheeks.

"She is gone?" Cree asked.

Elsa turned with a jump, Cree having startled her, and shook her head. "Not yet, but there is nothing more I can do for her."

Cree stared down at the young woman, no color to her face, as if death had already claimed her. A blanket rested over her chest, almost to her neck.

"Has she said anything?" Cree asked.

"Sorry. She keeps saying she is sorry," Elsa said, wiping away the tears that ran down her cheeks. "She has lost much blood. I do not think she will survive the night."

"Let me know if she wakes," Cree said and left the cottage. He tried to find it in his heart to forgive the dying young woman, but he could not. The past three months had been a living hell for him and even worse for Dawn because of Lara, and Fate had given her what she deserved.

Cree stepped out of the cottage to find Elwin talking with Sloan. Elwin was one of his most trusted and fierce warriors. He was a large man and had a kind heart, which is what had brought Dorrie and him together.

"A messenger from the Clan Macardle waits for you in the Great Hall," Elwin said.

"Sloan wait with the messenger in my solar. I will follow shortly," Cree ordered. "Elwin, find Henry and have him wait for me in the Great Hall."

Cree watched the two men go in opposite directions, then he turned to the woman on the bench, her weeping having subsided.

"Ann," he said and the woman jumped up off the bench, her eyes turning wide and her face losing all color. "Sit," he ordered and she nearly collapsed on the bench, as if her legs were simply too weak to hold her.

Ann shook her head. "I told her not to trust him, my lord, but she was so desperate for someone to love her. But I never ever thought she would betray her own."

"What are you talking about?" Cree asked, looming over her as he came to stand in front of her.

Ann shrunk back against the cottage wall, stumbling with fright as she tried to speak.

"Tell me what you know and no harm will come to you," Cree warned.

"I know nothing, nothing," Ann said, having seen the punishment Cree had imposed on those he deemed deserved it. "I am loyal to you, my lord, and the clan. Never would I betray you."

"Then speak up and answer me," Cree snapped, having lost all patience with the weeping woman. "Tell me of this man you warned Lara about."

Ann was quick to speak this time. "I know little about him. She kept him a secret."

"Why?"

"He told her to."

Again Cree asked, "Why?"

"I do not know. Lara told me it was not safe for her to say, but in time all would be known and all would see how much he loved her. I told her she was being foolish. That she should not trust him." Ann shook her head. "I am ashamed to say I began to believe it all a tale, that there was no handsome man whose garments were of the finest cloth. So one day I followed her. I caught a glimpse of him. He was wickedly handsome and his garments were of the finest cloth, but," — she shivered— "he had an evil grin. I warned her not to return to him, but she told me I was jealous and she spoke of him no more to me."

"Did you tell Lara that you saw the man?"

"I did and that was when she told me I was jealous of her."

"Do you know if she told this man that you saw him?" Cree asked.

"I do not believe she did. She got angry with me when I told her, saying that if he knew someone had followed her, then he would not trust her anymore."

"You should have come to me with this when Lara first told you of this man," Cree said with a harshness that brought fresh tears to the young woman's eyes.

"I thought it a harmless tale. When I heard that Lara was responsible for what happened to Lady Dawn, I feared I would be blamed, having known she was meeting someone in the woods. Please, my lord, forgive my foolishness," Ann begged.

"Did she continue to meet this man after Dawn was believed lost?"

"That I do not know. She never spoke of him again, though she did grow more and more solemn after Lady Dawn disappeared. I thought nothing of it since the whole village had grown solemn as well. Again, my lord, I beg your forgiveness."

"It was your duty to report this man hiding in the woods to Sloan or me. I will not abide duty being ignored or the excuse that fear stopped you. You should have feared more what I would do to you than your friend losing her lover. You will spend two days in the stock."

Ann paled worse than before. She had seen what had happened to Dorrie when placed in the stock. The villagers had thrown all sorts of rotted food at her and had spat on her.

Cree signaled one of his warriors with the snap of his hand. "Have this woman put in the stock for two days."

"What is happening here?" Elsa asked, upon hearing Cree's decree as she stepped out of the cottage. "Ann has harmed no one and I am in need of her. She is my only helper."

Cree turned a scowl on Elsa. "Her punishment could be far worse and I will hear no more from you."

"As you say, my lord," Elsa said, aware that she had already said too much.

Cree took strong strides to the keep, then stopped suddenly. He turned with hastened steps to make his way to the stocks. A crowd had formed, curious whispers circling the area as Ann's neck and wrists were secured in the stocks.

Silence took hold of the crowd as soon as Cree stepped forward. He stood tall, his shoulders back, his chest more powerful with muscle than it had ever been and his demeanor as commanding as ever.

82

"Ann chose to keep a secret of Lara's, not thinking it may have helped in finding Dawn when she had gone missing or to find Lara when she had disappeared. Her punishment is two days in the stock. It could have been far worse, but since she had the courage to finally tell me, I saw fit to lessen her punishment. You will not throw garbage at her or spit on her or you will join her in the stocks. Ann may have delayed coming to me, but in the end she did tell me what she knew. For that, I commend her. If you know something, even think you may know something, talk with Sloan or seek me out."

Cree turned and walked to the keep not expecting anyone to step forward and speak. They would all think on his words, then seek out Sloan if they thought they had something to share. They were too fearful to come to him.

"You will wait for me," Cree said to Henry his tracker as he passed through the Great Hall to his solar. Once he entered the room, he looked to the messenger weary from travel. "What word have you for me?"

Chapter Nine

Dawn woke with a small stretch and turned to see Beast, his chin resting on the bed and a whispery whine coming from him. He needed to go out, which meant no one had seen to his care since he had been left with the twins.

With another stretch, Dawn got out of bed, feeling much refreshed. She had to remember that her body still needed to heal and a nap helped with that. It took a moment for her to recall what had brought her to her bedchamber... a pain and a faint.

She patted Beast's head and patted her chest and pointed to the door, letting him know they would be leaving the room.

Beast danced around in circles, his happy dance that he let only her see.

She slipped on her boots and would have lingered to tend her braid, far too many strands falling loose, but decided not to delay. Beast looked far too anxious to go out.

When Beast finished outside, she would return and see to the twins, but right now she hurried through the Great Hall, greeting Henry with a smile and a nod as she rushed through the room and out the door. Beast took off as soon as his feet hit the keep steps.

It was then she remembered Lara. How could she have forgotten? But then the nap had left her feeling peaceful, content as she once had felt. Now, however, with Lara on her mind, that peace turned to troublesome thoughts. She made her way to Elsa's cottage, hoping she could talk with Lara.

Dawn was surprised to find Lara alone and one look made her think death had claimed the young woman. Guilt had her saying a prayer over Lara. There had been enough suffering, it was time for it to end.

Lara's eyes suddenly opened and when she caught sight of Dawn, her eyes spread wide. "Sor-ry," She struggled to speak or was it that she struggled for breath? "Fool. Never loved me. Please forgive…"

Dawn found her heart going out to the woman, struggling with every breath to beg forgiveness. Lara had realized her mistake too late and that mistake had cost her dearly, but then her poor choice had brought heartache and troubling times to many.

Lara continued to struggle for breath while her eyes continued to beg for forgiveness.

Forgiveness came easy to Dawn and yet she stood looking down at Lara with a heavy and not so forgiving heart. The last three months had been like a living hell that she would not soon, if ever, forget. However, she was home, reunited with her family, all those who loved her, and Lara was dying.

Dawn reached out and gently took her hand and smiled.

"You," —Lara coughed, blood dribbling from her mouth— "forgive me."

Dawn nodded, feeling her heart swell with sadness for the woman and glad to realize that she did actually forgive her.

Lara tried to smile, but she coughed, more blood spilling from her mouth and she gripped Dawn's hand tightly and mumbled something.

It took Dawn a moment to understand what Lara had said.

Frightened.

Dawn perched herself on the edge of the bed, keeping hold of Lara's hand, and rested her other hand on the young woman's chest, then on her own and back on Lara's chest once again, letting her know that she was there with her. That she was not alone.

Lara struggled to speak, but Dawn shook her head, letting her know it was not necessary, and brought their clutched hands to rest against her chest so Lara would know she was there and all was forgiven.

It was not long before Lara took her last breath, her hand going limp in Dawn's and a tear trickled down her cheek.

"You have a good and forgiving soul."

Dawn shut her eyes against the tears that had gathered there before she opened them, then laid Lara's lifeless hand on her chest and stood to turn to Elsa.

"Lara was very sorry for what she had done," Elsa said, tears in her own eyes.

Dawn nodded and wiped at the few tears that spilled free.

Elsa wiped her own tears away and straightened her shoulders, her chin going up. "I have a favor to ask of you."

***

Cree entered his solar to find the young messenger enjoying a tankard of ale with Sloan.

"What news do you have for me?" Cree asked, though it sounded more of a demand.

The messenger, not more than ten and four years, put his tankard down, and gave a respectful bob of his head. "I am Evin of the Clan MacLoon, Lord Cree. I have come with a request from Chieftain Walsh. He is concerned with the Clan Macardle. Chieftain Angus Macardle claims that a good portion of MacLoon land actually belongs to him and he has demanded the land be returned to his rule or he will claim all of MacLoon land and the clan with it."

Cree had helped the Clan MacLoon many years ago when his life had consisted of nothing but endless battles, and the stench of blood and death were everyday odors. Chieftain Walsh MacLoon was a good and honorable man, his clan not large, but proud and resilient. They had pledged their fealty years ago to the neighboring Clan MacFiere or as the powerful chieftain was known... *Tighearna an Teine.*

Lord of Fire.

When Cree had come upon the Clan MacLoon, there had been barely a handful of the neighboring Clan MacFiere left. He had been told that the Lord of Fire had left on a mission. It had not been long after that that his wife and son left and little by little the Clan MacFiere had dwindled. What went on there now, Cree did not know, though rumors had circulated that an illness had claimed the last few occupants of the MacFiere clan and fear kept the curious away from what many now believed a haunted place.

"Chieftain Walsh MacLoon has appreciated the help you have given us in the past and requests your help in keeping the clan safe against the Clan Macardle and says he will pledge his fealty to you."

"Castle MacFiere still remains empty?" Cree asked.

"Aye, my lord." Evin nodded and his thin frame shivered. "It's a frightening place, sitting there on the hill, as if staring down on all around it, brooding and waiting for its chieftain's return."

"This land that Macardle claims belongs to the Lord of Fire, has it ever been in dispute before?" Cree asked.

Evin shook his head. "No, my lord, it has always been MacLoon land. Chieftain Walsh MacLoon believes Angus Macardle looks for an excuse to battle and take possession not only of the Clan MacLoon and our land, but of the MacFiere castle and land as well."

87

While Cree had no desire to return to battle, he would not abandon the small MacLoon clan and their honorable chieftain.

"I will have a troop of warriors return with you and see your clan protected. I will also send along a missive to Angus Macardle and let him know that if he intends to battle with the Clan MacLoon he will also battle with me as well," Cree said and went to the door, opened it, and barely got Flanna's name out when the woman appeared. "See that this young man is fed and has a place to rest."

"Aye, my lord," Flanna said.

"The Clan MacLoon is most grateful to you, Lord Cree," Evin said his young face alit with relief as he gave a respectful bob before following Flanna.

Cree went and filled a tankard with ale and turned to Sloan. "I wonder what goes on with Angus Macardle that he should suddenly want to war with his neighboring clan."

"It's been what four or five years now since the MacFiere castle has been deserted?" Sloan asked, trying to recall. "Perhaps he feels this is his chance to gain more power in the area."

"Closer to six years I believe. Why now, though? Angus is not a young man and he has three daughters that are of marriageable age. Why not marry one of them to a MacLoon and unite the two clans? I recall meeting one of his three daughters. I believe her name was Willow."

"I recall some talk about her. She is the eldest of the three sisters," Sloan said and a quick smile appeared. "I also recall someone saying that her mum gave her daughters names to impart their nature on them. Willow was named after the willow tree that bends and sways and adapts to whatever must be weathered."

"So there is a good chance she will be a dutiful and uncomplaining lass. Traits that make for a good wife. Why would Angus not wed his eldest daughter to a MacLoon and settle this feud easily? Something does not seem right. We need to learn more." He took a swig of ale. "Send Tannin with a troop of warriors to accompany Evin home. That will make Angus Macardle think twice before he does anything. Also Tannin will deliver a message to Angus from me. Ready the troop to leave tomorrow."

Sloan left to see Cree's orders carried out.

Cree downed his ale and went to the Great Hall to speak with Henry.

"Tell me about finding Lara," Cree said and motioned for Henry to sit when he stood as he joined him at the table.

"I came upon her by accident, my lord. I had picked up signs of a trail, to the east of the village and was following it when I found Lara. From what I could see, she had been crawling. I believe she was trying to make her way back to the village. I thought she was dead and when I turned her over, she looked upon me with fright and was about to crawl away when she recognized me. She spoke only one word. "Home."

Knowing Henry well, Cree said, "You followed her trail after returning her here?"

Henry nodded. "I did but it ended abruptly almost as if the person realized he had left a trail and began covering it."

"You did well, Henry," Cree said.

"Thank you, my lord," Henry said with a nod. "One other thing, I have been backtracking, thinking on the day Lara had claimed Lady Dawn had fallen in the stream. The area she had pointed us to and also where I found Lara had spots that have no sentinels. Lara must have alerted this person to where our sentinels patrol."

Cree's scowl surfaced. "That will change today. You will also speak with Ann. She followed Lara one day. You can see if that is another area that lacks sentinels."

"Aye, my lord," Henry said.

"Ann is in the stocks for not telling me what she knew. Go and speak with her. I will join you there after I see to Lady Dawn." Cree stood.

"Lady Dawn?" Henry asked, appearing confused.

"Aye, she is resting."

Henry looked doubtful about speaking.

"Say what you will," Cree ordered.

"Lady Dawn passed through the Great Hall a while ago."

Cree shook his head, though a smile crept up to tease the corners of his mouth. His wife was healing well, her having ignored his orders to rest attesting to that. He turned to go find her just as the door opened and she entered, Beast at her side. Her presence surprised him. He had thought he would find her freeing Ann.

Henry hurried out of the hall as Cree approached his wife. Dawn was taller than most women and there were times after first meeting her that her posture had been that of most servants, head bent and body drawn in so as not to call attention to themselves. And he could well understand why, since she was more vulnerable than others, having no voice.

No more, though. She had gained courage and confidence in the two years they had been together, not that she never possessed either. It took enormous courage to face the world with no voice and she did it with tremendous confidence and a smile. So seeing her now, her head bent, her shoulders slumped, alarmed him. Something weighed heavily upon her and she had been through enough that she should carry another burden.

Even Beast worried over her, turning his head up to glance at her often as they slowly made their way toward Cree.

Cree did not wait. He went to his wife, his arm going around her waist, and placed a kiss on her brow.

Lara. Dead. She mouthed.

He tried to find it in him to feel some sympathy but he could not. "Lara had caused much grief and pain and also was the making of her own tragic tale. Say a prayer for her if you will, but do not let her death burden you. Come, we will sit and share a hot brew and you will tell me what else weighs heavily upon you."

She cast a faint smile on him. He knew her far too well. She gave no protest as he eased her along to a table to sit.

"A hot brew," he called out to a servant who had entered the hall and was about to take her leave, looking as if she did not want to disturb the pair.

She nodded and scurried off.

Beast kept close to Dawn, lying near to where she sat, his head on his paws and his eyes fixed on her.

"Tell me what troubles you," Cree said, slipping in beside her on the bench and wishing he could take hold of her hand, but she needed her hands to speak with him, and he needed to comfort her. He moved closer, their shoulders touching, and she slumped against him. His arm went around her. "Tell me," he urged again.

Dawn was not in a rush to speak with her husband. She was relishing his warmth and strength. She needed it. She had missed it. But she needed to share her concern. She reluctantly and slowly sat up straight and gestured being locked in the stocks.

"This is about Ann's punishment?" he asked.

Dawn nodded.

"Her punishment could have been far worse," he said and, thinking his wife too soft-hearted, since he assumed she was going to ask him to free the woman.

Dawn nodded again and mouthed Elsa and pointed to him.

"Did Elsa ask you to speak to me about Ann?"

Dawn tapped his arm once.

91

"Elsa should not have involved you. Ann is suffering far less than she deserves to and my word is law. I will not change the punishment."

Dawn nodded and patted her chest.

"You agree with me?" he asked surprised by her response.

She nodded again.

"Then what troubles you?"

Dawn's hands began to move and she lost the battle of trying not to cry, tears gathering in her eyes.

Cree had come to know her gestures and it had become easier to understand her, more so when she moved her hands slowly as she did now. The problem was what she was telling him.

He interrupted her. "Are you telling me that a rope was placed around your neck and your captives led you along by it?"

She nodded and pressed her wrists together, then gestured being in the stocks once again before pressing her wrists together once more and patting her chest.

The image of his wife being led around by a rope at her neck and wrists rushed a rage so strong through him that he wanted to roar with fury. He was going to find who did this to her and… he forced the thought away. There would be time for that, he would make sure of it, but now his wife needed his thoughts on her.

Cree wiped at her eyes, catching her tears before they could fall. He hated to see her cry and she had done so too often, mostly in her sleep since her return.

"Are you telling me that seeing Ann in the stocks reminds you of being tethered?" he asked.

She nodded vigorously.

"You went to see Ann?"

She kept nodding, though she clasped her hands together in prayer and raised them to her lips and lowered them, repeatedly.

"Ann repeatedly told you she was sorry and begged for your forgiveness?"

She stopped nodding and took a breath before responding with a quick nod.

Cree ran his hand gently along her cheek. "That is all well and good, but Ann's apology appeases Ann. How can mere words be sufficient enough for what her ignorance has cost you? And if she is not punished, what then will others do when faced with the same choice?"

Dawn's silent sigh, squeezed at his heart.

"I will see more suffer for what was done to you and I will not go so easy on them as I did Ann. After hearing what you suffered, Ann deserves much more. Ann may have been too frightened to come to me, and not want to betray her friend, but she could have easily told Sloan that a stranger lurked in the woods. That alone could have prevented your abduction."

Dawn understood the wisdom of his words and knowing, seeing it for herself, what a fair man her husband was to the clan, she could not deny his reasoning. And part of her agreed with him, Ann should be punished. Another part of her, the part that had suffered similar to Ann, being tethered and at the mercy of others, wished for her release. But as Cree said, his word was law and she would not defy him on this like she had done once not long after they had met. It was different between them then. She was finally finding her way with him, the mighty, fearless Highland warrior who had captured her heart forever.

Cree gently ran his hand done her smooth cheek. "It is time, wife, that you tell me everything that happened to you."

Chapter Ten

Dawn was not ready to confess everything. She was still trying to comprehend it and forgive herself. She had survived and that was what was most important or so she told herself.

Cree took her hand. "My solar offers more privacy."

Dawn was glad for that. This was between Cree and her. No one else needed to know.

Beast stretched himself to a stand.

"Guard Lizbeth and Valan," Cree ordered and Beast cast a questioning eye to Dawn.

She nodded and the large, black dog followed her command.

"I am curious to learn where and how you came by Beast," Cree said and called out to Flanna as she entered the Great hall. "A hot brew and food in my solar." As he returned his attention to Dawn, he felt her steps falter slightly. "Are you in any pain?"

Dawn did not want to admit her reluctance to speak to him about her ordeal. There were things she was willing to tell him and then there were things better left alone. The problem was that she had a difficult time keeping things from her husband. They had been honest with each other and the reason trust was something neither ever questioned. How could she even think of not telling him the whole truth?

But would the truth hurt their marriage?

The thought sent a shudder through her.

"You are chilled," he said and as soon as he got her in the solar, and sat her in a chair before the fireplace, he bent and stoked the fire in the hearth, so the flame's warmth would reach out and warm her.

Flanna arrived as he worked on the hearth, arranging a small table close to Dawn with food and drink. Once finished, she and the servants left as quietly as they had entered.

"Eat before we talk," he said, reaching to fill a tankard.

She stopped him with a shake of her head. She tapped her lips, then gestured shoveling food into her mouth.

Cree understood. She would eat after they talked.

She was all set to explain what had happened when she was first abducted but that was not the way of it. What she gestured even surprised her, her hands moving before she could stop them.

Cree stared at her, clearly understanding her, but surprisingly shocked by her unexpected question. "Why have we not made love since your return?"

She nodded, glad she had finally asked. It had been troubling her, the way he seemed to avoid any intimacy between them. That was not like her husband. They had made love often, all enjoyable and many more memorable and she wanted, actually longed, to make memories with him again.

She nodded, then tilted her head, showing how troubled she was by it, and waited for him to respond.

There was no hesitation in Cree's response. "You have yet to heal sufficiently."

It was a plausible excuse, yet somehow Dawn felt it was just that, an excuse.

A reason reared ugly in her head. Could he believe that other men had touch her and wanted nothing to do with her anymore? Could he think she could be with child and was waiting for her monthly bleeding to prove otherwise? Or did her questions come from her own doubts and fears?

Dawn silently admonished herself. If there was one thing she should never doubt, it was Cree's love for her. She was being foolish and yet the thoughts would not stop nagging at her. Cree was not one to go long without coupling and after three months of abstinence, how was it that he still abstained? Or had he? That was a question she had never given thought to until this moment.

If he had believed her dead, had he sought to appease his desire with another woman?

"Tell me of your abduction, everything you can recall about it, and what you remember about the men who took you."

Dawn fought against the thought that Cree had coupled with another woman, having thought her dead. He would have every right to, but had it not been too soon after losing her to seek another's bed? But then he had a fierce appetite for coupling. Three months would be long for him to abstain. She closed her eyes against the disturbing thoughts.

"Are you feeling unwell, Dawn?"

The concern, heavy in his tone, and how his hand reached out and slipped over hers, lacing his fingers tightly with hers, to bring up and kiss it vanquished her foolish thoughts.

She smiled and patted her chest, letting him know she felt fine. She tapped her temple, her smile fading.

"Your thoughts trouble you."

She nodded.

"If you are not ready to speak about your abduction, it can wait."

He was thoughtful of her and she felt guilty for thinking as she had about him. Still, the thought lingered and poked and one day she would have to ask him if she was to have peace of mind.

She shook her head, sighed, and settled back in the chair and let go of his hand so she could speak with him.

***

Cree sat in his solar alone. He had taken his wife up to their bedchamber to rest, her endless yawns having brought their discussion of her abduction to an end. He had tucked her into bed for a second time that day, an urge to join her, and not just in sleep, overwhelming him, and it was growing exceedingly more difficult to ignore it, but until she fully healed he would not touch her.

Every time the scent of mint drifted from her mouth close to his, he could think of only one thing, kissing her. When he held her in his arms and felt her soft breasts press against him, he ached to take them in his hands and feel their fullness and taste her sweet nipples. It was not only about slipping his manhood into her and seeking relief, though he looked forward to that, as it was about the intimacy they shared. A closeness that came with simple touches, faint kisses, teasing nips, and the feel of closing his hand around hers and knowing she belonged to him.

The look in her eyes when she had asked why he had not made love with her since her return troubled him. And he wondered if there was more to her question than she had asked. He had thought to ask her, but then thought it best to wait. It was a discussion left for a better time. Besides, after learning that her abductors had tethered her with a rope around her neck, he had been eager to know more.

His wife had been generous in the telling of her ordeal. Lara had told her she had found a patch of strong, young nettles and asked her to help collect them. When they reached the spot, two men where there and grabbed her. Lara had run and listening to the two men talk Dawn had learned that Lara had been part of the plot to abduct her.

Dawn had gone on to describe the two men as best she could. One fairly tall and lanky and the other short and round, opposites of each other in more ways than one; a pug nose compared to a crooked one, dark, long stringy hair compared to short hair with a bald spot at the top. Though, the men were both the same when it came to rancid breathes that had had her heaving, and they had laughed and joked repeatedly about her not having a voice. They had found it even more amusing that they could do whatever they liked to her and they would hear not a word of protest from her. Though, the one man had reminded that they were not to touch her or they would not get paid. The other man had insisted that there would be no way of him knowing and so the two had continued to argue back and forth.

It had been difficult for him to listen to her ordeal, imagining how helpless she had to have felt. What squeezed at his heart and twisted his gut the most had been when she said that she knew he would come for her. That he would rescue her. But when she heard the men talk of how they had no worries of being found that she had been thought to drown, Dawn had felt her only choice had been to rescue herself.

On the fourth day, after endless arguments between the pair, the two finally came to blows, and she made her escape the only way possible. She had jumped in a rushing stream that had swept her away. How ironic that would have been, the tale of her disappearance proven, in the end, to be true.

It was after that her yawns had started and Cree had claimed it enough for one day. They could continue the talk another day.

Cree rubbed his chin, thinking on how to find these two men. They had not delivered Dawn as they had been hired to do. Their type would be looking for another job to compensate for what they had lost. There were places they could go for that and Cree intended to trap them in a plot of his own.

A knock at the door and a shout from Cree had Sloan entering the solar.

"The troop is set to leave by mid-day tomorrow."

"I have another mission, an important one, for two men," Cree said and began to explain.

***

Dawn woke to find herself alone in bed the next morning just like last night when she fell asleep. She wondered if Cree had come to bed at all. When she rolled over on her side, buried her face in his pillow, his scent strong upon it, and the warmth of the bedding caressed her naked body, she had her answer. It had not been long since he had left their bed.

She hugged his pillow, wishing it was her husband she hugged, wishing to feel his powerful body slip over hers and… she buried her scream into the pillow even though it could not be heard.

With a toss of the blanket, she hurried out of bed and into her garments. She combed her long hair and braided it and after slipping on her shoes, continued her hurried pace as she rushed up the one flight of stairs to see the twins.

Beast greeted her with a yawn and a stretch from where he laid in front of the door. He had taken to sleeping there when Cree had informed him that he would not be sleeping in their bedchamber unless ordered. The dog seemed to have understood him and it had become routine for him to settle at night by the twins' door.

When she saw that the twins and Ina were still sleeping, she realized how early it was. She left quietly, Beast keeping stride with her, and once in the Great Hall saw that the room was just beginning to stir.

"Is something wrong, Lady Dawn? You have risen early."

Dawn turned with a smile to Flanna and pointed to the window, the overcast sky making it difficult to define time, and shook her head.

"You were unaware of the time. It is barely past sunrise, though the sun was not seen this morning," Flanna said.

Dawn nodded.

"You are healing well. It is good to see you looking better every day."

Dawn's smile widened and she patted her chest in appreciation of her thoughtful words.

Flanna looked about at the empty room, before taking a step closer to Dawn, and whispered, "Lord Cree is sending two of his warriors on a secret mission."

Flanna kept Dawn informed about all that went on in the keep and the village, the woman having the uncanny ability to find out anything.

Dawn pointed to Flanna's lips and motioned for her to tell her more.

"That is all I know of it… so far. Lord Cree also sends a troop of his warriors to the Clan MacLoon, the Clan Macardle threatening war with them, and with no Lord of Fire to protect the MacLoon Clan they requested Lord Cree's help."

That news was of little help to her, but she appreciated anything Flanna gave her and she thanked her. Dawn's stomach chose to rumble just then.

"Sit and I will get you a brew to quell the rumbling." Flanna urged.

Dawn sat and waited until Flanna left the Great Hall, then she rushed off, knowing there was only one person who could help her make sense of her worries.

She tried not to look anxious as she set a hasty pace through the village, Beast at her side, and was glad only few were about. Normally, she would be happy to see Paul, Lila's husband, but she was relieved to catch only his departing back as he walked to the fields to begin the day's work. She did not wish to stop and talk with anyone. She wanted to see Old Mary.

Dawn stopped before turning up the short path to Old Mary's cottage. She looked at Beast, patted her chest and pointed to the cottage, letting him know this was where she would be, then waved him off. He appeared reluctant to go. She patted her chest again, then crossed her arms over it, smiled, and pointed to the cottage again.

She smiled when he rubbed his head against her leg and took off. He had understood that he had nothing to fear in leaving her side, that she was visiting a friend. Dawn had no doubt he would be waiting for her outside the door when she was done.

She kept her steps quick up the path to the cottage that had once been her home where she had lived with her mum after arriving here. It had been her sanctuary, a place of love and acceptance, and she smiled at the memories.

The door opened before Dawn reached it.

"Come, I have a nice brew waiting for you and a sturdy shoulder for you to lean on," Old Mary said, with a smile and waving her in.

Dawn loved Old Mary. Some thought her a bit touched in the head and others whispered she was a seer and were frightened of her, but all respected the old woman, and sought her out in time of need.

Old Mary lowered herself with a wince to the chair at the small table. "These old bones continue to protest more each day."

Dawn reached for the pitcher and filled the two tankards on the table. She placed one in front of Old Mary, hoping the steaming brew would help ease her aches.

"Do you doubt Cree's love for you?"

Dawn was taken back by her question. It was not what she had expected her to say or ever question. Cree loved her and always would and that made her realize what the old woman was trying to say.

Dawn shook her head.

"And do you question your love for him?"

Again she shook her head.

"Then what troubles you should not trouble you at all," Old Mary said. "It is the strength of your love for each other that gave you the courage to find your way home. And I believe it was why Cree had such a difficult time accepting your death. I do not believe he never truly believed you were dead. Yours and Cree's love is like no other. Trust it. It will not fail you. And do not be so hard on yourself. You did nothing wrong."

Dawn patted her chest and frowned.

"You may feel like you did, but in truth you did not."

Dawn imitated her husband's scowl to show she spoke about Cree and nodded.

"You know your husband well. Of course he will be angry, but he will get over it, after he throws the man a beating."

Dawn paled.

Old Mary stilled, her eyes intent on Dawn.

Dawn waited, knowing Old Mary saw what she had been hiding.

Finally, Old Mary spoke. "Now I see what has been eluding me and why you worry and I will say again… trust your husband's love for you."

Chapter Eleven

"Flanna," Cree said, his tone sharp as he entered the Great Hall, seeing her speaking with some of the servants who quickly scurried away.

"What may I do for you, my lord?" she asked.

"My wife, have you seen her?"

Flanna gave a brief nod. "Aye, my lord. She was here about an hour ago. I went to get her a hot brew and when I returned she was gone. If I were to guess where she went, my lord, I would say—"

"Old Mary," Cree said and turned and left the Great Hall.

Cree had risen before sunrise this morning to speak with the two warriors before they left on their mission. It had taken longer than he had intended, but he had no worry about Dawn waking before his return. She had slept well past sunrise since her return home, so it had surprised him to find her gone. He had thought she might be with the twins, but had not found her there either. He had found Beast gone from where he slept each night in front of the twins' door and assumed his wife had been there and having found the twins sleeping, which was what their mum should have been doing, she took Beast with her.

He made his way directly to Old Mary's cottage and was pleased to see Beast sitting in front of the door that opened before he reached it. He stopped when he saw the smile that lit his wife's lovely face when she saw him. It spoke more clearly than words could. Her dark eyes sparkled with joy and love and he spread his arms out to her, arms that had missed the feel of her and since her return wanted to hold her forever.

He closed his arms around her, hugging her tight, and he was pleased that her arms returned the hug with a strength that proved she was growing stronger.

He gave her lips a quick kiss. "You are up early, wife."

Dawn's smile remained strong as she nodded and patted her chest.

"You are feeling good."

She nodded again, pleased that the aches that had haunted her every day were barely noticeable today. She truly was healing.

As if the heavens agreed, the clouds parted and the sun suddenly appeared.

"A walk through the village before the morning fare?' he asked and took hold of her hand, clasping it tight, leaving no room for her to refuse.

Dawn locked her hand around his just as tight, so as not to let him get away from her. This was something they had done often, just the two of them, and other times with the twins. It had been something she thought and dreamed about, while away, something that she held on to, told herself she would do once again with her husband, feel his strong hand wrapped around hers, holding tight, never wanting to let her go.

She smiled at her husband, pleased this time it was not a dream.

"I do not think I will ever be able to stop telling you how much I missed you," Cree said as they walked.

Dawn patted her chest and touched his arm, so he would know she felt the same.

The village had come to life with morning chores and many greeted the lord and his lady with smiles and well wishes.

"You have brought life back to the clan. I was a miserable bastard without you," Cree said.

Dawn scowled, tapped her lips, then pointed to him and shook her head.

He gave a chuckle. "You admonish my tongue, but bastard is the only word that suits my horrid nature in your absence."

Sadness filled her heart, thinking of what he had been through, thinking her dead. At least, she had known that he was alive and that somehow, someway she would return to him, but he had thought her gone forever. Her heart ached at the terrible thought.

"Worry not, she will be released tomorrow morning," Cree said.

Dawn looked to see Ann in the stock and realized he thought her sadness was for Ann. And while she was sad for the woman's plight, Cree had been right. If Ann had spoken up about the stranger in the woods, the secret Lara had kept, could have prevented the whole ordeal and saved Lara from dying.

If Ann had spoken up. If the secret had been revealed.

Was she not presently doing the same? Keeping a secret? Not speaking up?

She had to tell Cree. He had to know what happened before someone else told him.

Dawn realized they had stopped walking and when she looked to see why, she took a step closer to her husband.

A large man, thick with muscle, though not heavy in body was drawing the attention of many. He had long dark hair and his mouth seemed to disappear into a bushy beard that covered his lower face. A sword was strapped to his broad back and a knife handle protruded from his one boot. His plaid was dark green with what appeared to be lines of faded yellow running throughout. He walked with a slow, cautious gait, his eyes alert to his surroundings. But what caught the eye the most was the iron shackle attached to his one wrist.

"Go in the keep and wait for me," Cree ordered, not taking his eyes off the stranger as he let go of his wife's hand.

Dawn tapped her husband's arm twice after wrapping her arm around it.

Cree turned a scowl on her. "No?"

Dawn nodded.

"Dawn," he warned with a low growl.

She smiled and kept hold of his arm.

Sloan seemed to appear from nowhere, approaching the man. They exchanged a few words and the large man nodded and turned and made his way through the village again.

"What brings him here?" Cree asked as Sloan neared them.

"He is passing through and needs shelter for a night or two and some food if we can spare it," Sloan explained.

"Why does he wear a shackle?" Cree asked.

"He did not say and I did not ask."

"His name?"

"He did not offer and I did not ask," Sloan said.

"Give him what he needs and keep an extra watch on him, and see he does not stay more than two nights," Cree ordered.

Sloan nodded and took his leave.

"My stomach tells me it is time to eat," Cree said, hungry himself but wanting his wife to eat, her body still not having recovered the weight she had lost.

Dawn smiled at her husband's attempt to get her to eat, though it was not necessary. She found herself famished and was eager for the morning meal.

The twins joined them in the Great Hall and it was a lovely family meal with smiles and laughter, and Lizbeth sneaking Beast food. Dawn and Cree both saw, but said nothing, letting her enjoy her little secret.

Secret.

It kept coming back to secrets, reminders of what she needed to do, but finding her courage waning every time she thought of it. She could not say that there had not been times it had been easy to tell her husband something, that she had been with child had been one of them, since they had not been wed at the time. Time and circumstance changed much, but then so had this abduction. She would find the right moment and be done with it and leave it to fate to sought out.

After the morning meal, Cree and Dawn walked through the village with the twins. Lizbeth hung on to Beast the whole time and Valan charged ahead with his wooden sword as if in battle.

Dawn could not have been more content and because she was she grew anxious. It seemed when moments were the happiest, something dreadful always happened. She did not want to think that way, but it had been the way of things and she could not deny it.

Ina and Nell joined them, time for the twins' nap, and though the two protested, several yawns suggested it was necessary.

"You need a nap as well," Cree said, having seen Dawn yawn almost as much as the twins. "Go rest, I need to see my warriors off on a mission."

She was about to agree, feeling more tired than she would have liked when the bell in the village tolled, announcing the approach of a troop.

Cree's first thought was to see his wife safely in the keep, but one look at her and he could see that she was not going anywhere. She would stay by his side, but then she belonged there.

He walked her to the steps of the keep to wait and whispered, "Hold your tongue, wife, I will handle this."

She chuckled silently and shook her head at him as he smiled at her. She always found it funny when he told her to be silent, and she also found it heartwarming that he treated her as if she had a voice all could hear.

Sloan suddenly rushed through the village to stand in front of Cree, trying to ease his breathing so he could speak. "Macardle."

Cree stared at him a moment. "Are you saying a troop from the Clan Macardle approach?"

Sloan nodded, his breathing having yet to calm.

"Tannin has not left yet with Evin, has he?"

Sloan shook his head.

"Good, keep them here until we see what Macardle has to say," Cree said and watched as three men approached on horses. "How many in the troop?"

"About twenty wait outside the village."

"See that they remain there," Cree ordered and he kept his eyes on the approaching men while he spoke to his wife. "There is nothing for you here. Go and rest."

Dawn shook her head and moved closer to his side.

Cree wondered over her insistence. There was nothing here that concerned her so why was she so adamant about staying?

The three men dismounted once near the steps of the keep, two remaining by their horses and one approaching Cree. He was of fair height, with dark hair and dark eyes, and good features except for the crook in his nose. He was lanky, though had muscles and he carried himself with confidence.

"Lord Cree, I am James and I have come on behest of Angus of the Clan Macardle," he announced.

"What does Angus Macardle want of me?"

"He wants you to know that the Clan MacLoon lies to you."

"It is you who lies," Evin called out as he ran toward them.

"Silence!" Cree said, his shout carrying with strength over the crowd that had begun to form. "You both will join me in the keep to discuss this."

Keeping their distance, the two men glared at each other, but bowed to Cree's command.

Cree walked arm and arm with his wife a distance ahead of the two men. He kept his voice low as he said, "You will—"

Dawn squeezed his arm, interrupting him and pointed to an upper window in the keep.

"You are going to our bedchamber," Cree said pleased that she would take her leave of her own accord. He did value her opinion, having received invaluable insights from her on many occasions. But he preferred that she rest.

As Dawn went to let go of his arm after they entered the keep, he kept firm hold of it for a moment.

"We will talk later." Cree released her arm, giving it a gentle squeeze before he let go and as he continued walking through the Great Hall, he called out, "Flanna, drinks in my solar."

As usual Flanna appeared from the shadows, gave a nod, and the shadows swallowed her up once more.

Cree took a stance in front of the cold hearth and pointed to the two empty chairs after the two men and Sloan entered the solar.

The two sat, though James protested before taking a seat.

"This is not a matter to be discussed with a messenger."

"I came in the name of Chieftain Walsh MacLoon," Evin said, his young head held up high.

"Whether it is a matter to be discussed is for me to decide," Cree said, settling it. His hand went up when James attempted to continue his protest. "Question my decision and you will be escorted off my land."

James clamped his mouth shut, appearing to fight hard to keep it that way.

Flanna entered then with a servant who placed a pitcher and four tankards on the table between James and Evin. The lass filled all the tankards, picked up two and handed one to Cree with a bob of her head and gave the other to Sloan before serving the other two men, then took her leave along with Flanna.

"Tell me why you believe a parcel of MacLoon land belongs to the Clan Macardle," Cree said with a nod to James.

"A parcel, for now, it is all of MacLoon land we will claim shortly," James said and continued before any protests could be made. "The Clan MacLoon does not own that land." James turned to sneer at Evin. "And he knows it. The land was gifted to Angus MacLoon by the Lord of Fire on the day the Clan MacFiere was no more."

"The Lord of Fire will return home," Evin argued.

"It has been almost six or seven years since the Lord of Fire deserted the keep. And with the agreement the Clan Macardle had with the Clan MacFiere, that if there came a time the Clan MacFiere was no more, then the Clan Macardle would take ownership of the land and all its holdings. The same applied the opposite. If the Clan Macardle ceased to exist, then its land and holdings would revert to the Clan MacFiere. I believe the agreement was made by both previous clan chieftains to make certain that one of them would keep rule over the area. From my understanding, the last MacFiere is near death. When that happens, MacFiere land and all its holdings revert to the Clan Macardle."

"The last MacFiere has yet to die," Evin said.

"Twilla is old, ill, and feeble, she has little time left," James argued.

"Is that a threat?" Evin challenged.

"It is fact and it is of no difference to me at the moment. It is the parcel of land that is to revert back to the Macardle once the keep is no longer occupied by a MacFiere that concerns me now."

Evin tossed his chin up in defiance. "The keep is occupied."

That had James turning a startled look on Evin.

"Twilla occupies the keep," Evin said proudly.

"You let an old, ill woman live there alone?" James asked, shaking his head.

Cree did not care for Evin's smile, it boded trouble, and at that moment he wished he could ring the of Lord of Fire's neck for leaving him with this mess.

"Someone visits her often and tends her," Evin said. "Someone you know well."

James' brow narrowed in question.

"Sorrell," Evin said with a bigger grin.

James shook his head and rolled his eyes.

"Sorrell," Cree repeated, the name sounding familiar. "Is she one of Angus's three daughters?"

"The middle one," James admitted reluctantly. "Though her strong opinions and endless chatter will probably do the old woman in before any illness or age can get her."

Cree had to keep himself from laughing.

"She is a good woman," Evin said in defense of Sorrell.

"You are too young and inexperienced to have any idea what makes a good woman," James reprimanded. "Do you not see, Lord Cree, that he is just a lad who knows nothing?"

Cree held his hand up when Evin went to protest. "Evin is here on his chieftain's behest and will report back all that was said and happened here. So while he may be young, he

111

has ears to hear with and eyes to see things for himself, and his chieftain must have confidence in him to have sent him on such an important mission."

"What news will he take back with him?" James asked.

"Evin will return home with a troop of my men, led by Tannin, a warrior of mine who has proven his worth and skill. Tannin will talk with Chieftain Walsh of the Clan MacLoon and also speak with Chieftain Angus of the Clan Macardle and report back to me. Only then will I decide what is to be done."

James got to his feet. "You have no right in making any such decision. It has already been made by previous chieftains of both clans."

Cree took a quick step toward James, so quick that James startled and fell back, plopping down in the chair.

"The Clan MacLoon is under my protection, so until I can determine what you say is true, I suggest you do as I say. Or you will find an army of my warriors descending on the Clan Macardle," Cree said and was startled himself, though did not show it, when a loud bark sounded at the door.

Sloan swung the door open as Cree rushed to it, his stomach clenching, worried that something had happened to Dawn.

"Da," Lizbeth said, standing beside Beast, her small hand gripping a bunch of Beast's thick fur at the back of his neck as if she had used him to guide her there, and a huge smile on her pretty face.

Cree reached down and scooped her up in his arm and before he could say a word, she planted a big, wet kiss on his cheek, and, of course, his heart melted.

"Love you," Lizbeth said.

"I love you too," Cree said and kissed her cheek. "Did you come here alone?"

She shook her head and her smile grew as she pointed to Beast.

"Beast brought you here?" Cree asked.

She nodded and tapped his chest.

Cree had noticed how Lizbeth often used her mum's gestures, sometimes along with words and sometimes not, to speak with him and others.

"Did you ask Beast to bring you to me?"

She nodded again.

"Lizbeth! Lizbeth! Where are you?"

Cree heard the frantic shouts echo down the corridor.

Lizbeth giggled and buried her face against her da's chest as if trying to hide.

Nell turned the corner and her body sagged in relief and her eyes turned wide in fright, seeing Lizbeth tucked in her da's powerful arm.

Nell bobbed her head as she approached. "I am sorry, my lord, I do not know how she got away from us."

"Or down that long flight of steps?" Cree asked, his tone letting Nell know he was not pleased.

Lizbeth raised her head. "Beast helped me."

Cree looked to Nell.

Nell trembled as she spoke. "She sweet talks the dog, my lord, and he does anything for her."

Cree glared down at Beast and the large animal turned his head away as if not wanting his guilt to show.

"Where is my wife?" Cree asked.

"Lady Dawn grew tired and went to rest," Nell said.

"Go with Nell, Lizbeth, and stay with her until I come to speak with you," Cree said and handed his daughter to Nell, glad to hear his wife was resting.

Lizbeth threw him a kiss as Nell turned to hurry off with the little lass.

"You stay with me, Beast," Cree ordered as the animal went to follow Nell.

Beast gave a growl as he entered the room and James and Evin jumped out of their chairs.

"Sit!" Cree snapped sharply and the two men sat instead of the dog.

Sloan turned his head away not able to hide his laugh.

James stood when he realized his mistake and mortified at his quick obedience to Cree's command for the animal said, "Much luck with your daughter, you will need it. She has a mind of her own just like Sorrell."

Chapter Twelve

"Lizbeth has to learn she cannot go off with Beast on her own," Cree said, his arm around his wife and her head resting on his shoulder as they sat braced against a tree trunk watching Lizbeth and Valan running around in play.

Dawn glanced over where Beast lay, looking as if he rested, but he was not fooling her. She saw the way his eyes remained focused on the twins. He had taken to the pair, though mostly Lizbeth, but then she had taken to Beast as if they had been long lost friends.

Dawn nodded, agreeing with her husband.

"She could have fallen down the stairs and seriously hurt herself or worse," Cree said the idea of a senseless and avoidable accident claiming her life an unbearable thought. "She is as stubborn as her mum."

Dawn turned a grin on her husband and patted his chest.

"I am leader of this clan, I need to be stubborn… and obeyed," he said, tapping the tip of her nose playfully.

Dawn's grin widened as she tapped her chest and nodded.

"You think you obey me?" Cree asked with a laugh.

Her firm nod confirmed that she certainly did, but her growing grin spoke differently.

Cree took hold of his wife's chin in a loving grip. "I would not have you any other way than who you are." Keeping hold of her chin, he leaned his head down and kissed her.

His words touched Dawn's heart and his kiss sent a strong stirring through her that grew much too rapidly. She was sorry for the kiss to end, though she was content there in his arms and she rested her head on his shoulder once again.

Cree almost pinched himself to make sure he was not dreaming. This was real, his wife in his arms, his children running happily in play. Life had been restored. He had been restored and he appreciated his life and family more than ever.

He hugged Dawn close to him and she settled against him as she had always done and the familiar comfort of her tucked there filled him with a joy he had never thought he would feel again.

Cree caught the quick movement of Beast's head going up and the way his eyes seemed to follow something. He looked to see what had caught Beast's attention and saw the bulky, bearded traveler he had seen this morning, walking a bit of a distance away, a small sack gripped in his hands. He walked with his head bent, his gait slow and steady, and the shackle still attached to his wrist... and that disturbed Cree.

While the stranger's eyes might seem focused on the ground, Cree got the feeling his eyes kept watch on his surroundings and that his slow and steady gait was on purpose. Cree intended to confront the man and find out what he was doing in the area, though that would have to wait until his wife and children were not around.

He looked down at his wife, dozing in his arms and rested his head back against the tree trunk and closed his eyes. A warm breeze brushed his cheek and rustled the overhead leaves and, content, he let himself drift off in a light doze.

"Da!"

Cree barely got his eyes open when Valan plopped himself on his lap.

"Hungry," Valan said.

Cree poked his son's tummy. "So am I, son,"

Dawn stretched her head off her husband's shoulder and patted her stomach.

"Mummy hungry too," Valan said.

Cree was glad to hear that and looked around to see what his daughter was up to and his heart slammed against his chest. She was talking to the large stranger, Beast at her side. He hurried his son off his lap and into Dawn's arms, her own face showing alarm as her eyes went from his to their daughter's.

It seemed the talk he had had with his daughter had done little good. He had told her that she was not to go off with Beast by herself. She certainly was her mum's daughter since she had peppered him with endless questions as to why she could not do that. He had finally told her that she was to obey him and that was that. But here she was doing it again and only a short time later.

Cree scowled when he watched his daughter take the man's hand and start walking with him, and Beast just followed along with them. He was furious at his daughter and more so at Beast for doing nothing.

"Make it better," Cree heard Lizbeth say as he got near.

"Lizbeth," Cree called out and she stopped and turned with a smile. The large man, however looked perplexed and Cree realized his daughter could do that to people, have them following whatever she said and not realizing why.

Lizbeth held up the man's hand and said, "Elsa help him."

Cree saw that the man's hand wore a soiled bandage.

"Our healer can help you with that," Cree said.

"I take him," Lizbeth said and turned to walk away.

"No, Lizbeth, go to Mummy," Cree said.

She smiled and said, "Later." And went to walk away again.

"Lizbeth!"

The little lass turned, this time with wide eyes to face her da.

"You will go to Mummy *now*!" Cree ordered.

Lizbeth nodded and hurried around her da, calling out, "Beast."

The large dog hurried after her. Cree watched as his daughter did as she was told, and satisfied she was safe, he turned his attention to the stranger.

"Who are you and what brings you here?" Cree demanded, letting the man know he expected an answer.

"I am no more than a man passing through in search of a peaceful, isolated place to make his own. I mean you and yours no harm."

"Then why not offer your name?"

"John, my lord," the man said with a respectful bob of his head.

Cree did not believe that was his name, but there was little he could do about it.

"Elsa will see to your hand and you will be provided with food for your journey. One more day, then continue your quest for peace and isolation."

"Aye, my lord, I am grateful for your generosity."

"Do not make me regret it," Cree said and turned and walked away.

***

Dawn wore her nightdress not that she planned on keeping it on, her body had been humming with passion since her husband had kissed her earlier. She not only wanted to make love, but her body needed to. She ached for the feel of her husband's manhood deep inside her, for his intimate touches, the way he nipped at her nipples, teasing them hard. And for the powerful and pleasurable release, often more than once, that he had always brought her.

It was time. She would not let him thwart her plans. They would make love tonight. She would let nothing stop it.

The bedchamber door opened and Cree entered.

Dawn did not wait, as soon as he shut the door, she lifted her nightdress over her head and tossed it aside, then stretched her arms out to him.

Cree did all he could to control his desire, his manhood not agreeing with him and growing harder by the second. The bruise on her side had yet to heal completely and with his need so strong for her, he feared the pounding he would give her would only cause her pain and deter her healing.

Dawn stared at him, wondering what kept him from rushing to her as he had always done when she had greeted him naked. Whatever was the matter? Why had he not made love to her, been the least bit of intimate with her, since her return?

She lowered her arms and suddenly felt the fool for standing there naked, as if begging him to make love to her. Never. Never would she had thought her husband would deny her. She turned and reached down to scoop up her nightdress, her heart aching.

Cree cringed when he saw the faded bruise on her backside from the bite that was healing nicely and he hurried over to her, having seen the disappointment on her face.

"Dawn," he said, reaching out to her.

She pulled away from him and fought to get her nightdress back on, her annoyed attempts twisting the garment until it knotted up into almost a ball.

Cree snatched it from her hands and hope soared in her. Had she been too impatient? Had her actions surprised him so much that he had frozen? She got her answer when he got the nightdress untwisted and slipped it over her head.

She felt like he had punched her in the stomach.

119

"You are not well enough for us to make love yet," he said, hating to see the hurt in her eyes.

To Dawn it sounded more an excuse and she was tired of excuses. She shook her head strenuously.

"You may think you are well enough, but the bruises and marks on your body and your need to rest throughout the day say otherwise," Cree said, hoping to make her see reason.

She shook her head again, stepping away from him as she pointed at him, then herself, and shook her head.

"Are you saying I don't want to make love to you?" he asked, not believing she would ever suggest that, and her response stunned him all the more.

Dawn patted her chest, shook her head, then cupped her one hand turning it sideways and with her pointer finger from her other hand drove it in and out of the hole, and shrugged her shoulders.

Cree thought he comprehended what she gestured, but he had to be wrong, she would never ask him that. Finally, he said, "Are you asking if I have poked another woman in your absence?"

She gave a firm nod and folded her arms across her chest and glared at him, waiting for an answer.

Cree stared at her, but only for a moment.

He moved so fast, Dawn barely had time to draw back away from him. She did not get far. His hand shot out and grabbed her arm, yanking her up against him.

"Listen well, wife, for you have stirred my fury. I suffered the tortures of hell while you were gone. I dreamt of making love to you every night only to wake hard and eager to delve into you and find the spot where you once laid beside me cold and empty. I could think of nothing but you day and night, and how I would never again feel you touch me, kiss me, make love with me. It was like my heart was being torn from my chest piece by piece each day, until I begged for death myself.

"The thought of touching another woman never entered my head. The thought of even taking another woman's hand in mine turned my stomach. You and you alone are the only woman I ever think about, I ever want, I ever desire. And death did not change that."

Cree's lips came down on hers in a bruising kiss that she returned in kind. The kiss fed only a partial hunger and when Cree tore his mouth away from hers, Dawn rushed to slip off her nightdress.

"No," he ordered firmly, stilling her anxious hands with his. "You will leave it on and I will see to this hungry need of yours, but not to mine."

Dawn shook her head.

"It is this way or nothing. I hunger for you far too much and will pound you like never before and only cause you more pain, and you suffer enough as you heal."

She shook her head again, aching to feel him pound into her over and over again.

Cree scooped her up in his arms and carried her to the bed, stretching out beside her, and before she could protest more, he kissed her. A hard, thirsty kiss that could not be quenched easily. His hand ran down along her nightdress to grab a handful of cloth and yank it up far enough for him to slip his hand beneath and rest between her legs.

She was so wet and ready for him that he almost lost his resolve, but as he eased his finger into her, his body pressing tighter against her, he felt her flinch and he realized he had pressed to tightly against her injured side. He eased away slightly, silently cursing himself.

He needed this done. If he allowed himself to linger, he would be lost. He would not be able to stop himself from joining with his wife and her flinch had proven what he had thought… she had yet to heal enough for them to make love.

His mouth sought her nipple through the nightdress and with his teeth, lips, and tongue, he began to tease it unmercifully as his fingers worked magic on her.

Dawn wanted it to last, hoping the longer it did, her husband would not be able to resist and he would mount her and give her the pounding he had mentioned. But she could not wait. She had gone far too long without him and she soon felt herself splinter into a thousand glorious pieces as she burst in climax.

She let out a roar of pleasure that could only be heard in her head and when he continued to tease her into another climax, her silent gasp felt as if it echoed in her head that a tolling bell that went on forever.

She had not realized that she was tapping her finger against his arm over and over and over as if she was screaming out yes, yes, yes.

Later as they lay in each other's arms, Cree whispered, "I love you, Dawn, only you. My arms will only ever hold you. Never forget that."

Dawn cuddled closer to her husband, her secret rearing its head to torment her. Her husband's arms may never hold another, but she could not say that her husband's arms were the only ones that ever held her.

Guilt kept her awake as her husband dozed off to sleep. She had to tell him what happened. He had to know. With guilt weighing heavily on her, she drifted off to sleep.

***

Cree felt the hand stir him to life, not that it would take much. He had gone too long without. His need was too great and he would wake with his hand on his manhood, seeing to his need as he had done endless times when he thought Dawn gone.

122

But she was not gone. She lay beside him and it took another moment for him to realize it was not his own hand pleasuring himself.

"Dawn," he said, turning his head and meeting her lips.

It was a gentle kiss, Dawn smiling afterwards and tapping her chest, then his.

Cree understood. He had done for her and she wished to do the same for him. He thought to protest, tell her it was not necessary, but it was. He needed this joining from her, however he could get it, as much as she had needed it from him. It was a way for them to be close once again and share the most intimate of pleasures.

He did not, however, expect her to take him into her mouth, especially since her teasing strokes had sprouted him so large and thick, he thought she might choke. But she did not and he was glad of it. Like his wife, it did not take long, to his regret, that she brought him to the soaring heights of a climax that he feared just might kill him. But what a way to die.

He may have pleasured himself while Dawn was gone, but he had gotten little pleasure from it. What he experienced now felt miraculous, but then that was because he was sharing it with the woman he loved and always would.

His climax sent him tumbling in wave after wave of pleasure so intense that he let out a groan that seemed to go on forever.

It must have impressed since when his wits finally returned to him, it was to see his wife's chin perched on his chest and her lips spread wide in a satisfying smile.

Cree ran his hand down the side of her face and rested it against her heated cheek. "Now I know why I missed you so much."

She laughed and slapped his chest playfully.

Sometimes he could swear he heard her laugh, and it warmed his heart.

123

A crack of thunder had Dawn jumping and Cree's hand going to her back to stroke it. "A storm approaches, nothing more."

Dawn pushed herself off him and hurried out of bed, grabbing her garments to slip on.

"What are you doing?" Cree demanded.

Dawn made a gesture of being in the stocks.

Cree cursed himself, since it was his fault this tender moment between them was interrupted because he had Ann put in the stocks. And no matter that she was to be released this morning, Dawn would not abide Ann being drenched by the storm. It was easier to appease his wife, and then return to bed with her.

"I will see to it," Cree said, but, of course, his wife shook her head and was out the door before he finished dressing.

He caught up with her as she stepped outside the keep doors. At least, she had had the sense to slip on a cloak, a light rain having begun to fall, and she had taken one for Ann as well.

Light broke on the horizon, though the sun would not show itself this morning. Cree kept pace with his wife, still annoyed that they had to leave the intimacy of their bed.

As they got nearer the stock, and Cree caught sight of Ann, her head hanging down as if lifeless, he grabbed Dawn's arm. "Wait here."

Dawn shook her head and yanked her arm from his and ran toward Ann.

A wind kicked up and blew the cloak off Ann that someone must have placed on her.

Cree hurried after his wife and grabbed hold of her as her knees gave way, and held her close.

Ann was dead, blood soaking through the back of her garment.

124

Chapter Thirteen

Cree kept tight hold of his wife as he walked her to Sloan and Lucerne's cottage and pounded on the door and heard Sloan shout from inside.

"Wait, wife, I will see who is there."

This was one time Cree was glad Lucerne did not obey her husband, she opened the door and Cree hurried his wife inside.

Lucerne turned alarmed eyes on Dawn and rushed to pull out a chair at the table.

Cree lowered Dawn to the chair and kept his hand on her shoulder as he stood beside her.

"I will fix her a warm brew," Lucerne said.

Sloan rushed into the room from the other room of the two room cottage, tucking his plaid at his waist. One look at Dawn and his eyes went to Cree.

"Ann is dead, stabbed several times in the back," Cree said.

Lucerne gasped. "Good Lord."

Cree bent down beside his wife. "You will remain here with Lucerne until I return."

Dawn rested her brow against her husband's and kept patting her chest.

He easily understood the gesture since he knew his wife so well. "This is not your fault. You did not place Ann in the stocks, I did."

Dawn tried to argue.

"I will hear no protests from you. You are not to blame... I am. I will return as soon as I can." He kissed her cheek and stood.

Sloan went to his wife's side and pressed his cheek to hers and whispered, "A guard will be posted at the door to make sure you are both kept safe."

The two men were no sooner out the door, then Cree ordered the guard to be posted, Sloan having known that would be the first thing he would do.

"Why would someone kill Ann?" Sloan asked, shaking his head.

"Probably someone who did not want Ann to recognize him," Cree said.

"The man Lara was meeting secretly… Ann would know him."

"And expose him."

Both men were silent for a moment, lost in their thoughts.

"Do you think this man has returned and intends Dawn harm?" Sloan asked.

"The question is what was the intention of whoever planned Dawn's abduction. The two men who abducted her had orders to deliver her unharmed to him. What was it that he had planned for her?"

"And why return here if he would be recognized?"

"Unless, he returned to be rid of the last person who could identify him and leave him free to complete his plan."

"I will have extra warriors walk the village and the outskirts daily," Sloan said.

"Find that bearded stranger who calls himself John and send two men to remove Ann before the village fully wakes," Cree ordered.

Sloan nodded and took his leave.

Cree made his way to Elsa's cottage. He wanted her to hear about Ann from him, no one else.

Cree spotted Neil stepping outside the cottage door and giving a stretch, wincing as he raised his one arm. He had been one of Cree's seasoned warriors, having fought bravely in endless battles. After his injury healed, his arm never regained the strength to swing a sword the way it once had.

Neil went to greet Cree with a smile and stopped when he caught a seriousness in Cree's dark eyes that he did not often see.

"What is it?" Neil asked when Cree stopped in front of him.

"Ann was stabbed to death."

Neil stared at him a moment, then shook his head slowly. "She was a good soul."

The partially opened door swung open and Elsa said, "Who was a good soul?"

Both men looked at her.

Elsa paled. "Please do not tell me it was Ann."

***

Dawn hugged the tankard with both hands that Lucerne had given her but had yet to drink from it.

"How horrible for Ann," Lucerne said, a tear falling from her eye. "She was such a giving person. She would take the time to answer my questions about various plants. She had gained so much knowledge from Elsa." She gasped. "My lord, what will Elsa do with both her helpers gone?"

Dawn looked over at her and shook her head, her heart going out to Elsa. Whatever would she do without the two women to help her, two women who had become her friends. Cree may have told her not to blame herself, but she did. She should have gone and freed Ann from the stocks like she had done for Dorrie that one time. The problem was that she had agreed with Cree. Ann had deserved some punishment and at the time the stocks seemed the least harshest.

Never had she expected her punishment to turn deadly.

"Cree is right. It is not your fault," Lucerne said. "Ann should have spoken up when you were thought drowned. It might have helped find you and spared everyone the pain, especially Cree. And now with her death, it seems that there is more to your abduction than thought."

Dawn was so distraught over Ann that she had not given thought to what the woman's death might mean. Why was she killed?

Lucerne answered her unspoken question.

"Ann must have been silenced for something she knew or could reveal."

Lucerne was a far different woman then when Dawn had first met her. She had complained, cried, screamed like a spoiled noble, and though she had been promised to Cree in marriage, an arrangement made by the King for Cree to secure the Carrick lands, she had not wanted to marry him. Thankfully, it all worked out, but at the time Lucerne was her bitter enemy, not so any longer. Dawn had been thrilled when Sloan and Lucerne had finally gotten together and was even more pleased that they were expecting their first child.

And now she was grateful that Lucerne had got her thinking about Ann's murder. There would be time to grieve. Now it was time to discover who did this horrible thing to her.

"With the Macardle troop just arriving and a few travelers stopping, that big, bearded stranger everyone whispers about being one of them, there are numerous men it could be, since I cannot believe that anyone in the clan could do such a terrible thing to poor Ann," Lucerne said, wiping at the tears that threatened to fall.

Dawn had to agree with her assumption. She just wished there were not so many possible people who might be responsible.

***

"I want to see her," Elsa said, tears streaming down her cheeks.

"Once she is out of the stocks," Cree said.

"No!" Elsa shook her head and marched past Neil and Cree. "I will see her now."

"Please, my lord, let her have her way with this," Neil said when Cree went to stop Elsa.

Cree reluctantly nodded, seeing no point in making it even harder on Elsa, and followed after her with Neil.

Two men were at the stock, getting ready to slip out the metal pin and lift Ann out of it when Elsa approached.

"Stop!" Elsa shouted as she rushed toward them. "I will see to her first."

The two warriors looked to Cree and at his nod, they stepped aside.

Elsa cringed when she saw the young woman, her head and hands hanging lifeless. She went to her and slipped her hand under her chin… and heard a low moan.

"She is not dead! Hurry, get her out! Get her out!" Elsa yelled.

Cree and Nell ran forward to help.

Cree was the one to lift Ann and, following Elsa's orders, hurried to the healing cottage with her.

"Place her on the bed, on her stomach, and hurry and send for Lucerne. She has helped me before," Elsa instructed, then leaned down and gently pushed Ann's hair away from the side of her face to tuck behind her ear. "It is all right. I am here, Ann. I will help you."

Cree ordered one of the warriors to fetch Lucerne and told him to let Lady Dawn know that she was to come as well.

The warrior rushed to Sloan's cottage and when the warrior standing guard saw the urgency on his face, he opened the door.

The warrior braced his hands against the frame of the door as he tried to slow his breath and hurried to speak. "Ann is alive and Elsa requires your help, Lucerne. And you are to come as well, Lady Dawn."

Both women rushed out of their seats and quickly hurried out of the cottage, the warrior who stood guard keeping pace behind them.

"How can I help?" Lucerne asked as soon as she entered the Elsa's cottage.

"Fresh cloth and water," Elsa instructed while cutting away Ann's garment. "She has been stabbed more than once and I need to clean her back of the blood so I can see the wounds and determine how much damage she has suffered."

Dawn stepped forward, looking to Lucerne and patting her chest and pointing to Elsa.

"Dawn wants to know how she can help," Lucerne said and received a grateful nod from Dawn.

Elsa turned and Dawn could see she was ready to refuse her help. Dawn lifted her chin and narrowed her eyes, daring Elsa to refuse her.

"You have a gentle touch, help me with her garments," Elsa said. "The rest of you, please leave."

Cree had been ready to forbid Dawn to help, but when he saw her raise her chin and the resolve in her eyes, and knew the guilt she felt, he could not refuse her.

"I will be outside. Keep me abreast," Cree said and he and Neil stepped outside.

Neil stopped Cree from closing the door. "Elsa will need all the light she can get, even with the gray skies. If you need to attend to anything, my lord, I can send word to you as soon as something is known."

Cree did not want to leave his wife, but with Neil and a warrior standing guard, she would be safe, and he wanted to see if Sloan had discovered anything.

"Do not let my wife leave here without a guard," he ordered.

"I will make sure she is protected."

Neil had proven that he would protect Dawn with his life, so Cree had no trouble taking his leave.

Cree found Sloan talking with Tannin, a troop of warriors standing ready for the young warrior's command.

"Ann is not dead. Elsa works hard at trying to keep her that way. Lucerne and Dawn help her," Cree said, stopping in front of the two men.

"That is good to hear," Sloan said.

"Why are you here with Tannin instead of finding that bearded stranger who gives a false name?" Cree asked.

"Tannin came to me with news before I could see to that. It seems Evin left before sunlight and the Macardle troop left shortly after daybreak."

Cree turned to Tannin. "Evin said nothing of this to you?"

"Not a word, my lord," Tannin said. "My thought is he wants to get a head start on reporting back to his chieftain. I think James Macardle caught wind of Evin's departure and took his leave sooner than he had planned. There was much rushing around in their camp this morning from what the sentinels have told me."

"Or perhaps there was another reason the Macardle troop rushed out of here," Sloan said.

Tannin voiced Sloan's concern. "You think they could have had something to do with Ann being stabbed? What could possibly connect any of them to Ann?"

"Perhaps nothing or perhaps everything," Sloan said.

"Wait no longer, be on your way, Tannin, and find out all you can about both clans, and the dissent between them," Cree ordered.

"Aye, my lord," Tannin said with a bob of his head and turned to his troop. "Mount, we leave now."

"Did you send men to follow and take count of the Macardle troop?" Cree asked.

Sloan nodded. "I did. We will know if anyone joined them while here or was left behind."

A rider approached and Cree saw it was Leith, the messenger he had sent to inform his sister that Dawn was alive and healing from her ordeal. It surprised him that his sister and her husband Torr were not trailing behind him. He had thought for sure his sister would insist on seeing Dawn for herself. That she had not come, caused him to worry that something was wrong.

"My lord," Leith said after dismounting. "Your sister sends word."

Cree nodded for him to continue.

"Your sister is beyond thrilled that Dawn is alive and has returned home. She wishes she could travel here immediately, but her son is ill as is Torr's father and she cannot leave them. Besides, she feels it is best you have some time with Dawn and says she will let you know when all is well and she is able to travel."

"How ill is my nephew and Torr's father?" Cree asked concerned for both.

"She said to tell you that neither are in danger of dying, but that might change if the two do not behave better while recovering."

Cree chuckled. "And Torr? Did he have anything to say?"

It was Leith's turn to chuckle. "Only to tell you that he wished he was returning with me."

Sloan laughed along with Cree.

"Go get food and some rest, Leith" Cree ordered.

"Thank you, my lord, I have been thinking of Turbett's delicious food the whole trip home. There is no cook as good as Turbett."

"Tell Flanna that and Turbett will no doubt reward you with a special treat," Cree said.

Leith grinned and wasted no time in hurrying on his horse and taking off.

"Sometimes I wonder if my warriors remain faithful because of Turbett's skill with food," Cree said with a shake of his head.

"Could be," Sloan said, grinning, though it faded slowly. "But I would think they are faithful to you since after years of fighting alongside you that you have provided them with a permanent home, a clan… a family."

"We all worked and sacrificed for that together," Cree reminded him.

"But you made it happen."

"Now it is time to make sure everyone stays safe. I need to talk to the bearded stranger," Cree said and the two walked off to find him.

They had not gotten far when Old Mary called out to them.

They walked over to her as she shuffled slowly toward them.

"You look for that big, bulky stranger," Old Mary said.

Cree was used to Old Mary's knowing, not so Sloan. He seemed uneasy with it.

"You know something, Old Mary?" Cree asked.

"I do," she said with nod. "I saw him before daybreak. He looked like he was sneaking out of the village, wanting no one to know he was taking his leave."

Chapter Fourteen

"You are not going anywhere but to bed," Cree ordered, pointing to the bed behind Dawn.

She pinched her lips shut and crossed her arms over her chest as if stopping herself from arguing with him, though she did narrow her eyes at him.

"You have spent nearly the entire day at Elsa's cottage helping with Ann and with what little time you took for yourself, you spent with the twins. It is time for you to rest." His hand went up when he saw her ready to protest. "You will be of help to no one if you exhaust yourself and delay your own healing." He stepped away from the door he had blocked, keeping her from leaving, and took gentle hold of her shoulders. "You have been of substantial help to Elsa and she has told you there is no more that can be done for Ann today. She sleeps and God willing does not die." He turned her around and marched her to the bed. "Into bed with you."

Dawn sat on the bed, pointed to her husband, then patted the spot beside her.

"I will join you as soon as I finish speaking with Sloan."

Dawn yawned and as much as she did not want to admit it, her husband was right. It had been a busy and challenging day and it had grown late and she needed to sleep.

Cree helped his wife slip into her night dress, then beneath the blanket, tucking it around her. He leaned over and kissed her lips lightly. "I better find you here when I return."

Dawn covered her mouth as a yawn hit her and she nodded and patted her chest, then the bed.

"Good, I am pleased and relieved you will stay in bed. I am going to leave Beast here with you until I return. Then he can go to the twins."

Dawn nodded.

Cree kissed her again. "You are mine, wife, and I love you."

Dawn smiled, patted her chest and pressed her hand to his chest to let him know she felt the same.

"Guard Dawn, Beast," Cree ordered before walking out the door.

Cree took the stairs down to the Great Hall his mind on earlier today. When Old Mary had told him that the bearded stranger had taken his leave, he had ordered Henry to track him. He wanted him found and he wanted to know why he had snuck away when he had one more day before Cree had ordered him gone. Why give up one more day of food and shelter, especially with the day that had promised a storm from the start?

Though it was late, he hoped there might be word from Henry and he also wanted to know if there had been any odd movements from a couple of travelers that had sheltered here for two days and would leave tomorrow. He had told Sloan to also keep watch for any travelers seeking shelter today. There was no better place for the offender to hide but then among his enemy.

Sloan was at the table by the hearth, getting warm, the storm having brought a chill with it.

"Any news?" Cree asked as he joined him at the table.

Sloan handed him a tankard of ale. "None from Henry on the bearded stranger and while two new travelers stopped here today seeking shelter from the storm, neither would be suspect. They are both clergymen. One is old, his hands gnarled, leaving him incapable of stabbing anyone. The other one appears worn and tired from the miles he has traveled. I also spoke with the men who patrolled the village last night and they saw nothing that gave them pause. One had stopped and given Ann water like you had ordered be done throughout the day. He told me that she was looking forward to sunrise when her time in the stocks would be done. He said she had appeared fine when his time had finished and the next sentries were set to patrol."

"Which means that whoever did this was familiar with the timing of the guards' rounds," Cree said. "Someone who may have spent a few days observing our ways or someone already familiar with them."

"You cannot think that someone in the clan did this to Ann?" Sloan asked shocked at the thought.

"I would be foolish to rule out any possibility."

"You never did trust easily."

"Only fools trust easily," Cree said, "and I can see by your grin that you intend to remind me that I trust my wife."

Sloan chuckled.

"The time Dawn and I spent in that small hut when I was held prisoner here gave me the opportunity to come to know her well as surprising as that might be since she has no voice."

"It no longer seems that way—that she has no voice— most understand her hand gestures now. And I believe the clan remain grateful to her for having tamed the mighty Cree," —Sloan held up his hand when Cree turned a scowl on him— "enough that they don't fear you when you walk through the village."

"It is better they fear me, then they will not fail to obey me."

"That obedience was enforced with what happened to Ann. Everyone fears the stocks now."

"The stocks are a good deterrent for minor offenses, though from now on when someone is placed in the stocks a guard will be stationed there the whole time."

Sloan nodded. "I thought that may be your order. The clan will be relieved to hear that."

"And you will be relieved to hear that we are done for the night since you must be eager to return home to your wife."

Sloan grinned. "I never imagined marrying Lucerne let alone being content with her."

Cree laughed. "You might not have imagined it, but most everyone else did."

Sloan laughed along with him. "When I realized it myself, I wondered how I had not seen it sooner."

"I think when we fall in love we are often the last ones to realize it or accept it. You and Lucerne fought it every step of the way, she insisting that she loved another and you, after proving the fool she believed she loved a rake, not admitting you did it because you loved her. I am just glad it is done and you two are together."

"As am I," Sloan said, standing. "I will bring word to you as soon as I get it."

Cree nodded and continued to sit at the table well after Sloan was gone.

Something was disturbing him, something to do with his wife. It was easy for him to see when something troubled her. Her brow would knit and she would appear lost in her thoughts, troubling thoughts as she gnawed on her bottom lip, leaving it plumped and much too kissable. Though it was her worrying thoughts he wished to kiss away, but he always held his tongue until she finally spoke to him about whatever was upsetting her. This time, however, she had not done so and he wondered why.

She had yet to tell him about her time after escaping the men who abducted her and he wondered if it had something to do with that. If she did not speak with him soon about it, he intended to ask her. He did not like that she suffered alone in her worry. Or that she did not seek help from him. Which had made him begin to wonder if she feared telling him something.

That thought had not set well with him. He never wanted her to fear speaking to him about anything and he never thought she would. So it was all the more disturbing to him that she held her tongue.

Cree stretched himself off the bench and went to his bedchamber. He shed his garments and slipped naked under the blanket to wrap himself around his wife. He hated that she wore a nightdress, and at his insistence, though more so for his sanity. It would not be long before she could shed it permanently. She was growing stronger by the day and Elsa had only recently assured him that no more than another week and she would be well healed.

He could not wait. She had made it easier on him this morning when she unselfishly saw to his needs. And as much as he had enjoyed it, he could not wait to make love with her. There was an intimacy about joining with someone you loved that could not be denied and never matched. It was a lasting intimacy that went far beyond that movement of satisfying pleasure and he had missed it terribly while Dawn had been gone.

Cree closed his eyes and smiled as he rested his face near his wife's hair and the scent of lavender drifted off it to tickle his nose. She was home, in his arms where she belonged and he could not be happier.

***

Cree was not happy when he woke the next morning and found Dawn gone. He was, however, pleased that when he went and found the twins still sleeping, that Beast was gone which meant he went with Dawn when she came to see the twins.

He did not need to worry where she might be, he knew.

Beast was sitting outside Elsa's healing cottage, his eyes alert.

"Go get your food, Beast," Cree ordered as he approached and the large dog did not wait, he hurried off toward the kitchen.

Flanna made sure the dog was fed in the morning and again in the evening. Cree was pretty sure others fed Beast as well, his daughter being one of them, since most of the clan was growing accustomed to him and how he protected Dawn and the twins.

Cree rapped on the door before opening it and with no one denying him entrance, not that it would matter if they did, he would enter anyway.

His wife stood at the table blending herbs in a bowl while Elsa attempted to spoon broth into Ann's mouth, her eyes drifting open only to close again.

Cree went to his wife. "You will tell me where you go before leaving our bed."

Dawn's first thought was to ask why when she had not done so before, but with what had happened she understood her husband's need to know her whereabouts.

She nodded and with her one finger traced a cross over her chest.

"I am pleased by your promise," he said and kissed her cheek before turning to Elsa. "How does Ann do?"

"It is too soon to say. She tries to wake now and again, but to no avail. So far her wounds show no signs of turning putrid, but again it is too soon to tell."

"Let Dawn continue feeding her. I need to talk with you," Cree said.

Dawn went and took the bowl from Elsa and sat, leaving Elsa free to leave the cottage with Cree.

Cree walked a few steps away from the cottage door before stopping. "Ann has not spoken a word to you?"

"No, my lord," Elsa said, a tear appearing in her one eye. "She barely has the strength to open her eyes. She suffered two wounds that concern me. A third only broke the surface of her skin."

"The other two wounds, are they deep?"

"Not as deep I expected, which bodes well for Ann and gives me hope that she will survive."

"That is good to hear, but Dawn cannot keep helping you. She has yet to heal completely."

Elsa nodded. "I told her the same myself, but her guilt keeps her here, though it is misplaced. I am, however, going to need help since Ann requires care and there will be those who seek my care throughout the day. Lucerne I am sure will help—"

"As much as you need me."

Cree and Elsa turned to see Lucerne approaching, Sloan beside her shaking his head.

"Her food revolted on her this morning," Sloan said.

"Some morning unease. It is to be expected," Lucerne said, dismissing it as if it meant nothing.

"True enough," Elsa said, "though it will do you no good to tire yourself out working here all day."

"I will find you help," Cree said.

"I am still going to help," Lucerne insisted.

Sloan was ready to argue when Cree spoke up, "Only if I permit it."

Lucerne sent her husband a scathing look.

Sloan threw his hands up. "I said nothing."

"Lucerne can help me now, my lord, if you permit," Elsa said, "so Dawn can go eat and rest since she has been here well before sunrise. I will go get her."

Cree nodded, annoyed that he had not known his wife had left their bed far earlier than he had thought.

Lucerne followed Elsa into the cottage.

"Cree!"

That Elsa screamed his name without proper title, shot fear through him and he ran into the cottage to find his wife lifeless on the floor.

"No!" Elsa cautioned when Cree went to scoop her up. "Let me make sure she suffered no injury." As soon as she bent down, Dawn began to stir. "A faint, I believe." And motioned for Cree to scoop her up.

Cree lifted her gently and once cradled in his arms, her eyes drifted open.

"Did you faint?" Cree asked, his heart still pounding with fear.

She nodded.

"Lucerne, stay with Ann. I want to go see that Dawn is settled in bed and check the bruise at her side," Elsa said.

"I will remain with her until you return in case she requires help," Sloan said.

Cree nodded his approval and hurried out the door, keeping a quick and steady gait to the keep. Elsa had to rush her steps just to stay a few feet behind him.

Once in their bedchamber, Cree deposited Dawn gently on the bed.

She went to push herself up.

"You will stay put," Cree ordered and slipped his hands beneath her arms to lift her carefully and place two pillows behind her head.

Knowing there would be no convincing her husband otherwise, she did not respond.

Elsa approached the side of the bed as Cree stepped aside, but before she could say a word, Dawn began to gesture.

She patted her side and turned her head fast.

Elsa nodded. "You moved fast again and you were hit by a pain in the area that is bruised."

Dawn nodded, patted her chest and smiled.

Elsa smiled along with her. "Otherwise you feel well."

Dawn nodded and looked to her husband.

"I do not care if you believe you feel well. You will rest."

That did it for Dawn. She did not care if she fainted again. She was tired of resting, being told to rest, and being forced to rest. She pressed her hand against the bruise, swung her feet off the bed, and stood before anyone could stop her.

Elsa hurried out of the way and out of the room, seeing the two were about to argue.

Cree went to lift his wife to put her back in the bed and she swatted at his arms.

"You will get back in that bed," he ordered.

Dawn pursed her lips, narrowed her eyes, and defiantly shook her head.

"You either get back in it or I will put you in it," Cree warned.

Dawn shook her head even more defiantly.

Cree growled like an angry dog and went to scoop her up.

"Cree!"

Sloan's shout had Cree and Dawn turning as he came rushing through the door.

"One of the men who abducted Dawn has been found and will arrive here shortly."

Chapter Fifteen

"You will confirm that this man is one of your abductors, then you will return to our bedchamber and rest," Cree ordered after Sloan had left to see to the prisoner's arrival.

Dawn nodded, then shook her head.

"Dawn—"

She raised her hand in front of her husband's face, stopping him from saying another word and her hands started flying.

"You are talking too fast I cannot understand you."

Dawn threw her hands up. She was far too annoyed, leaving her far too impatient to temper her frustration. It was at times like this that she wished she had a voice so Cree did not have to interpret what she was saying.

"You will do as I say, wife," Cree said his own frustration heard in his clipped tone.

Dawn shook her head and threw her hands up again.

"Excuse the intrusion."

Cree and Dawn turned to see Old Mary in the open doorway.

"The village worries over Dawn after seeing you carry her to the keep, as do I. I came to see how Dawn fared, and I see for myself she is doing well."

Dawn sighed, the only indication of it the heaving of her chest, and pointed to Cree.

Old Mary smiled softly and looked to Cree. "She is frustrated with you."

"Frustrated with me?" he asked and raked his hand through his hair and addressed his wife. "You are still healing and refuse to rest. If you will not do what you should, I will see it done for you."

Dawn started gesturing at her husband, her face pinched with annoyance.

Old Mary remained in the doorway as she interpreted. "She says stop ordering me to rest, to eat, to sleep. I know what I need to do to heal."

"Then why do you not do it?" Cree demanded, then answered for himself. "Because you are too stubborn."

Dawn's hands moved even faster.

Old Mary had no trouble interpreting for her, having known her since she was young. "You are far more tenacious than me and I will have no more of it."

Cree stepped closer to his wife. "Are you dictating to me? And think wisely before you answer that."

Old Mary continued interpreting. "*You* are dictating to *me*."

"I rule here, therefore I dictate."

Dawn tapped her chest and shrugged and that gesture needed no interpretation.

"Yes, I dictate to you when necessary. When you are too stubborn to know what is good for you. Like that day you were abducted. You insisted you needed no guard, you would be only a short while and what harm could come from collecting a few plants. Elsa and Lara did it all the time without incident, not so the day you joined them. I failed to dictate that day. I will not fail you again."

Old Mary backed out of the room, knowing it was time to take her leave, and quietly closed the door behind her.

Dawn had known her husband blamed himself for what had happened to her. She had known he would even before returning home. She did not, however, realize that it would make him even more overly protective of her than before.

She tapped his chest and shook her head.

"I am at fau—"

Dawn pressed her finger to his lips, shaking her head. She would not hear him say again that he was at fault for what happened to her. She tapped his chest, then hers and shook her finger.

"You may believe neither of us are at fault, but I believe differently. I am not only your husband but the leader of this clan and it is my responsibility to keep you and the entire clan safe. No matter what you say, I failed my duties and that is unacceptable. And I will not let it happen again."

Dawn realized then that she would never change his mind. But then how could she? Did she not love her husband for who he was? A loving husband and father, a protector, a warrior, a leader, the defender of his clan. He did what he did to keep her safe and to see her from harm, to see that he never lost her again.

She pressed her hand to his heart and then to hers, letting him know she loved him and his arm went around her waist.

"Even when we argue," —he grinned— "due to your stubbornness. I never doubt you love me." He kissed her softly. "And that you know my love for you grows stronger by the day."

She smiled and nodded, then tapped his chest and pointed around the room and mouthed, *prison.*

"You feel our bedchamber is a prison?" he asked as if he did not quite believe it.

She shook her head, tapped his chest, folded her hands to her cheek and shut her eyes as if sleeping, then rolled her hand around and around and around.

"It feels like a prison when I tell you rest again and again and again."

Dawn smiled and nodded.

"I worry you do too much and not heal as you should and believe me when I tell you I want you to heal since it is not rest you will be getting in our bed once you do."

145

Dawn's smile grew.

"You are no fool, wife, so promise me that you will rest when you know you should and I will not order you to do so."

Dawn crossed over her heart with her finger, nodded, then sealed their pact with a tender kiss.

When her lips left his, he rested his cheek to hers and whispered, "I grow hungrier for you by the day."

Dawn brushed her lips over his once more and patted her chest, letting him know she felt the same.

Cree wisely stepped away from her and Dawn did not object. Though she did take hold of his hand and cherished the way his strong fingers wrapped around hers to grip her hand lovingly.

"As I said before, you will confirm the identity of this man… and take your leave. And I will brook no arguments on that."

Dawn nodded, knowing her husband did not want her witnessing what he would do to the man.

***

Dawn stared at the man. She recognized him immediately, short, round, a pug nose, and a bald spot at the crown of his head, but she made no move to confirm it. His arms were drawn back behind the wood post and secured tightly. A rope around her waist and at his ankles secured him even more tightly to the wood post. His garments were filthier than she recalled and what hair he did have grimier. He had a pungent odor before and even more so now.

A shiver ran through her from the memories that assaulted her and she leaned against her husband when his arm went around her.

"He is the one?" Cree asked, his wife's discomfort confirming it for him.

Dawn nodded.

"Beast will follow wherever you choose to go," Cree said.

Her husband was letting her know it was time for her to take her leave and go where she pleased and she was grateful for that. She raised her arm and cradled it, rocking it back and forth.

He kept his voice low when he said, "I am pleased you tell me that you go to the twins."

Dawn kissed his cheek, patted Beast's head, and left without glancing at the man tied to the post.

Cree gave a nod to one of the warriors nearby and he followed a distance behind Dawn. With his wife's safety secured, he turned his attention to the prisoner.

"Mercy, my lord. Mercy. I have done nothing," the man begged.

"Speaking false words to me is not wise. It will only earn you endless suffering, whereas the truth will bring you a less painful death," Cree said, his hand going to rest on the hilt of his dagger tucked in the sheath at his waist.

The man paled. "Death? But I have done nothing."

"More false words, more suffering," Cree reiterated. "You abducted my wife. I want to know why."

He made no mention that he knew someone had hired the man. He wanted to see what the man would offer of his own accord.

"I know nothing of what you speak," the man said.

"Then you say my wife lies when she identified you as one of her two abductors?"

"She must be mistaken. I—"

Cree's fist slammed into the man's mouth before he could finish. "More lies, more suffering." And Cree's fist struck him again.

The man gagged on the blood that filled his mouth and after spitting it and a tooth out, he finally spoke. "I wanted

147

nothing to do with it. It was all Gille's doing. He comes to me and tells me, Bram, I need help. There's a debt I owe this man and if I do not repay it, he will do me in. so what choice did I have but to help Gillie, being he is my cousin."

"That is not what my wife tells me, Bram."

Bram crinkled his face. "She is struck dumb, has no voice. How can she tell you anything?"

Cree's fist came down on Bram's nose so hard it shattered bone and cut flesh. "My wife is not the dumb one. By the time I get done with you, you will have no face and no voice either since you will lose your tongue for all the lies you spew."

Bram's head hung down, blood spilling from his nose and moans from his lips.

Cree grabbed him by the hair at the lower back of his head, snapping his head back. "My patience is gone. The truth or I will beat you unmercifully until you beg me to die."

Bram's face was a bloody mess and he struggled to speak. "A man hired Gillie to abduct a woman. Told him it would be easy. She would give him no trouble since she was dumb—"

Cree's fist came down on Bram's jaw, knocking him out.

Cree nodded to Sloan and stepped aside as he picked up a bucketful of water and a warrior grabbed Bram's hair at the nape and yanked his head back. Sloan did not hesitate, he threw the water in his face, waking the man.

He spurted and coughed blood while the warrior kept tight hold of his hair, forcing him to face Cree.

"Call my wife dumb again and I will use my dagger on you and relish every moment of it," Cree said. "Who hired you?"

Bram shook his head.

Cree pulled out his dagger.

"Gillie knows, not me."

"Where do I find Gillie?"

Bram spoke with haste. "Bertie. With Bertie."

"Where is Bertie?"

"Take you."

"You will tell me," Cree ordered.

"Hard to find."

Cree stepped forward.

Bram turned his face away with a groan. "Truth. No pain, I beg. Please no more pain."

Cree stepped away from the man and Sloan joined him.

"I would worry it was a trap," Sloan said, "but he is far too ignorant to plan anything. A small troop of warriors could escort him and bring both of them back."

"Give the task to Elwin and—" Cree glared at Sloan. "Why do you shake your head at me?"

"Elwin will obey and see to the task, but reluctantly. Dorrie is due to birth their bairn soon and he will not want to leave her."

"Then choose someone and I will speak with him before he leaves. Tomorrow is soon enough. Have Elsa see to him," Cree said with a nod toward Bram. "I do not want anything to happen to him before he leads us to this man Gillie. I also do not want him to have an easy death. He will suffer for what he did."

"And rightfully so," Sloan agreed.

Cree left Sloan issuing orders to the men and walked to the practice field. The few warriors there fled before he entered the area. He did not blame them. His fury was there for all to see, he could no longer hide it and he was having a difficult time containing it, which was why he had come to the practice field. He needed to release it.

He wanted revenge for his wife's ordeal and the suffering it had caused so many. But now, at this moment, he was furious that Bram had called his wife dumb. That the ignorant man could not see beyond what was in front of him, a courageous, strong, intelligent woman who was able to escape him and his cohort.

He grabbed one of the swords that rested in the wooden holder that was brought to the practice field each morning. He swung with ease and skill as he approached the post in the ground. He had not battered another post since the day Dawn had returned, his anger having abated, though not entirely gone.

Someone had to be held accountable for what had happened and made to pay the consequences. Until that time, anger would stalk Cree.

He let that anger reign now, grabbing the hilt of the sword with two hands and delivering blow after blow to the thick post wrapped with rope.

His warriors and some of the villagers watched from a distance with fear and admiration of their chieftain. His proficiency and strength with a sword was unsurpassed and they could not take their eyes off him. He was truly remarkable to watch in action.

Cree swung and swung again until his fury died to an ember and the strain and ache in his arms warned him to stop. But he needed one last, good, hard swing and he took it, lopping off the top of the post.

He lowered the sword, his chest heaving like it had done so many times at the end of a battle, and this had been a battle for him, a battle to not let his fury rule and kill Bram too soon. He needed more information from him and he needed the man Gillie so that he had the two men who had abducted his wife. Somewhere between the two the truth would be discovered.

Cree took a deep breath, rolled his head and his shoulders, and when he turned, it was not the group of warriors and villagers watching him that drew his attention, it was his daughter walking toward him with Beast at her side… alone again.

He rested the sword against the post that now tipped to the side and had chunks missing from it and went to his daughter who was running toward him, Beast keeping pace at her side.

While he wore a scowl, his daughter greeted him with a cheerful smile.

"What did I tell you about going off on your own?" Cree said sternly.

"With Beast," she said and gave the large dog a hug.

Beast at least understood that Cree was annoyed and avoided looking at him.

"Where is Mummy and Valan?" Cree asked.

"Turbett," she said and scurried around him to hurry toward the battered post.

Cree shook his head and scooped her up before she reached it.

She giggled and grabbed his face to kiss his cheek.

"Kisses will not work this time, Lizbeth," he said but damn if she was not melting his heart like she always did. "You have disobeyed me again."

She scrunched her face. "Sorry." Her small hand pressed against his chest, then pressed it to her chest.

How could one tiny lass get to him so much? That she used her mum's gestures to tell him that she loved him tore at his heart and made him proud. His daughter was definitely going to be a challenge.

"You broke it," Lizbeth said, pointing to the post.

"I did and Uncle Sloan will see it gets fixed." The post was not a subject his daughter needed to know about. "Have you eaten?"

She shook her head. "Come find you to eat."

"You cannot go walking around alone," Cree said as he started walking, Beast following alongside them.

151

She sighed dramatically and raised her small hands. "With Beast," she said as if she needed to explain it to him again.

He tapped the tip of her nose. "Beast is a dog—"

She grabbed his face in her small hands, stopping him from saying another word and shook her head. "Beast my friend."

Cree could see this was not going to be easy. His daughter had as strong, if not stronger, independent streak and stubbornness in her than her mum did.

"Aye, Beast is your friend, but you cannot go off with only Beast, and you cannot simply go off on your own. If you do not obey me on this, Lizbeth, I will have one of my warriors follow you at all times."

"Which one?" She turned her little head around searching for one. "He take me in woods. Pick flowers."

"No!" he said with a sharp sternness that wiped the smile off his daughter's face. "You will listen to me, Lizbeth or you will spend more time in your room."

Her bottom lip began to quiver.

His daughter's tears could do him in easily, so he was quick to say, "Tears will not help you, Lizbeth. Obey me or else."

She sniffled back tears that had yet to spill and nodded, then slipped her hands around his neck and kissed his cheek. "Mad?"

"Not if you obey me," he said, wanting to hug her tight and ease her worry, but it would do no good. She had to learn.

She nodded and kissed his cheek again. She kissed it at least six times by the time they reached the keep. And it touched Cree's heart that her kisses were her way of saying she was sorry.

152

Dawn rushed out of the keep, her eyes wide with fright, just as Cree reached the steps and she sighed with relief when she saw her daughter in her husband's strong arms.

"She is safe. You just realized she was missing?" he asked, wondering what had happened, since Dawn kept a good watch over the twins.

Before Dawn could gesture, Lizbeth spoke.

"Mummy with Valan. Me with Ina."

Dawn nodded, confirming what her daughter said.

Cree placed Lizbeth on the ground, the little lass taking his hand as if she intended to keep him by her side.

"After we eat, I will speak with Nell and Ina," Cree said to his wife and she nodded, looking relieved.

***

The two women stood in front of Cree visibly shaken and he had yet to say a word to them.

"Sit," he said, pointing to the two chairs not far from where he stood in front of the hearth and the two woman immediately did as he said.

"Lizbeth may be a handful, but it is your responsibility to watch over her. And since she escaped your sight twice now in a short time, it would seem that neither of you are doing what is expected of you."

"For a wee lass she is willful," Ina said, a tremble in her voice. "She smiles that sweet smile of hers and you think she will obey what you tell her and then off she goes, doing whatever strikes her fancy. Valan is forever shaking his head at her. He is a purposeful lad. He can sit for hours with the many wooden figures Elwin has carved for him. Or play in battle with his sword. Though at night, his little head keeps popping up to make sure his sister sleeps before he does."

"Aye he is a good lad," Nell agreed.

"And Lizbeth?" Cree asked.

153

"Perhaps more curious than willful, my lord. But, truthfully, she is only a wee bairn and a happy one at that."

It was Ina's turn to agree. "That is true. She wakes with a smile and wears it throughout the day."

Cree did not need to ask about Valan. While the lad did not wear a scowl like his da, he could often be found deep in concentration, a crinkle to his small brow. And then there were times he smiled and laughed, something Cree was glad to see.

"Regardless how willful, or curious, my daughter is, it is both your chore to make certain she does not wander off alone."

"Beast goes with her," Nell said and cringed at her own words.

"My daughter's sentiments exactly," Cree said, a glare surfacing.

Ina tried to rescue her friend. "The wee lass always goes on about her not being alone since Beast is with her more often than not."

Her words gave Cree an idea. "You both will make sure Lizbeth does not wander off again or there will be consequences."

Both women nodded vigorously.

"You may go, though one of you bring my daughter to me. I will remind her to obey both of you."

The two women nodded again and looked somewhat relieved as they hurried to the door.

He waited, hoping the idea he had would solve the problem of his daughter wandering off with Beast.

Sloan entered the solar and did not get a chance to say a word since Lizbeth, giggling non-stop, came barreling in with Beast, the large animal shoving Sloan out of his way to keep up with the wee lass. Nell came in right behind her and stopped beside Sloan.

"Da!" she cried out with a laugh and threw herself at Cree.

Cree scooped her up and while he wanted to return her smile, he kept a scowl on his face.

Lizbeth rubbed at his scrunched brow just as Dawn did when she tried to ease his annoyance.

"You will obey Nell and Ina and not wander off with Beast or on your own. And you must share Beast with mummy. Beast will make sure mummy gets help in case she should ever need it."

Lizbeth scrunched her brow as if thinking over her da's words, then her face brightened in a smile. "When mummy has Beast, me have warrior. Pick flowers."

Damn if his daughter was not negotiating with him.

"No, Lizbeth. No Beast. No warrior. No flowers. You do as Nell and Ina tells you."

She kept her smile and nodded, then tapped his chest and her own. "Pick flowers."

He could not keep the smile off his face. "Aye, I will take you to pick flowers, but not today."

Lizbeth's little arms went around his neck, squeezed tight, then she kissed his cheek.

Cree kissed her cheek, then set her on her feet.

"Bye," she said with a wave to her da and to Sloan as she hurried past him, Nell following with haste after her and Beast.

Sloan was smiling and shaking his head. "She is a handful now. I can only imagine what she will be like when she is grown."

Cree grinned. "That will be your son's problem, since Old Mary predicted my only daughter would wed your son."

Sloan laughed. "He will tame her easily enough, since he will have my charm when dealing with women.

"Like Lucerne who insisted she would marry anyone but you?"

155

Sloan spread his arms out. "But look whose charm she could not resist."

Cree laughed and shook his head. "What brought you here?"

Sloan's smile faded. "One of the warriors who was sent to follow the Macardle troop returned with news. It seems that along the way the troop increased by one man."

Chapter Sixteen

Possibilities of what that one warrior who had joined or rejoined the Macardle troop could mean occupied Cree's thoughts as he walked through the village toward Elsa's healing cottage. As soon as he had entered the Great Hall, and without even asking, Flanna had informed him that Dawn had instructed that he be told that she went to see how Ann fared.

Cree was pleased his wife kept him apprised of her whereabouts, but then he had warriors watching her, not following—at least not all the time—but he had eyes on her at all times so that he could track her movements if ever necessary. And never again would he allow her to go off anywhere, with anyone, without the protection of his warriors.

With that worry aside—not that it was gone or ever would be—he could concentrate on other matters like the increase of one warrior to the Macardle troop. Where had the fellow come from and where had he been? Could he be a Macardle scout? Had James sent someone ahead to scout the area and see what he faced before arriving?

That was something Cree had done numerous times, but would James?

Or could he have planted the man there before arrival and to leave a day or so afterwards to see what might follow their departure? Another thing Cree had done in the past and had proved beneficial.

His men would continue to follow the Macardle troop and report back as would Tannin. He would have to wait and see what other news followed before it all could be sorted out.

He was pleased to see Beast rise up in a stretch outside Elsa's cottage just before Dawn stepped outside. When she saw him approaching, her face brightened in a smile.

God but he loved this woman. He sometimes thought of when they had first met and how frightened she had been when Colum, the liege lord at the time, had forced her to tend his wounds. He had been shocked when he had discovered she had no voice, though knew it was the very reason she had been chosen to tend him.

The more he had learned about her, the more he witnessed her courage, the deeper he fell in love with her. And he wanted nothing more than at this moment to take her in his arms.

He hastened his steps and seeing her do the same had him realizing she wanted the same. She wanted to be in his arms as much as he wanted her there.

He reached out and as she got closer his arm snatched her up in a tight hug. He relished the feel of her warm body and while she was still thinner than before, her face had plumped some and there was color to her cheeks and happiness had replaced the fear that had lingered for days in her dark eyes.

She kissed him, a light kiss, and pressed her cheek to his as her hand pressed against his chest, then pressed her own chest, telling him as she had done so often since returning home that she loved him.

"I will never grow tired of hearing you tell me you love me and I will never grow tired of loving you."

Her smile grew and she gestured for them to walk and took his arm.

It was on his tongue to ask if she needed to rest, but kept hold of it. He had given his word he would leave it to her to decide if she needed to rest and she did not appear tired, and, truthfully, he wanted to walk with her as they had often done.

"Ann does well?" he asked.

Dawn tilted her head and closed her eyes briefly.

"She continues to sleep."

Dawn nodded.

"No changes?"

Dawn shook her head.

She tapped her lips and cradled her free arm, rocking it.

"Aye I talked to Nell and Ina about our daughter and told them there would be consequences if Lizbeth wandered off again. I also talked with Lizbeth and warned her again about going off with Beast or on her own. I also told her that she was to share Beast with you, hoping that without Beast she would not wander off." He looked down at the dog. "I am glad to see she listened and that Beast is with you."

Dawn mouthed Lizbeth, tapped her mouth, pointed to Beast and tapped her chest, then rested her hand to her cheek and shut her eyes briefly.

"Lizbeth told Beast to go with you as you put her down for a nap?"

Dawn nodded.

"Good. I am glad she finally obeys me."

Dawn smiled playfully and tapped her chest.

"Like you obey me? That is humorous, wife, truly humorous."

Her chest shook with silent laughter.

It felt so good to talk and laugh as she walked with her husband. There had been times while away that she feared she would never get home, but she had always managed to push the fear away and remain determined. She was ever so glad she did.

There was, however, still one thing that had disturbed her and she could put it off no longer. She had to talk to her husband and explain what else had happened to her. The problem was that it would take some explanation and she feared he might misinterpret what she said, and that could prove upsetting.

Dawn kept a smile on her face, though worry and guilt nagged at her. She should have seen to this sooner. It did no good to wait. It only made it more difficult.

"You smile, but I can feel your body grow taut beside me. What bothers you, Dawn?"

Before she could answer, Sloan approached with Henry.

"Sorry to disturb, my lord," Sloan said, "Henry has news."

"Wait in my solar," Cree ordered.

Cree walked Dawn over to a spot that afforded them some privacy.

Dawn gestured before Cree spoke. She tapped her lips, then his chest.

"You want to talk to me and I sense it is about something important."

She confirmed with a nod.

"I will talk with Henry, then you and I will talk undisturbed," he said and seeing the worry on his wife's face, he grew concerned. His hand slipped around her waist, drawing her closer. "You can talk with me about anything, wife, for there is nothing, absolutely nothing that will make me love you less."

She smiled after she brushed her lips across his. She expected him to say as much and his words did ease her worry, but not her guilt.

Dawn gestured that she would go and visit Lila and Cree walked her to Lila's cottage.

"I do not know how long this will take, but I will come find you when I'm done," he said.

Dawn pointed to the cottage, then to the keep.

"When you finish here you will be in the keep."

She nodded and after a hasty kiss, Cree walked off and Dawn walked up the path to the cottage door.

"I am so pleased you stopped to visit," Lila said, after opening the door and stepping outside. "Thomas just went down for a nap so we have some quiet time to talk without the wee bairns."

Lila left the door open and the two went and settled in the grass near the garden.

"You wear your worry on your face, you always have," Lila said. "What concerns you?"

Dawn voiced her troubling thoughts through her gestures.

"I can understand your concern that your husband might interpret your gestures wrong since it will take a bit of time to explain it all and especially since it is important to you. But that is easily resolved. I can interpret for you," Lila offered.

Dawn scrunched her brow as she gestured.

"Oh, it is of a personal nature. That could be a problem and even more of a problem if your husband misunderstands you or me hearing what is said between you two?"

Dawn sighed and shrugged, having no answer.

***

"He discovered you were tracking him and confronted you?" Cree asked, not sure he had heard Henry correctly. That was something that had never happened to Henry and made Cree more curious about the bearded man.

Henry nodded, then lowered his head, shaking it. "I was shocked when he came upon me."

"And you asked him why he left sooner than planned?" Cree asked.

"I did and he told me that there were too many people and too much noise for him."

161

Cree wondered over the man's aversion to people and noise and propensity for solitude. It was a trait found often in men who had seen much battle and death. Or men who had been shackled to other prisoners and crammed into small cells. He, himself, had longed for solitude at one time, battles having seemed endless, but he had a responsibility to the men who fought with him and their families. He was now glad he never took that path, since he would have never met Dawn.

"He told me if you wished to speak with him, he would wait, where he is camped, one more day. After that, he would take his leave. He says he will speak to no other but you."

"Did he say why he would speak to only me?"

"No, my lord, but he strikes me as a man of his word. When he came upon me it was not with vicious intent. It was simply to let me know that he knew I was following him. And he offered to wait on his own accord and made it known he was willing to speak with you, though he also made it clear he would not return here."

"Did he say why?" Cree asked.

"He said he has had enough of people. He prefers the silence of his own company."

"How long to there and back from where he is camped?" Cree asked.

"If you leave now and not spend too much time with him, you can be back by tomorrow evening."

Cree did not like the thought of leaving Dawn alone, but there was no reason to have the man forcibly returned here if he was willing to speak with Cree. And not knowing if the man had any involvement in Ann's attack or by chance what he may have seen it would be wise of him to talk with the bearded stranger.

"Prepare a small troop of warriors," Cree ordered Sloan.

"I will prepare a larger troop… in case a trap awaits you."

"I saw no signs of anyone else about when I followed him," Henry said.

"Yet he managed to discover your presence," Sloan reminded.

"I would have found signs of troop movement and I found none," Henry argued.

"I will take a small troop and Henry will scout for me." Cree raised his hand to silence Sloan when he went to object. "You will send another troop to follow a distance behind us and not make itself known unless necessary."

"That will work," Sloan said, appeased with Cree's decision.

"We leave within two hours, see it done," Cree ordered and Sloan headed to the door, a wave of his hand ordering Henry to follow.

"A word, my lord?" Henry asked.

"Henry will follow shortly and, Sloan—"

"I know, order extra sentries posted while you are gone and keep an extra watch on things, especially your wife. Worry not, all will be protected in your absence."

"I never doubted it would be," Cree said, though still did not feel comfortable leaving Dawn. He turned his attention to Henry. "Something troubles you, Henry?"

"I am sorry for failing you, my lord."

"You did not fail me, you simply met your match and the experience will make you an even better tracker than you already are."

"Thank you, my lord, but I wanted to speak to you about my wife, Nell. I went to see her for a moment to let her know I had returned and she was very upset. She worries you no longer trust her and what you may do to her and Ina if your daughter slips away again."

"Nell and Ina can prevent that from happening," Cree said, impressed that Henry approached him about his reprimand of Nell and Ina. He was defending his wife, something Cree respected him for.

"True, my lord, but Lizbeth is a curious bairn, from what Nell tells me and from what I have seen, and having been a curious bairn myself, I often wandered off to explore without thinking of any dangers I might face."

"What have you seen concerning my daughter?" Cree demanded and was surprised when Henry smiled.

"Lizbeth is as charming as she is curious and she asked me what I was doing one day when Nell had her and Valan out for a walk. I was studying some tracks like I always do, honing my skills, seeing if I could determine who the tracks belonged to. Lizbeth asked me what I was looking at and I explained to her about how the marks in the dirt spoke to me. Her questions continued one after the other. She has a sharp astuteness about her for one so very young."

"Are you saying you believe my two-year-old daughter can outwit Nell and Ina?" Cree asked disbelievingly.

"I would not dismiss it lightly, my lord," Henry said.

"I appreciate you sharing that observation with me, Henry."

"I worry that my wife worries about your daughter and keeping her safe and I cannot imagine what it will be like when we have a daughter of our own."

Cree rested his hand on the young man's shoulder. "Beyond, difficult, Henry. Beyond difficult."

***

Cree was surprised to find Lila sitting with Dawn in the Great Hall, then it struck him. She wanted Lila to interpret for her, which meant it was important to her that he not struggle to understand or misinterpret her gestures.

Cree stopped in front of the table where Dawn and Lila sat and pointed. "My solar."

Lila was quick to bow her head and stand. Dawn rose more slowly and once in Cree's solar, she went to the hearth, her hands stretched out to the warmth of the fire.

"Sit," Cree said and his wife shook her head and gestured, Cree easily understanding that she felt it better if they stood for easier interpretation.

Cree remained standing as well and kept his eyes on Dawn. "Tell me what has so disturbed you, wife, that you have delayed telling me and that you feel it necessary Lila interpret for you."

Dawn began, Lila interpreting. "I want no misunderstanding in what I tell you about what happened after I escaped the two men who abducted me."

Cree nodded. "I have been patient, not an easy thing for me. I want to know, tell me."

Lila spoke as Dawn gestured. "I ran to get as much distance as I could from the two men. They realized quickly that I had made an escape. The tall, lankier of the two was fast on his feet. I knew I would never out run him. My only choice was to take a chance with the rushing stream. I jumped in and tried to swim, but the turbulent waters had other ideas. I had all I could do to keep my head above water." Dawn's hand paused, the memories taking her back to that moment, then she shook her head and brought herself back to the present, her hands moving once again. "I truly thought I would die."

Lila snuffled back tears that threatened to fall when Dawn paused again.

Cree could see his wife was struggling to continue and he spoke up. "I want to hear all of what happened to you, but if it bothers you to speak of it, the telling can wait for another time."

Dawn shook her head and began to gesture.

"The water finally had its way and swallowed me. I woke—" Dawn's hands stilled and it took several moments before she continued. "I woke wrapped in a blanket, naked beneath, before a burning hearth, cradled in a naked man's arms."

Cree looked to Lila. "*Naked?* In a *naked* man's arms?"

"Aye, my lord, that is what she said," Lila said and Dawn confirmed with a nod.

Endless, angry thoughts of what it might mean whipped through his mind, not at Dawn, but at the naked man. As difficult as it was, he kept them to himself. He wanted to hear what else his wife had to say.

Dawn was well aware of the anger that stirred in her husband. She could see it in the tight set of his jaw and the way his eyes narrowed ever so slightly. She also was aware that his anger was not meant for her.

"Did he release you once he saw you were awake?" Cree asked.

Dawn shook her head, and Cree's nostrils flared.

"It took a bit to sort things out, to make him understand that my lack of a voice had nothing to do with me almost drowning. And also to make him understand I had no difficulty hearing."

Cree's anger mounted with the man thinking his wife deaf besides voiceless or dumb as most people referred to someone who could not speak. He could only imagine, though he preferred not to since the very idea stoked his anger even more, how difficult and frightening the situation must have been for her.

He warned himself to hold his tongue, but that was impossible. He needed to know. "Did he have his way with you?"

She shook her head, then shrugged.

"What does that mean?" Cree asked, not able to keep his anger out of his voice.

Lila was quick to explain as Dawn's hands began to move.

"I do not believe he did, since he was the one who rescued me from the stream, but I do not know how long I was out or what happened during that time. I was assured by one of the few women in the troop that I had been treated well and that the man allowed no harm to come to me and that he had wrapped himself around me so that his heat and the fire's heat would stop me from trembling so badly."

"The man's name who rescued you?" Cree asked more concerned with him at the moment than the mention of a troop.

"Tarass, that is how he introduced himself, though he offered no more than that nor did anyone else. I got the feeling that he preferred I learned little about him."

"Did you tell him you were my wife?"

Dawn shook her head.

Before she could explain, Cree demanded, "Why not?"

"I was not sure if he was friend or foe to you, or a stranger, and I did not want to take the chance. I requested he help me get home to my husband and bairns."

"A wise decision, wife," Cree said, glad his wife had had the wits to contemplate that before saying anything and to let this Tarass know she had a husband and bairns. "So he refused your request and you left to journey home on your own?"

"No, he told me he would see me escorted home safely after he saw to a matter that required his immediate attention. I realized after a couple of days that we were traveling further away from where I wanted to go. I asked him how long he thought it would be before he could see me home and when he told me a month at the least, I knew I could not wait that long."

"So you left," Cree said.

"I tried—"

167

"Tried? He would not let you leave?" Cree asked, wishing this Tarass was standing in front of him.

"He stopped me when I tried to leave. He told me it was not safe for me to travel on my own that I was to be patient and he would make sure I got home safely."

"So you snuck away?" Cree asked.

Dawn nodded and held up two fingers.

"Twice?"

"Aye, he found me the first time I tried. I would have been home a month sooner if I had been successful. The second time I planned my escape better."

"How did he find you the first time?" Cree asked.

Dawn pointed to Beast laying near her feet.

"Beast tracked you?"

Dawn nodded.

"Beast belongs to Tarass?" Cree asked.

Dawn nodded again.

"How is it that Beast is with you if he tracked you the first time and you were found?" Cree asked.

"I had been gone a few days before Beast showed up and, at first, I thought I would be found, but when no one appeared, I realized that Beast had escaped as well. Tarass had told Beast to look after me, let no harm come to me. He spent all his time with me and we grew more attached than I believe Tarass expected."

Cree looked at Beast sleeping beside Dawn and was grateful that the animal had grown so fond of Dawn that he continued to protect her and the twins as well.

A hard rap at the door reminded Cree that he would be taking his leave soon.

Sloan confirmed that when he entered and said, "All is ready for departure."

"I will be there soon," Cree said and turned to Lila. "You may leave us now."

Lila nodded and Dawn thanked her with a tight hug.

Cree went to his wife as the door closed and took her in his arms. "You feared telling me this?"

Dawn nodded.

"I would ask you why but since I know you well I would say it was because you feel guilty, though you have no reason to. And while I do not like that this Tarass had you naked in his arms and refused to escort you home right away, I am also grateful to him for saving your life and to the addition of Beast to our family."

Dawn forced a smile, not feeling as relieved as she had thought she would. And while her husband's words consoled, they also cautioned. He might be grateful to the man for saving her, but there were still some things he did not like, did not have clear answers to, and she was sure her husband would get his answers.

"No matter what you would have told me, wife, it would have changed nothing between us. You have no reason to feel guilty or worry over it any longer. It is over and done."

Dawn knew her husband as well as he did her and she did not believe this was the end of it, but for now it brought her a modicum of peace of mind that she had told him all she had gone through. She now kept nothing more from him.

This was not the time to leave his wife. She had harbored this unnecessary guilt when all she had done was fight to return to her family. Yet the information he might gleam from this man could help solve the mystery of her abduction and the murders.

"I have to go, not that I want to. Henry tracked down the bearded man and he will talk to me and only me. He refuses to return here and I do not think it would be wise to force his return."

Dawn nodded her head, agreeing with her husband, and already feeling his absence.

169

She might agree, but her reluctance to his sudden departure was there in the slight slump of her shoulders.

"I will be gone but a day—" His words stilled on his tongue. A day was far too long to be gone. "I will return tomorrow evening and Sloan will see you and the twins are kept safe."

The disappointment that filled her eyes poked at his heart and made him think he would not go. It was too soon after their forced separation to leave her. And with what she had just told him, she needed him there now with her, proving that nothing she had said changed anything between them.

"I will not go. I will not leave you," Cree said, taking tighter hold of his wife as if his grip confirmed his decision.

Dawn would prefer her husband to remain with her, but it was a decision of the heart that drove that thought when a sensible decision was needed.

She gestured, needing to know how long he would be gone.

"I would be home by tomorrow evening," he said, "but that matters not. You need me here."

She gestured again.

"Aye, it is important to speak with him. He could be involved in Ann's stabbing, though I doubt that, but he could have seen something that could be helpful in solving what happened to Ann."

Dawn gestured and pointed to the door.

"Are you telling me I must go?" Cree asked, his wife's strength continually surprising him.

Dawn rested her cheek against his, keeping it there for a moment, then nodded her head.

That she would miss him and was reluctant to let him go was obvious, but she also understood the benefits of him seeing to this matter.

"I will miss you," he said and kissed her.

He meant it to be a light kiss, but when their lips met it sparked his passion that he had attempted to control far too long. Her lips never felt so luscious, the taste so delicious, and her response so damn inviting.

Her arms hugged his neck so tight that he thought she would never let him go and her body melted against his in complete surrender, not only to him but her own passion.

Cree found it nearly impossible to ease her away, returning again and again after trying to separate from her, until finally he shoved her gently away.

"When I return, wife, be ready, for I am done being celibate," he said and took hasty steps out of the room, yanking the door closed on his smiling wife.

He was glad Sloan waited for him in the Great Hall.

"There is an important matter I want you to see to," Cree said as he neared Sloan and he joined steps with Cree as he walked through the Great Hall.

"A man named Tarass. Find out all you can about him. I have questions for him."

Chapter Seventeen

Cree faced the bearded stranger, a cold campfire separating them. They had arrived at his camp before mid-day the next morning as he appeared ready to take his leave.

"What is it you wish of me, my lord? I am eager to be on my way," the bearded man said.

"You left my village suddenly, why?"

"Too many people and too much noise, I prefer solitude," he said.

He may have given the impression of focusing on Cree, but he could see the man's eyes shifted now and again to the warriors a short distance behind Cree. He kept a good watch on them and something warned Cree that he was not a man who would surrender easily.

"Why?"

The man appeared puzzled by the question.

"Why do you prefer solitude?" Cree asked.

The man settled his bold blue eyes on Cree. "I find no one to my liking. Now what is it you wish of me, my lord, as I said, I am eager to be on my way."

"Were you aware of the woman in the stocks?" Cree asked, ignoring his wish for their talk to be over.

"I was, though I paid her little heed. It did not concern me."

"When you took your leave that morning, did you pass by the stocks?"

"I did."

"Did you see anything that gave you pause?" Cree asked.

His brow wrinkled as he pondered the question, then he gave a slight nod. "A moving shadow caught my eye in the dark spots that hugs the night, but it was not my concern."

That the man had caught a moving shadow in the darkness told Cree that there was more to this man than he wanted anyone to know. The ability to detect a shadow among night shadows was a skill attributed to seasoned warriors.

"Anything you can tell me about this shadow?"

"It was quick. All I caught was a hasty glimpse of the hem of a cloak."

That was more than Cree expected and most importantly it gave him someplace to start… a cloaked person lingering in the shadows, perhaps waiting for the perfect time to attack Ann.

"A worn cloak, the hem ragged," the man added.

That gave Cree even more pause. He had made sure worn garments were a thing of the past when he took over the title of the clan and land.

"The woman in the stocks, Ann, looked well to you when you passed by her?" Cree asked.

The man turned his eyes to the sky. "She was looking up. I assumed she was waiting to see the sun rise and her punishment to be over."

"You knew her punishment was to come to an end that day?"

The man lowered and turned his head to Cree. "There are few secrets in a village. Tongues keep busy minding other peoples' lives."

"What else did you hear?"

"Nothing I paid mind to."

"Nothing that might help me to find out who attempted to kill Ann?" Cree watched for the man's reaction to the news of the attempted murder, but he showed no trace of one.

"I told you what I know, my lord. I have nothing more to offer you."

Cree disagreed. He had another question for the man. "Why would you only speak to me?"

"I do not trust another to repeat my words correctly. They have a way of getting twisted when others speak for you."

Cree wondered over the man's distrust. Had someone betrayed him, had spoken his words incorrectly on purpose? Could it have caused him to be accused of something? Something he now hid from? The reason for the shackle on his wrist?

"If that is all, my lord, I would like to be on my way."

Cree had studied the man as they had talked. His full beard hid a good portion of his face and his long dark hair fell loose along the sides concealing his face even more. His layers of garments gave the impression of a thick man beneath, but it was difficult to tell. He was hiding from something and well before he arrived at the Village Dowell.

One other thing that made Cree believe the man had nothing to do with the stabbing was that a man of his size would need only one thrust to see the chore finished. It would be deep and it would be fatal.

"We are finished," Cree said, dismissing him and with a brief nod the man turned and walked away.

Cree wanted nothing more than to leave for home right away. But they had stopped only once for a brief repast and rest. The men and horses needed more rest and food before returning.

"Set a fire burning, we eat and rest," Cree ordered and while not one of his warriors would have complained if he had ordered their immediate return home, he could see the relief on their tired faces.

He, however, had a reason to return as soon as possible. He wanted to make love with his wife. They may have been reunited when she returned home, but joining with her, feeling as if they became one was a true reunion and besides, he had missed making love with her terribly. He never felt as whole, as alive, as loved as he did when they made love. It was a bonding that went beyond the norm and deep down into their souls.

He had never thought that way before when he had joined with other women. He had coupled to satisfy a need. That was not the way with Dawn. The need was there, but it was different and it had taken him a while to understand it, though more to admit it. Admit that he had fallen in love with a voiceless woman. But then Dawn had never truly been voiceless. She might not have a voice people could hear, but she certainly made herself heard.

He was proud of her, proud to call her wife, proud she belonged to him and always would. His thoughts had stirred his needs and he decided to rest along with his men, since he would set a good pace home and once there, he would seek his bed, though not to sleep.

***

Dawn sat with Lila outside her cottage in a patch of grass while their children played. She kept a watchful eye on Lizbeth as did Beast from where he laid beside Dawn. Where she had ordered him with a firm hand and a look to stay put, since she did not trust him from surrendering to the whims of her daughter.

The sky was a bit overcast, the warmth having vanished with the sun that had shined for barely an hour earlier in the morn. Still, it was a pleasant day to be outdoors and for the children to have time to play.

"You have avoided talking about it and you always talk with me when something troubles you," Lila said.

Dawn's chest heaved in a sigh, grateful to her friend for recognizing her need.

"It must not have been easy for you," Lila said. "But then you are a brave one. I remember being so frightened for you when Colum sent you to tend Cree in that small hut when he arrived here as a prisoner. I thought for sure he would harm you."

Dawn smiled, recalling her short time spent there with Cree, and gestured.

Lila smiled as she spoke her friend's response. "They are better memories than expected." She reached out to lay a comforting hand on Dawn's arm. "Cree loves you beyond measure. There is nothing that should worry you unless... you are not with child, are you?"

Dawn looked appalled as she shook her head.

"I do not mean to upset you, but you did say you woke naked in that man's arms and you only have the word of women, who you know not at all, and who supposedly tended you. So how can you be sure?"

Dawn rested her hand on her stomach and shook her head firmly.

"You have bled since arriving home?" Lila asked.

Dawn shook her head and moved her fingers as if walking.

"On your journey home?"

Dawn nodded.

Tears collected in Lila's eyes. "I do not know where you get the strength. You are so brave."

Dawn gestured.

"You say what choice do you have, but you have done things many women would dare not do, would be far too frightened to do... me being one of them."

The children squealed in laughter drawing theirs and Beast's attention, his large head shooting up to stare at them.

176

"He watches over you and the twins. It is good you have him." Lila's eyes rounded. "This man... he would not follow after Beast would he?"

Dawn's eyes widened as well.

"You have thought the same," Lila said and Dawn nodded. "Is that what worries you, that he will come here one day?"

Dawn tapped at her temple.

"You have thought on it. I do not see how you could not give it thought. The man might believe you robbed him of his dog, giving him an excuse to track you down."

Dawn's head drooped as if the weight of it all was too much.

Lila squeezed her arm. "I am sorry. My tongue speaks before I think."

Dawn shook her head, then tapped her lips, pointed to Lila and rested her hand to her chest.

"I do speak from the heart to you, but it does not always help."

Dawn nodded and patted her chest.

"You are being kind saying it does help just as you always have when my mouth says too much."

Dawn smiled.

"You did say this man had an important matter to take care of, so he probably will not waste time tracking down his dog," Lila said, trying to reassure her friend.

Dawn nodded, appearing to agree but not sure if she did.

"But if he does show up..." Lila words trailed off as she swallowed hard. "He will face the mighty Cree."

***

It was late, the light just fading, everyone asleep except for the sentinels posted throughout the village.

Dawn stood on the top step of the keep, her shawl wrapped around her, warding off the chill as she looked in the distance, hoping to see her husband. She had grown impatient waiting in their bedchamber, not a bit tired, eager for her husband's return.

She turned to go back inside and stopped. She did not want to return to an empty bedchamber or to sit in the silence of the Great Hall. Beast was not with her, having gone as he did every night to sleep near the twins.

The fast encroaching darkness gave her no pause as she descended the steps and entered the village and even though the darkness seemed to fall faster with each step she took, it caused her no fear. More sentinels had been posted and having seen warriors linger in her steps every time she left the keep, she had no doubt her husband had ordered her watched.

She headed toward the healing cottage. Lucerne had been helping Elsa throughout the day, but in the evening Elsa would stay and look after Ann, even if there was little she could do for her.

Dawn was drawn to a halt a few steps from the healing cottage, by the flash of a dark shadow in the darkness. She stared at the spot she had seen it, a dark swirl of sorts, and seeing nothing, she questioned if she had seen anything at all.

A chill settled around her and the night suddenly took on an ominous feel, making her hurry her steps to the cottage door. She rapped softly on it, thinking perhaps it had been foolish of her to come here so late.

The door opened slowly and Elsa's head peered from around it.

"Dawn, whatever at you doing here? Are you not feeling well?" Her eyes turned wide. "Forgive me, my lady, for addressing you improperly."

Dawn shook her head and waved her apology away, then patted her chest and smiled to let Elsa know she was fine.

Elsa opened the door and waved her hand. "Please, my lady, come in."

Dawn wished Elsa would call her by her name, at least when they were alone as Lila did, but she had not been successful in convincing her.

Dawn pointed to Ann.

"She wakes, takes some broth, and sleeps again."

Dawn tapped her chest.

"Aye, much like you did after returning home," Elsa said.

Dawn pressed her hand to her brow.

"No fever so far and her wounds show no signs of turning putrid, but it has not been that long since the attack." Elsa looked to Ann. "She has a fight ahead of her."

Dawn pointed to Elsa and shrugged.

"How am I?"

Dawn nodded.

"Worried for her," Elsa said with a nod to Ann.

Dawn placed her hands together as in prayer and rested them to her cheek.

"I am used to little sleep. Besides, I cannot sleep knowing Ann fights to live."

Dawn patted her chest and pointed to the chair.

Elsa turned a soft smile on Dawn. "I appreciate your offer to sit with Ann, but you still heal yourself," —Elsa held her hand up when Dawn attempted to protest— "Your husband would not be pleased with me if I allowed it this late at night."

Dawn could not argue with that and she did not want to cause Elsa anymore worry.

"Tomorrow you can sit with Ann while I see to tending to some things," Elsa offered.

Dawn nodded and went to the door, leaving Elsa to return to the chair by the bed where Ann lay sleeping.

With nothing left for her to do, Dawn returned to the keep, her eyes watchful for any moving shadows. Once in the keep, she questioned if perhaps her eyes had played tricks on her. Or perhaps the night shadows had played tricks on her.

She recalled the many times on her journey home that she had thought she had seen something moving in the darkness of the night. After a while, she had realized that if Beast did not stir, then there was nothing to worry about.

Still, sleep had not come easy and she had avoided well-worn roads frequently traveled for they were treacherous for a woman traveling alone. It had added time to her return home, but if she had not taken precautions she may have never made it home.

Dawn sat at a table near the burning hearth. A night chill had swept over the land and the warmth of the keep was welcoming. After another yawn surfaced, she lowered her head on her folded arms resting on the table and was soon asleep.

***

Cree handed the reins of his horse to one of his warriors and headed up the steps to the keep. He was bone tired, something he did not want to admit. He had pushed his warriors and himself to get home, and not a one of them had complained. They had been in more battles than most and finally having a permanent place to rest their heads, a place that welcomed—a home—none wanted to be gone long from it… he being one of them.

He had thought of nothing but making love to his wife, but with the lateness of the night, he knew he would find her

180

sleeping and he would not wake her. She might argue, but she needed her rest.

He rolled his shoulders, easing the ache between them, then rolled his neck to ease the ache there as well. He was brought to a stop at the sight of his wife, sitting at a table near the hearth, her head pillowed on her folded arms that rested on the table.

She had waited for him and it warmed his heart.

He went over to her and eased her dark red hair away from her face. She slept peacefully, content and safe, and he intended to keep her that way. He lifted her gently in his arms, reminded of the weight she had lost and thought how she needed to eat more, but right now, she needed to sleep.

He carried her slowly up the stairs to their bedchamber, cherishing the feel of her in his arms, tucked against him, her hair tickling at his nose. He would wrap himself around her once in bed, but wanted to linger in this moment and enjoy the simple pleasure it brought him.

He laid her on the bed and quickly shed his garments, then ever so carefully and gently he began to disrobe her. He lifted and shifted her around with tender care, doing his best not to wake her. Or did he hope he would?

He ran his hand down her naked arm when it was free of the sleeve and lingered in the soft feel of her. How many nights had he dreamt of doing just that, feeling her silky skin as if she was real and lying there beside him in bed only to wake and feel the punishing ache of discovering yet again that she was gone?

No more though, she was here and real and warm and so very soft.

Once he discarded the last of her garments to the floor, he stared down at her and reveled in her beauty. Her stomach was as flat as it had been before she had the twins and he could not help but think of her growing round with child once again.

The urge to plant his seed deep inside her grew along with his manhood.

"Mine. Always mine," he whispered, whishing she was awake, wishing he could make love to her repeatedly. He closed his eyes and shook his head.

Another day.

He opened his eyes, ready to drop down in bed next to her, take her in his arms, and attempted to sleep.

He found himself staring at his wife, her eyes open and her arms spread out to him.

Chapter Eighteen

Cree dropped down over her and as her arms circled him, he rolled to his side, his arms going around her and taking her with him. His hand drifted in a soft caress down her back, rediscovering the feel of her and possessively reclaiming every inch of her. When he reached her backside, he gave it a firm squeeze and adjusted her to fit snug against his hard manhood.

He continued to stroke her slowly, her arm, her waist, the curve of her hip.

"I have missed this, you here, naked in bed beside me, pressed against me," —he eased his hand between her legs, slipping his finger inside her— "wet an eager to have me inside you."

He could almost hear her silent gasp and felt her head nod against his shoulder and that she let him know she felt the same only fired his passion more.

She reached down and tried to move his hand away, worried it would be over too fast if he continued to tease her.

"No, wife," he whispered in her ear, then nipped playfully at the lobe. "I will make you come more than once this night."

Dawn nodded as she turned her head away from his shoulder to smile at him while her hand wasted no time in taking hold of his manhood.

"It is a challenge you want," he said with a rumble of low laughter as he pushed her onto her back with the weight of his body. "And a challenge you will lose for I will see you pleased again and again and again before I seek my own release."

183

Dawn released his manhood, reluctantly. She loved the feel of him, big and powerful, in her hand and yet vulnerable to her touch, her command, until he had no choice but to surrender, something not easy for Cree. But then he had had no choice when it came to love.

She rested her hand to his cheek and mouthed, *I love you, always.*

"I have said it many times before and will continue to say it, especially since I thought I would never hear you say it again, that I will never grow tired of hearing you tell me that you love me."

He settled his mouth on hers in a kiss that left no room to his intentions. He wanted her to know he intended to possess her, make her his, leave his mark so that there would never be a fraction of a doubt that she belonged to him and always would.

Between the kiss and the way his fingers pleasured her, Dawn felt herself much too close to climax. She wanted this time, this night to last, but then she recalled his words… *I will see you pleased again and again and again.*

And she let go.

Cree felt her climax shatter her body and he lifted his head, ending the kiss, to watch his wife toss her head back, her eyes tighten shut, her mouth drop open in a silent scream, and her hand grip his arm tightly as pleasure rocked her body.

As sanity returned to Dawn, passion still lingered on the fringes, and she smiled realizing why when she felt her husband's mouth at her breast teasing her nipple with his tongue and felt his manhood rubbing between her legs, not allowing the ember of passion that still burned in her to die.

She ran her hands over his broad shoulders, his muscles taut and thicker than she remembered, but then he had grown in size since she had been gone. He was powerful before and even more so now, and feeling the strength of him as he hovered over her flared her desire.

He pushed himself off her, his hands braced on the bed to either side of her shoulders and settled his manhood between her legs.

"I want to plant a bairn inside you. What say you, wife?"

That he should ask her and that he did not even give thought to her possibly being with another man but accepted her word filled her heart with joy.

Dawn smiled, nodded, and patted her chest, letting him know she would love him to give her another bairn.

Cree smiled, a wicked smile, and teased her with a kiss that stirred her senses and promised so much more.

"I will keep you busy day and night, wife, getting you with child."

Dawn crossed her heart.

"Aye, wife, I promise," Cree said and as he claimed her lips in another kiss, she spread her legs welcoming him, and he entered her slowly.

Too slowly for Dawn. She arched her back and he sank deeper into her and she smiled, having waited as if forever to feel him there inside her once again.

She tapped her mouth so he would look at her lips, then gripped his arms as she mouthed, *need you, want you, love you.*

Cree answered with a sharp thrust, entering her and tossing his head back to release a rumbling groan. He remained still for a moment, savoring the feel of her, and wanting to feel more, so much more.

He began to move as did Dawn and they set a rhythm familiar to them both, slow and steady at first with Cree lowering his head now and again to tease her neck with nips and nibbles.

185

It spiraled Dawn's passion like it always did and she quickened the pace of their rhythm.

Cree obliged her, moving faster, his own need growing rapidly and when Dawn began to tap his arm with her finger over and over, her gesture for yes, yes, yes, he took charge. He plunged in and out of her, the force of his movement rocking them back and forth on the bed, and still he felt he could not bury himself deep enough in her.

He watched her, making sure he was causing her no pain, but he saw only pleasure as she crunched her eyes and her mouth dropped open in silent groans that would have surely echoed throughout the keep if she had a voice.

He let himself go just as she did, enjoying every thrust, every sensation, every moment of joining with his wife once again.

Her hands gripped his arms tight just as he felt himself on the verge of climax and knew she would join him, and she did.

His roar filled the room and Dawn was sure it could be heard throughout the keep and she wished her scream of pleasure could be heard along with his. But her silence in no way lessened the never-ending spiral of pleasure that consumed her nor did it rob her of the joy of seeing her husband's pleasure as he emptied into her, leaving his seed to take root.

"You are mine," Cree said as he dropped down over her as if he had claimed her for the first time.

Dawn smiled and wrapped her arms around her husband, for those words meant more to her than anyone would know.

They soon fell asleep in each other's arms, but sometime later Dawn woke in the throes of passion, her husband's hands working their magic once again. When he realized she was awake, he was quick to pull her up onto her knees and with her hands braced on the mattress, he entered her from behind, gripping her backside as he drove in and out of her until they once again exploded together in climax.

Cree promised himself he would not touch her again that night, seeing her yawn soon after he had settled her in his arms, and feel how limp her body rested against his. She was tired and needed to rest. Tomorrow would be soon enough to make love to her again.

But he woke how long later, he did not know, his manhood stirring once again. He eased his wife out of his arms, much too tempted to wake her, and went to sit in the chair by the fire, adding logs to the dying embers before he sat.

He shook his head. He had been wise not to join with his wife too soon upon her return. He knew once he did he would not be able to get enough of her. He never seemed to be able to get enough of her, and was pleased she felt the same. But now that he had, it would be difficult, if not impossible, to keep his hands off her, and she still had to heal more.

It had felt so good, so very good, to join with as one once again. It was like nothing he had ever experienced before and had missed beyond measure when he had thought her dead. And it felt even more special knowing they were making another bairn together.

The twins had been a surprise, since he had thought Dawn had taken the brew Elsa had given her to keep from getting with child. He had not wanted her to get with child then, since he had been promised to another. But in the end it had helped him make a decision, regarding him and Dawn and all had worked out well. Not that he would have had it any other way.

Now, though, this time was different. They were wed, settled with a home, a family, and they had chosen to add to that family. He was more than pleased. Though, he would be even more pleased when he solved the puzzle of Dawn's abduction and the consequences that followed, Lara's death being one of them, the man Tarass being another.

He pushed the disturbing thoughts away. He would not let anything ruin this night and its memories. His wife was home, truly home now. They were one once again and that was all that mattered.

He smiled, hearing his wife approach from behind him and placed his hand over hers after it settled on his shoulder. He was not surprised when she linked her fingers with his and walked around to stand in front of him.

The fire's light cast a glow over her, outlining the subtle curves of her body that was still sluggish with sleep. Her dark red hair was a mess of tangles, several strands falling around her face, and her dark eyes—the corners of his mouth lifted ever so slightly—burned with passion.

He pulled her to him and her body quickly lost what sleep lingered as she fell against him, making sure she landed in his lap and she rubbed herself against his rising manhood.

Her arms went around his neck and she pressed her lips to his in a kiss that was far from tender.

It did not take long for either of them to grow impatient and Cree suddenly stood, his hands slipping under her backside, taking her with him while their lips remained locked in a punishing kiss.

Their lips separated when Dawn was jolted back against a wall.

"Hold tight," Cree ordered. "I am going to ride you hard."

Dawn kept her arms firm around her husband's neck and he lifted her slightly and fitted himself inside her with ease, but then she was ready for him, having woken from a dream wet and eager to join with him.

He was true to his word, he slammed into her hard again and again, her back repeatedly hammered against the wall with his forceful thrusts. She was soon lost in pleasure, always enjoying the times there was no preamble to their lovemaking. He would do nothing but enter her quick and with a fierce need that had him driving deep and fast into her, until...

She heard his groan before she realized he was climaxing. He never climaxed before her, not ever, and she smiled and tightened around him, enjoying this unexpected moment.

"You think you will not come with me," he said in a growling tease and cupped her bottom with his arm as his other hand slipped between them to tease her sensitive nub that was already throbbing, and she exploded in climax. Not once but twice, Cree driving into her until she came again.

Cree braced his one hand against the wall as the last of his climax faded, Dawn's head resting on his shoulder as her second climax faded away.

He waited a few moments, his climax so hard that it robbed him of some breath and strength. It did not take long for him to regain both and he carried her to the bed, lowering them down on it.

Their hands remained locked together as they lay side by side until Dawn shivered, then Cree turned, pulling the blanket over them and hugging her close. Sleep claimed them quickly and it was well after sunrise before they woke.

"Where are you going, wife," Cree asked, rubbing the sleep from his eyes to see Dawn hurrying into her garments.

Dawn gestured fast and Cree pieced together what he caught, his eyes still blurred from his heavy sleep.

"You go see the twins, then Elsa." His brow wrinkled at what she added. "You do not feel well?"

Dawn smiled wide as she hugged herself.

"Feeling good today." He corrected and grinned, feeling good himself.

Dawn rushed over to him, kissed him quick, patted his chest, then pointed to her smile.

"I put the smile on your face this morning?" he asked, knowing it was what she meant but wanting to hear it from her.

She nodded and rolled her hand around and around, her smiling growing.

"Many times over," he said with a chuckle.

She nodded again and looked as if she chuckled along with him.

Cree grabbed her around the waist and pulled her down on the bed. "Shall I add another time to it?" His hand slipped beneath her garment, but when he touched her between her legs, she stiffened. A reaction he had never gotten from her. He looked at her and her wince told him everything. "You are sore."

She nodded, looking almost apologetic.

"I should have been more tender with you."

Dawn shook her and gestured, letting him know she did not at all agree and that she had been just as eager to make love as he had been. She finished with a wave of her hand as if her discomfort was nothing and would pass.

"You will see if Elsa has anything that will help you," Cree ordered and I will not touch you for a day or two."

Dawn sat up and poked him hard in the chest, shaking her head.

"You are sore," he reminded. "I will not make it worse."

Dawn tapped her chest.

"You think it is for you to decide?"

She nodded and pushed herself off the bed, but Cree caught her arm before she could stand.

"My decision, wife, since you are too stubborn to do what is best for you."

Dawn looked about to argue when she turned a grin on him and nodded, then gave him a kiss on the cheek, eased her arm out of his grasp, and slipped off the bed to hurry to the door.

Cree jumped out of bed. "I know that smile, Dawn. You will not have your way."

Dawn turned and even wider smile on him and pointed between his legs, then tapped her chest, letting him know she would have her way and rushed out the door before her husband could stop her.

Cree looked down at his jutting manhood and growled, "Traitor."

***

The twins took up more of Dawn's morning than she had planned. It made her realize how they had grown in her absence. She loved that Cree made sure to spend time with them in the morning before he saw to his duties. It was not until the twins settled in to play with Nell and Ina that Dawn was finally able to go see Elsa.

"Oh, Dawn, I am so glad you came," Elsa said and waved her into the cottage.

When Elsa did not correct herself for calling Dawn by her name, she knew the healer was upset.

"Lucerne is not feeling well," Elsa said, pointing to a pale Lucerne sitting at the table.

"It is nothing more than a roiling stomach. Something I have grown used to since I am with child," Lucerne insisted.

"Perhaps, but you cannot see to these few visits alone," Elsa said. "And I cannot leave Ann. She is warm to the touch and I fear a fever may be setting in."

Dawn tapped her chest and pointed to the healing basket.

191

"It is settled then, Lady Dawn will help me," Lucerne said, standing.

Elsa nodded her head. "And if your stomach grows worse, you must give me your word you will return home and rest."

Dawn nodded, patted her chest, and walked her fingers, then pointed to Lucerne.

"You will make sure to see her home," Elsa said with relief.

Dawn nodded and reached for the healing basket before Lucerne could.

"Tend Ann and worry not about me," Lucerne said with a pat to Elsa's arm before she and Dawn left the cottage.

"It is good to see you do so well," Lucerne said as they walked through the village.

Dawn nodded with a smile and stretched her hand out over the village.

"You are glad to be home," Lucerne said, understanding her. "I am sure those we visit today will be pleased to see you doing so well."

Dawn enjoyed the time she spent with Lucerne, amazed at how caring she was with the people she tended and how right she had been about the people being pleased to see her. It made her realize how many of the clan truly cared about her. It had not been like that a few years ago, few if any would acknowledge her, fearful they would catch whatever afflicted her. Some had believed her cursed and did not want the curse passed to them. She was relieved that that had all changed.

They were finished, about to return to the healing cottage when Sloan approached, looking none too pleased.

"Elsa tells me you are not feeling well," Sloan said, reaching out to gently tuck a stray strand of his wife's blonde hair behind her ear as his brow wrinkled with concern. "And you are pale."

Lucerne smiled. "Paleness and nausea are constant companions of mine since I have been with child." She continued, stopping her husband before he could respond. "And please do not tell me to rest. I not only feel worse when I rest, I feel useless."

Dawn nodded and patted her chest, feeling the same when told to rest.

A sharp bark caught their attention and Dawn saw Beast running toward them and she worried something was wrong. And when he reached her and sat to lean against her leg and whine, she definitely knew something was wrong.

She crouched down and hugged him, burying her face in his fur, letting him know all was well. His shiver told her otherwise.

"He misses you when you're not near," Lucerne said.

It was more than that, but Dawn did not want to discuss it with Lucerne or Sloan. She stood, Beast's big body continuing to lean against her leg.

A quick hand to Lucerne's face, could not hide the deep yawn that surfaced.

Sloan took his wife's arm. "You will rest."

"A brief nap," she conceded.

Dawn waved her away with a smile, recalling how she would suddenly grow tired while carrying the twins.

Once the pair was a distance away, she crouched down again. She took Beast's face in her hand, tapped the top of his nose gently and then her chest. She repeated it several times, letting him know that he belonged to her now and nothing would change that.

Beast licked her face and his shiver calmed, but Dawn wondered over it. What was it that had upset Beast? What had he sensed?

Chapter Nineteen

Dawn wished it could always be the way the last week had been, the days passing by without conflict or concern. The weather was surprisingly lovely, even allowing a couple of days of unusual warmth, though the nights remained chilly. Ann was improving slowly after spending two days fighting a fever and Elsa had hoped she would recover. Cree had spoken with Ann once and there was nothing she could tell him. She remembered feeling a searing pain, then nothing until waking in the healing cottage.

Still, though, that day Beast had been so upset continued to weigh heavily on Dawn. Something was brewing, Beast had sensed it and she worried over it.

"Did you get no pleasure from our lovemaking, wife?" Cree asked, leaning up on his elbow beside her in bed to rest his head on his hand as he traced her lips with his finger. "You frown."

He need not ask her, he had seen and felt for himself how much she had enjoyed it. So what was troubling his wife that it brought a frown to her face so quickly after making love?

Dawn shrugged.

He leaned his face down until their noses nearly touched. "Are you telling me nothing or that you do not know? And let me remind you that you have never lied to me and I do not expect you to start now."

Her husband was right and she would expect the same from him.

A sharp rap at the door prevented her response.

After a mumbled oath, Cree called out, "Who disturbs me at daybreak?"

"Someone who was not happy about being disturbed either," Sloan shot back. "Evin from the Clan MacLoon and one of our warriors have returned with news that cannot wait. I will wait in your solar with them."

Cree dropped on his back annoyed that this time with his wife had been interrupted.

Dawn turned and rested against him, tucking herself in the crook of his arm to lay her head on his shoulder and drape her arm over his naked chest.

"Not letting me go, wife?" he asked, stroking her arm and as always loving the feel of her soft, warm skin wrapped around him.

Dawn tapped his arm once, signaling yes and gave him a squeeze to once again confirm she preferred he remain there with her.

"Tell me what troubles you, for I have seen your worry on your face and have waited for you to talk with me about it, but I have grown too impatient to wait any longer," Cree said.

Dawn pointed to the door.

"They can wait."

She voiced her concern. A concern she had not even wanted to admit to herself. She kept her gestures slow, pausing now and again so that her husband could fully comprehend her.

"Beast has been upset?" Cree shook his head slowly. "Strange as that sounds, I have noticed a difference in him of late. He stares in the distance when outside as if expecting someone to arrive. And he stays closer to my side when he is with me and I have seen him do the same with you and the twins. Almost as if he fears losing us."

Dawn nodded, pleased he not only understood but he had seen and sensed it for himself. She gestured again.

195

"You believe Cree's master will come for him and will demand his return?" he asked to be sure he understood her.

Dawn nodded.

With Sloan having found out nothing about the man Tarass so far, Cree would be only too pleased to have him arrive of his own accord. "I would be pleased to meet Tarass and thank him for helping you and I will make certain Beast remains here with his new family."

Dawn's smile barely reached her lips. While she was overjoyed that Cree would see that Beast remained with them, not doubting for a moment her husband would get his way, she worried about him meeting Tarass, if her suspicions proved correct and he was to arrive here.

Would Cree thank the man or did he have other plans for him?

Cree took hold of Dawn's chin and with a gentle tug forced her to look at him. "I feel your worry and see it in your dark eyes that refuse to meet mine. What will be, will be, wife, and you can do nothing about it."

Was that a warning that she was to leave it be, that it was in his hands now?

"I need to go and see to this matter. I will meet you and the twins in the Great Hall for the morning fare."

Dawn reluctantly let him go, though took pleasure in watching him don his garments. She did not think it possible but she firmly believed her husband's already fine features had improved in her absence. Or perhaps it was the joy that her return had brought him that graced his good features. Either way, he was a fine looking man and he belonged to her.

Dawn pointed to him and, fixing a slight scowl on her face, she thumped her chest and pointed to him again.

He sent her a deeper scowl, though a hint of a smile shined through it as he approached the bed. "Are you telling me I belong to you?"

Dawn gave him a firm nod, thumped her chest again, then hugged it.

"I am all yours?" he asked, placing his knee on the bed.

She nodded, a playful smile surfacing to chase her scowl.

Cree dropped down over her, planting his hands to either side of her head, as he hovered over her. "Aye, I belong to you, wife, and you belong to me. You are mine and always will be."

He kissed her, a mistake, and one he purposely made since his wife's sudden possessive nature had aroused him and with her naked beneath him, what choice had he but to show her just how much they belonged to each other.

**

Cree entered his solar some time later, Evin jumping out of his chair and appearing anxious to speak with him. And Cree obliged him.

"You have news that cannot wait, Evin?" Cree almost found himself smiling since it had waited and for an extremely important matter.

"Aye, my lord," Evin said eagerly.

Cree leaned back against the edge of the desk and signaled Evin over to stand in front of him while Sloan and the warrior waited to the side.

"Tell me," Cree ordered when Evin came to a stop in front of him.

Evin beamed as he said, "The Lord of Fire has returned home."

Cree turned to his warrior, Dylan, for confirmation.

"The son inherited the father's title and lands and has returned to lay claim," Dylan confirmed.

197

"With the Lord of Fire in residence now, the Clan Macardle has no claim on our land," Evin said as if it was all settled.

Again Cree turned to Dylan.

"Tannin assumed the same, but James Macardle continues to claim that the one particular area of land belongs to the Clan Macardle."

Cree looked to Evin. "With the Lord of Fire in residence, it falls on him now to protect your clan since you were under fealty to me only because there was no Clan MacFiere to protect you."

"But the Clan MacLoon's fealty is still with you and we wish to remain under your protection. You have always been there for our clan. We trust and respect you."

Cree looked to Dylan for an explanation, sensing Evin was not telling all.

"A reputation has followed the Lord of Fire. It seems that he is a fierce warrior, trained by barbarians or so the tale goes."

"Has Tannin met with him?"

Dylan nodded. "He has, my lord, as soon as he learned the Clan MacLoon intended to remain loyal to you. The Lord of Fire demands you release the clan of their pledge."

"Demands?" Cree asked, not taking kindly to the mandate.

"He sends his warriors into our village with orders, demanding that every able bodied man must help restore the MacFiere keep," Evin said. "We have our own village to tend to before harvest is upon us and winter sets in."

"You pledged your fealty to the Clan MacFiere and they saw you kept safe longer than I did. It is your duty to help them now," Cree said.

Evin disagreed with a sharp shake of his head. "The Clan MacFiere deserted us, left the Clan MacLoon to fiend on their own for far too many years. We owe them nothing."

"The Lord of Fire vehemently disagrees," Dylan said. "He also disagrees with the Macardle claim that part of MacLoon land belongs to them and has made it known there will be no negotiating the claim. The situation is not a good one."

"Does Tannin fear there will be trouble?" Cree asked.

Dylan nodded. "Tannin is trying to ease tempers and encourage discussion, but with it being only a few days since the Lord of Fire and his troop arrived, it does not look promising. The Lord of Fire is adamant in his decisions."

"He says he will come here and tell you himself that the Clan MacLoon owes the Clan MacFiere their fealty and he intends to see that we keep our pledge," Evin said with a bit of a quiver in his voice

It seemed the Lord of Fire had left an impression on Evin and not a good one. However, Cree knew all too well the necessity of taking command and letting all know what is expected of them. Still, he had invested time and warriors in seeing the Clan MacLoon safe in the absence of the Lord of Fire. For that, he should be rewarded at least respect and gratefulness, rather than a demanding command.

"Return and tell Tannin that I *demand* the Lord of Fire present himself here at my home to settle this dispute," Cree ordered Dylan.

"That will not be necessary, my lord. Tannin sent word to me not long after we left. The Lord of Fire and a troop of his men left shortly after we did. Evin and I rode hard to get here, but from what I have seen of the Lord of Fire and his skilled warriors I doubt they will be far behind us."

Sloan spoke as soon as Cree turned to him. "I will find out how far out they are."

Before he could take his leave, Cree ordered, "Take Evin with you and see that he is given food and drink."

Evin cast one more plea to Cree. "Please, my lord, do not desert us. We need your protection now more than ever."

199

"I will see what can be done, Evin, but your chieftain is well aware that he pledged his fealty to the Lord of Fire and that would extend to any who held his title and land."

Evin appeared as if he was being led to his execution, his shoulders drooping along with his head as he took slow steps to Sloan.

The door had barely closed when Cree turned to Dylan. "What else have you to tell me?"

"Tannin's message to you about the Lord of Fire is that he is a man who cannot be swayed from his decisions. And he believes that there is more to his return home than only to claim his father's title and lands."

"Has he surmised what that might be?"

"Tannin thinks it could possibly be revenge the Lord of Fire seeks. He has brought a small group of people with him, perhaps what is left of his clan. It is difficult to say since none will offer any words about the Lord of Fire. And nothing has been said of where they have been all these past years."

"But people speculate," Cree said, recalling the many tales that had spread about him.

"They do," Dylan said with a nod. "But I believe they are wild tales spread by fear."

"Why? His father was a respected warrior. Why fear the son?"

"There is talk that his mother was a descendent of barbarians and some believe that she left her home after receiving word of her husband's demise and took her son to be raised among her people."

"Gossiping tongues can do much damage," Cree said, again thinking of the gossip, lies, and secrets that had first plagued him and Dawn when they had gotten together.

"Some claim to have seen proof of her barbarian heritage."

"What proof is that?"

Dylan lowered his voice as if revealing a secret. "A painting on her upper arm."

"They believe her a descendent of the painted people... the Picts?" Cree asked, shaking his head. "They have been long gone from this land."

"Some believe the last of the Picts went north and survived."

"Does the Lord of Fire wear a painting?"

"There has been no word of it."

"The Picts were a ruthless, barbaric people, my lord," Dylan said.

"How ruthless would you be to fight to keep this land, the home that we have built for ourselves?" Cree asked.

Dylan thought on it a moment, then slowly nodded. "I see what you mean. I would do whatever was needed to keep my land, my home."

"Tannin has given me fair warning and no doubt he continues to find out what he can. We will be well prepared for the Lord of Fire's arrival."

***

Cree watched his daughter snatch up her brother's wooden sword and swing it around as if fighting a foe. Valan did not take kindly to it and slipped off the bench to chase after her. Lizbeth, the true warrior she was, did not surrender it, though she did screech with laughter as her brother chased her.

"I think our daughter needs a sword of her own," Cree said, turning to his wife.

Dawn smiled and nodded.

"Help, Beast, help!" Lizbeth yelled and laughed.

The large animal barked and looked from Cree to the twins, not knowing what to do.

"Enough, Lizbeth," Cree called out, seeing Beast growing upset and understanding his quandary. Who did he protect when he usually protected them both?

Lizbeth stopped running and Valan grabbed his sword and gave her a shove, knocking her on her bottom.

"Valan!" Cree snapped and stood.

His son turned a scowl on him. "*My* sword."

Cree walked over to him, a scowl growing as he did and overshadowing his son's. "Help your sister up and do not shove her like that again. You are to protect her, not hurt her." He waited until Valan did as he was told, then he pointed to his daughter. "And you, Lizbeth, will not take your brother's sword without asking him." Cree raised his hand to silence his daughter before she could speak. "I will see that you get your own sword."

She smiled at that.

"And, Lizbeth, do not dare call for Beast to help you against your brother. He is here to protect both of you."

Lizbeth went to Beast and flung her arms around his neck. "Sorry, Beast. Love you."

Cree shook his head. "It is your brother you should be telling you are sorry."

"Why?" Lizbeth asked, turning wide, innocent eyes on her da.

Dawn stepped around Cree and stretched her hands out to her daughter and son. She crouched down and tapped each on the chest and locked two of her fingers together. Then with fingers from her other hand, she tried to separate the two but they would not budge. With the two she tapped the twins repeatedly on the chest, then joined their hands.

Valan tapped his chest. "Keep Lizbeth safe."

"Me too," Lizbeth said and gave her brother a hug.

Cree smiled, watching his son squeeze his eyes closed tight and grow rigid as his sister hugged him senseless. He was pleased and relieved that they understood their mum.

Dawn had gestured to them since they were tiny bairns and he did at times as well. He wanted to make certain they had no trouble communicating with their mum and it appeared they had no problem with it.

Sloan entered the Great Hall and Cree could tell from his scrunched brow that the news would not be to his liking.

Dawn saw it as well and signaled Nell and Ina to take the twins.

"A walk outside," Nell said and the twins hurried ahead of her to the door, Lizbeth stopping to talk with Sloan for a moment.

"That daughter of yours is far too observant for her years," Sloan said, a smile having replaced his frown.

"What did Lizbeth say to you?" Cree asked curious.

"She told me that da wears a mad face too."

Cree shook his head while Dawn smiled.

"So what is it that has you mad?" Cree asked and pointed to the bench for Sloan to sit. He took his wife's arm and assisted her to sit before he did.

Dawn was pleased that her husband included her in the matter, but then he had asked her advice occasionally, though she gave it to him whether he asked her or not.

"Not mad, concerned, though it is thanks to Tannin that we know what goes on. He sent two men to follow the Lord of Fire. One rode ahead after a while and arrived here to let us know that if the pace continued, the Lord of Fire would arrive sometime tomorrow morning… with fifty warriors. That is my concern. Why bring fifty warriors if you simply want to talk with you?"

"Show of strength," Cree said. "And since he feels it necessary, we shall do the same. Have the men don their battle weapons for his arrival."

Sloan grinned. "Now that is a show of strength."

"Pardon, but Lady Dawn is needed."

The three turned to see Flanna.

"Elsa requests your help. Ann has worsened."

Chapter Twenty

"You were there helping with Ann until late last night, you need more sleep," Cree said, wanting to reach out and stop his wife from leaving their bed before daybreak, yet knowing it would prove useless.

Dawn gestured after donning her shift, letting her husband know that Elsa would have been up all night with Ann and would need rest herself.

"There are others willing to help Elsa. Ina said she would sit with Ann while the twins sleep."

Dawn shook her head and gestured.

"She does not require healing knowledge to sit with Ann. She could fetch Elsa when necessary."

Dawn shook her head again and finished dressing

"I could order you back to bed," Cree said, a scowl surfacing.

Dawn's shoulders sagged and she walked over to sit on the bed beside her husband. He was sitting up, the blanket resting past his waist, and his naked chest reminding her how comfortable it had felt only moments ago when her head rested upon it.

She rubbed at the scowling crease between his eyes, then rested a finger to his lips, then to hers and shook her head slowly.

"I do not want to argue either, but my concern is for you. You spent nearly the entire day yesterday helping Elsa with Ann. And while I know you have mostly healed from your ordeal that does not mean you should work until exhausted."

Dawn patted her chest and nodded.

205

"You may think you will take care, but I know you well, wife. Sometimes, you push yourself beyond where you should go." He pressed a finger to her lips when she raised her hands to speak. "The Lord of Fire arrives today. I want you by my side when he does."

Dawn nodded and pressed her cheek to his.

Cree closed his eyes for a moment, his wife's cool cheek feeling good against his warm one and the scent of their recent tender lovemaking lingering on her. It always amazed him that his love for this woman continued to grow by the day and he slipped his arm around her, wanting to keep her close.

"I know I must let you do this," he whispered, "but promise me you will take care."

Dawn nodded as she moved her cheek away from his to settle her lips on his in a gentle kiss that sealed her promise.

Before she stood, she tapped his lips, then her chest and gestured as if riding a horse.

"Aye, I will let you know when our visitor approaches," Cree said.

Dawn gave him a quick kiss and hurried off the bed and out of the room. She loved lingering in bed with her husband, making love with him just before sunrise, and dozing in his arms afterwards. She hated leaving him now, but she was needed and she was grateful Cree understood that.

She hurried through the quiet keep. No one would be stirring for at least another hour. She thought of taking Beast with her, but he was intent on staying with the twins until they woke. And she felt no fright in walking through the village, Elsa's cottage being close to the keep.

It was early morning, though the light had yet to break and the sky did not look promising, dark clouds dotting an already dark sky. A rainy day most likely.

Dawn kept her shawl tight around her, cool air chilling her as she approached the cottage. She stopped abruptly, thinking she spied movement. A swirl of something dark? Similar to what she had seen that one time. Or were her eyes playing tricks on her?

She stared, trying to make sense of what she had seen or if she had seen anything at all. When all remained still, not a sound being heard, she shook her head and went to the cottage door, opening it slowly, not to wake Elsa in case she had fallen asleep in the chair beside Ann's bed.

Dawn froze for a moment, seeing Elsa collapsed on the floor. She rushed to her side and seeing blood pooling by her head, feared the worst. On closer look, Dawn saw she had suffered a huge bump to her head that had split open. She quickly got a cloth and wrapped it around Elsa's head to stop any further bleeding. She then hurried to Ann and her heart gripped with pain. The young woman was dead, her head hanging off the bed, the pillow on the ground. Her first thought was that someone had suffocated her.

Help. She had to get help.

Neil? Had Neil suffered a similar fate as Elsa? He was in the cottage nearly attached to this one. She rushed next door and entered without a knock. She was relieved to see Neil asleep in bed. It took quite a bit of shaking to wake him and when she finally did, he stared at her in shock.

"Lady Dawn, what is wrong?" A thought hit him and with an agonizing twist to his face, asked, "Elsa. Something has happened to Elsa?"

Dawn nodded, pointed next door, and waved her to join him as she ran out.

Neil hurried into his garments and joined Dawn, seeing her bent over Elsa.

"Oh my God, Elsa," Neil said as he hurried to squat down beside his wife.

Dawn hoped Neil understood what she gestured, telling him she would go for help. She was relieved when he told her to hurry and that was just what she did.

Her shawl fell off her one shoulder, trailing behind her as she rushed through the village and strands of her hair fell loose from her braid. She bumped into the edge of a bench when she entered the Great Hall as she made her way to the stairs.

She took the stairs as fast as she could and flung open the door to the bedchamber to find her husband almost dressed.

Cree's heart slammed against his chest as he hurried to his wife standing in the doorway, her hand gripping the edge of the door so tight it turned her knuckles white, and her face pale.

"What is it?" he asked. "Are you hurt? Did someone harm you?" He looked her over, searching for an answer.

Dawn shook her head and waved her hand, letting him know she was fine. She grabbed his hand and tugged.

"Is it Ann?" he asked.

Dawn held up two fingers.

It took a minute, then Cree said, "Elsa. Has something happened to Elsa?"

Dawn nodded and hit the top of her head with her hand a couple of times and ran her fingers down her face slowly.

"Someone has harmed her? She is bleeding?"

Dawn nodded again and tugged for him to hurry.

He slipped on his boots and they were out the door.

Flanna approached them once in the Great Hall.

"Elsa has been hurt and Ann is—" Cree looked to his wife.

Dawn shook her head, unshed tears shining in her eyes.

"Oh my lord, Ann is dead," Flanna said.

A bark had them turning, Beast, having heard the commotion, had come to see what was about.

Cree pointed to the steps. "Guard the twins now!"

Beast did not hesitate, he rushed back to the twins.

"Find out what servants have been up and about," he ordered Flanna, then he took his wife by the arm and they left the Great Hall.

Dawn was not surprised when he stopped first at Sloan's cottage.

Cree banged on the door. "Trouble, Sloan. Meet me at Elsa's cottage and bring Lucerne."

"Aye," Sloan yelled through the closed door as Cree and Dawn walked away.

Cree grew incensed when he saw his healer lying on the floor of her cottage, a bloody cloth around her head and blood in a small pool beneath it, and an upset Neil kneeling beside her.

"She just started groaning, but has not spoken," Neil said, looking ready to shed a tear.

"Let me get Elsa in your bed in the other cottage where Dawn and Lucerne can look after her."

Neil nodded and stood aside, and Cree leaned done and lifted his healer up in his arms.

Dawn hurried out to the other cottage and pulled the blankets down on the bed, then placed a couple of towels on the pillow, knowing Elsa would have done the same.

Cree placed Elsa down on the bed and she groaned.

"Oh my God, what happened?" Lucerne asked, entering the cottage in front of her husband.

"From what I can see, someone smashed Elsa in the head," Neil said.

"Was Ann harmed?" Lucerne asked.

"Ann is dead," Cree said.

Lucerne gasped, her hand going to cover her mouth and tears rushing to her eyes.

"Dawn needs help tending Elsa," Cree said and Lucerne nodded and joined Dawn at Elsa's bedside.

Cree placed a firm hand on Neil's shoulder. "Leave the women to tend Elsa and let us see if we can discover what happened."

Neil looked to his wife.

"We will take good care of her," Lucerne assured him.

"You will come get me when she wakes?" Neil asked.

Dawn nodded while Lucerne spoke. "I will fetch you right away."

Neil gave his wife's hand a squeeze. "I will not be far, my love."

Sloan and Neil followed Cree into the healing cottage. Cree went directly to Ann and bent down to have a look at the lifeless young woman. The way her head hung off the bed, the pillow on the floor. It was obvious she had been suffocated.

"This makes no sense," Sloan said. "It was common talk in the village that you had spoken to Ann and she did not know who had harmed her. So why kill her?"

"Unless she could say and was too frightened to do so," Neil said.

Sloan disagreed. "That is not likely since Ann knew as do all that Cree would have seen to the culprit immediately. The very reason she had not said a word about Lara meeting an unknown person in the woods. She knew Lara would face punishment."

Neil shook his head. "Then why kill Ann if she knew nothing?"

Cree stood. "And how did the culprit get in here without being seen by the sentinels?"

"That is impossi—" Sloan shook his head, not believing his own thought. "No one unknown could get past our sentinels. That would mean—"

"Someone known to us, known to Elsa, did this?" Neil asked, anger sparking on his face.

"While I would prefer not to believe it, it would be the most logical conclusion," Cree said.

***

Lucerne sat on the bed beside Elsa, gently cleansing the wound while speaking softly to her. "It is not a deep wound and I remember you once telling me that head wounds can fool you. That a minor head wound can bleed a lot."

Dawn could not help but envy Lucerne, sitting there comforting Elsa as she worked. Without a voice, she could never console like that, and when trying to fight your way out of heavy darkness, a voice could be the light that led you out of it. Lila's constant talking had done that for her.

"After I cleanse the wound, Dawn will help me bandage it and hopefully by then you will wake," Lucerne said.

"Ann," Elsa mumbled.

Lucerne looked to Dawn.

Dawn almost shook her head at Lucerne, warning her not to tell her that Ann was dead, but Elsa would not want it that way.

Dawn nodded and Lucerne agreed with her own nod.

"I am sorry to tell you that Ann is dead."

Elsa's eyes fluttered open as she fought to break out of the fog. "No. No. She was doing well."

When Lucerne looked to Dawn again, Dawn covered her nose and mouth with her hand and widened her eyes as if fighting to breathe.

Lucerne shook her head, her eyes filling with sadness. "Someone smothered her, Elsa."

Elsa's eyes opened wide. "Oh, good Lord, poor Ann. Who would do that to her and why?"

"Lord Cree will find out and see the person punished, but right now, I am relieved that you have woken," Lucerne said.

Dawn stepped closer, smiled, and nodded, letting Elsa know she felt the same.

"Let me get, Neil," Lucerne said. "I promised him I would fetch him as soon as you woke."

"First tell me about the wound and bandage it, since I would like a little time for this fog to leave my head."

Lucerne detailed it for her and answered her questions while she finished cleaning it.

"Your mind is far from foggy," Lucerne said as Dawn helped her wrap the wound. "Does your head pain you?"

"It does, but that is to be expected," Elsa said with a wince.

"You will rest and sleep—"

Dawn interrupted, shaking her hands and head.

"Dawn is right. Sleep will not help right now. I have seen too many sleep after a head wound never to wake from it. I will take things easy, rest a bit, but not sleep. Late tonight will be time enough for me to sleep. You can get Neil now. I have left him worrying long enough."

Lucerne stood and Elsa patted the spot for Dawn to sit as Lucerne left the cottage.

Elsa took Dawn's hand, squeezing it. "I thought it was you who came to help me, since not a word was spoken as the door creaked open. I was about to turn and send you back to bed when I felt a pain and all went black until waking up here. I don't understand it. Why did someone want Ann dead?"

Dawn shook her head and shrugged, telling Elsa she was just as puzzled over it.

"Elsa!" Neil called out in relief as he hurried into the cottage.

Dawn quickly got out of his way as he rushed to his wife to sit at her side.

"I am fine, do not fuss," Elsa ordered gently, though relief at seeing her husband was apparent in her eyes.

212

"I will fuss all I want," Neil said and kissed her cheek.

Dawn went to Cree as soon as he entered the cottage and his arm went around her waist. Sloan did the same with Lucerne after he entered the cottage.

Cree waited a few moments, then said, "I am glad you woke and look well. I will not tell you to rest since you are the healer and know better than anyone what you must do to heal. But do tell me what happened."

"There is not much to tell, my lord," Elsa said. "Ann's fever had gone down and I was hopeful the worst of it was over. I dozed while she slept. It was mostly a quiet night. I felt safe with the sound of the sentinels passing by the cottage several times, the peaceful hoot of an owl and the crackle of the fire. All was well. When the door opened, the only sound a creaking noise, I assumed it was Dawn, returning to help. I was about to turn and send her home when I felt a blow to my head and all went dark."

"So you saw nothing," Cree said.

"Nothing, my lord, though I wish I had. Something. Anything that would have helped."

"I am glad you did not see anything," Neil said, relief obvious in his voice. "If you had, the crazy person would not have allowed you to live."

A tear caught in the corner of Elsa's eye and Neil wiped it away with his thumb and rested his brow to hers.

"I will stay in the healing cottage and look after whoever seeks your help today," Lucerne said.

"I can rest in there as well as here," Elsa said and rested her hand to her husband's mouth before he could protest. "I am a healer and I will heed the advice I would give to others if they had received such a blow to the head."

"If you recall anything else, Elsa, let me know," Cree said, then looked to Neil. "Keep her here until I send word that all is taken care of in the healing cottage."

Neil nodded and Elsa remained silent, understanding that Ann's body had yet to be moved.

Cree stepped outside with his wife and Sloan and Lucerne just as Ann's wrapped body was being carried out of the cottage by two warriors.

Dawn gestured to Cree that she would help Lucerne clean the healing cottage.

Cree reluctantly agreed. She had been through enough and the sun had just risen. "Once you finish, return to the keep and prepare for the Lord of Fire's arrival."

He eased her closer to him and while it was on his tongue to tell her she had been through enough for so early in the day and she should rest, he held his tongue. He had made her a promise and he would keep it.

He smiled when he saw her brow narrow and he knew her thought, which would have been correct if he had allowed his thought to reach his tongue.

"I love you, wife," he whispered and kissed her cheek and he got what he wanted from her… a smile.

She tapped his brow, then his lips and shook her head, continuing to smile.

"Are you saying that was not what I was thinking?" he asked with a soft chuckle.

She nodded.

He kissed her cheek, then nipped playfully along her ear before whispering, "You know me too well, wife."

Dawn was well aware of what her husband was doing. He was trying to chase her sorrow away and she was grateful to him for it. It had been a difficult morning and she did not want to bring her sorrow to the twins when she saw them. There would be enough of it once word spread of Ann's death and Elsa's close brush with it. And with the Lord of Fire's arrival that would not be good.

She nodded and tapped his brow again, then hers.

214

"Aye, I know you just as well." He let her slip from his arms after she kissed his lips lightly and watched her and Lucerne enter the cottage, then he turned to Sloan. "Do you know what is wrong with what Elsa told us?"

Sloan nodded. "Aye, our sentinels are silent in their rounds of the village. She would have never heard one, which means someone else was prowling about outside the cottage."

Chapter Twenty-one

Dawn headed back to the keep, Lucerne having chased her off after they both helped Elsa get settled in the bed they had dressed with fresh bedding, in the healing cottage. People started arriving just as she was taking her leave, not looking for the healer to tend them but to pay respects to her and see for themselves that she was well. All were worried for their healer. Seeing Elsa sitting up in bed and giving advice to those she knew needed it, did well to alleviate their fear of losing her.

With thoughts heavy on Dawn's mind, she went to visit Old Mary.

As usual Old Mary opened the cottage door before Dawn reached it. "I am glad to see you."

Her words made Dawn realize she had not spent enough time with the old woman who meant so much to her.

"You have much on your mind. You do not need to worry about seeing how I fare," Old Mary said, as if hearing her thoughts.

Dawn smiled and shook her head, making it clear she did not agree. By the time she got done gesturing, Old Mary was in tears.

"I am pleased to know I am like a mum to you, for to me you are the daughter I never had, though it seems I have one after all."

Dawn gave her a hug and gestured again.

"Aye, I am now a true grandmum and pleased I am to be, though I think Lizbeth will be a handful, far wiser than I first believed, just like her mum."

Dawn beamed with pride.

216

"What worries you, Dawn?"

Dawn was startled by Old Mary's direct and unexpected question and giving it thought, she wondered what did worry her. There were many things she could choose from, but what one troubled her the most? She could not say.

"There is something unsettled in you and soon you will have a chance to see it settled," Old Mary predicted. "I wish I could be more clear, but for some reason Fate will not let me see all of it."

Dawn gestured and Old Mary nodded and smiled.

"You are right. Fate serves us many challenges, what we do, how we approach them, how we handle them, is inevitably ours and ours alone, and in the end the choice lies with us as to how we will deal with them. It is obvious where Lizbeth gets her wisdom."

Laughter shook Dawn's chest as she gestured.

Old Mary laughed along with her. "You are right again. Wisdom comes to us in ways we do not expect and often do not want." Her laughter faded along with her smile. She reached across the table and rested her hand over Dawn's. "Fate has not been easy on you, but you not only survived Fate's barrage you have thrived and I am so very proud of you."

Tears tickled Dawn's eyes and she squeezed Old Mary's hand, then gestured.

"It is I who am lucky to have you," Old Mary said.

Dawn continued talking with Old Mary, sharing memories of her mum. Lizbeth was named after her and while the woman had not given birth to Dawn, she might as well have, for she had been Dawn's mum in every sense. And Dawn missed her to this day.

"Your husband searches for you," Old Mary said and chuckled.

"Dawn!"

She jumped at the roar in her husband's voice as he called out for her. She stood to hurry to the door, but it burst open before she reached it.

"You were to go to the keep. I looked for you and you were not there."

He sounded as if he accused her of purposely disobeying him, but she was used to that since she usually did ignore his orders. But this time was different. It had been different since her abduction and return home. Having been ripped away from her family, from Cree, had been more heartbreaking than she had ever imagined and she never wanted to experience it again. And she understood that Cree felt the same.

She felt bad that she had been the cause of his fright when he could not find her, even more so now with Ann's death and Elsa's attack.

She was quick to apologize to him.

He was just as quick to take her in his arms and hug her tight. "Not one sentinel could tell me that they saw you after I discovered you were not at the keep. It will not go unpunished."

His words gave her pause.

"Dawn has duties to see to," Cree said to Old Mary in a way of them taking their leave.

Old Mary nodded. "Aye, much goes on today and you thrive once again, Dawn."

A slight shiver overtook Dawn. If Old Mary predicted she would thrive today, then that meant she would need to survive something to do so? What more had Fate in store for her?

Cree kept hold of Dawn's hand as they walked toward the keep.

Dawn signaled with one hand, once again that she was sorry.

"I know it was not intentional," Cree said, squeezing her hand as if reassuring himself she was there beside him.

Dawn did her best to speak with one hand. She pointed back toward Old Mary's cottage and shook her head, then pointed to the keep.

"I understand that you did not intend to go there that it was a moment's decision and I imagine you did not intend to stay long."

Dawn nodded, having planned to let him know that time had gotten away from her.

"It will take time for fear not to grip and squeeze relentlessly at me when I cannot find you."

Dawn grabbed his hand that held hers and brought it to her chest.

"You feel the same," he said, releasing a pent up breath of relief. "I wonder if that fear will ever leave either of us, though I think what happened to Ann and Elsa worsened it."

Dawn stopped, recalling his words in Old Mary's cottage that had given her pause. She slipped her hand out of his and gestured.

"Are you asking me why no sentinel saw you?" Cree asked.

Dawn nodded.

"It is a question I intend to find out and punish whoever failed their duty."

Dawn gestured and Cree followed along with questions.

"You are telling me there were no sentinels around when you went to Elsa's cottage this morning?"

She pointed to her eyes and shook her head.

"You didn't see any?"

She nodded, letting him know that was what she meant, then she gestured again.

"You saw something in the shadows?" he asked.

She nodded and continued, detailing what she had seen, then held up two fingers.

"You saw what you think may have been a swirl of the hem of a cloak twice now in the darkness?"

She nodded.

"The bearded man told me he saw the same in the early morning hours Ann was attacked. He also told me that the hem of the cloak was well-worn."

Dawn gestured again.

"I thought the same. The clan all were given new cloaks two years now, but that itself cannot rule out anyone in the clan since many kept some of their worn garments. What does give me reason to believe it could be someone in the clan is that this person seems to move unnoticed throughout the village and only a clan member can do that. Those who arrive here seeking a day or two of shelter would not know that the sentries' routine changes each day. And when Elsa told me she heard the sentinel moving about—"

Dawn grabbed his arm and shook her head.

"Aye, the sentinels do not make a sound on their rounds."

Dawn stepped closer to her husband and cast a suspicious eye around her.

"I am wondering the same. The person who killed Lara and Ann could very well be a member of the clan."

***

"Flowers, Da," Lizbeth cried out when Cree and Dawn entered the Great Hall. She scurried off the bench before either Nell or Ina could stop her and ran to her da.

Cree scooped her up and as was his way, and she planted a kiss on his cheek as her little arms went around his neck to squeeze tight.

Cree hated to disappoint her and was glad for the gray skies and promise of rain, rather than telling her he was far too busy to take her flower picking today.

220

"It is going to rain, another day," Cree said and got a frown form his daughter.

Ina approached. "I could take her to the edge of the woods, my lord, where a few wildflowers grow."

Lizbeth nodded. "Ina take me."

Cree saw his son, sword in hand, and Beast by his side approach.

Valan stuck out his little chest and raised his sword. "Me and Beast go."

"You will protect your sister?" Cree asked proud of his son, so young, yet so brave.

"Aye, da," Valan said with a firm nod.

Cree signaled one of his warriors sitting at a table. "Gather two more warriors and escort Ina, my daughter and son to the edge of the woods so she can pick flowers." He turned a stern look on Ina. "None of you are to go into the woods."

"Aye, my lord," Ina said with a bob of her head.

Cree lowered his daughter to the floor and crouched down beside her and his son. "Do not go into the woods. Stay at the edge or you will not pick flowers again." He turned to Lizbeth when he said that and she nodded and kissed his cheek again.

Dawn bent down to the twins and reaffirmed what their da had commanded, the pair responding in words and gestures. She kissed them both and stood.

"Flowers for mum," Lizbeth said and Dawn smiled and nodded, letting her daughter know she would like that.

Cree looked to Beast. "Guard the twins well."

Ina took Lizbeth's hand. "You will stay close, Lizbeth."

And before the warrior could follow behind Ina and the twins, Cree stopped him.

"Keep close watch on my daughter, Reed, and do not let her sweet talk you," Cree ordered.

"Aye, my lord," Reed said and hurried off.

Cree turned to his wife. "I have matters I must see to. Eat, I can hear your stomach grumbling, then be ready for when our visitor arrives."

Dawn smiled, nodded, and patted her stomach.

Cree pressed his cheek to hers and whispered. "You see to satisfying one hunger and I will satisfy another hunger of yours later tonight."

Cree scrunched his brow when he stepped back and saw she wore a frown.

She pressed two tips of her fingers together from either hand, then drew them a distant apart.

Cree chuckled. "Far too long for you to wait?"

Dawn smiled and nodded.

"I will see what I can do about that," Cree said and gave her a quick kiss and left the Great Hall.

Dawn's smile faded as she watched him walk away and she did not seek a bench at one of the tables until the door closed behind him. It was not a time to be thinking of making love with all that had happened so early this day. But she was glad he had made mention of it. It made the day seem like any other day, chasing some of the sorrow away, but not the worry that the culprit might very well be among them.

No doubt, he was on his way to talk to the sentries on duty last night until early this morning and see what he could piece together. And what about that worn cloak?

Most of the garments the clan had possessed before Cree had claimed title to the Clan Carrick had been so threadbare and patched that they had been beyond salvageable. Some had even burned garments that might have seen another year or two, wanting to be rid once and for all of the harsh memories associated with them.

Dawn ate while she thought it all through, relieved at least a few things had been discovered. though growing ever more concerned that if it did turn out that someone from the clan had killed Lara and Ann, then it was possible that a clan member had part in planning her abduction.

Lila entered the Great Hall just as Dawn finished her meal and she looked concerned.

Dawn was quick to gesture, asking what was wrong?

"Dorrie is in labor and Lucerne is having a difficult time keeping Elsa from going to her and with Elwin insisting Elsa needs to tend his wife, Lucerne does not know what to do. She asked me to fetch you to see if there was some way you can help."

Dawn nodded and stood, her hands moving, asking where Thomas was.

"Bless Ina, she took him along with the twins. They are all busy at the edge of the woods picking flowers, though Valan is standing guard with his sword, looking much like his da."

Relieved to hear all was going well with the twins, Dawn went with Lila.

The crowd that had gathered earlier had dissipated, word having spread that Elsa was well and resting.

Elwin had other thoughts. "Dorrie needs Elsa. You have not given birth, Lucerne, and you do not know anything about birthing a bairn."

Elwin was a large man, his features plain. He had once guarded Dorrie only to fall in love with her. And to everyone's surprise Dorrie, an attractive lass with lovely features and beautiful blonde hair, but not a nice nature, had fallen in love in return. Her unkind nature, especially toward Dawn, had changed through a series of events and due to Dawn's thoughtfulness and ability to forgive.

Dorrie was now a true friend and Dawn wanted to help her.

Lucerne was relieved to see Dawn enter the cottage. "Elsa should not get out of bed. She tried once and got dizzy."

223

"I am fine. It does not help lying abed all day," Elsa argued.

"Like it or not that is where you will stay," Neil ordered after entering the cottage.

"Dorrie needs her," Elwin argued.

"There are more than enough women capable of helping Dorrie give birth," Neil said and nodded toward Dawn. "Dawn one of them."

Dawn nodded and patted her chest.

"She agrees," Neil said.

"I can gather some women who would help," Lila offered.

Elwin shook his head. "Elsa is a healer. She knows best."

"My wife is not going with you, Elwin. Either Dawn tends Dorrie or you deliver the bairn yourself," Neil said in a stern voice that left no room for argument.

Elwin looked to Dawn. "You can do this?"

Dawn nodded.

"She can," Elsa confirmed. "She has helped me with quite a few births."

Elwin capitulated with a nod.

Lucerne joined in in helping Dawn gather what she needed and she was soon out the door.

"I will fetch some other women capable of helping you. Then I am going to get Thomas. I will see the twins returned to the keep as well, and shall I see that Cree is told of your whereabouts? Lila asked.

Dawn could have hugged her friend for reminding her that Cree should be informed of her whereabouts. She nodded and patted her chest in appreciation, then hurried to keep pace with Elwin.

***

Cree was not too pleased when he had learned that his wife was delivering Dorrie's bairn. Any other day and it would not have mattered, but with the Lord of Fire minutes away from arriving, he would have preferred his wife to be standing by his side.

He had made a point of having Dawn present when any titled man arrived at their home. He wanted it clear from the beginning that he did not hide his wife away because she could not speak and that he had pride and respect for the woman he loved.

It had been several hours since he had gotten word of what his wife was doing. He had hoped the bairn would deliver fast, and Dawn would have time to join him, but the bairn had yet to be born.

Cree stood on the top step of the keep alone as the Lord of Fire approached. He entered the village with six of his warriors, the remainder of his troop waiting on the outskirts of the village. He kept a steady eye on the Lord of Fire as he drew closer.

From the way he sat his horse, Cree could tell he was a man of sizeable height. He dark hair was short, cut high on his neck and around his ears. And he was a man of fine features, the women giving proof to that since they could not seem to take their eyes off him. The men on the other hand eyed him with suspicion.

He had a lean, defined build, and wore the MacFiere plaid over a white shirt that fit a bit snug. And for some reason Cree got the impression that the garments did not suit the man. That he was not comfortable in them and he wondered what type of garments would suit him.

He kept his eyes on him. He would reach the bottom of the keep steps in a few minutes, so he was more than pleased when he caught sight of his wife rushing through the village toward the steps. She was trying to reach the steps before the

Lord of Fire so that she would be by his side as he had asked of her.

Her hands were freeing her hair of its braid, her fingers combing through the strands so that her dark red hair fell around her shoulders. He loved when she let her hair loose. It was soft and silky and fell over her shoulders and down along her chest in waves after having worn a braid for a while. Her cheeks were flushed red, giving her some color and though her garments were a bit disheveled, she never looked more beautiful to him.

Cree stretched his hand out to her as she rushed up the keep steps and she took it, locking her hand tight with his.

He smiled at her. "Dorrie and her bairn is well?"

Dawn gestured.

Cree smiled. "A tiny daughter Elwin fears he will break if he dares touches her." He chuckled at the thought of the big warrior fearful of picking up his daughter. "He will grow used to her."

His wife gestured placing the bairn in Elwin's big arms and her eyes going wide, demonstrating Elwin's reaction.

"Cree," Sloan called out.

The chuckle that was about to leave Cree's lips at Elwin's startled reaction disappeared. Sloan was letting him know the Lord of Fire was almost upon them. He turned as the man came to a stop at the bottom of the keep steps.

Suddenly, Beast burst out of nowhere and rushed up the steps to take a warning stance in front of Dawn, baring his teeth in a threatening growl.

Cree looked to see all color drain from his wife's face and he turned to look at the Lord of Fire. He was grinning.

"It is good to see you again, Dawn," the Lord of Fire said with a wicked grin. "I have missed you and *my* dog."

Chapter Twenty-two

"I gave you no permission to speak to my wife," Cree said and without taking his eyes off the Lord of Fire pointed to the snarling dog. "Quiet, Beast."

The animal obeyed and remained where he was in front of Dawn, his eyes fixed on the Lord of Fire.

"I meant no disrespect," the Lord of Fire said though his tone held no apology. "And my dog's name is Demon."

"Not any longer," Cree said, suspicious of the way the man's eyes narrowed, the firm tenor of his tone, and that he did not actually apologize.

"There is much for you and I to discuss, including who Demon belongs to," the Lord of Fire said.

"And why you did not return my wife to me immediately," Cree challenged.

"As I said, there is much for us to discuss."

"Sloan," Cree said, nodding his head to where he stood at the bottom of the steps, "will show you to my solar. I will join you there shortly. Your men will be given food and drink while they wait for you in the Great Hall."

The Lord of Fire nodded and Cree could see anger stirring in his bold blue eyes.

Cree turned, took his wife's hand, and signaled for Beast to follow them. Once in the Great Hall, he called out to the warriors who had been positioned there. "Keep a keen watch." And to Flanna, he said, "Keep them well fed and with drink."

Cree ushered Dawn up the stairs to their bedchamber, Beast following on their heels.

"That is Tarass, the man who rescued you from the stream?" Cree asked, after closing the door.

Beast once again took up a protective stance by Dawn while keeping his eyes on Cree.

Dawn nodded.

"He is the naked man whose arms you woke up in?"

Dawn nodded again, relieved her husband did not question her as if he was accusing her of something, but as if he simply wanted to confirm what she had already told him.

"He did not harm you in anyway?"

Dawn shook her head.

"But he would not return you home when you asked?"

Dawn nodded, pointed to her husband, then to herself and shook her head.

"I remember you telling me that you told no one you were my wife, not knowing if they were friend or foe of mine."

Dawn nodded.

Cree stepped closer to his wife. "Is there anything you have not told me that I should know before I speak with this man?"

Cree was pleased when she did not hesitate to shake her head, but it gave him pause when she held up one finger.

"You have something to say about him?" he asked.

She nodded and tapped her lips rapidly.

"He is quick with his words?"

She nodded, then tapped her eye and her ear, and spread her arms.

"And sees and hears much. He is observant."

She nodded, glad he understood her.

"Did he find it difficult to communicate with you?"

Dawn pretended to draw.

"You communicated through your drawing."

Dawn nodded.

"Did he ever show any anger toward you?" Cree asked.

Dawn held up one finger, then ran in place, turning her head over her shoulder as if looking to see if someone chased after her.

"When you left on your own and he came after you, he got angry with you?"

She nodded again, narrowed her eyes and shook her finger.

"He yelled at you?" Cree asked, his own temper firing.

Dawn held her hand up, seeing the anger flare in his eyes and worried he misunderstood. She patted her chest, then acted as if she was fighting off someone and narrowed her eyes and shook her finger again.

"He was angry because you could have been harmed going off on your own?"

Dawn nodded.

"Well, he is right about that," Cree said and was surprised when his wife agreed with a nod.

Dawn patted her chest, then stepped closer to her husband, and rested her hand to his chest.

"You wanted to come home to me."

Dawn nodded, tears glistening in her eyes as she spread her arms.

"Very much wanted to come home to me," Cree said and took his wife in his arms. "And I very much wanted you to, but I hate thinking of what you went through to return home or what could have happened to you."

She patted her chest and shook her head, reminding him that nothing happened.

"Things did happen to you and if it were not for Beast, you would not have made it home."

Beast looked up at Dawn and she smiled down at him and patted his head, understanding now what had agitated him recently. He had sensed Tarass was close. Her smile quickly faded when she looked to her husband. She shook her head frantically, pointing to Beast.

"Do not worry. I will not let him take Beast from us."

Dawn hugged her husband, laying her head on his chest as she did. The strength of him always comforted her and she needed that now more than ever. But she was also concerned over what would happen between him and the Lord of Fire.

"All will go well, wife, do not worry," Cree said, keeping his arms tight around her, aware she sought solace in his arms from the uneasiness he felt in her tense body.

Dawn stepped back, patted her chest, pointed to him, then the door.

"You want to be there when I speak with him?"

Dawn nodded.

"I understand you wanting to be there, wife, but this is something between him and me."

Dawn stepped away from her husband, shaking her head and patting her chest.

"Aye, it is about you," Cree said, "but it is between Tarass and me to settle it."

Dawn shook her head again, refusing to accept that, patting her chest harder.

"I understand—"

Dawn waved her hand furiously at him, cutting off his words. Then shook her finger, letting him know he did not understand.

"You need to obey me on this, Dawn," Cree said. "I do understand why you want to be there, but it is best that I speak with him alone. I do not do this to upset you, but to protect you."

The glare that Dawn turned on Cree surprised him and what she did next caught him off guard.

Dawn rushed around her husband and out the door.

"Dawn!" Cree yelled as he chased after her, knowing where she was headed.

He could not believe how fast she took the steps down, though it did make him realize she had healed well.

Beast burst past Cree when he reached the bottom step, almost knocking Cree off his feet.

Cree stopped himself from falling and those few lost minutes delayed him from reaching his wife before she got to his solar. He was not surprised when he saw her standing outside his solar door and even less surprised when she opened it just before he reached her side and stepped in.

It appeared as if Cree allowed her to enter first while Beast had squeezed himself in along with Dawn and remained close by her side.

"Demon certainly has attached himself to you," the Lord of Fire said with a hint of a smile.

Cree did not fail to catch that he called the dog by the name he had given him, marking the animal his property. Or that his slight smile vanished quickly when Beast growled.

"With your wife present, I assume you wish to discuss the time she spent *with me*, Lord Cree? Then we can discuss what has brought me here."

Cree did not care for the way he made it sound as though Dawn's time spent with him had somehow been intimate.

Cree nodded. "Aye, since I am trying to decide whether to express gratitude or seek revenge, against you, Tarass."

That Cree did not address him with respect, as he had done with Cree, was not lost on Tarass. His jaw tightened and his right hand fisted at his side.

Cree was pleased to see it unnerved the man and to discover he was right handed. He had learned long ago to learn all he could about anyone who might prove a foe.

"I am sure your wife told you, *Cree*, that she was treated well."

Cree expected Tarass to address him as such after not addressing him properly and it did not disturb him in the least. He also was not surprised when his wife stepped forward and nodded, confirming what Tarass had said.

"You should not have gone off on your own, Dawn. I would have seen you home safely, though it is good to see you made it home unharmed," Tarass said, then looked to Cree. "Your wife is far from obedient.

"Dawn obeys only me," Cree said and tried not to choke on his words since Dawn barely obeyed him. Though, he was pleased she did not argue the point in front of Tarass.

"Is there anything in particular you wanted to know about her time spent with me?" Tarass asked.

Cree once again did not like the way Tarass made it sound as if she had been with him and him alone.

"Dawn told me that your people treated her well," Cree said, making it clear that Tarass had not been alone with her.

"They did when they finally reached me."

Cree saw his wife's body tense and so did Tarass.

"I can see you did not realize it was almost a full day before my people arrived at the campsite," Tarass said. "I had gone on ahead and settled in a spot waiting for them to meet me when I saw you draped over a large branch in the stream. "You were unresponsive and your lips blue. I did not think you would survive. I believe the heat I provided you with spared your life.

Cree fought the anger rumbling in him. While Tarass had saved his wife's life he had left one thinking as to how he had provided the heat that had spared Dawn. Had he done it on purpose? Did he want Cree to think he had been intimate with his wife?

Dawn shook her head and looked to her husband, tapping her lip, pointing to him, then to Tarass.

Cree understood what she wanted him to say. "Dawn was told by your women that they tended her after you found her."

232

Tarass turned to Dawn. "They did once they arrived at camp, though I can understand you thinking otherwise. You woke periodically, though not fully, and your affliction made it difficult to understand you."

That did not satisfy Dawn. She was blunt, tugging at her garments and shaking her finger back and forth at him.

Cree did not have to interpret her gestures. It was obvious she disagreed with him about the removal of her garments.

"Your wet garments had to go and quickly if you had any chance to survive. I built a strong fire first, stripped you, and wrapped you in a blanket. I stripped myself as well, my garments soaked. I wrapped myself around you when you remained unresponsive, doing all I could to heat you and keep you alive."

Cree saw how upset his wife was at Tarass's explanation and Beast's low whine confirmed it, feeling it himself, as did he. Tarass provided some details of what had happened, but he left more unsaid and Cree wondered if it was on purpose. Did Tarass feel somehow that it would give him an edge over Cree? If so, he had thought foolishly. Cree would leave it be for now, though he much preferred to beat the man senseless, which had been why he had not wanted his wife present when he spoke with Tarass. There were just some things that needed to be handled between men and men alone.

Tarass looked to Cree. "Dawn told me that two men took her from her family. Have you found the ones responsible for her abduction?"

"Not yet, but I will" Cree said concerned for how still his wife had become.

"If I can be of any help," Tarass offered.

Dawn turned to Cree and gestured and, without looking at Tarass, she left the room, Beast following close beside her.

She went straight to their bedchamber and sat in the chair by the hearth, needing to chase the chill that had taken hold of her. Beast licked her hand, then sat down to lean against her leg. She rested her hand on his head, petting it slowly.

She felt at a loss. She had hoped she had been told the truth. That there had been others there when he had pulled her out of the stream. It did not matter to her if he had seen her naked. Other men had seen her naked the time she had bravely gone into the dungeon where Cree had been taken prisoner to help him escape. Old Mary had saved her from the prison guards having their way with her, and that was what mattered to her.

She had never been with any man before Cree. Colum, the liege lord at the time, had forbid any of the men to couple with her. He had worried she would produce more dumb ones like herself.

Dawn had possessed scarcely anything in her life, anything she could truly call her own, so when Cree and she had finally made love, it pleased her to give him something that was hers and hers alone to give, something she had never given to another. It was her gift to him and she did not want to be robbed of that gift.

But now, with Tarass telling her what had happened, how would she ever know for sure if that special gift had been taken from her?

***

Cree was at odds with himself. Tarass had saved Dawn's life but he had also left a question hanging in the air. He might have made it seem he was the hero, rescuing and keeping Dawn from death, but was there more to it than Tarass had said?

"I am here to discuss the Clan MacLoon pledging its fealty to you," Tarass said. "I will see it settled and be on my way in the morning."

That was fine with Cree, but he planned on getting an answer, for the taunting question he had purposely left hanging between them, from the man before he left.

Cree approached him. Though, Tarass might be lean, they were almost equal in height and there was a solidness to the man that warned he was no less powerful. He would make a worthy opponent.

Cree remained standing and as did Tarass. Sloan remained off to the side, if Cree should need him.

"Have your say," Cree ordered.

"While I am grateful to you for protecting the Clan MacLoon in my family's absence, I have now returned and their fealty is owed to me," Tarass said as if Cree had no recourse.

"I have spent time and coin on seeing them kept safe while your clan land and responsibilities remained unattended. What is my compensation for that?"

"I can offer my friendship and warriors if ever you are in need," Tarass said.

"You will pledge your allegiance to me?"

"I pledge my allegiance to no man or clan," Tarass said with a strength in his voice that made it clear he would lead, never follow.

"Then how do I trust you?"

"My honor is my word. I would not betray my honor," Tarass said.

Men may claim their word was their honor but Cree had seen too often the opposite. So it remained to be seen if Tarass was as honorable in word and action as he claimed to be.

"So you say," Cree said, letting the man know that he was yet to believe him. "What of the Macardle situation and the piece of land they claim belongs to them?"

"They are mistaken about that. It does not belong to them."

"From what I hear it has caused quite a problem," Cree said.

"Nothing I cannot settle with little difficulty," Tarass said confidently.

Cree thought of a solution, though he did not think Tarass would take to it, but it could work to calm the unrest in that area. "The Clan Macardle has three daughters of marriageable age. You should wed one and unite the clans. It will strengthen your rule in that area."

"I know of the three daughters, Willow lacks strength, bending far too easily to others, Sorrell," —he rolled his eyes— "does not hold her tongue enough, and Snow, unfortunately was blinded in some accident at the keep."

"Snow may not suit you, but one of the other two could prove a good wife and secure peace for all concerned."

"When I wed it will be to my benefit. Marriage to a Macardle daughter provides little benefit to me and I do not need to wed one of them to secure peace there. Of course, I would not mind having a wife with Dawn's mettle, venturing off on her own to return to you took great courage, though I could do without her disobedience."

That he praised Dawn in one breath and faulted him in another for not controlling his wife was not lost to Cree.

"Dawn belongs to me and always will," Cree said. "So I have your word—your honor—that you offer me your friendship and warriors if ever needed."

"Aye, you have my word on it and again my gratitude for looking after the Clan MacLoon in my family's absence," Tarass said.

"There is one more thing I will have from you before this agreement is sealed," Cree said.

Tarass smiled. "You want Demon."

Donna Fletcher

Chapter Twenty-three

After ordering Sloan to keep a close watch on Tarass and his men, Cree went to find his wife. Not that he had to look far, he knew she would seek solitude in their bedchamber.

She turned and looked at him when he entered the room

He was glad there were no tears in her eyes, though it troubled him to see the sadness there.

"Beast, come here," he ordered.

The large dog turned sorrowful eyes on Dawn, rubbed his face against her hand as if bidding her farewell and reluctantly left her side, taking slow steps to Cree.

Beast stopped in front of him to await his fate. Cree crouched down and took the animal's face in his hand. "*We, me, Dawn, the twins, Lizbeth and Valan* are your family now. You will remain with us. You are Beast and will remain Beast. Now guard the twins."

Beast's eyes widened and his tongue shot out and caught Cree's cheek in a wet, sloppy kiss before he could avoid it, then with a spry gait left the room.

Cree shut the door and turned to Dawn. "Come here to me, wife."

Dawn rose and went to her husband, his arm reaching out to snatch her around the waist when she got close. She settled against him, the warmth of his hard body and the strength of his powerful arms engulfing her with love as they always did when he embraced her.

Cree pressed his cheek to hers. "I care about one thing and one thing alone. That you returned home to me. I thought I knew heartache, but I was wrong. I did not know

238

the tormenting hell of heartache until I believed I had lost you. I cursed the Heavens for taking you away from me, then I begged them to give you back to me. And here you are and nothing—absolutely nothing—matters except you being here safe in my arms."

Tears filled her eyes, she could not keep them away, his loving words tugging at her heart.

"You belong to me. You are mine always," he said with a roughness that challenged anyone to deny it. "You are the gift in my life I will always be grateful for and will cherish forever."

Those words melted her worries and seeped deep into her heart.

She was the gift and no one could take that from them.

Cree kissed her, not softly, but with a firmness that felt as if his lips had sealed something for all eternity between them, a bond of sorts that could never be broken.

The sense of such a deep rooted love between them fired Dawn's passion for her husband like a spark set to dry kindling, blazing hot in seconds. And she felt it do the same in him, his manhood sprouting hard against her.

This was not the time for them to make love. Her husband had important matters to tend to. It was enough that he had known she was upset and had taken the time to come to her to chase away her worries, though it would take much strength to let him go when her need for him so overwhelmed her.

She lingered with her cheek resting against his after their kiss ended, trying to calm her thudding heart and ease the ache that had grown her wet. She told herself to hurry and step away, be done with it, release him to his duties.

Her body thought differently, begging her to press closer, tease him into making love to her, for she knew if she did, he would not deny her. But it would be a fast joining, since duty presently took priority, and she did not want a fast joining. She wanted to linger and enjoy each other.

Before she could surrender to her own maddening passion, she went to take a step back away from him.

"Oh, no, wife," Cree said with a soft chuckle, tucking her back close against him. "You will not turn me rock hard and walk away from me."

Dawn smiled and did her best to explain she needed more than a quick one.

Cree nibbled at her ear. "I agree. A quick poke will not suffice."

She scrunched her shoulders against the tormenting tingle that raced through her from his nibbles that he continued delivering down along her neck.

"I want you naked," he whispered.

Dawn tapped his chest.

"Aye, me to."

They both got busy getting each other out of their garments and when done, Cree lifted Dawn in his arms with a playful bounce and carried her over to the bed and laid her down. He placed his knee on the edge of the bed and looked her over.

"I do not tell you often enough how beautiful you are," he said.

She smiled softly and stretched her arms out to her husband.

Cree leaned down slowly over her. "I am going to kiss every inch of you."

Dawn shivered at the thought and, shaking her head slowly. did her best to let him know she would never last that long.

Cree chuckled. "I intend to have you climax more than once, wife."

And it was not long before she did.

***

Cree lay on his back, his body covered in a fine sheen of sweat, his breathing finally calming, along with his racing heart, and his hand locked with his wife's lying beside him. He had had various types of climaxes from not so great to satisfying ones through the years with women before Dawn came along. Once he had made love to Dawn, he knew there would never be another woman who could satisfy him the way she did. That had been proven true over and over again through the last two years and even more so a few moments ago when he climaxed for a second time, leaving him completely spent.

"Love," he said between breathes that continued to calm.

Dawn turned her head to look at him, her own breathing still rapid and her heart thumping rapidly. Her husband had brought her to climax three times, the last one leaving a sensual tingle that still rippled through her.

Cree turned his head to look at his wife. "I love you, wife."

Dawn smiled, patted her chest, turned on her side and laid her hand on his chest.

Cree rested his hand over hers and chuckled. "With the way you just rode me, I would say you love me an awful lot."

Dawn's silent laugh shook her body gently, and she nodded.

Cree turned on his side, facing his wife, his hand slipping down between them to rest on her flat stomach. "I planted my seed deep and it is bound to take root. It will be a spring bairn we have."

Dawn knew without a doubt that the bairn would be his, but she wondered if Cree had even a brief doubt that it could

241

be otherwise. The thought disturbed her even more so now that Tarass had left an inkling of doubt to linger in him.

"Do not let Tarass rob us of what we have," Cree said when she failed to smile.

Her brow scrunched in question.

"Love and trust," Cree said. "Do not let him take them from you."

Dawn smiled then and gestured, tapping his temple, letting him know how wise he was.

"Of course I am wise," Cree boasted playfully. "And lucky you are to have such a wise man for a husband."

Dawn chuckled, though it ceased quickly when a knock sounded at the door, and Sloan called out.

Cree hurried his wife into his arms and yanked a blanket over them as he shifted them to sit up in bed, then bid Sloan to enter.

"Sorry to disturb," Sloan said.

"A problem with Tarass and his men?" Cree asked.

"No, they eat, drink and get on well with our warriors," Sloan informed him. "It is Dawn who is needed."

Dawn turned questioning eyes on Sloan.

"Elsa has ordered Lucerne to rest, the bairn having made her ill too often today. Now Elsa is insisting she, herself, tend those in need."

Dawn shook her head.

"Neil agrees and asked me to see if you could help."

Dawn nodded and shooed him away so she could get out of bed and dress, but Sloan did not move. She was quick to turn to her husband. It was his permission Sloan waited for and Dawn tapped his chest and pointed to Sloan.

Cree looked to Sloan. "Have a warrior follow her."

"As you say, but our warriors are busy keeping watch on all of Tarass's warriors and we have extra warriors patrolling the village, then there are those who patrol the outlying areas to make certain more of his warriors do not

242

wait to attack. And even more that have traveled a distance beyond our boundaries to make certain no more of his warriors have followed. There is no reason she should not be safe in the village with so many patrolling it."

"Fetch Beast, he guards the twins," Cree ordered and wait outside the door until summoned.

"Aye, my lord," Sloan said.

Dawn threw the blanket off herself and her husband as she went to slip over him and out of bed, but his strong hands clamped around her waist, stopping her.

"I do not think Tarass means you harm, but I will take no chances. You will give me your word that you will keep Beast close at all times and you will not venture out of the village."

Dawn nodded, crossing her heart in a promise.

"Where is Lila? Can she help you?" Cree asked annoyed at himself for having yet to get Elsa help. He would talk with Flanna. She would know who would make good helpers for Elsa.

Dawn cradled her arm carefully as if holding something tiny.

"She is with Dorrie and the new bairn," Cree said and Dawn nodded.

Dawn felt his reluctance to let her go, his grip a bit snug at her waist. She understood his worry and shared it. Only time would heal what her abduction had stolen from them.

She tried to assure him that she would be fine and that he was not to worry.

"Keep Beast with you," he reminded and after a quick kiss released her.

Cree opened the door after they were both dressed to find Beast sitting there and Sloan beside him.

"Guard Dawn well, Beast," Cree ordered firmly.

Beast barked and moved to stand beside Dawn.

"Be safe, wife," Cree said, kissed her again and watched the pair disappear down the stairs.

"Dawn is safe in the village, especially with all the warriors about," Sloan said, "and with their show of weapons. I think that has impressed and warned Tarass's warriors more than we realize."

"I am glad of that, but the memory of losing her lingers and strikes fear in me when she is gone from me too long."

"I understand that fear now that I have Lucerne," Sloan said. "Your warriors know without it being said that she is to be watched over. She will have many eyes on her in the village today."

"I have no doubt of that," Cree said and headed to the stairs, still he would make sure to check on his wife himself, more so with Tarass here.

***

The sky remained overcast throughout the day, but Dawn paid it little attention. She was far too busy tending to those in need, mostly minor issues. She had stopped to see how Dorrie, Elwin, and their tiny daughter were doing and was pleased to see that all was well and that Elwin had gained more confidence in holding the little bairn. She was also pleased that Lila suggested she help Dawn, since Dorrie was doing fine and the other women who helped with the birth would continue to look in on her.

Dawn returned to the healing cottage every now and then to let Elsa know how things were going and to ask for advice even though she had not needed it. Lila also chatted with Elsa, detailing all they were doing and keeping her talking while Dawn collected what they needed.

Neil had ushered Dawn quietly outside the last time they had stopped, Lila and Elsa too busy chatting to pay them heed.

"I want to thank you for returning here now and again and let Elsa know what goes on. She would be lost without tending people and you stopping to ask her questions, get her advice, has helped to ease her concerns and allow her to rest comfortably. It does her well to know you will seek her out when necessary." He smiled. "And sometimes when it is not at all necessary."

Dawn had smiled and patted her chest and pointed at the healing cottage, hoping Neil understood that she was saying she was glad to be of help.

"We appreciate the help," he said.

Dawn's smile spread, pleased he had understood her.

More villagers began approaching Dawn when word finally spread that she would be tending those in need today, more so since Lila had joined her making it easier for Dawn to be understood.

"Do you realize your husband has made his presence known around you four times now since I have joined you," Lila said in a whisper, though Cree was too far for him to hear her.

Dawn smiled, nodded, and waved to catch her husband's eye as they made their way through the village.

He waved back and Dawn almost chuckled, knowing he had been watching her out of the corner of his eye the whole time. He returned talking with Sloan, but Dawn knew his eyes followed her as she and Lila continued walking.

Dawn would not have spotted Ina walking through the village if she had not felt Beast's wagging tail brushing against her leg and looking down to see what had caught his eye that pleased him.

"What is Ina doing about? She should be with Nell tending to the twins," Lila said and when she saw Dawn's eyes narrow in concern, she called out to the woman. "Ina."

Ina stopped and seeing Dawn, hurried over to her. "I have a sour stomach, my lady, and thought Elsa or Lucerne

245

might be able to help me." She shook her head and a smile lit her face. "My own fault since I indulged in the sweets the twins did not finish last night."

"Neither are up to tending anyone today. Dawn is seeing to those in need," Lila explained and smiled. "And I would indulge myself in anything that Turbett made."

Dawn reached into the healing basket, picked out a small pouch, and handed it to Ina, then gestured.

"Make a brew from some of these mint leaves," Lila interpreted. "It should help your stomach as will rest. I will find someone to help Nell with the twins for the remainder of the day."

"Are you sure, my lady, I can return to the keep after a small rest," Ina said. "It is my fault and I should not benefit from being foolish."

Dawn shook her head, then smiled softly as she gestured.

Lila continued to be Dawn's voice. "No, rest and feel well and return in the morning."

"I am most grateful, my lady," Ina said and after a respectful bob of her head to Dawn, walked off toward her cottage.

Lila poked Dawn in the arm with her elbow. "Look at the way the men watch her. I am surprised she is not wed by now. Though, I do recall hearing she is fussy when it comes to a man. Wants what she wants." Lila shrugged. "But then why not? I wanted Paul and only Paul." She grinned and poked Dawn again with her elbow. "And I got him."

Dawn nodded and laughed, happy Lila had joined her and brought humor to the task.

When all was finally done, no one left to tend, and Lila gone to retrieve Thomas, visiting with Old Mary, Dawn spoke one last time with Elsa.

Her head pained her and she asked Dawn to brew her a tankard of chamomile. She did and settled Elsa in the bed for the night, and told the couple that she would have Flanna send them supper.

"You do not have to fuss," Elsa said.

Neil was quick to disagree. "Nonsense, we cannot refuse such kindness."

Elsa laughed though winced a bit as she did. "You just want Turbett's food."

"Of course, I do," Neil said, grinning and rubbing his hands together in anticipation.

Neil thanked her again after stepping outside with her and watched as she and Beast walked off.

The village was quiet, but then the overcast sky had darkened bringing with it the chance of rain. She was eager to return to the keep, see the twins since she had barely seen them today. A friend of Nell's, Bartha, had approached her and offered to help with the twins. Dawn had been relieved to have that settled, knowing the twins could be a handful for one person. She was also eager to see her husband, and she smiled at the thought.

Her mind was so busy with thoughts of her family that it startled her to hear Beast growl and she almost bumped into him when he ran in front of her, stopping her from taking another step.

"He does protect you, but then it was me who ordered him to do so from the start."

Dawn watched as Tarass emerged from the shadows on the side of one of the cottages.

"It is not easy getting a moment alone with you," Tarass said as he approached Dawn.

Beast snapped at Tarass, warning him not to get any closer.

"You are a traitor. It is good to be rid of you," Tarass snarled back.

Dawn pointed at Tarass, then at Beast, hugged herself, then shook her finger at Tarass.

"Are you telling me that I cared nothing for that dog?"

Dawn gave a firm nod.

"He is a dog. How much can you care for a dog?"

Dawn spread her arms wide, then dropped them to her sides before pointing to him, then to herself and gave a shrug.

"Let me see if I understand you correctly. You are saying you can care much for a dog, which is evident, and you are asking me what do I want from you?"

Dawn nodded.

"Again you speak to my wife without permission," Cree roared after coming around the corner of a nearby cottage and took quick strides toward them, Sloan and two warriors following behind him.

"A friendly chat no more," Tarass argued, annoyance sharp on his tongue.

"Good job, Beast," Cree praised and the dog quieted as Cree stepped close to Tarass. "My home, my rules. Obey them or suffer the consequences."

"Like your wife, I do not obey," Tarass challenged, taking a step closer to Cree.

"My wife is not your concern," Cree warned.

"I disagree. We spent time together and I got to know her *well*."

Cree had had enough. He jabbed his finger in Tarass's chest. "Not well enough since she recalls nothing about you."

Tarass fisted his hand at his side. "Perhaps it is better that way or she would be disappointed on her return home."

Dawn would have gasped if she could at such a blatant and challenging remark. She knew an altercation would ensue, her husband sure to retaliate, and possibly a full battle, warriors of both clans gathering along with the villagers. She quickly stepped between the two men, her arms stretching out from her sides, pressing a hand to each chest to keep them apart. She shook her head, warning them the best she could to stop.

"This is between him and me, wife," Cree said.

"Aye, obey your husband as you first did me," Tarass said with a snide smile.

Dawn almost got crushed between the two men when her husband lunged forward fast. She shook her head again and nodded toward the keep.

"Your wife is right. We should take this inside, a crowd gathers," Tarass said.

Cree did not care who gathered around them. He wanted nothing more than to land a blow on Tarass that would knock him out cold, the bastard deserved it. Why he was taking a chance provoking him, Cree did not know and did not care. If Tarass wanted a fight, Cree would give him one and enjoy beating the hell out of him.

But not at the expense of his wife. Dawn was clearly upset and he understood why. This matter was private and should be discussed in private.

"My solar," Cree commanded and placed his hand at his wife's waist to ease her to his side.

"It is good you obey your wife," Tarass said with a chuckle.

That was it, Cree had enough. He gave his wife a slight shove to move her out of the way, bringing his arm around with such force as he did that when it connected with Tarass's jaw, he felt the blow clear up along his arm and watched with pure joy as it lifted Tarass off the ground and propelled him in the air to land with a hard bounce on the ground, knocking him out cold.

Chapter Twenty-four

"It was well worth it, leave it be," Cree ordered as his wife fussed over his bruised knuckles.

He silently cursed his snappish remark, seeing the unshed tears that had lingered in her eyes since entering his solar. He reached out, his hand going around the back of her neck and brought her close to rest his brow to hers as he reassured her. "I am fine, wife, and all is well. Worry not." He kissed her gently.

Dawn shook her head and patted her chest.

"This is not your fault. I will not hear that from you. You did nothing wrong. His own warriors did not even come to his defense when I hit him."

That was something that puzzled Cree. There was only one reason why that would be since loyal warriors always defended their commander, and Tarass's warriors did seem loyal, unless he gave orders otherwise. He puzzled no more on it when Tarass appeared in the open doorway.

"My warriors had orders not to interfere in any altercation between you and me," Tarass said, rubbing his jaw that had darkened with a large bruise.

Sloan stood behind Tarass and Cree gave him a nod and he closed the door, leaving the three alone.

"Sit, wife," Cree said, taking her hand and walking her over to one of the chairs by the hearth, having felt the chill in her and wanting to get her warm. "Tarass is going to tell us why he has been such an *arse* since his arrival."

A knock at the door annoyed Cree. They were not to be disturbed, so who had dared to disturb them.

Flanna entered and gave a respectful bob of her head. "My lord, a hot brew for my lady."

Cree nodded and was pleased she had thought of Dawn, but then they had been friends before he had ever entered their lives.

She was quick to give the brew to Dawn, squeezing her hand in a silent message of comfort and support as she handed her the tankard.

Dawn smiled and patted her chest in appreciation.

"I could use a drink myself, though preferably ale," Tarass said.

Cree gave a nod to Flanna and she filled two tankards from the pitcher on the sideboard and handed one to Cree before handing the other to Tarass. With another respectful bob of her head to Cree, she left.

Cree took a deep swallow, needing to wet his dry throat, or was it that he needed to do something, anything, to avoid surrendering to the urge to beat Tarass senseless? It did help seeing him wince while drinking.

"Explain yourself," Cree ordered.

"Explain how you let your wife be taken from you," Tarass shot back.

Dawn bolted out of her chair to once again come between the two men as her husband lunged forward and Tarass jumped out of his chair. She looked from one to the other, shaking her head. The hand that rested against her husband's chest, she moved to raise in a fist and shake her head, then tapped her lips with her finger and nodded. Then she turned to Tarass tapped her mouth, scowled, pointed around the room, and shook her finger at him.

"She is warning you to watch what you say in her home," Cree said and was surprised when, in a way, Tarass apologized.

"You are right. I should not have provoked."

Dawn nodded and pointed for Tarass to return to his chair while she remained by her husband.

Annoyance pinched at Tarass's face, but he sat.

Dawn returned to her chair once he sat and gave her husband a gentle smile.

Cree was proud of his wife. Her actions made it clear that she defended her husband while chastising their guest for his rude behavior.

"This needs to be settled so you can take your leave at sunrise," Cree said, letting Tarass know he was not welcome after that.

"My intentions all along," Tarass said, then continued. "I was shocked to see that Dawn was your wife, though pleased to see she had survived, not so much that my dog had betrayed me. Beast, as you call him, was ordered to watch over Dawn, not take his leave with her the second time. But I should have known better. The dog had grown ever closer to her, never leaving her side."

Dawn gestured at Tarass.

"My wife says that she tried to get him to return to you, but he would not leave her."

"I do not know what it is the dog found in you that made him desert me, but he is more loyal to you than he ever was to me," Tarass said.

A caring love, Dawn thought and felt pity for him that he could not understand that.

"Why did you not bring my wife home when she first asked?" Cree said.

"I had someone I had to meet and that meeting could not be delayed."

"Why not let Dawn go when she left you the first time? She was nothing to you. Why waste your time chasing after her?" Cree asked.

The scowling pinch between Tarass's eyes had Cree thinking the man was contemplating on whether to respond or not. Or was he conjuring a lie?

Tarass gave an almost unnoticeable shake of his head as if he was not pleased with what he was about to say. "She had information I needed."

"Information?" Cree asked, thinking the information had to hold a good bit of importance to Tarass for him to go after Dawn.

Tarass nodded and seemed to surrender to the fact that whether he liked it or not he had to explain things to Cree.

"Shortly before Dawn took her leave from me the first time, I talked with her about her abduction. She drew a picture in the dirt of the two men who had abducted her. I recognized the one man as the one I had hired to get information for me on someone and had failed to meet with me. I needed to know where she had been abducted, so I knew where to start searching for him, but she would point in a direction, tap her lips, then walk her hands, which I came to understand meant she would tell me as we went. I understand now her reluctance to tell me and to name her family. She did not know if I was friend or foe of yours, though it would not have mattered since I knew nothing of your reputation until I returned home and learned that you are known as a powerful and fearless warrior."

"Why did you not tell me this when you first saw Dawn?"

Tarass took a swallow of ale before answering. "I did not know you and I do not share private matters with strangers. Also my pride had been wounded. How would you feel if a woman bested you, a voiceless one at that and," — he shook his head— "that she also made off with your dog."

Cree looked to Dawn and grinned. "My wife is a remarkable woman."

"I came to realize that quite early upon meeting her."

253

"Finding Dawn here gave you the information of where to begin your search for the man you had hired. Why not let things be and take your leave?"

"I never got to ask Dawn one important question."

Dawn tilted her head in question at Tarass while Cree waited for him to continue.

Tarass looked to Dawn. "Did either man ever mention the name Slatter?"

Dawn scrunched her brow, giving it thought until she finally shook her head.

"Are you sure? Think on it more," Tarass urged.

"Dawn has given you her answer," Cree said, annoyed that Tarass sounded as if he badgered her.

"She may not remember," Tarass snapped.

"Dawn remembers everything," Cree argued

"She does not remember struggling with me when I tried to get her wet garments off and striking me repeatedly. I do not know where she got the strength to battle me as she did. The exhaustion from her ordeal and her expending the last of her strength on me took its toll and she once again fell unconscious. I hurried to strip her and get a blanket wrapped around, then myself since by that time night had settled in with a chill and I was growing cold. I wrapped myself around her still having a bit of body warmth left and knowing the fire would warm me even more and in turn warm Dawn as well."

Dawn nodded, gesturing to her one arm, running her finger up and down it, then pointing to Tarass.

"You remember that," Tarass said, pushing up his shirtsleeve.

Dawn nodded staring at the drawing on his arm and cringing as if in fear.

Cree could understand why. There on Tarass's one arm was a drawing of an arrow, the head of it reaching just below his wrist, pointing to the palm of his hand.

Cree understood the significance of it immediately. "In your confused state, you thought an arrow was ready to strike you."

Dawn nodded, remembering, and rolled her finger around and around.

"Repeatedly," Cree said and Dawn nodded again.

"I never thought of that," Tarass admitted. "My sleeve got snagged on the branch when I pulled you out of the water and tore it clear off. You saw only the arrow again and again."

Dawn nodded and tapped her head.

"You remember that now," Tarass said, understanding her.

Dawn gestured again and this time Tarass looked to Cree to interpret.

"My wife says she now recalls how when you left her side to keep the fire going strong, she would shiver and was glad when you returned to keep her warm."

Dawn gestured again and from where she pointed and then shook her head it was easy to understand what she said.

"I am glad you remember that I never touched you improperly," Tarass said. "I am not the kind of man who would force himself on a helpless woman, only a coward does that."

Dawn crossed her hands over her chest and patted it, then pointed to Tarass.

Her gesture did not need interpretation, but Cree wished to add his own words. "My wife thanks you for saving her life and I am glad to know you are an honorable man."

"Then we are friends?" Tarass asked with a sly smile.

"We shall see," Cree said.

Tarass turned to Dawn to ask again, "You truly do not recall any mention of a man called Slatter?"

Dawn thought again on the name, but shook her head, expressing her regret that she could not help him.

"Worry not, I will find who I look for," Tarass said.

Cree held his hand out to his wife and Dawn took it and got to her feet.

"There are some things I need to discuss with Tarass," Cree said.

Dawn nodded and cradled her arm.

"You go to the twins," Cree said.

Dawn nodded again and thanked Tarass one more time.

He stood. "I am glad you survived and reunited with your family."

Cree spoke after Dawn shut the door behind her. "Since you finally turned civil I will share news with you that may help you."

"Any help you can give me would be appreciated."

"My warriors captured one of Dawn's abductors, Bram is his name. The other one is called Gillie from what Bram told me."

"Gillie is the one I hired," Tarass confirmed.

"Bram claimed ignorance. According to him, Gillie was the one hired to abduct Dawn and asked him to help. He had no knowledge of the man who had hired Gillie. He did, however, know Gillie's whereabouts. My warriors have taken Bram there to collect Gillie and bring them both here. They should return soon. If you wish to remain here until then, you are welcome to."

"I am grateful for your offer and accept it."

"This man Slatter, you look for, could he have anything to do with Dawn's abduction?" Cree asked.

"Anything is possible when it comes to Slatter. He is an evil man in many ways. He can talk anyone into anything. He charms the women and uses them, pits people against one another to gain power, and lies with every breath he takes."

"He has harmed you in some way?"

"He has information I need," Tarass said, "or I would not bother with the likes of him."

One more thing," Cree said, "You do not strike me as a man who lets his pride get in the way of anything. So, tell me the real reason why you were such an arse upon discovering Dawn here and that she was my wife."

"You are an observant man, Cree."

"The same can be said of you."

Tarass nodded. "True enough."

"So why act as you did? Why provoke me as you did?"

"When Dawn told me that she had been abducted, but evaded my questions about her husband, I wondered if it had been her husband who had arranged the abduction and eventually what would lead to her death. I thought perhaps that her husband did not care for a wife who could not speak. It was obvious she was a brave woman and I wanted to make certain no harm came to her. I wanted to return her home and see for myself that her husband wanted and loved her."

"So you provoked me to see how I would respond?"

"I had little time to make sure Dawn would be safe here. There was no other way, though I admit, seeing you two together, it appears that you truly love each other."

"But you needed to be absolutely certain," Cree said.

"I did."

"Which is why you attempted to speak to Dawn alone when you could have easily asked her that question in my presence."

Tarass nodded. "I knew your warriors would see me speaking to her and go straight to you."

"They alerted me immediately."

Tarass rubbed at his bruised jaw and winced as he smiled. "And I got a definitive answer. You love your wife very much."

"I do, though I need not prove that to you. You came close to losing your life," Cree said.

"At least I know when I leave here that I am leaving Dawn in the arms of someone who would give his life to see her safe."

Cree held his hand out to Tarass. "Now we are friends."

Chapter Twenty-five

"A day's time you say," Cree said as he returned to the village from the fields with Sloan the next morning.

"That was the message received," Sloan confirmed. "And from what our warrior said our men will be glad to be rid of the two since they squabble worse than two women."

"Has Tarass been informed?"

"Aye, and he was pleased with the news. I believe he is eager to take his leave."

"Have you learned much about Tarass?" Cree asked.

"His warriors are tight-lipped, though several of our warriors have caught Tarass's warriors speaking the Viking tongue. They change tongues quickly, and none, not a one of them, offer a word as to where they come from or anything about Tarass."

"He has taught his men well," Cree said.

"Do you trust him?" Sloan asked.

"I trust that he means us no harm. I wonder, though, of his plans for those clans that surround his land and what will happen if they show him no friendship."

"You think he would war with them?"

"It would be no war. He is a fearless warrior as, I believe, are his men. Victory would be his soon enough. I would hope he would show some diplomacy, but I think because of his long absence, he is more prone to a hasty solution. It is not for us to interfere and he offered me his support if needed, which I accepted."

"But that would mean he would expect the same of you."

Cree nodded. "Aye, it would, which is why I agreed."

"You would go fight with him?"

"I would go and make certain things did not escalate, elsewise, I would have no say in the matter. But if I raise my sword alongside him, then I can speak my piece."

"A wise move."

"How goes the search for the worn cloak?" Cree asked, having given orders to see if the mysterious tatty cloak could be found.

Sloan shook his head. "Impossible. I and several of our sentinels have seen cloaks with worn hems. Even though the people have been given new cloaks, they still cling to their old ones as if waiting for them to wear out completely. But then they had been a deprived clan before we came along so I cannot blame them for clinging to whatever little they have."

"Keep note of all those you have seen with tatty hems. It may lead to something."

"Already done," Sloan said.

"What is on your mind that you are not saying, Sloan?" Cree asked, stopping and walking off to a more private area to talk.

"You read me too well."

"It got easier and became more pronounced when you set yourself the task of finding out about the man Lucerne had planned to wed. Though, from the start it was actually to sabotage her plans since you refused to admit that you loved her." Cree smiled. "But then she refused to admit she loved you as well. Dawn and I enjoyed watching both of your antics during that time."

"I saved her from a man who did not love her," Sloan argued.

"Nor did she love him no matter how she tried to convince herself and everyone else, mostly you though. She made you jealous enough to finally admit to her that you loved her. Not an easy thing to do for someone who had no intentions of ever falling in love let alone marrying.

"I never was partial to the whole love and marriage thing, especially spending the rest of one's life with one woman. It never made sense to me until I met Lucerne. Well, not when I first met her. She was a nightmare, though through no fault of her own. Having been fed a potion by her mother that made her ill, only to find out the woman was not her true mother had to have been devastating. It was the strength I saw in her in the time that followed her ordeal that made me see her differently."

"And now you would do anything to keep her from ever suffering again."

"Aye, I would, which is why I am desperate to find two women who can replace Lara and Ann. Lucerne wakes with a sour stomach every morning and still she goes and helps Elsa. Sometimes she is ill throughout the day and into the evening as well and does not eat. I worry over her and our bairn. I do not want to lose either of them."

"Have you spoken to Elsa about this?" Cree asked.

Sloan shook his head in frustration. "Lucerne will have a fit if I did that."

"You are her husband. It is your right and your duty to make decisions for her when she is too foolish to do so herself."

Sloan chuckled. "And how has that worked for you with Dawn?"

Cree stopped himself from responding in haste, his brow crunching in thought.

"You have to think about it," Sloan said, chuckling again.

"Women," Cree said, shaking his head.

"My point exactly," Sloan agreed.

"I have spoken with Flanna and she knows of three women who have expressed interest in working with Elsa. I will speak to Elsa about them without making any reference to Lucerne… for both our sanity," Cree said.

"You are a wise man," Sloan said relieved.

Cree spotted Old Mary making her way slowly toward them.

"I should have listened to her when she kept telling me that Dawn was not dead that she would have known if she had died. I thought she could not accept her death." Sloan looked to Cree. "Much like you who continued searching, not giving up, continuing to hope."

"Until I finally did."

"Not that long before Dawn returned and besides, I always believed you were too stubborn to ever truly give up hope that Dawn would return to you."

"I begged for a miracle," Cree admitted.

Sloan slapped Cree on the back. "And you got your miracle, but then I do not think the Heavens want you and the devil sure in hell wants nothing to do with you."

Sloan acknowledged Old Mary with a nod when she got close and slipped away, leaving her to talk with Cree.

"Something troubles you," Cree said, seeing her concern in the way she worried her gnarled hands.

"There is something in the woods," Old Mary warned with a shudder.

"What," Cree demanded, ready to dispatch his men.

"I do not know. I saw nothing but I felt it." She shuddered again. "Danger lurks there as if in wait."

"I will send my warriors."

"I do not think you will find anything. I warned Dawn since I saw the twins with Nell at the edge of the woods. She ran to collect them."

Cree left Old Mary without a word, his stomach twisting in fear as he hurried to join his wife, to protect his family.

262

His heart slowed its pounding when he saw his wife holding each of the twins' hands and walking them away from the woods. She looked as relieved as he felt when she spotted him and he hurried his steps to his family.

Cree was proud of his son, holding his sword up as his eyes scanned the area. He was ready to fight, ready to protect even as young as he was. Lizbeth on the other hand was pouting. He scooped her up as soon as he got close.

She pointed back over his shoulder. "Woods, Da, flowers."

"No woods," Cree said firmly.

Her pout grew.

He ignored it and turned to Nell who walked to keep up with them. "The twins are not to go into the woods or at the edge of the woods. And no woman will go into the woods alone until I say otherwise."

"Forgive me, my lord, I thought it was all right to take them there since Ina has brought them twice now," Nell said, a tremble to her voice.

"No more," Cree said with a strength that made Nell shudder.

"Aye, my lord, I will make sure of it," Nell said, then rushed to say more before her courage failed her. "You should know, my lord, that Ina went into the woods to get other types of flowers for Lizbeth."

"I will see to Ina," Cree said and turned, hearing his daughter's whimper. As soon as he did, Lizbeth broke into tears.

She sobbed between trying to say flowers, which sounded nothing like flowers, though Cree understood her. He felt for her, but it mattered not. He would see her kept safe.

"No tears, Lizbeth," he said. "Da will take you, but not yet."

His words did nothing to temper her tears. Instead, they increased.

Cree ignored her as they walked back to the keep, not so Dawn.

She grabbed her husband's arm stopping him, turned a scowl on her daughter, slapped her hands together loudly and gave one sharp snap of her finger at Lizbeth's face. The little lass's tears stopped immediately. Dawn took hold of her son's hand again and walked ahead, though Valan turned to send his sister a grin.

Cree followed behind her, Lizbeth's head going to rest on his shoulder and her little arms slipping around his neck, and he tried to keep from smiling. His wife might not have a voice, but she certainly made sure that the twins heard her and obeyed her.

***

Dawn set a quick pace to Old Mary's cottage. She had to speak to her and set her own suspicions to rest. The twins had been settled in their room and Cree was busy leading a small group of warriors into the woods not only to locate Ina but to see what he could discover for himself. He also had Sloan busy spreading the word that no woman was to go into the woods alone. Of course, that created a stir among the people, keeping gossiping tongues busy.

Old Mary was sitting on the bench, Paul had made for her, braced against the cottage wall not far from the door. Her head was bent, her attention appearing focused on her lap and she did not raise it as Dawn's approached.

It was strange to Dawn that the woman did not move, did not seem aware of her presence. It was unlike Old Mary not to realize that she was there, a short distance from her, waiting to greet her.

It was not until she stood in front of Old Mary that the old woman lifted her head.

Old Mary patted the spot beside her on the bench. "Sit. I know you have questions, I do myself, but Fate refuses to reveal them."

Dawn sat, her hands resting in her lap, ready to listen.

"There was a darkness—no—an evil in the woods I could not explain. It surrounded me suddenly and I feared I could not escape it. Then it either released me or I escaped it, since I could not truthfully tell you if I had taken a step or I had been frozen in place. Something lurks there, but how to find it, I do not know."

Dawn patted her chest.

"I wondered myself if it could have anything to do with your abduction, if the evil has returned to attempt once again to claim you. But I cannot say. It is not clear. Fate will not show me, though I wonder if Fate cannot see through the heavy darkness herself."

Dawn took Old Mary's hand and gave it a squeeze, attempting to reassure the old woman who had done the same for her countless times.

"I know one thing," Old Mary said with certainty. "This darkness comes and goes at will. There one moment and gone the next. How can something so elusive be found?"

Dawn stuck her chest out and held her hand up high, signifying her husband, and nodded firmly.

"Cree is a wise warrior and I know he has faced evil before, but this evil is different," Old Mary said, shaking her head. "Far different. It cannot be seen. It evades the eye."

Her words kept ringing in Dawn's head long after she left Old Mary. The whole time she had been gone, she had wondered over her abduction. Why had someone taken her? What had been the person's intentions? She recalled the one abductor reminding the other several times that she was not to be harmed and they were not to have their way with her. So what had been the reason for her abduction?

"My lady."

Dawn startled, losing her balance and Tarass's hand reached out quickly to steady her.

"I did not mean to frighten you."

Dawn shook her head, then tapped her temple.

"You were deep in thought."

Dawn nodded.

"Something troubles you?" Tarass asked as he followed alongside her when she continued her slow pace.

Dawn had found it easy to talk with Tarass during the time spent with him, though she minded her tongue when speaking with him. Still, she had found that though he had a quick tongue, he listened well.

Dawn nodded and crossed her wrists, pressing them against each other.

"You think of your abduction."

She nodded again.

"I thought on it much myself when you were with me and then after you were gone. Truthfully, I was concerned that your husband had you abducted with the intention of seeing you dead."

Dawn smiled, shook her head, and patted her chest.

"I realize now seeing you and Cree together that I was wrong. The man adores you and would give his life for you. That kind of love is rare. I understand now why you wanted so badly to return home. But someone meant you harm."

Dawn shook her head. She reached her hand out and pulled it back toward her several times.

"You believe you were abducted because someone wanted something."

Dawn nodded.

"Do you have any idea what that might be?"

Dawn shook her head.

"My lady."

Tarass and Dawn turned to see Ina hurrying toward them.

"Forgive me for disturbing you, my lady, but Lord Cree hurried me out of the woods fast, warning me not to go in the woods again alone and that the twins were not to go near the woods. What has happened?" Ina asked, standing there with a bouquet of a variety of woodland flowers clutched tightly in her hand and worry heavy in the deep lines between her eyes.

Dawn pointed to the bouquet and held her hand down low to demonstrate height.

"Aye, my lady, these are for Lizbeth. She wanted some different flowers so I went into the woods to get them for her. But what has happened? Did I do something wrong?"

Dawn shook her head, pointing to her.

Ina looked relieved, understanding she was not at fault.

"Do they search for someone in the woods?" Ina asked, looking to Tarass.

"I am not aware of what goes on," Tarass said.

Dawn found that difficult to believe. Nothing had gone on in his camp that he did not know about, which had made her escape more difficult. And while this may not be his camp, he kept a watchful eye and ear and no doubt knew what had taken Cree to the woods with his warriors. So why say otherwise.

I trust few. You should do the same.

The words came back to her suddenly. Tarass had said them to her one time when they had talked. She wondered what had happened to Tarass that he trusted so few.

Dawn smiled and shook her head at Ina, hoping to reassure the young woman that she had nothing to worry about.

Ina nodded and held up the bouquet. "I will take these to Lizbeth so she has them when she wakes from her nap."

Dawn's hand shot out to take hold of Ina's, her eyes full of concern seeing the blood that covered her one finger.

"A scratch, nothing more," Ina insisted.

Dawn shook her head, disagreeing, rested her hand under Ina's elbow and pointed at Elsa's healing cottage.

"If you insist, my lady, I will have Elsa look at it."

Dawn nodded, then turned and gave a nod to Tarass.

"My lady," he said with a respectful nod and walked off.

"It is not necessary for you to come with me, my lady," Ina assured her.

Dawn would not be dissuaded, keeping her hand to Ina's elbow she walked with her to the healing cottage.

"Truly, my lady, I can see to this myself," Ina said as they got closer to the cottage. "You must have things that require your attention. Please do not let me keep you from them."

Dawn recalled that she wanted to speak with Lila and warn her about the woods and that was something that could not wait.

Smiling, Dawn nodded, pointed to the bouquet of flowers and patted her chest thanking her for collecting them for Lizbeth.

"Lizbeth does love flowers," Ina said and after a bob of her head to Dawn, continued on to the healing cottage.

Dawn hurried off to see Lila.

"Lila is not there," a voice said when Dawn went to rap on Lila's door.

Dawn turned to see Cleva, one of the women who tended to the spinning of the cloth along with Lila.

Cleva was quick to tell her where Lila had gone. "She went to collect some shellock in the woods."

Dawn cradled her arm and shrugged, hoping Cleva would understand that she asked about Thomas and trying to keep her worry from showing.

"Thomas joins in play with the other spinners' bairns."

Dawn smiled, patted her chest in thanks, and walked off, worried for her friend. She could send word to Cree and

268

have him see to it, but it would take time for the message to reach him and he was not familiar with where the shellock grew. She was and could reach Lila in no time.

She thought to go and collect Beast to take him with her, but he was protecting the twins and she much preferred he remained with them. Cree would not be happy with her going off on her own and if she requested one of his warriors to accompany her, he would prevent her from entering the woods. But there was Lila's safety to consider.

She had only one choice, though she had given her word to Cree that she would let him know of her whereabouts. That was easily solved.

Dawn rapped on Old Mary's cottage and it took a few minutes before the door opened and she could see that she had disturbed the old woman's rest. She did not wait. She told Old Mary where she was going.

"You cannot go there," Old Mary argued. "Let Cree see to it."

Dawn remained steadfast, her gestures firm.

"I do not care if it is Lila. You cannot leave yourself vulnerable to danger."

Dawn would not waste time arguing with Old Mary, Lila could be in danger. She gestured for the woman to tell Cree when he returned if she, herself, had yet to return.

Old Mary went to argue and Dawn held up her hand to stop her, then pressed it to her heart. She was letting Old Mary know that Lila meant too much to her not to help her, then she simply walked away, slipping behind the cottage to enter the woods.

Chapter Twenty-six

With every step Dawn took, she berated herself. This probably was not a wise thing to do, but she could not stop herself. Lila had defended her against endless taunts through the years and even went after a young lad who had come up behind Dawn one day when they were about twelve and shoved Dawn so hard, she hit the ground, splitting her lip.

Lila had been furious and had unleashed that fury on the lad. She swung her fist, hitting him with such force that it knocked him out, suffering far worse pain to his pride than the wound itself.

She would be devastated if anything happened to Lila, especially if she could do something to prevent it. She would collect Lila and hurry out of the woods before her husband got word of where she was. Or so she attempted to convince herself.

Dawn often picked the pot herb shellock for her mum along with Lila. The best place to find the herb was not far into the woods and keeping a quick pace, she should be done and back to the village with Lila in no time.

She rounded the tree where she knew she would find Lila and would have let out a scream if she could.

Lila lay prone on the ground, not moving.

Dawn rushed to her, dropping down beside her, feeling as if she choked on her silent gasp when she saw the pool of blood beside Lila's head. She gently lifted her head to get a look at the wound in the back, hoping it would stir Lila awake, but her eyes remained closed. The wound was similar to Elsa's, a bump and a gash, though this gash did not seem as bad as Elsa's, giving Dawn hope that Lila wound do well.

She ripped a piece of cloth from the hem of her shift and did the best she could to fashion a bandage around her friend's head even though the bleeding looked to have stopped.

The problem now was how did she get Lila home. She was unable to call out for help and she would not leave Lila here alone while she went to get help for fear the culprit would return.

The thought had Dawn looking hastily around. She could be leaving herself vulnerable as well. She gave another quick glance over the surrounding area and gathered any large stones she could. She spotted a few larger stones a short distance away and went to gather the only weapons available.

She spotted the blood on a large stone before reaching down for it. It had to be the stone used to hit Lila. She did not pick it up, she left it lying there as she glanced back and forth between Lila and the stone. Whoever hit her had walked away with the stone in hand and dropped it before disappearing into the woods.

Dawn jumped at a noise, her hand gripping a large stone and instinctively shooting up in the air, ready to throw and defend her and Lila. She was greeted with silence. She waited listening and finally when she heard no sound that brought her alarm, she returned to Lila. She tried tapping her cheek to wake her. If she could get Lila on her feet, she could help her to walk, but she did not respond.

Carrying her was not a possibility, she simply did not have the strength. And if she attempted to drag her through the woods, she could chance doing Lila more damage. Her only recourse was to wait for help. But how long would it take and did the culprit still linger nearby?

Her head shot up, hearing another sound and this time the sound did not stop. It remained steady and grew.

Dawn positioned herself in front of Lila, a stone in each hand, prepared to fight, to defend them both.

She grinned, seeing a big ball of black fur burst past the trees... *Beast*.

She dropped to her knees in relief, releasing the stones, to bury her face in Beast's fur and wrap her arms around his thick neck. The dog licked her face enthusiastically when she finally released him, his tail wagging rapidly.

Dawn felt safe with Beast there, but he could not stay. He was her only hope in getting her and Lila help. It took a few repeated gestures to get him to obey her, more so from his reluctance to leave her than him not understanding her.

Beast took off in a run, barking as he went.

***

"My wife is in the woods," Cree repeated, having heard his warrior who had delivered the message from Old Mary, but repeating it to make sure he had heard him correctly.

"Aye, my lord, she went to find Lila," his warrior said a bit out of breath from running. "Old Mary says to hurry."

"Did she say why?" Cree asked.

"No, though it seemed that she just realized that you needed to hurry as she spoke with me. She shooed me away, urging me to hurry, not waste a minute."

Something was wrong if Old Mary rushed the warrior off. And Cree's stomach twisted in fear. He let out a yell and his warriors rushed from all directions toward him. He was about to give orders when he heard barking.

"Beast," he shouted and the barking stopped for a moment, then started again and did not stop.

Cree realized the dog had no intentions of coming to him. He waited for Cree to find him.

Cree took off, his men spreading out to follow, covering a good portion of the surrounding area, leaving no places uncovered in case of attack.

His gut continued to twist and tighten as he worried over his wife. She should have come to him. She should not have gone into the woods alone, not after Old Mary had warned them against it. How would he ever keep her safe when she often plunged ahead without thought or consequence?

Never.

The thought struck him like a severe blow to his midsection. He could never keep her completely safe no matter how hard he tried. It was an impossible task. That was the most frightening thought he had ever had and also the most truthful.

It was not long before he came upon Beast and the animal did not wait, as soon as he spotted Cree, he took off and so did Cree.

He felt another hard blow to his gut, but this one was one of relief when he saw his wife standing, unharmed, though anger took quick hold of him when he spotted Lila on the ground, not moving.

He was relieved to see that Lila was not dead, but seeing her head bandaged, he guessed she had suffered a similar blow to Elsa's.

Dawn hurried to explain to her husband, first though, he embraced her, hugging her tight, the strength of his arms letting her know she and Lila were safe now and all would be well.

"At least you had the sense to bring Beast with you," Cree said, taking a step away from her and growing annoyed when the look on his wife's face told him otherwise. "You did not bring Beast with you?"

Dawn pointed to Lila, reminding him that she was what was important right now."

"Later, wife," he said with a snarl that sounded similar to Beast's.

Dawn paid her husband no heed. She was too concerned with Lila. She tapped her husband's chest, pointed to Lila, and moved her fingers as if they were running feet.

"You want me to rush Lila back to the village," Cree said and he saw then the worry on her face, the hint of tears in her dark eyes, and how they pleaded with him.

Dawn held up two fingers, wrapping them around each other and pointed them to Lila, then to herself.

Cree stepped closer to his wife, his hand going to rest gently on her arm. "I know she is like a sister to you and we will do everything we can to see her safe and help her heal."

Dawn threw her arms around her husband to let him know how grateful she was for his words, his support, his love.

Cree would have loved to let her remain wrapped around him, but what she needed from him right now was to get her friend to Elsa.

He eased her away from him. "We need to get Lila home."

Dawn nodded firmly and stepped aside.

Cree issued orders to one of his warriors to go get Paul from the fields and have him waiting at the healing cottage. He also ordered his men to spread out and see what they could find while six of his men were ordered to follow him back to the village.

He also took a moment to praise Beast. "You did well, Beast. You will be rewarded. Now protect Dawn on our way *home*."

Beast took a protective stance beside Dawn, a wag to his tail that Dawn knew meant he was glad to be returning home.

Cree leaned down and lifted Lila up into his arms, then turned to Dawn. "Stay close, wife."

Dawn pointed to Lila, then to him, and then to Beast and herself.

274

"Are you telling me to protect Lila over you?"

Dawn nodded and pointed to Beast.

"She is pointing to Beast is she not?" Lila asked with a moan. "Dawn would do that, expecting you to help me over her, but she should not expect that of you, my lord. You are her husband and you would protect her first as you should."

Dawn grinned as Lila continued to talk, knowing she would be all right, that no one could silence her, though by the time they reached the village, she was sure Cree would have had enough of her endless chatter.

***

"You saw nothing?" Cree asked of Lila, sitting up comfortably in her bed, her son snuggled next to her in the crook of her arm and Paul sitting on a chair beside the bed, holding his wife's hand, grateful Elsa felt that with a few days' rest she would be fine.

"Nothing, my lord. As I said, I thought I heard a voice and before I could turn, I was struck on the back of the head and that is the last I recall until I woke just before you lifted me in your arms." Lila's cheeks reddened.

"A single voice or more?" Cree asked.

"I cannot be sure, my lord," Lila said.

"You have done well, Lila," Cree praised. "Rest, and if you recall anything more, let me know."

"I am most appreciative of what you did for my wife, my lord," Paul said with a respectful nod of his head.

"I do far less than what you and Lila have done through the years for Dawn. It is I who am eternally gratefully," Cree said.

"Lady Dawn is family to Lila and me, my lord, and you protect your family, as you do for all of us," Paul said.

Dawn sent Paul a smile, a tear threatening to spill, pleased that Paul acknowledged what he and Lila had told

275

her through the years. The three of them were family and always would be.

"I am pleased that my wife has such a caring and loving family," Cree said. "I will see that the culprit, who harmed your wife, is made to suffer for his ill deed."

"I had no doubt you would, my lord," Paul said.

Dawn gave Lila a kiss on the cheek and Paul too, crossing her arms over her chest and letting them both know that she loved them before she took her leave with her husband.

Silence followed Cree and Dawn after they left Lila's cottage, Beast keeping steady pace with the pair. It was not until the cottage was nearly out of sight that Cree spoke.

"It was foolish of you to go into the woods."

Dawn sighed and tightened her grip on her husband's hand as she rested her head against his arm as they walked.

"I understand you were worried about her," Cree continued, "but you placed yourself in danger."

Dawn gestured and it was easy for Cree to understand.

"I know Lila would have done the same for you, but you should have sent word to me."

Dawn nodded, agreeing.

"What am I to do with you, wife?" Cree asked with a shake of his head.

Dawn gestured.

"Love you?" Cree asked in a whisper. "I do that every minute and second of the day and will continue to do so long after I am gone from this earth."

Strong words that stirred an already simmering passion. Without a voice, making love with her husband was one of the ways she could express her deep love for him.

"The fiery heat in your eyes speaks more loudly than a voice and ignites my own need. To our bedchamber wife," Cree whispered, then muttered beneath his breath when he saw Sloan approach.

Cree stopped and was pleased to see his wife looked as annoyed as he did by the interruption.

"Six travelers, not together, have arrived today seeking shelter for one to two days. I thought it odd with the incident in the woods and thought you might want to speak with them," Sloan said.

Dawn responded for him, nodding, then patting her chest, then her husband's.

"You will come with me?" Cree asked.

Dawn nodded again.

"I do not recall extending an invitation," Cree said.

Dawn smiled, patted her chest, and shook her head.

"You do not need one?"

Dawn smiled, letting him know he had understood her.

Cree brought his nose to rest close to hers. "You will go wait in our bedchamber."

Dawn grinned and tapped her chest hard, then laid a hand on his own chest.

"Are you telling me to make you go to our bedchamber?"

Dawn grinned again and nodded.

Sloan chuckled and took several steps away from the couple after Cree turned a threatening scowl on him.

Cree pressed his nose to his wife's. "You dare challenge me, wife?"

Dawn pressed her hand to her chest, then to his and kissed his cheek.

A deep grumble rumbled in Cree's chest as he interpreted. "You dare to love me."

Dawn nodded, intent on stealing this time alone together to join as one, to love, to let all that had happened this day drift away if only for a short while.

"Let us see how much you dare to love me," Cree whispered and grabbed his wife, flinging her over his shoulder, then spoke to Sloan. "I will speak to the travelers who seek shelter in good time."

Sloan laughed and watched as Cree carried his wife into the keep.

Chapter Twenty-seven

Once in their bedchamber, Beast dispatched to the twins' chambers, Cree lowered his wife to her feet. His need for her had grown with each step he had taken up the stairs, but now that he was here, seeing her gaze at him with such heated desire, the memory of losing her assaulted him with a vengeance.

He grabbed the back of her neck with both hands and rested his brow to hers. "Your word, wife, that you will never do something so foolish again."

Dawn felt his worry in the grip of his hands and the forcefulness of his command. And as much as she did not want to add to his concern, she also could not lie to him.

She eased her head away from him and shook it.

Cree found himself speechless, though only momentarily, that she refused to give her word to him.

He kept his hands firm at the back of her neck as if by sheer force he could make her obey. "It is a command, not a request."

Dawn laid a gentle hand on his arm and shook her head again.

"I will not lose you again. You will obey me," Cree snapped and turned, taking a step away from her, needing to calm the anger that the harsh memories sparked in him.

Dawn stepped in front of him and gestured slowly, knowing this was not about her disobeying him. It was about something they both someday would face and her abduction had forced them to experience it.

Cree threw his hands up and stepped away from her again. "I do not want to hear about death, about us being

279

separated. I barely lived through it once, I do not want to think of living through it again or even dying before you, for wherever death takes me, I will rage against them for taking me from you."

Dawn went to gesture again and Cree grabbed her wrists, stopping her.

"There is nothing you can say that will change it."

Dawn eased out of his grasp and gestured.

"And nothing I can do to stop death," he said, understanding her gestures all too clearly. "But I can try to prevent it by keeping you safe, if only you would obey me."

Dawn did her best to help him understand how she felt.

Cree listened and did not speak until she was done. "I know by telling Old Mary where you were going, you kept your word about letting me know where you would be. I even understand why you would go into the woods to warn your dearest friend, but the thought of you continuing to do something so foolish that it puts you in danger rips at my heart and gut. I also know that at times you will not see it as foolish and rush headlong into it. I will forever live in torment that your foolishness will be the cause of me losing you. And what of Beast? He is there to protect you when I am not there. He should be with you at all times."

Dawn gestured.

"I know he was protecting the twins, but they were safe in the keep. You should have taken him with you."

Dawn placed her hand gently on her husband's arm. She hated that she was the cause of his distress and promised what she could.

Cree shook his head slowly. "I am pleased that you promise to do better at not being so foolish. It gives me hope that you will live a long life and I will live one with less worry of losing you."

A rap at the door had Cree shaking his head again and demanding to know who disturbed him.

"Forgive me for disturbing you, my lord," Flanna called out. "Elsa sent word that it is important she speak with you."

Cree saw the gentle cringe of disappointment on his wife's face and felt it himself.

"I will be there shortly," Cree said, knowing Elsa was not one to bother him with trivial matters.

"Aye, my lord, I will tell her," Flanna said, her footsteps heard hurrying off.

Dawn forced a smile and mouthed *later*.

Cree chuckled and wrapped his arm around her waist, easing her close to him. "You think I would leave you unsatisfied?"

Dawn teased with a gesture that there was not enough time.

Cree grinned. "There is always time to make you come at least once."

Dawn smiled and held up two fingers.

"You are a greedy one wanting to come twice."

She nodded, slipping her hand beneath his plaid and taking hold of him, her smile spreading, feeling how hard he was.

"If you want to come twice, wife, I would be careful how you tease me," he warned playfully.

Dawn brought her face close to his and mouthed, *Not. Up. To. It?*

Cree laughed. "You have the answer in your hand, wife, though it is a challenge I will not refuse."

He hoisted her up, her feet not touching the floor as he walked over to the bed and dropped her down on it, then flipped her over on her stomach, and pulled her to her knees.

Dawn scrambled to balance herself on her hands and smiled when she felt his hand push her garments up, exposing her bare backside. Her head shot up when she felt his finger slip into her and she bit on her lower lip when his thumb connected with that small spot of pleasure that stirred

281

such passion. Not that it needed much stirring since she had felt herself not far from climax as soon as he had dropped her on the bed.

Cree had no wont to linger and after feeling how ready she was for him... he did not hesitate.

Dawn's head shot back and she squeezed her eyes shut, immense pleasure shooting through her as her husband rammed into her with a forcefulness that would have had her screaming out his name if she had had a voice.

Cree groaned as he kept a firm grip on her backside, keeping her steady against his rapid, hard thrusts. He would not last long, feeling her close ever tighter around him, but she wanted to climax twice and he would see that she did.

A sudden deep thrust had a climax rushing up, shattering his restraint, and exploding with such forceful pleasure that it buckled his knees and he had to fight to remain steady. He was pleased when he saw his wife drop her head down then it shot back up, and he could almost hear her scream his name as she joined him in an explosive climax.

When his wits finally returned, he was quick to slip his hand between her legs, to tease her nub while he gave a few final thrusts and felt her shiver in climax again.

Out of breath and spent, Cree pulled out of Dawn only after he saw her head lower slowly, knowing the last of her pleasure had drifted off. She turned as soon as he did and reached up to pull him down beside her and rest against him to linger in the satisfying aftermath of their hasty lovemaking.

They locked hands and lay there, not moving, not speaking, not gesturing, simply relishing the moment.

"You are mine and I love you. Never forget that," Cree said after a while.

Dawn let him know she felt the same, patting her chest then his. And as much as she would have loved to linger there with him, he was needed elsewhere. Dawn reminded him that Elsa wanted to speak with him.

"I forgot," Cree admitted. "And since Elsa does not bother me with frivolous matters, it must be important." He sat up and reached down to help her up. "Come with me." He grinned. "I know you want to."

Dawn smiled, nodded, and gave him a quick kiss.

After straightening their garments and making themselves presentable, they left their bedchamber and headed to the healing cottage.

Elsa hurried over to Cree when she saw him approach and spoke before he could say a word.

"One of the travelers who arrived today may be sick with fever," she said.

"You have not seen this person for yourself?" Cree asked.

"No. One of the other travelers brought it to my attention when she came to me for a minor problem. She believes this man has a fever and tries to conceal it. If it is a fever he suffers from, my worry is I have no idea as to the cause and, therefore, no idea how dire it may be to the clan unless I speak with him. You know yourself how disastrous a fever can be to a village."

Cree certainly did know, having seen a village almost wiped out due to a fever left by a man who had spent one night there.

"I would like to speak with this man, but I thought it best if you went with me," Elsa said.

"You have mentioned this to no one?" Cree asked, knowing what could happen if she did.

"Not a word, my lord," Elsa assured him, "though I did have all those around him moved elsewhere."

"Wise decision," Cree said and turned to Dawn.

She held up her hand and gestured that she would wait for him in the keep.

283

Cree pressed his cheek to hers and whispered, "I am grateful for your wise choice and will confide all in you as soon as I am done."

Sloan was summoned and alerted as to what was happening.

"I will accompany you and Elsa along with two other warriors," Sloan said.

"You will accompany us, but you will keep your distance once there," Cree ordered. "If this man does suffer a fever, I will not take a chance of it spreading. And you have Lucerne and your unborn child to consider."

"And you?" Sloan asked.

"If Elsa deems it necessary after speaking with the man, I will keep myself removed from everyone."

"I do not like it, but I see the wisdom of your decision," Sloan said. "I will remain at a distance and await your orders."

Elsa clutched her healing basket tightly as they walked to the area in the village where those who requested temporary shelter were placed.

"You are worried," Cree said.

"Until I know the cause of the fever, aye, I am worried."

Elsa said no more as they walked and there was nothing Cree could say that would ease her concern. He had concern himself, for his whole clan, and he would do whatever was necessary to keep the fever from spreading.

Elsa approached the man lying on a blanket that had been placed over a bed of straw in one of the lean-tos for use by those who asked for a day or two of shelter.

"I am the clan healer. I have come to tend you," Elsa said, stopping a short distance from him.

Her response was a groan.

Elsa looked to Cree. "I implore you, my lord, please stay back unless I need you."

284

"You leave yourself vulnerable going to him while still healing from your own wound," Cree argued.

"I am a healer and you lead this clan. Let us both do what we do best," Elsa said.

How could Cree argue with such a reasonable response? "I am here when needed."

Cree paced, watching Elsa speak with the man, then gently lifting the cloak that partially covered him. After a moment, Elsa waved him over.

"The fever will not bring harm?" Cree was quick to ask.

Elsa shook her head. "No, his fever is from a wound turned putrid. He was stabbed in the side and came here so that his body would not be left for the beasts of the forest to feed on but to have a proper burial. He requests that in return for the information he has for you."

"Can you help him?" Cree asked.

Elsa shook her head. "I believe it is too late, but that does not mean I will not try to help him."

"I will have him moved to your healing cottage, after I speak with him," Cree said.

Elsa nodded and moved away.

Cree crouched down. "I am Lord Cree. You have news for me?"

The man struggled to open his eyes, then struggled to speak, a moan the only thing that spilled from his mouth.

"Can I be of help?"

Cree and Elsa looked up to see a clergyman standing a short distance from them. His arms were crossed in front of him and his hands disappeared into the wide sleeves of the brown robe he wore and his hood drooped over his head, concealing part of his face.

It unnerved Cree that he had not heard his approach, but the men of cloth were known for their silent movements.

"I could offer prayers and peace," the clergyman said.

"Not now," Cree said and ordered him away with a wave of his hand.

"I am near if you need me," the clergyman offered and stepped aside.

"You will be summoned if needed. Take your leave now," Cree ordered.

The clergyman bobbed his head. "As you say, my lord."

Cree looked to Elsa. "When did he arrive?"

"I believe he and a fellow clergyman arrived sometime this morning."

Cree turned his attention back to the groaning man. "Tell me what information you have for me."

Cree listened as the man fought to speak through his groans of pain and his anger grew with every word he heard.

He sprang to his feet when the man had no more to say. "I will send men to take him to your healing cottage. No one is to speak with him."

"Aye, my lord," Elsa said.

Cree took rapid steps to Sloan a distance away. "It is safe. His fever is from a wound that has turned putrid. Have men take him to the healing cottage, then send a message to Tannin." His anger showed in his deep scowl. "I want him to return home with his troop and he is to bring James Macardle with him, whether he wants to come or not."

Chapter Twenty-eight

Dawn leaned back in the chair to stare up at her husband and shook her head.

"I could not believe it myself when he told me that James Macardle paid to have you abducted," Cree said, pacing in front of the hearth in his solar.

Dawn shrugged.

Cree stopped, her shrug saying what he himself thought. "I wonder why myself. What possible reason could he have had to abduct you? And what were his plans for you?" A deep scowl surfaced. "There is no reason that would be acceptable. He will be punished for the hell he has put us through."

Dawn shrugged again and pointed at the floor, then at her husband, then held her side as if wounded.

Cree understood that she asked why the injured man had come to him and he explained, "For a proper burial from what he told Elsa, though I doubt that had been his original intention. I can only assume he had been given partial coin to abduct you and he would get the remainder of it once he delivered you to Macardle. Your escape cost him and I suppose he figured he could get coin from me for the information without implicating himself. We will learn the truth of it when Gillie and Bram arrive shortly."

Dawn shrugged again and her gestures were clear.

"My thought as well, wife. How did Lara get involved? There are many questions that still need to be answered. For now, I must go see about those who have recently arrived, seeking a brief repast and shelter, especially now with this man's arrival. Macardle could have had him hunted with the intentions to silence him. I want to see if any who arrived here might be capable of that."

Dawn tapped her chest and gestured that she would go see Elsa and the wounded man.

Cree nodded. "Aye, do that, and see if he has said anymore to Elsa. And take Beast with you."

Dawn smiled, stood with a nod, and kissed her husband's cheek.

Cree grabbed her around the waist and with a chuckle asked, "Why is it you always seem obedient but seldom are?"

Dawn feigned innocence with a look that was anything but innocent and gave his lips a quick kiss.

Cree let her go and warned, "Be good, wife."

Dawn smiled, nodded, and patted her chest, letting her husband know that she was always good as she walked backwards to the door, blowing him a kiss before she turned around once she reached the door.

Cree smiled and shook his head, the smile fading when his thoughts went back to the moment when he realized that he would never be able to keep Dawn entirely safe. It was an impossible task. Fate possessed a far more powerful hand then he did. He could only do so much and he would, but he also realized that the most important thing he could do was to live every day to its fullest with Dawn and his children. To enjoy, to love, to cherish every moment. Only then would they forever remain in each other's hearts.

"The message was sent to Tannin," Sloan said from the open doorway."

"You made it clear that the only response I expect is for him to arrive here with James Macardle as soon as possible?"

"Extremely clear," Sloan confirmed.

"Now I will speak with those who recently arrived here. Perhaps one of them can tell me about the wounded man," Cree said, approaching Sloan.

"Or perhaps one of them is the one who wounded him," Sloan suggested.

"I thought the same myself," Cree said.

***

Dawn asked after Elsa first when she entered the cottage, Beast remaining outside and stretching out not far from the door to wait for her.

"I do well, he does not," Elsa said, pointing to the man on the narrow bed.

Dawn pointed to him and tapped her lips.

"His name is Rutland and he has said nothing since speaking to Cree."

Dawn pointed to Elsa, tapped her lips, shrugged, then pointed to the man.

"You want me to ask him something for you?"

Dawn nodded and mouthed *Lara*.

"Lara?" Elsa asked, a bit confused. "What has Lara to do with him?"

Dawn nodded vigorously, her eyes going wide.

"Oh, I see what you mean. That is what you want to know."

Dawn confirmed with a nod.

"I will see if he will respond to me," Elsa said and walked over to the bed to sit in the chair she kept close to it to tend the ill.

She squeezed the cloth that soaked in a bucket of water by the bed, then dabbed along his brow with it as she spoke. "Rutland, do you know Lara?"

He did not respond.

She kept her voice soft and continued dabbing the cloth along his face. "Is Lara a friend, Rutland? Is that how you know her?"

He stirred a bit.

"You are safe here. No one will harm you," Elsa assured him and rinsed the cloth to dab at his brow again. "Rutland, is Lara a friend of yours?"

"Lara?" Rutland asked with a labored breath.

"Aye, Lara, how do you know her?"

Rutland shook his head and fought to speak. "No Lara."

"You do not know Lara? She is from our clan?" Elsa asked.

He shook his head again.

Elsa turned a puzzled look on Dawn.

Dawn gave a nod to Rutland, held her side, and shrugged.

Elsa nodded in return, understanding, and asked, "How did you come by your wound, Rutland?"

He struggled to get the words out. "On… the road… robbers."

Elsa turned to Dawn and whispered, "He grows weaker. No more questions."

Dawn nodded, seeing for herself how the few questions had robbed him of strength.

"How long?" Rutland managed to ask.

Elsa turned to him. "How long for what?"

"Death."

Elsa dabbed at his brow again with the wet cloth. "Worry not, rest."

Her gentle words seemed to appease him or perhaps it was that she did not confirm the inevitable that he settled back to sleep.

Elsa stepped outside with Dawn, Beast getting to his feet as soon as they did.

"If he does not know Lara, then how did she get involved with your abduction?" Elsa asked.

Dawn shook her head and shrugged, wondering the same.

"It makes no sense. She helped your abductors. How could he not know her?"

It was a question that plagued and Dawn hoped it was one that her two abductors could answer when they finally arrived here.

***

Cree looked over the people who were settled in the lean-tos he kept near the outskirts of the village for anyone seeking shelter for a day or two. Most were travelers with destinations, like now. There was a crofter returning home to his family, a warrior to his clan, a woman and her son who sought safety for the night. And there were the two clergymen, one old, bent with age, the other on his way there, his head bowed some and his shoulders slumped as he walked.

He was the one who had offered to help when Cree spoke with the wounded man.

"Is the man doing well? Can I be of any help?" the clergyman asked, lifting his head.

"The healer sees to him," Cree said and noticed an intense unrest in his dark eyes, not something one would think to see in a pious man of the cloth.

His fine features also caught Cree's attention, striking the eye and making one take note of him. He wished he could see his hands, but he kept them crossed over his arms and buried in his sleeves. Hands told much about a person. A warrior's hands bore the marks and scars of battle, a farmer's hands bore the results of working in the fields and with the

291

earth. For some reason, he did not strike Cree as a pious man.

"I can offer prayer and sanctuary for his soul," the clergyman said.

"Do not waste your breath, clergyman, hell awaits him," Cree said. "What brings you here?"

"We travel the area to bring comfort to those in need of guidance," he said.

"You have been here before?" Cree asked, having seen clergymen here one other time but not knowing if he had been one of them.

"We have. It is kind of you to offer food and shelter to those who seek it in their travels. And if you are in need of guidance—"

"Spare me, clergyman, I need nothing from you," Cree said.

"We are all in need in some way."

Cree ignored his preaching and asked, "You will be leaving soon?"

"Newlin," the clergyman said, nodding to the older man resting in the lean-to, "is not feeling well. A day or two of rest and his old bones should be well enough for us to take our leave."

"My healer will tend to him," Cree said.

"That is not necessary, your healer must be busy, rest will suffice," the clergyman was quick to say.

"If I say it is necessary, clergyman, it is," Cree said, reminding the man his word here was law.

"As you say, my lord," the clergyman said with a slight, reluctant bob of his head.

Cree walked away, Sloan at his side.

"He never gave his name," Sloan said.

"It does not matter. He would not speak the truth if he did. He is no clergyman," Cree said. "Keep watch on him."

***

Cree watched with pride as his wee son stood, his small chest out, his shoulders drawn back, his face scrunched in a scowl and his small hands gripped tight to his wooden sword as he swung at an imaginary foe. He would make a fine warrior one day and a wise leader, Cree would make sure of it.

He shook his head when he looked upon Lizbeth, sticking flowers in Beast's fur. He looked like he had run through a field of wildflowers and every one of them had stuck to him. She had the large animal completely mesmerized with her sweet chatter, telling him how handsome she was making him and how much she loved him and always would.

Where his son, Valan, would conquer with a sword, his daughter, Lizbeth, would conquer with words and her foe would never see it coming.

"Where did she get so many flowers?" Cree asked, turning to his wife sitting beside him in their favorite spot beneath the big oak tree as the twins played.

Dawn pointed.

Cree followed her finger to Ina, talking with one of his warriors who seemed as mesmerized with her as Beast was with Lizbeth.

"See to your duties, Reed," Cree called out sharply and the warrior bobbed his head and walked off without a word to Ina.

Ina turned away as well and joined Nell where she stood not far from Lizbeth.

"Ina went in the woods?" Cree asked, turning to his wife.

Dawn nodded and pointed again.

Cree did not have to look where she pointed. "Reed took her."

Dawn nodded and smiled.

"I do not need my warrior distracted," Cree complained.

Dawn continued smiling and patted her chest.

Cree kept his voice low. "It is not the heart he thinks with."

Dawn's silent laugh shook her chest.

"Reed will not find it humorous when he feels the consequences of not tending to his duty. Now, wife, tell me how Lila does."

Dawn answered with a huge smile.

"She heals well. I am glad to hear that," Cree said pleased, his wife's worry having been apparent with the many times she had gone to Lila's cottage to see how she felt and if she needed anything.

Dawn patted her chest, nodding, letting him know how much she was relieved that her friend did well.

"How was your visit with the wounded man? Were you able to learn anything from him."

Dawn looked around for something to write with, forever grateful to her mum for having taught her. She reached for a twig and cleared a small area of earth to write.

"Rutland," Cree said. "That is his name?"

Dawn nodded, then brushed his name away and wrote, *Lara*, then shook her head.

"He did not know Lara?"

She shook her head again.

"He could be lying," Cree suggested.

Dawn scrunched her face slightly as if thinking over his words, then shook her head.

"You do not believe so?"

She gave another shake of her head and shrugged.

"A good question. Why lie now when he is dying?"

Dawn walked her fingers, then tapped her side, and wrote… robbers.

"He was stabbed by robbers while on the road?"

Dawn nodded.

Cree thought a minute. "It might not have been robbers. Macardle could have sent someone to kill him to keep him silent."

Dawn agreed with a nod.

A wail brought Cree and Dawn quickly to their feet to find their daughter crying and Beast looking on helpless.

"Beast shook," Valan said, going to his sister and picking up one of the flowers, that had gone flying off Beast when he shook his entire body, and handed it to her.

She took it and continued to cry.

Cree went to his daughter and scooped her up in his arm and wiped at her tears. "Beast was very patient with you, Lizbeth. You cannot expect him to sit still that long."

She sniffled back her tears. "No more flowers."

"You still have flowers. You only need to pick them up just as your brother did."

"I will pick you more," Ina offered.

"I go too," Lizbeth said with a cheerful smile.

"No," Cree said firmly. "You have enough flowers for today."

"More," Lizbeth said, then kissed her da's cheek.

"Another day," Cree said firmly and placed her on the ground. "Now pick up your flowers."

Cree was pleased to see his son help his sister and before returning to his wife, he gave Beast a pat on the head, wanting him to know he had done nothing wrong. "Good job, Beast."

That had his daughter hurrying to the dog and hugging him tight.

"Love you," she said and kissed the top of his snout.

The dog licked her face and Lizbeth giggled, then returned to the task of gathering her flowers.

Cree joined his wife where she sat and she rested her shoulder to his and smiled.

"Finally, our daughter listens without debating the matter," he said with a chuckle.

Dawn's smile grew, finding the humor in it as well.

Cree took his wife in his arms and settled back against the tree to watch the twins work together picking up the flowers. He was content and glad for this time spent with his family.

He was not, however, glad to see Tarass approach, his face pinched with annoyance.

Cree raised his hand when Tarass went to speak after stopping in front of him. The man was not pleased, his annoyance turning to anger.

"Is this something that should be discussed in front of my family?" Cree asked.

"It would need not be if you had informed me that it was Macardle who had your wife abducted."

"That does not concern you," Cree said, getting to his feet.

"It most certainly does. No doubt you will punish him severely and I need to know if you intend to take his land in retribution."

Cree walked away from his family, forcing Tarass to follow. He would not discuss this in front of others and certainly not in front of the twins.

"That would depend on if Angus Macardle was aware and approved of his nephew James Macardle having my wife abducted," Cree said once they were a distance away.

"I wonder if Angus even knows what James does," Tarass said.

"What do you mean?"

"After returning home and learning of the land dispute, I went to see Angus Macardle to settle it. I never got to meet with him. James gave the excuse that he was not feeling well. I attempted two more times to speak with Angus and twice it was James who met with me. I began to wonder if he was holding the old man prisoner."

"What of his daughters? Would they not speak up in defense of their father?"

"They continue to recover from the fire that ravaged part of the keep and surrounding buildings and left Angus's wife dead and several in the clan injured, including his daughters."

"James made no mention of this when he spoke with me," Cree said.

"Which is suspicious in itself," Tarass suggested. "From what I have learned, since few of the Clan Macardle will speak about it, six or more months ago fire ravaged the Macardle keep. Now think about it. Life was lost, injures suffered, and suddenly a nephew arrives and takes command of the clan."

"That does seem suspicious," Cree agreed.

"And I believe that there is more to that land dispute than James says. The piece of land is not that large, not at all vital, so why does he so desperately claim it belongs to the Clan Macardle? And now the abduction of your wife. What is James Macardle up to?"

Cree was suspicious at heart. He had learned to be from the endless years of lies and deceit from those who had hired him and his warriors to fight for them. It was the reason he had demanded payment before he agreed to battle for anyone and because of his fierce, unconquerable reputation he had gotten what he demanded and he gave what they expected in return... victory.

He had hoped that was all behind him now, that he was settled, but once again he found himself faced with lies and deceit. The question was who was the most deceitful?

"James Macardle will tell me the truth, of that there is no doubt," Cree said.

"I want to be there when you speak—" Tarass stopped as soon as Cree turned a scowl on him that would drop most men to their knees in fright. He, however, was not most men, though he was a man who respected Cree. "I would appreciate it if I could be present when you speak with James Macardle. It could help settle the stirring unrest in my area."

"I will think on it," Cree said and he thought it wise of Tarass to say no more on it.

"My lord," Sloan called out as he approached.

Cree and Tarass both turned.

Sloan looked to Cree, ignoring Tarass. "Our warriors have returned with Gillie and Bram."

Chapter Twenty-nine

Cree went to his wife and reached down to take her by the arm and help her to her feet. "Gillie and Bram have arrived. I will speak with them and tell you what they say."

Dawn nodded, aware that it would not be a pleasant sight to witness her husband speak to the two men and he wanted to spare her from seeing it. She gestured, pointing to the twins and resting her joined hands to her cheek.

"You are going to take the twins in for their nap," he said.

She nodded again, then mouthed, *Lila*.

"Take Beast with you when you go see Lila," Cree ordered.

Dawn nodded once again and gave him a quick kiss.

Cree hooked his arm around her waist before she could step away and whispered playfully, "You forever tempt me with your teasing kisses.

Dawn chuckled silently, then leaned close, so no one could see what she was doing, and ran her finger slowly around her moist lips before slipping it inside her mouth to suckle on it for a moment, then slowly removed it, and mouthed, *later*.

"Damn it, wife," he grumbled beneath his breath, trying hard to control his rising arousal and trying even harder to keep the image of what she intended out of his thoughts. Though, now he had even more reason to beat the two men senseless, since they were keeping him from enjoying a pleasant romp in bed with his wife.

Cree walked off still grumbling beneath his breath.

Tarass joined him, keeping step beside him.

"You will say not a word to either one of them until I am done with them," Cree ordered, knowing without saying what Tarass wanted.

"I fear that when you are done with them neither one of them will be able to utter a word," Tarass said.

"Would it not be the same if it were your wife?"

"I do not seek a marriage born of love. Love gets in the way of things. I would, however, see the men suffer for daring to touch what belonged to me."

Cree turned a grin on the man. "I thought that way once about a wife." He laughed. "Fate had a different idea… she sent me Dawn."

"Fate does not rule me."

Cree laughed again. "Much luck with that."

"Let me speak to Gillie first, then do what you want with them," Tarass said annoyed.

"Do not take long," Cree ordered.

Tarass nodded. "I will be brief."

Cree saw that Bram had barely recovered from the beating he had given him and the other man, Gillie, had a few bruises on his face as well, no doubt from his attempt to avoid Cree's warriors.

"I found him for you, that has to mean something," Bram said as soon as he spotted Cree.

"Traitor," Gillie spat, then his eyes looked as if they bulged from his head when he spotted Tarass.

"I paid you good coin for information, do you have it?" Tarass demanded of Gillie.

Gillie shook his head. "No one would speak his name let alone speak of him."

"That is not what I asked. Do you have what I seek?" Tarass snapped.

"Given more time, I could find him for you," Gillie said, hope heavy in his voice that this man could help free him.

"You found nothing?" Tarass asked curtly.

"I heard one thing, but it cannot be true," Gillie offered, again hoping it would spare him.

"Tell me," Tarass ordered impatiently.

"Someone said that the thief Slatter had been taken prisoner and was not there long when a fellow prisoner broke them free of their chains, not that that is possible. No man can break free of iron chains," Gillie said.

"Where is it that he supposedly broke free of these chains and who is Slatter?"

Gillie shook his head.

"I do not know where it was he was imprisoned."

"You did not ask?" Tarass accused.

"I did not believe the one who told me."

"Who told you?" Tarass demanded.

"A man not to be believed, a beggar who wanted coin."

"Who is this Slatter and where can I find him?"

"He is a sly one, able to talk his way out of anything. He charms men out of their coins and women out of their garments. I was surprised to hear he had been caught."

"Where can I find him?" Tarass demanded.

"No one finds him. He finds them, which is why I question if it was really Slatter who had been caught."

"Enough," Cree ordered. "Your time is done with him."

"No. No." Gillie begged. "I can still help."

"Not any longer," Cree said and he was glad that Tarass stepped aside, though he did not take his leave.

"I got Gillie for you, my lord, please have mercy on me," Bram begged.

"I will have mercy on you," Cree said. "You will have a swift death."

"No, please, my lord, I beg you," Bram said, starting to cry.

"Tell me how you know Lara?" Cree demanded.

"Lara?" Gillie asked as if he did not know the name.

Bram sniffed back his tears. "The woman who helped us."

"Why did Lara help you?" Cree asked.

"That woman?" Gillie said and looked at Cree. "Why ask us how we know her when you can ask her yourself?"

Cree walked over to the man and delivered a punch to his jaw that flung his head back against the post knocking him out.

Bram was quick to talk, all too familiar with Cree's devastating punches, his broken nose a mess and still painful. "We spotted her in the woods talking with a man. He sweet talked her, promised her all sorts of things as he encouraged her to tell him about her work with the healer and if she tended any of the travelers that stopped here. I got the feeling he was looking for someone."

"Lara did not help you plan my wife's abduction?" Cree asked.

Bram shook his head. "No. We did not know how we would capture your wife. We were waiting, trying to come up with a plan. Then one day Gillie got an idea. He figured we could threaten her that we would tell you that she was meeting someone secretly and supplying information to the man about the clan and you. Gillie figured, she would get frightened, knowing harsh punishment awaited her, and she would do as we asked. And he was right, she did and without so much as an argument."

"I told you love got in the way of things," Tarass said from behind him.

Cree paid Tarass no heed. "Were you not concerned Lara would tell this man and he would come after you?"

Bram shook his head. "Gillie heard him tell her that he had to go away for a few days, no more than week, then he would be back for her and they would go off together. Me and Gillie knew he was never coming back, but she believed him."

Cree stepped forward. "You could not tell me this the last time I asked you?"

Bram realized his mistake too late and he cringed as Cree's fist came swinging at him, connecting with his nose once more.

Gillie had come around, after two buckets of water had been thrown in his face.

Cree nodded to his warrior standing by the man and the warrior yanked the man's head back.

"Who hired you?" Cree asked, walking over to stand in front of Gillie, his cheek and jaw already bruising and his lips split.

Gillie did not hesitate. "Rutland. Mad as hell we failed."

"Who hired him?" Cree demanded.

"He never said and it was no concern of mine," Gillie said.

"Which one of you intended to force himself on my wife?" Cree asked.

"Bram," Gillie shouted.

Bram, dazed and bleeding, did not understand what was said.

"You do realize my wife will confirm or deny what you say," Cree said.

Gillie went ghostly pale.

"That is what I thought," Cree said and walked over to Bram. "Your fate is in my wife's hands since you warned Gillie against touching her. She will decide if she wants you dead or not."

Bram just stared, still not comprehending what was happening.

"And me," Gillie asked fearfully.

"You die, after you suffer," Cree said and went to walk away.

"I know more than Bram," Gillie said. "Spare me and I will tell you."

"You will tell me regardless if I spare you," Cree said.

Gillie realized what he meant. "Please, my lord, please, I beg of you, do not torture me."

"What is it you know that Bram does not?"

***

Dawn was relieved to see Lila looking better than when she had visited her earlier in the morning and she let her know.

Lila smiled and hugged the tankard of chamomile that Dawn had brewed for her. "I know, Paul says the same, and I feel my old self. I want to get back to doing all the things I do, but Elsa says I should take it slow since I am with child. She also told me that the bump and cut to my head was not as bad as hers." Her smile waned. "I cannot help but wonder who would do this awful thing. I know Elsa was assaulted so that the person could kill Ann, but why did someone come after me? And do I now need to worry it will happen again?"

Dawn reached her hand out to lay on Lila's arm as she shook her head.

"How can you be sure someone will not come after me?"

Dawn patted her chest, pointed to Lila, tugged at her ear, then shook her head.

"You think I was not supposed to hear whoever it was I heard talking and that was why I was hit on the head?"

Dawn nodded, pointed to her eyes and her body sagged in a sigh, as if relieved.

"I agree that it is good I did not see anything or I probably would not be sitting here talking with you," Lila said, tears springing to her eyes. "And I am glad to have a friend who would come to my rescue even at her own peril."

Dawn got teary-eyed herself and pointed to Lila, then patted her own chest.

"Aye, I would do the same for you."

The two women locked hands and let a couple of tears fall.

"Enough of this," Lila said, brushing away the last of her tears. "Tell me what I have missed since being stuck in here."

Dawn was about to gesture when there was a rap at the door and Lucerne entered.

"I am sorry to disturb, but would you have some time to sit with Rutland while Elsa sees to someone that I do not have the skills to tend, though she requires my help?"

Dawn nodded and after giving Lila a hug and promising to return later, Dawn followed Lucerne out of the cottage. Beast stretched his way up on his paws and went to walk at Dawn's side.

"Elsa waits for you," Lucerne said.

Dawn nodded and the two women went in separate directions, Dawn taking a quick pace to the healing cottage.

"I beg your pardon, my lady."

Dawn stopped and turned and was surprised to see a clergyman, though she was more surprised when Beast jumped in front her to snarl at him.

The clergyman took a hasty step back. "I mean you no harm."

Two of Cree's warriors appeared out of nowhere, taking a stance beside her.

The clergyman removed his hands, buried in his sleeves, and held them up. "I mean her no harm. I only wanted to let her know that I am here and pleased to offer help to anyone who might be in need."

Dawn tilted her head slightly, not able to get a clear look of the clergyman's face, the hood of his robe almost covering his eyes. It was as if he tried to hide and she wondered if Beast had also sensed that and was the reason for his snarl.

Curious, Dawn pointed to his hood and motioned pushing it back.

"Remove your hood," one warrior ordered, making it clear to the clergyman is was not a request.

"As you wish," the clergyman said, raising his hand to push his hood off his head.

Dawn caught a quick glance of his red, swollen knuckles on his right hand and thought it odd that a man of the cloth would raise his hand against another. She was also surprised by his fine features, they captivated along with his intense dark eyes that once focused on refused to let go.

"I only wish to help however I can," the clergyman said.

He seemed insistent on helping and that had her recalling what Cree had told her of the two clergymen who had stopped for a night or two of shelter, the older of the pair needing rest. He had shared his opinion on the other of the two, believing the man was not truly a clergyman. She could see now why he had thought that. The clergyman's bruised hand alone spoke otherwise.

Dawn pointed to him, then tapped her lips, and pointed to him again.

The one warrior interpreted. "Lady Dawn will summon you if needed."

Dawn grew more surprised by the day with how many of her clan understood her gestures and she turned a smile and a nod of appreciation on the warrior.

"You carry your heavy burden well," the clergyman said. "I am here, if you wish to seek counsel."

Dawn nodded, his dark eyes might be intense, but his voice was soothing, understanding, almost mesmerizing. He would be a man easy to talk with and one who could easily manipulate.

"How does the wounded man do?" the clergyman asked as Dawn turned to walk away.

One of the warriors spoke up. "You have taken enough of Lady Dawn's time, clergyman, be on your way."

Dawn was glad the warrior sent the clergyman on his way. She had to get to the healing cottage so Elsa could take her leave and she also had no wont to continue to speak with him. Her husband was right. There was something about the clergyman that did not ring true.

***

Cree glared at Gillie. "I am waiting to hear what you know that Bram does not."

"Your wife was to be returned to you unharmed," Gillie said.

Cree's scowl deepened. "Yet you intended to force yourself on her."

"Lies. He always lies," Bram said, his head clearing.

"I am not lying. Rutland told me he would give me extra if I delivered her unharmed," Gillie said.

"Then why did you talk all the time about poking her?" Bram asked. "That was constantly on your mind and tongue."

"There is no harm in a poke. She would have been delivered without a bruise or mark on her," Gillie said. "Rutland would have never known."

"She would have told him," Bram said.

"She is a dumb one. She cannot speak and who would believe her anyway?"

"I would."

Both men looked to Cree, Gillie's eyes going wide when he saw Cree's face twisted with rage.

"You tricked me into saying that, Bram," Gillie accused

"You did that yourself since you never mind your tongue," Bram said, wincing when he tried to smile.

"You wanted to poke her too," Gillie accused again.

"Lady Dawn can say who speaks the truth," Bram said.

"Rutland is here as well," Cree said.

Gillie once again did not mind his tongue. "You lie. He is dead."

"Not yet, but he will be soon, I assume thanks to you," Cree said.

Gillie was quick to point the finger elsewhere. "I did not stab Rutland, that was Bertie's doing. She got mad that I failed to deliver your wife to him and refused to give me some of the coin he had already been paid. Bertie sent her two sons to get it from him. They told Bertie they left him for dead and took what coin he had, though it was far less than expected."

"Have you told me all now?" Cree asked, closing his hand in a tight fist.

"I would not have harmed your wife. I wanted the extra coin," Gillie said, his voice trembling with fear.

"But you would have poked her," Cree said, his fingers digging into the palm of his hand as he squeezed his fist ever tighter.

"I would not have harmed her," Gillie said again as if it would make a difference.

"But you did harm her and you harmed me when you took her from me." Cree stepped closer to Gillie. "And that you even thought of touching my wife…" His nostrils flared, anger consuming him like hungry flames devouring a dry log. "You will suffer for it, then you will die… slowly."

Gillie went to speak, but Cree's fist crashed into his mouth, knocking several teeth out and shattering his jaw.

Chapter Thirty

"He asked for a clergyman," Elsa said when Dawn entered the cottage. "I will have the clergyman who stopped here brought to him. He does not have long."

Dawn nodded and felt a slight shiver run through her. There was just something about the clergyman that did not set right with her. Or perhaps she felt suspicious of everyone who was not familiar to her. While she had known Lara, it had been more an acquaintance than a friendship. She had thought on that during her time away. Lara had been friendlier than usual that fateful day and Dawn had thought nothing of it and had gone willingly with her when she had claimed to have known where a batch of young nettles grew abundantly.

It had been as if Lara had walked her into a never-ending nightmare. She had grabbed Dawn's shawl and walked away. Not once did she look back after leaving Dawn struggling against the two men who had jumped out of the bushes and grabbed her. She had said nothing to Dawn, nothing to the two men. She had simply turned and walked away, not caring what happened.

Dawn shivered again, the memories still vivid as well as the fear. It had gripped and twisted at her and it had been made worse by not being able to scream out for help.

The thought of being left that vulnerable again had her suddenly feeling trapped as she had that day and she rushed to the door. She stopped abruptly once outside, taking a deep breath.

Beast sprang to his feet, ready to defend and protect her, and hurried to her side.

Dawn dropped down beside him and rushed her arms around his neck in a tight hug, burying her face in his fur for a few moments, cherishing the calm and comfort it brought her, then kissing him atop his snout.

She would have never made it home if it had not been for Beast. She had come to depend on the animal and to love him more each day. She did not know what she would do without him, especially at a time like this when she was feeling far too vulnerable, and Cree was not beside her. She knew it would take time to regain that sense of safety and security she had had before her abduction as would Cree. Time would heal them both and Beast would be there to help her.

"My lady."

Dawn turned to see Ina walking toward her, clutching her stomach and Dawn went to her, concerned.

"I fear whatever ails my stomach has not left me and it is not fair to leave all the work to Nell. Bartha enjoys tending the twins and says she will help until I am well enough to return, if that is all right with you, my lady?"

Dawn nodded, agreeing and thinking how excited Valan would be since Bartha loved to help him set up battle scenes with his wooden figures and then do battle.

Dawn hoped Ina understood when she gestured that she would send Elsa to tend her as soon as she was available.

"Elsa is busy and I have some of the brew left you gave me. I will take it and rest as instructed," Ina said, wincing in pain.

Dawn shooed her away to get rest.

"Thank you, my lady," Ina said with a bob of her head and turned to walk away.

Dawn saw the clergyman approach, his hood up on his head, but not covering his face as it did before. His expression was stern, his jaw set tight, his brow scrunched, and his arms were crossed in front of him, his hands disappearing into his wide sleeves.

A pious man, it would seem, but one she felt was hiding something.

Ina steps suddenly faltered and the clergyman hurried to steady her. They exchanged some words and he nodded before releasing her, though his hand did not let go until he was sure she was steady on her feet.

"I am here to administer to the dying man," the clergyman said as he came to a stop in front of Dawn.

Beast remained close at her side as she entered the cottage after the clergyman and stood aside while he sat in the chair beside the bed and spoke quietly with Rutland.

She could not make out Rutland's mumbles, though she did hear when his voice grew agitated and the clergyman responded in a soothing tone.

It had been some time since she had heard Latin spoken, her mum having taught her and having spoken it with her frequently so that she would remember it. While the clergyman kept his voice to a soft whisper, she caught a few words now and again.

It was not long before Rutland took his last breath and the clergyman leaned over him, his hand blessing him, his lasts words barely a whisper.

"*Et putredo in infernum.*"

Dawn scrunched her brow, questioning what she heard. Had she misunderstood the clergyman? Had she heard it wrong? She had to have misunderstood. Why would a clergyman pray for the dead man to *rot in hell*?

***

Cree washed the blood off his bruised hands, wanting them to look as presentable as possible when he saw his wife. He could already see her eyes light with worry for him and he did not want her to concern herself with something so minor. Besides, it had felt great to punch the two bastards that had abducted her. He would feel even better when he sent warriors to deal with Bertie and her sons. She was as guilty as Gillie and just as greedy, having known about it and going after Rutland. It was because of her and her sons that Cree was not able to learn more from Rutland. And he doubted James Macardle would be forthcoming with the truth, but he would get it from him one way or the other.

"They remain tied to the posts until I say otherwise and see that there are sufficient guards around them at all times," Cree ordered Sloan as he dried his hands on a cloth.

"As you say," Sloan said, having already anticipated his orders and set them in motion.

"I will speak with Rutland. Fear of eternal flames eating away at the flesh, often have men speaking the truth on their deathbed."

"Then you best hurry. Elsa sent word that Rutland does not have long and has asked for a clergyman."

***

"He is at peace now," the clergyman said.

Dawn nodded and was about to point to the door for him to take his leave, when he bobbed his head and hurried out the door without saying another word. And when she stepped outside the cottage, she was surprised to see that the clergyman was nowhere to be seen.

"Is he dead?"

Dawn turned with a soft smile, pleased to see her husband and nodded.

"Did Rutland say anything before he died?" Cree asked, his arm going around her waist.

Dawn instinctively went into the crook of his arm. It was as if after being separated for even a short time, more so

312

since her abduction, they needed to reunite, join close, be as one.

Dawn gestured with one hand as if pulling a hood over her head and slipping her hand in her sleeve.

"He spoke to the clergyman," Cree said.

Dawn nodded and pointed in the distance, letting him know the man had taken his leave. Then she took his hand and went to a spot of clear earth, picking up a small rock and using it to write in the dirt.

"Latin," Cree read before she even finished the word. "He spoke Latin to Rutland."

She nodded, brushed the word away with her foot and wrote again.

"Rot in hell?" Cree asked. "I had forgotten you know Latin, French as well, if I recall correctly."

She confirmed with a nod.

"Are you sure you heard him correctly?"

Dawn nodded and shrugged.

"Not completely sure," Cree said.

Dawn nodded again.

Cree signaled to one of his warriors. "Go get the clergyman who was just here and bring him to me."

"Aye, my lord," the warrior said and hurried off.

"See to moving the body," Cree ordered two other warriors.

Cree slipped his arm around his wife's waist once again, eager to hold her close. "We will go to my solar and I will tell you what Gillie and Bram had to say."

They had taken only one step when one of the warriors rushed out of the cottage.

"He is not dead!"

Cree and Dawn hurried into the cottage, Beast following them.

Cree went to the bed and leaned down. The man's breathing was short and rapid, and he struggled to speak.

"Cur..sed.."

"Who cursed you?" Cree asked, realizing his wife had interpreted the Latin correctly. "Who cursed you to rot in hell?"

Rutland continued to struggle to breath and speak. "Pra..y."

"Tell me who cursed you and you have my word I will pray for your retched soul," Cree said.

"Slat..t…"

"Slatter?" Cree asked, recalling the name of the thief Gillie had mentioned. "What did he want from you?"

The man gave a brief nod, confirming it was Slatter. "Search…"

"Search for what?" Cree asked, but saw the man barely had any strength left to speak

"Pra…" Rutland barely managed to say.

An honorable man never gave his word falsely so Cree gave what he had promised. "May you find forgiveness where you go, for you will get no forgiveness on this earth."

Rutland could say no more, his breathing low, and while he took his last breath, Cree turned away from him, and spoke to one of his warriors.

"Make sure the clergyman who was here a short time ago and the one who travels with him are found and brought to me." Cree turned to another warrior who stood near the end of the bed. "Have Elsa confirm he is dead, then take him and see him prepared for burial."

Cree took Dawn by the arm and guided her out of the cottage, Beast staying close to her.

"I have to see to this Slatter who is posing as a clergyman," Cree said once outside. "Gillie mentioned him. He is a thief, sly from what Gillie says. I need to find out what he is doing here and what he wanted from Rutland."

Dawn tapped her chest and shrugged.

"Gillie made no mention of him being part of your abduction and with what the man suffered, I do not think he would have kept that from me."

Dawn took hold of his one hand, careful not to touch his red and swollen knuckles, though she did place a tender kiss on the bruise.

"It was worth it," Cree said, "and I am not finished with him yet. We will discuss their fate later."

Dawn was not surprised that her husband would consult her on what was to be done to her abductors. After all, she had been the one to suffer at their hands, but in the end the decision would be her husband's and she was good with that.

Cree slipped his hand out of hers and placed it on his wife's soft cheek to cup her chin. "This will all be done soon. With what Rutland, Gillie, and Bram told me and having sent word for James Macardle to be brought here, we will have heard from all those involved with your abduction and I will make certain that every one of them suffers the consequences."

Dawn turned her head and kissed his palm, closing her eyes briefly to linger in his gentle strength.

"I look forward to our time alone, wife," he whispered and nuzzled her neck, pleased to see a smile creep along her face.

Dawn took hold of his arm as he turned to walk away.

"What is it?" Cree asked, turning back to face her.

She scrunched her brow and shrugged as she mouthed *Lara*, then *Ann*.

"Are you asking me who killed the two women?"

She nodded.

"That, wife, remains a puzzle."

315

Chapter Thirty-one

A chilled rain had started falling, sending most people scurrying for shelter. Weather was unpredictable in the Highlands, sun one minute, rain the next, or endless clouds and a sudden chill even in the summer.

Cree stomped through the village and wondered if it had been the rain or his frightening scowl that had chased everyone. It was evening and the two clergymen had yet to be found. His warriors had searched the entire village, then extended their search into the woods. Tarass and his warriors had even joined in the hunt once he had found out that the clergyman was actually the man called Slatter that Gillie had mentioned. He hoped once caught, this Slatter could provide information about the man Ruddock he searched for.

It was as if the two men had suddenly disappeared. No one had seen them leave. No one had spoken to them and how was it that the older clergyman could take his leave when he was so worn out? Or had he been? Had it been a ruse to seek shelter here? If so why? What was the man searching for? And did it have anything to do with his wife's abduction?

Cree spotted Sloan hurrying toward him and he hoped he brought good news with him.

"Tell me the clergymen have been found," Cree said.

Sloan shook his head. "Not yet, but I just received word that James Macardle will arrive tomorrow."

"How can that be? The messenger has not had time to reach Tannin yet."

Sloan grinned. "The messenger met Tannin and Macardle on his way to see them. It seems James Macardle is eager to speak with you. And with the Lord of Fire's return Tannin concluded that it was best he returned and spoke with you as well."

"Macardle has much to account for."

"It is his word against a dead man's word," Sloan said. "It will not be easy to prove Macardle had anything to do with it. And he is a titled man. You cannot tie him to a post and beat it out of him."

"True," Cree said, "but there are other ways to get what I want from him."

A warrior came rushing at Cree and Sloan. "We got them, my lord. We got the clergymen. Henry picked up their tracks and led us right to them. They will arrive in the village shortly."

"Good work," Cree said, "The warriors will eat extra well tonight."

The warrior's face lit with glee, knowing Turbett would be instructed to prepare a special meal for them.

"We are grateful, my lord," the warrior said with a bob of his head.

"Have the clergymen brought to my solar," Cree instructed to the surprise of Sloan and the warrior.

"Why your solar?" Sloan asked once the warrior left them.

"I will treat them with respect until they give me reason not to."

Sloan grinned. "You are giving them time for their lies to reveal themselves."

"They will dig their own graves."

Both men turned at the sound of the keep door opening.

Dawn smiled at both men as she tugged her shawl around her and approached them.

"Where are you off to on this chilly evening?" Cree asked, thinking Beast should be with her, then realizing he would be with the twins now.

317

She pointed at him.

"You came looking for me," Cree said.

She nodded and slipped into his arm that reached out to welcome her.

"I will see you shortly, my lord," Sloan said and, with a nod to both Cree and Dawn, took his leave.

Dawn turned a questioning glance on her husband.

"The two clergymen have been found and will arrive here shortly," Cree explained.

Dawn smiled to show how pleased the news made her. She tapped her chest, then his, pointed to her lips and held up two fingers.

"You want to be with me when I speak with them?"

She nodded.

"Is that a request or a demand?" he asked.

Dawn could hear the teasing in his voice. She softened her smile before mouthing... *hope*.

He had had no intentions of denying her, but that she should offer a silent plea of hope had him lowering his brow to rest on hers and admitting, "You tug at my heart far too often, wife."

Her smile grew and she pressed her cheek to his, then kissed his lips ever so gently.

"There you go tempting me again with those demanding kisses."

She laughed, the slight shake of her body the only evidence of it.

He kissed her just as gently and briefly. "You have no idea how much your innocent kisses arouse me."

She brushed her lips over his in a feather-light kiss, then tapped her chest.

"Now that I know they arouse you as well, I will kiss you that way more often."

Dawn hurried to draw a cross over her heart with her finger.

"Aye, wife, I promise," Cree said with a tender laugh before he kissed her again, though not as lightly as before.

They entered the keep together. Once in the Great Hall, Cree called for warm brews to be brought to his solar.

Cree saw that his wife was settled in a chair near the fire and a hot brew placed on the small table beside her. He was telling her about James Macardle's arrival tomorrow when there was a rap at the door.

The two clergymen were escorted into the room by two warriors and Sloan. When the door closed behind the two warriors, the younger clergyman spoke.

"Why were we forced to return here, my lord? We have duties to see to."

"I have a few questions for you," Cree said and pointed to two chairs. "Sit."

The commanding tone let it be known that it was not a request.

Both clergymen nodded and sat, though the younger of the two kept poised on the edge of his chair, appearing ready to take his leave or run if necessary.

Cree looked to the older clergyman. He had never gotten a good look at him. His short hair was completely white, pure white like the stark white clouds. He had multiple lines and wrinkles, though they did not distract from his fine features. And Cree noticed that he held himself with distinct dignity, no longer slumped over like when he had first seen him.

"You are feeling better?" he asked the man.

"Aye, my lord, thanks to your generosity," the man said with a nod.

Cree turned to the other clergyman. "It was good of you to ease the wounded man's suffering as he took his last breath."

"It is what we do, my lord," the younger clergyman said.

"Did the man say anything to you before he died?" Cree asked.

The clergyman shook his head vehemently. "It is forbidden to reveal anything that is confessed."

"I did not ask you to reveal a confession. I asked if the man said anything to you," Cree said and saw the man tense, his shoulders drawing back defensively.

"He wanted absolution and I gave it to him."

"You blessed his soul," Cree said.

"Aye, my lord, I sent his soul where it belonged."

"To rot in hell, Slatter?" Cree asked and watched the man change before his eyes.

His head went up straight, his shoulder drew back even more, his chest broadened, and he removed his hands from his sleeves.

He looked to Dawn and grinned. "You know Latin."

"You will address me, not my wife," Cree ordered.

"You know who I am," Slatter said and went to stand.

"Do not dare get out of that chair," Cree warned and took a step closer to him. "What role did you play in my wife's abduction?"

"Abduction? I had nothing to do with any abduction," Slatter said as if affronted to be accused of such a crime. "Rutland had information I needed, nothing more."

"What information?" Cree demanded.

Slatter shook his head. "That is not your concern."

"Everything here is my concern!" Cree all but bellowed, causing the older man to jump. "Is it the same information you wanted Lara to get you? Is that why you returned here and killed her?"

Slatter once again looked ready to pound out of the chair, but a sudden, sharp rap at the door interrupted his response, then the door flew open.

"I gave you no permission to enter, Tarass?" Cree snapped.

"I heard you had Slatter here. I need to speak with him."

"Take your leave and wait until I summon you or I will deny you time with him," Cree ordered.

Tarass looked ready to argue, clamping his lips shut for a moment to get control of his tongue. "I will wait outside the door."

"You will wait in the Great Hall," Cree commanded.

Sloan went to the door and instructed one of the two warriors stationed outside it to escort Tarass to the Great Hall.

"I do not know that man," Slatter said.

"That matters not to me," Cree said. "I want the truth and I want it now."

"The truth is I know nothing about your wife's abduction or this Lara you mentioned."

"I have two men who say differently about Lara and how you enticed her to do your bidding and get information you wanted. Now she is dead."

"Not by my hand," Slatter insisted with a firm shake of his head.

"We will see who tells the truth," Cree said and turned to his wife. "Wait here."

She nodded.

Cree looked to the two men. "Follow me."

Sloan followed behind the two men and the two warriors followed behind him until they left the keep, then they walked alongside either of the two prisoners.

Tarass wasted no time in tailing the group.

"Rouse them," Cree ordered the warriors who stood guard over Gillie and Bram.

It took a few moments for the two men to gather their wit and focus after having water thrown in their faces.

Gillie was the first one to call out, wincing with every word, his face a bloody mess. "That is him. That is the man who met with the woman in the woods."

321

Bram nodded. "Gillie's right. That is him, but he was not wearing the robe of a clergyman."

"What do you have to say now, Slatter?" Cree asked.

"You caught me," Slatter said with an indifferent shrug. "What is there for me to say."

"I beg mercy, my lord," the white-haired man said, his hands clenched together begging. "I had no part in this. He demanded I repay him for saving my life from robbers."

"You are a sniveling coward, Newlin."

Newlin continued to beg. "Truly, my lord, I harmed none and I know nothing of this woman called Lara."

"What of my wife's abduction? Do you know if he had any part in that?"

"I told you he had no hand in that," Gillie said.

"Do you want to feel my fist again?" Cree asked, turning a fierce scowl on him.

"No, I beg you, my lord. No."

"Then hold your tongue unless spoken to," Cree warned.

Gillie clamped his swollen mouth shut with a wince and a nod.

Cree looked to Newlin.

"He spoke of no abduction to me, my lord."

"How long have you been with him?"

"Two weeks now, and hopefully by your mercy I will be free of him. I have a sister who offered to take me in. I am not well and she will look after me. I was on my way there when our paths crossed."

Cree signaled one of his warriors. "Take him to the Great Hall to wait and do not leave his side."

"I am most grateful, my lord," Newlin said and before leaving, turned to Slatter and spat at him. "You lying bastard. Now you will get what you deserve."

"And so will you," Slatter said in warning.

"Secure his wrists," Cree ordered and once done turned to Tarass. "Ask what you will of him."

"What do you know of a man called Ruddock?"

"I know no such man," Slatter said.

"You are lying?" Tarass said.

Slatter shrugged. "Believe what you will. I care not."

"From what I have learned you were imprisoned with him."

Slatter remained silent.

"Do you owe him something that you protect him?" Tarass demanded.

Slatter continued to remain silent.

"What price to tell me where he is?"

"Now you have my attention, though where will I spend my newfound wealth when I am kept prisoner here?" Slatter asked and looked to Cree. "And for what? Having some fun with a woman?"

"Gillie says you were looking for someone," Cree said.

"I was playing with her, bringing some excitement to her dull existence until the person I waited for arrived and I took my leave."

Cree turned to Gillie again. "Did you see him with anyone besides Lara?"

Gillie shook his head, but Bram spoke up.

"I caught sight of a cloaked figure in the woods one day."

"Who did you speak with?" Cree asked.

"It had to have been Lara since I spoke to no one else," Slatter insisted.

"What about the person you waited for?" Cree asked.

"We took our leave immediately and neither of us wore cloaks. We were eager to be on our way." Slatter shook his head and sighed. "Really, my lord, I happened upon an imminent abduction I had no part of and cared nothing about. I had important matters to deal with elsewhere and did not want to linger. Lara was nothing more than a simple distraction and I wished her no harm."

"Then why did you return here?" Cree asked.

"Rutland's tracks lead me here."

"As you said before, he had information you wanted. Do not bother to tell me again that it is none of my concern, for I have yet to decide what to do with you," Cree warned.

"Rutland was a wealth of information... for a price. Always for a price."

Cree crossed his arms over his chest and glared at him when Slatter grew quiet, saying not a word, just waiting.

"I had heard that someone had set a price on my head and I wanted to know who since I could find out nothing about it," Slatter informed him reluctantly.

"Did Rutland know?"

Slatter shook his head. "He found nothing. There is no price on my head. It was a rumor set by someone who believed I wronged him."

Cree could not be sure if Slatter was telling the truth, but he planned to eventually find out.

He ordered his warriors to secure him in one of the huts and to keep two guards on him at all times.

"I have done nothing wrong that you should keep me prisoner," Slatter protested.

"You will be judged in due time," Cree said.

"For what?"

"That is what I will decide," Cree said and motioned for Slatter to be taken away.

"He lies easily," Tarass said as they walked back to the keep.

"I will get the truth from him," Cree said with strong confidence that had Tarass believing him.

**

Dawn laid in Cree's arms, listening to all he had to say. It had been a long, tiring day and tomorrow would be no different with Macardle's arrival. She was impatient for this whole matter to be settled so their days could settle as well. At least their nights had returned to normal, making love and sleeping wrapped in each other's arms.

"Slatter lies on top of lies," Cree said.

Dawn nodded, agreeing.

"He knows something, he is not saying but I do not know if it concerns your abduction, Lara, or if it is separate from everything. I do not even know if I believe Newlin, the man with him. Is he a cohort of his or an innocent victim?"

She tapped his chest and smiled.

"You believe I will find out."

She nodded, having not a doubt.

"In time perhaps, unless of course there is a price on his head. Then I may just hand him over to whoever wants him and collect the coin."

She smiled, shaking her head, then tapped her lips and pointed to him.

"You know me far too well, wife, and you are right. Until I feel he has told me all I want to know he will remain a prisoner. One thing I feel he may speak the truth about is Lara."

Dawn scrunched her brow, asking why?

"The way he spoke about her, she mattered not at all to him. He was simply having fun with her to pass the time. And if he had wanted her dead why wait? Why not take her life before he took his leave?"

Dawn mouthed, *Ann,* with a questioning tilt of her head.

"She was never mentioned, though Bram did say he spotted someone wearing a cloak in the woods. Perhaps it was Ann the day she had seen Lara and Slatter together." Cree shook his head. "I feel like a piece is missing to the puzzle. James Macardle had you abducted and we will find

325

out more about that tomorrow, though there is no excuse he can give that would make it right and keep me from punishing him. Rutland is the man he hired to do the deed and Gillie and Bram are the men Rutland hired to do the dirty deed. They in turn got Lara to help them. If what Slatter says is true, then he accidentally happened upon the impending plan and had no part in it at all. That would mean all who took part in your abduction have been accounted for. I can see someone killing Lara to keep her from saying what she knew, but why wait three months, giving her time to rethink what she had done and confess? It makes no sense. It does not seem to fit."

Dawn listened to her husband go on about it, content in his arms. The three months she had been away, she had thought of moments like this she had shared with him and missed them terribly. He would speak about matters in the clan, she would ask him questions or give her opinion, and more often than not reasonable solutions were reached.

Not so this time, though like many times before, she agreed with him on this. Something was missing that would tie it all together.

Cree suddenly rolled Dawn onto her back, leaning over her. "Enough talk, those tempting kisses of yours today have left me ravenous for you."

Dawn reached down to take hold of his manhood and see how true his claim, and her smile spread across her face.

"I will have you screaming out my name soon enough, wife. You have my word on it."

If only, she thought.

Her smiled faded slightly, but Cree noticed and brushed his lips across hers as if trying to seal what was left of it. "I hear you, Dawn. I hear it in my head just as you do." He grinned. "And it is a good thing no one else hears you, for you would bring every stone of the keep down on our heads."

326

They both laughed and as usual Cree kept his word.

Chapter Thirty-two

Cree waited on the steps of the keep, his wife beside him, as Tannin and James Macardle approached on their horses. Macardle's warriors were detained outside the village and Macardle made no objection. Cree sensed the man was here to confess. Perhaps he had learned that his plan had been exposed and he hoped to beg for Cree's forgiveness.

Macardle would be wrong to think that. Cree intended to see him suffer for what he had done.

Cree took his wife's hand and squeezed it as he turned to her. She was beautiful, standing tall and proud. She wore a soft yellow tunic, cinched at the waist with a knotted plaid belt. Stripes of the yellow cloth were wound in her long braid, her dark red hair glistening more red when the sun fell upon it. Her face was flushed from the kisses he had planted on it before they had left their bedchamber this morning and her lips were plump from his numerous kisses. This day would not be easy for her and he had wanted her to start it knowing how much she was loved.

"You are beautiful, wife," he said.

Dawn smiled, rested her hand to her chest, then to his.

"I love you too," he said and they both turned to face James Macardle.

Tannin went up the steps quickly while, James Macardle climbed the keep steps like a man with a heavy burden to carry.

"My lord," Tannin said with a bow of his head. "Macardle has something of great importance to tell you."

"We will speak later. Go and get food and drink for you and the men."

Tannin bobbed his head and went to his horse, taking the reins of Macardle's horse with him and the animal followed along peacefully.

"My solar," Cree said before Macardle could say a word.

Sloan joined them in the solar, closing the door after everyone entered and stood in front of it.

Cree offered Macardle a drink, seeing that the man could use one and he accepted without hesitation.

Macardle sat, a slump to his shoulders and his head slightly bent as he focused on the tankard of ale in his hands.

Cree stood at the end of the fireplace, near the chair where his wife sat and waited as the man took several swallows of ale. He was reminded of the men he had seen doing the same, fortifying themselves before going into a battle they feared would not be victorious.

Macardle took one last swig before he raised his head high and drew his shoulders back. "I have something to tell you and I hope you will find it in your heart to forgive."

"I am told I have no heart," Cree said.

"Then I hope you will understand."

"How could I ever understand or forgive you for having my wife abducted?" Cree said, sharp anger punctuating his every word.

"You know?" Macardle asked shocked.

"I know," Cree said, but offered no more, wanting to hear what Macardle had to say. "What I cannot understand, and doubt I ever will, is why you did it. Why have my wife abducted?" He took an abrupt step forward. "And what truly was the purpose of your first visit? Did you wish to see for yourself that your plan had failed?"

James Macardle stood, keeping his voice tempered. "I did not have your wife abducted. Angus Macardle had your wife abducted. I only found out about it."

Cree glared at him. "You blame it on your uncle?"

James Macardle's shoulders slumped once again, he shook his head slowly, and closed his eyes briefly. "There is much for me to explain."

"Then explain it," Cree said and returned to stand near his wife.

Macardle sat and took another swallow of ale, then looked to Cree. "What I say here, I ask it stay among those in this room."

"You have no room to bargain," Cree warned.

"I know, but it is something I ask anyway."

"I will decide that after I hear what you have to say," Cree said, leaving no doubt that his decision was not negotiable.

Macardle nodded, having no choice.

Loud voices outside the closed door interrupted them, and Cree's displeasure could be seen in his deep scowl as he nodded to Sloan to see to the matter.

Sloan opened the door to the two guards blocking Tarass from entering.

"I need to hear what Macardle has to say," Tarass demanded, his anger evident in his demanding tone.

"This does not concern you," Cree said.

"Anything that my neighboring clan has to say, especially since he disputes land that is rightfully mine, concerns me," Tarass called out.

"He is right. This does concern him and as much as I do not want to admit it, I may require his help," Macardle said.

"What help? You will swing from a tree when this is done and the Lord of Fire will claim your land," Cree said.

"Then it is best he hears what I have to say," Macardle said, as if resigned to his fate.

Cree motioned for Sloan to let Tarass enter.

Tarass went to remain standing at the opposite end of the mantel from where Cree stood.

"Sit and not one word," Cree ordered, pointing to a chair. "Or I will have you removed."

Tarass shot him a glare, but did as he said.

Cree looked to Macardle. "Now tell us this tale."

"It is not a tale. It is the truth," Macardle insisted. "Many months ago, I received a missive from my uncle requesting my presence. When I arrived, he was surprised to see me and I wondered who had sent the missive if not him. My first night there a fire broke out in one of the storage sheds and it spread to two more. While the clan fought to stop it from spreading further, a fire broke out in the keep."

Cree wondered where this long-winded tale was going and listened, while fighting to keep hold of his irritation.

"Snow, the youngest of the three Macardle daughters was in the keep and somehow managed to rescue her da and mum before the flames got to them, but at a price. It left her blind. Part of the keep was destroyed and three outbuildings and two cottages burned to the ground. Angus recovered nicely from the ordeal, but not so Lady Belle, Angus's wife. That was when she told me the truth.

"Lady Belle had been the one who had sent me the missive. She explained that Angus Macardle was having lapses in memory and became incoherent at times. She had hoped my visit there would enlighten me to the problem and I would agree to lead the clan. She worried what Angus would do during a memory lapse, since he had mentioned it was time he found husbands for his daughters. She feared the choices he might make when his mind was not what it should be.

"I gave my word to Lady Belle that I would stay and do what I could. She died shortly after. It took time to sort through things and it was only recently that I discovered Angus had arranged for your wife's abduction."

"He admitted it?" Cree asked, not sure whether to believe the tall tale or not.

"He blurted it out one night, telling me he had forgotten to advise me of his plan to have the Clan Macardle gain prestige and strength once again. It seems he paid a man named Rutland to abduct your wife with instructions she was not to be harmed in any way." Macardle shook his head. "How he ever thought that would matter to the man made me realize just how much he had lost his senses. The Uncle Angus I knew would never have done such a horrible thing.

"Rutland was to leave your wife in a specific area where Angus planned to come upon her as if by accident and he would return her to you. You in turn would be grateful and be forever in his debt and help him with anything he asked of you."

"You expect me to believe this ridiculous tale?" Cree asked, still questioning his excuse.

"I tell you this so that you know how much Angus has lost his mind. It was two days after he told me that he recalled it again and remembered Rutland's name. It was only when he had a truly lucid moment that he realized the magnitude of what he had done and told me I was to go to you and tell you the truth. And that he would face whatever punishment you decreed. He also recalled accidently setting the fire in the keep. The fire that eventually took his wife's life. It was that moment, he signed a document naming me heir apparent and Chieftain of the Clan Macardle."

"A fancy tale that most certainly benefits you," Cree said.

"Come and see Angus for yourself and decide if it is truth or tale that I tell you," Macardle said. "Or speak with Snow. She is the one daughter who clearly understood what was happening to her da and suffered for it. I am not making an excuse for him and either is he. What he did was wrong. He knows how terribly wrong it was, when he is lucid enough to remember it, and I cannot express his regret enough." He grew silent a moment, sorrow filling his eyes. "I truly believe that Angus hopes you take his life as punishment. The shock of what is happening to him made him realize that he cannot live with the man he has become, the man who grows worse by the day, the man who will soon not know himself at all."

Cree did not need to look at his wife to know what he would see on her face... sympathy for the old man and his family. He was not that forgiving.

"Lady Belle must have complete trust in you to have turned to you for help," Cree said, still not satisfied with his explanation.

"Lady Belle was a unique woman, loving and forgiving beyond measure and possessed of the most calming nature."

"You thought highly of Lady Belle and she of you, since she thought you a good choice to lead the clan," Cree said and a strange thought popped into his head.

"Lady Belle had a generous heart, forgiving and accepting things most wives would not?" Macardle said.

Cree stared at James Macardle. Could it be? He swore silently. "You are not Angus's nephew. You are his bastard son."

Macardle nodded and kept his head high, showing no shame in who he was. "And Lady Belle knew it and still she reached out to me and asked me for help. While lucid, Angus recalled how Belle had told him to claim me as his son and make me chieftain before it was too late. Angus did not want his daughters to know. He felt they had been hurt enough with their mum's death and I agreed, which is why I asked that what I say in this room not leave this room. I gave my father my word and I intend to keep it."

333

Cree felt his wife tug at his hand. He was surprised she had remained silent this long. He only had to look at her to know what she would say. There were tears in her eyes.

Cree turned to Macardle. "Can Tannin confirm any of this?"

"Tannin made it known to me that he thought there was something amiss with Angus. I am sure when you speak to him, he will tell you about what he has seen for himself."

"I will speak with him and let you know what I decide," Cree said.

"I do not mean to rush you, my lord, but I cannot be away from home too long. Angus can be too much for his daughters to handle and they have suffered more than their share of pain already."

Dawn stood and gestured.

Cree interpreted. "My wife wants to know how we can help."

"You have a generous and forgiving heart, my lady, to extend a helping hand to one who wronged you," James Macardle said.

Cree knew he was lucky to have fallen in love with Dawn, but at that moment, seeing not for the first time how forgiving his wife could be, he felt himself more blessed than he deserved.

"I was, however," —Macardle turned to Tarass— "hoping you might be interested in uniting our clans. I am concerned for my clan's safety since I discovered that the fire in the outbuilding had been purposely set and someone recognized the man who set the fire, then fled. He is a man known for offering his unscrupulous service for a tidy sum. His name is Slatter."

"I am sure we can reach some agreement and we can take care of the Slatter problem as well since he is here... imprisoned in one of Cree's huts," Tarass said and stood. "If you are finished with James, he and I can talk."

"For now," Cree said. "If I need him, I will summon him."

"We will be in the Great Hall," Tarass said.

James Macardle stood. "I cannot express my regret enough for what my father put your wife, you, and your family through. I would have no trouble hanging a man who did that to my wife and family. But my father would never do this if in his right mind and when in his right mind, he insists he must be punished for his wrong doing. So please, I beg for mercy on his behalf. If you did decide to punish him, God forbid hang him, unless lucid, he would not understand why. He would cry out for justice and wonder why no would come to his defense." Macardle shook his head. "And you would have to fight his daughters, for they would not stand by and let it happen. So again, please have mercy not only on my father, but my sisters as well."

Cree stepped in front of his wife to stop her from gesturing, knowing her intention. She would assure James that that would not happen.

"You will have my answer by nightfall," Cree said.

Macardle bobbed his head and left the room with Tarass.

"I will get Tannin," Sloan said, following the two men out.

Cree turned to his wife to find her arms crossed over her chest and a threatening gleam in her dark eyes.

"This is my decision, wife," he said.

She tapped her chest.

"It did not only happen to you. It happened to me, the twins, your friends, the clan. Angus deserves to be punished."

He. Already. Suffers. She mouthed slowly.

"And no doubt will suffer even more... but not by my hand," Cree said.

Dawn let out a silent sigh of relief.

335

His arm went around her waist. "I might want to hang him, kick the barrel out from under him myself, and watch as the noose does its job and chokes him to death, for the hell he put us through, but that does not mean I would. And that, dear wife, is your fault. You turned me soft… you gave me a heart."

Dawn pressed her hand to his chest, then to hers.

"A heart you love," Cree said, easily understanding her and gave her waist a tug so that she fell to rest against him.

She nodded and spread her hands wide.

"A heart you love very much."

She nodded vigorously.

He said aloud what had lingered in his mind. "I am more blessed than I deserve."

Dawn's nod turned to a shake and her brow creased deeply. She pointed back and forth between them rapidly.

"We deserve each other?"

She smiled and nodded vigorously again.

Cree grinned and brought his face close to hers. "That is because we are the only fools who would dare love the likes of either of us."

She laughed and nodded, then threw her arms around him and kissed him.

"Now take yourself off while I speak with Tannin," he said after the kiss ended. "Or I will neglect my duties and rush you back to bed."

Later, she mouthed.

"You can count on that wife," he said just as a knock sounded at the door.

Dawn went to open it, but first motioned cradling a child.

"You go to the twins," he said. "Make sure Beast stays with you after that."

She nodded and greeted Tannin with a smile when she opened the door, then out she went.

Dawn hurried upstairs to see her son and daughter only to learn that Nell and Bartha had taken them outside, Beast having gone with them.

The weather was fair today, the sun peeking out past the clouds now and again. They would go to their favorite spot under the large oak tree. She saw Bartha sitting in the grass engrossed in a serious battle with Valan and his wooden figures. She looked around for Lizbeth, but did not see her.

Dawn approached Bartha and Valan.

"Busy, Mummy," Valan said, not wanting to be disturbed during battle.

Dawn let him be and gestured to Bartha, pointing to Valan, then holding up two fingers tight together and folding one down.

"You want to know where Lizbeth is," Bartha said. "She was restless, so Nell took her for a walk."

Dawn nodded, pointed to herself, and walked her fingers to let Bartha knew she would go and leave them to their battle. Bartha barely paid her heed, intense on protecting her troop.

As she left the pair, she thought to talk to Cree about keeping Bartha and moving Ina to some other duty. Valan truly enjoyed her and she would not want to take that from him.

Rounding a cottage, she spotted Nell and grew alarmed when she did not see Lizbeth with her. She quickly asked where her daughter was.

Nell was quick to explain. "She is with Ina, my lady. Lizbeth was excited to see her and Ina had missed her so much that she joined our walk, but I was soon ignored and Ina shooed me away and told me she would bring her back shortly. Beast, of course, would not leave Lizbeth's side."

Dawn was relieved to know Beast was with Lizbeth and smiled and nodded at Nell.

"Dawn!"

337

She turned to see Lila heading her way and Nell hurried off.

Dawn was shaking her head and her finger at Lila as she approached.

"Stop that. I am feeling fine and I will return home and rest some more after I tell you what I recalled just moments ago." She shook her head. "How I forgot it I just do not know. Before I was hit on the head I got a strong whiff of flowers, like someone had just pick a bunch of them and was holding them in their hand."

Dawn scrunched her brow. Something was familiar about that and then in an instant her eyes went wide and she gestured fast, relieved Lila would understand her.

"It is Ina who hit me? She is with Lizbeth?"

Dawn nodded and gestured some more, though it was not necessary, Lila thought as she did.

"Go get Lizbeth. I will get Cree."

The two women ran in opposite directions.

Chapter Thirty-three

Dawn ran to Nell, her gestures frantic.

"Forgive me, my lady, I do not know what you are saying," Nell said.

Valan jumped to his feet. "Lizbeth."

"She is with Ina as I said," Nell was quick to say.

Dawn swung her hand out toward the village.

"Where are they?" Nell asked and answered. "Ina mentioned about taking her to her cottage for a treat after they walked a bit."

Dawn pointed to her son, then toward the keep.

Bartha immediately scooped Valan up and started running toward the keep.

Nell ran with Dawn to Ina's cottage. It was empty but draped over the lone chair was a cloak and Dawn saw that the hem of the cloak was worn ragged. She shook her head as she recalled the blood on Ina's finger that day as she clutched the bouquet of flowers she had picked… Lila's blood. How had she not realized it when it was right there in front of her?

Her heart pounded so badly with fear she thought it would burst. Why did Ina do what she did and why would she take Lizbeth?

"I should get Henry. He can try to find their tracks," Nell said.

Dawn nodded eagerly. She waved her off and followed Nell out the door, though she would not wait for him. She had to do something. She ran to the one place she thought her daughter might be… the edge of the woods where she liked to pick flowers, and where Ina had often taken Lizbeth.

339

Her fear escalated when she found no one there. Ina had killed Lara and Ann and had harmed Elsa and Lila, what would she do to Lizbeth?

A bark echoed in the woods—*Beast*—and hope surged through Dawn. She did not wait, she ran. A second bark followed and she blessed Beast for staying with Lizbeth. He would protect her. The third bark sounded more like a growl and Dawn hoisted her tunic and ran with all the speed she could muster.

Her heart slammed against her chest when she heard Beast's sharp cry of pain, then silence.

No! No! No! Dawn screamed in her head.

It was not long before she came upon Beast's body lying on his side, blood soaking his fur on the side of his face. He was not moving and his eyes were closed. She placed her hand on his side and felt his heart beat.

She kissed the top of his snout and gently tapped the top of his head, then pressed her cheek to his face, hoping he understood she would return for him and get him help. Then she scrambled to her feet and ran like the devil was chasing her.

"Beeeeeeeast, help!"

Fear tore at Dawn's heart, hearing the terror in her daughter's frightened voice as she pleaded for Beast, and she pumped her feet faster. She ducked under branches, sprinted over fallen trees, avoided large rocks with quick maneuvers all the while praying for her daughter to stay safe. Her heart pounded viciously in her chest and her limbs felt as if they were on fire, but she refused to slow down.

"Daaa! Daaaa!"

That her daughter cried out for Cree had tears threatening Dawn's eyes. She had to get to her daughter. She had to save her.

She rounded a group of trees and her heart leapt when she spotted Ina and Lizbeth not far from her. Her daughter was struggling to break free of Ina's hand clamped around her small, skinny arm. Dawn's anger soared when she watched helpless as Ina brought her hand down across Lizbeth's small face and her daughter cried out in pain.

Dawn wished her furious scream that echoed in her head could echo through the woods. A small smile did come to her face when her daughter spotted her and screamed out loud, and it echoed through the woods.

"Mummyyyyy!"

Ina turned and seeing Dawn, scooped Lizbeth up and took off running.

***

Lila burst into the Great Hall and pushed her way through the warriors congregated there. When she did not see Cree, she knew there was only one other place he could be and she hurried to his solar.

Two guards stood in front of the door, barring entrance.

"Take yourself off, Lord Cree cannot be disturbed," the one guard ordered sharply.

There was no time to argue or explain to these warriors. Lila yelled out as loud as she could. "Lord Cree, Lizbeth is in danger!"

The door swung open before the guard could turn around.

"Tell me," Cree demanded.

"You must hurry," Lila said. "Ina has taken Lizbeth and means her harm. Dawn searches for them now."

Cree roared with fury and when he entered the Great Hall all his men were standing, hands on the hilt of their swords ready to battle for him.

Bartha entered the Great Hall then, clutching Valan protectively in her arms.

"Lady Dawn has gone with Nell to Ina's cottage to look for Lizbeth," Bartha said.

"Comb the village and find my daughter and Ina," Cree called out and hurried out of the keep.

Cree grew numb, knowing if he let fear and anger rule this could end badly just like the day he was made to believe Dawn had fallen in the stream and drowned. If he had turned numb, he would have seen the truth, but he had let his heart and fear rule him.

Not this time.

One of his warriors shouted out. "Henry has picked up tracks in the woods."

Cree ran, thinking Beast was with Dawn. He would protect her and their daughter and alert him. He kept his ears sharp for Beast's bark as he rushed into the woods.

It was not long before Henry notified him of Beast.

"He is dead?" Cree asked.

"Not yet, my lord," Henry said.

"Leave him," Cree ordered. "I will see to him when this is done."

And to the one who did him harm, Cree thought and forged ahead.

***

Dawn caught up with Ina and Lizbeth and froze in her tracks when she spotted Ina standing near the edge of the stream, her hand gripping the back of Lizbeth's tunic as she held her dangerously close to the rushing water. One small push and she would fall in.

"Mummy," Lizbeth said, a quiver in her voice and tears rolling down her cheeks.

"Come any closer and in she goes," Ina threatened when Dawn approached and gave the small bairn a slight push.

"Mummy!" Lizbeth screeched with fear

Dawn stopped, stretching her hands out pleadingly.

"Do not dare come any closer," Ina warned.

342

Dawn assured her with a shake of her head that she would not take another step. She cast a quick glance to her daughter and gestured that she would get her soon. Her heart hurt when Lizbeth nodded, her tiny bottom lip quivering as she did and fear turning her eyes wide.

She needed to keep Ina placated, giving Cree enough time to reach them. Though, she worried how they would get Lizbeth from the crazed woman before she could push her in the stream. With Lizbeth so small, the rushing water would sweep her away before they could reach her and she would drown in no time. The thought frightened her so badly, it turned her limbs weak and she fought to stay strong.

"I want Slatter released," Ina demanded. "He belongs to me like you and Lord Cree belong to each other. He never wanted Lara. She chased after him. He only wanted me. It was her fault he left. We would be together now if not for her and for you. My limbs grew weak when I saw him in the clergyman's robe. I could not believe my eyes. He told me we would meet and talk as soon as possible. He came back for me. *Me!*"

Dawn nodded and tapped her lips, encouraging her to say more, gaining as much time as she could for Cree to find them.

"I knew as soon as you returned home Lara would confess her guilt and mention Slatter, and Lord Cree would think him guilty of your abduction when he had nothing to do with it. It was those two idiots who were to blame and Lara, of course, for helping them. I saw her talking to them one day in the woods. I thought she knew them but could understand why she would not want anyone to think she did. They were filthy men. I did not realize what she had been up to until you were abducted. I said nothing for the same reason I silenced Lara. I had to save the man I loved. We deserved a life together. I could not have him blamed and punished for something he did not do. I could not lose him.

343

"That was why Ann had to die. She told on Lara and left Slatter vulnerable. I did not want to harm Elsa but I had to make sure Ann did not ruin everything. And Lila should not have been where I met with Slatter."

Dawn was too astonished to make a gesture. All this time Ina knew about everything and had said nothing. Then she went about silencing anyone who knew anything. She wanted to beat the woman senseless, but first she needed her daughter safe.

Her eye caught movement past Ina's right shoulder, in a grouping of trees, and as difficult as it was for her to do, she kept focused on Ina, when she would have rather had shouted with joy at seeing Sloan.

That meant Cree was here.

"I took good care of the twins for you," Ina said as if that somehow made up for what she had done.

"Then continue to do that and release Lizbeth, Ina, and we will talk. I promise no harm will come to you," Cree said, stepping out from behind a large bush and going to his wife's side.

Dawn silently thanked the Heavens her husband was finally there and blessed him for those words until…

Ina gave Lizbeth a hard shove and yanked her back before she could fall in the stream.

"Daaa! Daaa!" Lizbeth cried out, fear turning her eyes as wide as full moons.

"I am here, Lizbeth. Ina will not harm you," Cree said, fighting the anger and fear twisting inside him. He would not lose his daughter to this mad woman.

A spark of anger nearly erupted his temper when he saw that his daughter's one cheek was swollen. Ina had struck her. His hand fisted for a brief moment, fighting the urge to rush at the woman, a foolish move. He had to be patient for his daughter's sake, then he would see that she paid dearly for what she did.

344

"Bring Slatter here to me and I will let Lizbeth go once we are safely away from here," Ina demanded.

"Let her go, Ina," Cree ordered, "and I will bring Slatter to you."

"No! No! No!" Ina shouted. "You will bring Slatter to me, then I will let her go."

Dawn watched her husband's eyes dart from Ina to Lizbeth, then the stream. He was seeing for himself what she had already determined, Lizbeth could not be reached in time to stop Ina from pushing her in the stream. She caught a barely noticeable movement to her husband's head and watched as Sloan and a few other warriors inched closer to Ina.

"Bring him here now!" Ina screeched.

Cree had to delay until his men could get into positon where they would be close enough to reach Ina and his daughter before she could push Lizbeth in the stream. Once his daughter hit that water, it would swallow her up and rush her away. She would be dead in no time.

"Daaaa!" Lizbeth wailed, suddenly struggling to break free.

His daughter's terrifying plea tore at his heart and her struggle frightened him. She could slip from Ina's grasp and stumble into the stream. "Stay still, Lizbeth."

His sharp tone brought the little bairn's struggles to an abrupt halt. and the sorrowful look she sent her da pierced his heart. She needed comfort from him not harsh words, but he could not risk her falling from Ina's grasp.

"All will be well, fear not, Lizbeth, be brave," Cree said with a strength in his voice he hoped would help his daughter.

She sighed back her tears as she patted her chest and pointed to him, telling him she loved him.

He fought all the feelings rushing through him, trying desperately to remain numb, so he could do whatever was necessary to save his daughter. But his heart, once silent and cold, could no longer turn numb. He simply could not hide or ignore his love for his daughter.

"I love you much, Lizbeth," he called out with strength. "You are my brave one."

"Enough!" Ina screeched. "Send one of your warriors to—" she stopped abruptly as if hit with a sudden, shocking thought and turned her head just enough to see Sloan and several warriors not far from her.

She moved quickly, turning so she could see anyone lurking behind her, and lost her balance and would have sent Lizbeth and herself into the stream if she had not steadied her footing hastily.

Dawn's hand rushed to her mouth as if stopping herself from screaming. For a moment, frightened she would see her daughter tumble into the stream. She felt hope fade when she saw it would now be impossible for Sloan to reach Lizbeth in time to save her.

Ina looked frantically around, her eyes darting from one to another, and realized she was surrounded, the stream her only escape.

"Do not be foolish, Ina. Put Lizbeth down and I will take you to Slatter," Cree said.

"For what, a moment to say goodbye before you hang me?" Ina said, shaking her head. "If I am to die for my love, then I will see you suffer as well."

Cree's arm shot out when his wife went to rush forward, stopping her. He could not blame her for her sudden move, he wished to do the same, but it would not save their daughter.

"I give you my word I will not hang you," Cree said. "I will take you to Slatter and set you both free, if you release Lizbeth."

"You will hunt us afterwards," Ina said.

"My word, I will not hunt you."

346

"Someone will."

"I cannot stop others, but I can see you safely off my land," Cree said, "just free my daughter and I will see it done."

"How am I to believe you?"

"Have you ever known me not to keep my word?" Cree asked, not wanting to let Ina and Slatter go, but their release was a small price to pay to save Lizbeth. Besides, Tarass would probably find them with little difficulty.

He could see her giving his proposition thought and continued to try and convince her. "Slatter must surely fear for your safety. Release Lizbeth, let this be done, and reunite with the man you love," Cree said.

Dawn tapped her husband's arm, then gestured.

"My wife says that even a small moment spent with the one you love is better than no moment at all."

A tear slipped down Ina's cheek. "You are right

Ina took a step forward away from the water and lost her balance. She jerked and flung her arms wide, trying to stop from falling, and Lizbeth went flying up and over the bank of the stream.

All watched with horror as in a split second Ina fell into the stream and Lizbeth small body went a short way up in the air, then fell toward the rushing water.

Before anyone had time to react, a big ball of black fur came sailing through the air and snatched Lizbeth's tunic in his mouth and landed with her on the bank of the stream.

Cree and Dawn rushed to their daughter, Cree scooping her up in his arms and grabbing his wife to wrap them all together in a tight hug.

"Beast," Lizbeth cried. "Beast hurt."

Dawn took Lizbeth in her arms, so grateful to be holding her, and hugged her tight. Her little arms went around her neck and squeezed like she never wanted to let go of her mum.

347

Cree bent down to Beast lying on his side, whining softly, and thumping his tail on the ground.

He ran his hand over the large dog and felt his heart steady and strong and he saw that the wound to his head was not that bad. He patted Beast gently on the head. "You did good, Beast. You shall be rewarded, and Elsa will have you well in no time."

He ordered two of his men to get the animal to Elsa. He was about to order Sloan to search along the stream for Ina and saw that he was already busy doing just that.

He turned and took his daughter from his wife. "Beast will do well, Lizbeth. He is brave like you. Now home we all go."

He reached out and took his wife's hand and they walked through the woods together.

After taking only a few steps, Lizbeth raised her head off her da's shoulder. "Flowers, da." She pointed to the yellow wildflowers growing in bunches. "For Beast."

Cree had to smile. After what his daughter had gone through, she still wanted to pick flowers and for Beast. She truly was a brave one. So, how could he deny her?

"We will pick flowers for, Beast," he said.

Lizbeth grabbed her da's face in her small hands and planted several kisses on his cheek.

Cree's heart swelled with love and relief to feel his daughter's kisses on his cheek after almost having lost her. He was ever so grateful to that big black dog for not only saving his wife's life, but his daughter's as well.

He set Lizbeth down on the ground and never had he thought picking flowers with his daughter and wife could bring him so much joy.

Chapter Thirty-four

Cree stood over the bed looking down at his wife, the twins snuggled in her arms, sleeping. With all that had happened today, he and Dawn wanted the twins with them safe in their bed and in their arms for at least this one night.

He would join them soon enough.

He turned and went to Beast curled up on a soft blanket in front of the hearth, the bunch of flowers they had picked in a crock not far from him and wilting from the heat. He bent down and patted the dog gently on the head, and Beast gave a wide yawn. Elsa had cleaned his wound and claimed him well, though ordered some rest. Lizbeth had fussed over him and Valan had helped.

Cree had been touched by the way his son had hugged his sister tightly upon her return home and how he had stayed by her side, his small wooden sword in his hand ready to protect her. The lad had even helped her put the flowers in the crock.

"Rest," he said and gave Beast one more pat on the head and the dog closed his eyes.

Cree left the room, closing the door quietly behind him.

It was late, everyone home and no doubt asleep, but there was one more thing he needed to do before he could join his family in bed.

He stepped out of the keep to a night without a cloud in the sky, the nearly full moon bright, and the air crisp as he walked through the quiet village. No one stirred except for the night sentinels that patrolled the village. All was well and all safe.

It did not take him long to reach his destination and he was not surprised to see the door to the cottage open as he approached it.

"Come in, I have a hot brew for us on this chilly night," Old Mary said, greeting him.

Cree sat in silence, his hands cupped around the tankard Old Mary had waiting for him.

"All is done," she asked, sitting across the small table from him.

"Aye, Ina's body was found and will be buried quietly. Slatter says he never met the woman until today when she spoke to him as if he knew her. He had no idea what she was talking about and told her he would speak with her another time since he had been anxious to talk with Rutland before he died."

Old Mary shook her head. "The poor lass. It was all in her head."

"It would seem that way. Dawn and I believe Ina must have seen Lara with Slatter in the woods one day and that was when her fantasy began."

"And Dawn's return brought it to light again," Old Mary said.

"I believe so."

"And this Slatter? What will you do with him?"

"Slatter will return with James Macardle to face punishment for the fire he set there, since there is little I can punish him for here. Newlin the man with him will be set free."

"What of the two men who abducted Dawn?"

"Gillie has but one sunrise left. Bram will be given a chance to redeem himself thanks to Dawn's generosity, though he will face punishment."

Old Mary scrunched her brow, sensing something. "There is one more who deserves punishment?"

Cree nodded, thinking about Angus Macardle. "Aye, the one who arranged the abduction and his punishment is severe."

Old Mary studied Cree for a moment. "Yet you have no hand in it."

"I could do no worse to him."

"Tarass?"

"Macardle and he will talk."

"Tarass is not a man to take lightly," Old Mary warned.

"He is not my problem now. Let Macardle deal with him."

Old Mary smiled. "You did not come here to tell me all this."

Cree shook his head.

Old Mary waited.

Cree stared at her a moment, then leaned forward. "I need to know."

"There is a reason that it is left unknown," Old Mary cautioned.

"I do not care. You never believed Dawn was dead, which means you know something about her death. There is no hell that can be as worse as that time I spent thinking Dawn dead, thinking I would never see her again, hold her again, love her again. Tell me of her death. Tell me we will join again elsewhere. Tell me I will not lose her forever."

"Did I not tell you once you would grow old together?"

"If you did, I do not recall, but I need more than that. Tell me if I take my last breath before she does."

Old Mary reached across the small table and took his hand. "You are sure of this."

"Aye, I want to know."

Old Mary nodded. "As you wish. You both have many years ahead of you. You will see many grandchildren born and you will share much laughter and tears. Dawn will be at your bedside, holding your hand, tears in her eyes when you take your last breath." Old Mary sniffed back her tears. "She will rest her head on your chest, and take her last breath as well, and follow with you into the afterlife." She squeezed his hand. "Your souls will unite time and again, for the love you and Dawn have is eternal."

Cree felt the fear that had gripped him since the day Dawn had vanished finally fade away.

He stood, a flood of feelings leaving him speechless.

Old Mary stood as well and smiled as she walked to the door and opened it. "Sleep well, my lord."

Cree stopped in front her and did something he rarely did except with Dawn and the twins, he wrapped his arms around the old woman and hugged her tight.

Old Mary's smile turned wide and a single tear caught in her wrinkles, sending it rolling haphazardly down her cheek as she watched him walk away. She thought to call out and tell him that he would have another son come this spring, but that was better left for him and Dawn to discover for themselves.

Cree returned to the keep and hurried through it and up the stairs to his bedchamber to find his daughter curled up against Beast's large body. He smiled and shook his head. The lass was definitely going to be a handful. He lifted her gently, Beast opening his eyes for a moment, making sure all was well, and seeing Cree closed them again.

He placed his daughter beside her brother cuddled in the crook of Dawn's arm, then slipped out of his boots and his shirt and wearing only his plaid climbed into bed beside his wife. He stretched his arm around her and the twins and tucked them close to him.

All was good now, he had his family safe in his arms, and he closed his eyes and slept peacefully.

THE END
Not really… look for more Cree & Dawn adventures
coming your way!

Donna Fletcher

The Cree & Dawn Series
(in order)

Highlander Unchained/Forbidden Highlander
Book 1 & 2

Highlander's Captive
Book 3

My Highlander
A Cree & Dawn Novel
Book 4

Highlander's True love
A Cree & Dawn Short Story #1
Follows Book 3

Highlander's Promise
A Cree & Dawn Short Story #2

Highlander Winter Tale
A Cree & Dawn Short Story #3

Highlander's Rescue
A Cree & Dawn Short Story #4

Highlander's Magical Love
A Cree & Dawn Novella
Follows Book 4

For a complete listing of Donna's books visit her
website… www.donnafletcher.com

Made in the USA
Middletown, DE
12 August 2022

71266702R00210